# Tobias' Spark

## The Kin Chronicles
## Book Two

A novel by:

Samantha Marshall

STARDUST
EMPIRE
PUBLISHING

# Love a Free Book?

---

**Learn to let go… or burn.**

Dating Noah Acheson has always been gentle, predictable and above all, safe – but when the softly spoken foxkin breaks the rules of their carefully crafted relationship, Deanna cuts him off, retreating to her private sanctuary deep in the Australian bush.

Stinging from Deanna's rejection, Noah returns from a brief stint fighting fires in New South Wales to face an infinitely more vicious fire front in Victoria. Though his broken heart still very much belongs to Deanna Schellponte, he's determined not to chase her – until the wind changes, turning the fires towards pack land, and Deanna is reported missing.

With fire raging all around, Noah races into the bush to find the wolfkin he loves. To survive, Deanna and Noah must confront not only the fury of Mother Nature… but the ghost whose memory tore them apart.

---

## Get your FREE copy here:

https://sliceofsammy.com/contact

# Acknowledgements

To my loved ones, who pushed me to make this crazy dream into reality and share it with the world. Thank you for the endless hours of tea, cake, laughter and listening to my crazy ideas.

# One

Aislinn had never been so glad to collapse as she was right then, tumbling into a heap on the soft training mats in Tobias' rumpus room. Flynn stretched out alongside her in his tiger form, tail flipping idly back and forth while his head nudged one lupine shoulder.

The run back from Old Tom's Hollow had been long, tiring and blissfully uneventful - just what she needed to get her thoughts into some semblance of order following the confrontation with Olaf. With any luck, the bearkin General and all-around asshole was off licking his wounds somewhere cold and dank, with useless minions and his own failure for company.

A girl could hope, at any rate.

Tobias' voice floated out from the kitchen. "Drink?"

"Something good," Aislinn returned, shimmering back into her human form and reaching up to scratch underneath Flynn's chin. She lowered her voice and said; "You better behave, or I swear I'll throw you outside."

Flynn whuffed indignantly, eyes sparkling with mischief. *As if I would even consider misbehaving.*

"Don't think you can charm me," Aislinn growled, her scratch turning into a firm poke. "I'm immune."

*Not to **him**, it seems. His scent is all over you.*

"Jealous?"

*Maybe.* One feline ear flickered. *Maybe not. He's very…* *wholesome.*

Aislinn burst out laughing at that, sitting up as Tobias came into the room with three glasses balanced between his fingers. "Flynn thinks you're wholesome," she said by way of explanation.

"Wholesome?" Tobias screwed up his face. "Like bread?"

*Goody two-shoes,* Flynn clarified - and by the way Tobias startled, he'd widened his speech range to include the other Alpha.

"One of Flynn's Sabre abilities is that he can communicate in animal form," Aislinn said, accepting her glass with a smile and sipping. "Oh, it's good."

"Of course it is." Tobias looked down at his spare glass and back at Flynn. "You want this in a bowl or what?"

Flynn yawned and shimmered back to human form. "Glass. Sticky fur is a bitch." Aislinn prodded him and he grunted. "Thank you."

"No worries." Tobias handed over a glass, hesitated, then sat cross legged on the floor beside Aislinn. She scooted closer, dropping her head on his shoulder as she watched Flynn take a tentative sip.

"Bourbon," the tigerkin rumbled appreciatively.

"Locally made." Tobias raised his glass and took a long drink, his free arm wrapping casually around Aislinn's waist.

Flynn noted the movement and smiled into his bourbon. "I'm not going to kidnap her, little Alpha. She'd cut my balls off."

"Both of you are reacting to each other's transitional energies," Aislinn cut in over Tobias' growl. "If you need, I can find a ruler and we can get the cock-measuring over with straight off the bat."

Flynn reclined on one elbow with a rumbling laugh. "Careful, Ash, it's been a while since I've had a nice tickle. I might enjoy it." Aislinn narrowed her eyes and he flashed a wicked grin. "So, you want the story now, I guess."

"Damned right I do - what are you doing here?"

"You mean apart from being transitional and you still on the register as my damper?"

"Apart from that, yes." She hesitated and frowned. "Gods above, you didn't kill anyone, did you? The episodes had pretty much settled, so I assumed -"

"Relax, nobody died." The tigerkin's eyes narrowed, as though he wasn't sure if that was a good thing or not. "After I wrecked your hospital room and got thrown out, the Council sent the team off on some bitch-ass recon mission. When we came back, you were already gone. I might've been okay with it - maybe - until I found out Jacques knew you were leaving the whole fucking time and was deliberately extending the mission so that Andre could ship you out alone." Flynn gnashed his teeth a moment, then took a sharp breath and continued; "I kicked his fucking ass and left that night."

"Jacques is one of our other team members," Aislinn murmured to Tobias. "Owlkin. Sharp eyed, but a real stickler for the rules."

Tobias snorted. "He must love you two."

"I've been saying for years he's only there to report on us," Flynn grumbled. "Brown-nosing busybody."

Aislinn blinked and sat up very straight. "The rogue Kin agent," she whispered. "It was *you*."

"No wonder Grandma didn't know about it - Andre must've been worried word would get back to us," Tobias said.

"He knew I'd have gone looking for Flynn," Aislinn nodded. "I'll add it to the list of his sins."

Flynn's elfin face crinkled in amusement. "There's a list now?"

"You bet there is," she growled - and quickly explained how Andre and Rupert had conspired to keep Aislinn and Tobias apart for so many years.

"Mother*fucker*," Flynn slugged the remainder of his bourbon and then wheezed a laugh. "That's a lot of string pulling. I don't know if I should be pissed off or impressed."

Aislinn sagged. "I'm sorry you ended up dragged into this because of me."

"Don't you dare," Flynn growled. Before Aislinn could as much as blink, his forehead was pressing against hers, his breath tickling her cheek. "I made my own choices, princess, and they all began and ended with you. Your useless piece of shit of a father might have made life hard but you know what? The two of you are here, now - and I'm right beside you, where I belong. Andre might *think* he and the Council are some top notch shit but they're just pissing in the wind when it comes to creatures like us." He leant back and gave Tobias an assessing look. "I guess I can't really speak for you, but I'm gonna assume you've got something interesting under that pretty-boy exterior or Ash would've eaten you by now."

"I'm not as tasty as I look," Tobias returned, rubbing his cheek against Aislinn's hair. "And, much as I may regret admitting it, you're right. Whatever plans Andre had in place, for whatever strange reasons, are irrelevant now. Although I'm interested to know how a volatile tigerkin got out of Ireland under the High Council's nose."

"I have connections," Flynn rumbled, sitting back on his heels. "Council never even knew I was gone until Kaira found Jacques tied up in the roof."

Aislinn frowned. "Kaira tattled?"

"No - she was just stupid enough to untie him." Flynn rolled his feline eyes and backflipped neatly to his feet. "Too late by then of course, I was already most of the way here. Did make getting out of Melbourne a little tricky, but Kaira called ahead to alert my contact and he was able to create a distraction at the airport. It meant extra overland travel on foot, but I like a challenge. Possums, by the way, are not half bad eating. Kind of taste like rabbit."

"You do realise," said Aislinn slowly, "That you could very well be listed as in breach of contract and imprisoned?"

"Screw that shit." Fur rippled over Flynn's body in an elegant wave, then settled as though it had never been. "Don't forget what I saw in that hospital, Ash. All those tests and medics and science assholes constantly asking questions, making you relive the whole ordeal over and over. You didn't need to be locked up, you needed someone strong at your back to pick up the pieces and keep 'em safe until you were ready to be put back together." He paused, staring up at the ceiling. "Civilised society my ass - they've got a lot to answer for. Where I grew up, we lived and died for each other, and I'll be damned if that's going to change because of some jerk in a suit with a bit of fucking paper. So yeah, I do realise they could list me as in breach of contract but you know what? I'll kill anyone who tries to put me in prison because I belong with, to use your wolfkin word, my pack." Flynn curled a lip and gave Tobias an odd look. "Which I suppose now includes you, too."

"It always did," Aislinn murmured.

"I *know* that!" Flynn roared, then raised his arm and bit viciously into his own flesh, chest heaving as blood trickled over his skin.

"Easy, tiger." Aislinn rolled to her feet, crossing the room to smooth her hands - and her shadows - over the tigerkin's chest. "Breathe. I'm glad you came."

Flynn retracted his teeth, grimaced at the puncture marks and spat blood on the floor. "I thought I was past all this, Ash."

Aislinn's heart contracted as he said her name and she realised just how much she'd missed the prickly tigerkin. "I know, but I'm going to go out on a limb here and say it's probably got something to do with Tobias - I don't have a reader out here but his energy is almost as strong as yours."

"Almost, eh?" Flynn threw an inflammatory look across the room. "Nice try."

"I didn't set out to be this way," Tobias growled from his place on the mat. "Every time I turn around it's like I'm drowning in an ocean of sensation and there's nothing I can do to stop it."

Flynn huffed. "You can't stop it, you idiot, it's part of you. Better off embracing it and going with the flow." He leered down at Aislinn. "Some mighty good fun to be had if you ride the wave."

She turned away, cheeks heating - and found Tobias' golden eyes blazing. *Mother Moon,* one voice whispered, while the other simply laughed. "Stop it," Aislinn hissed, rubbing her temples with shaking fingers. Her blood was beginning to pound again, a sure sign that the calming effects of the long run home were wearing off.

"Tonic got you?" Flynn asked, his voice full of amusement. "It's normally the only reason you talk to yourself."

"Yeah. It's been, what, almost twelve hours since Jemima gave it to me?" Aislinn sighed, looking anywhere but directly at Tobias whilst she waited for her blush to fade. "I've got at least another eight hours before I collapse. I'm going to need to run it off again."

Unsurprisingly, both Tobias and Flynn spoke simultaneously. "Where to?"

A moment later one growled and the other huffed a laugh - which turned into a yowl as two large bodies thumped down on the mat. Aislinn turned to see the two men tumbling across the floor, flashing into their animal forms as they yipped and snapped at one another. She considered wading in and dragging them apart by their ears - or maybe the organ that seemed to be driving them both to act like adolescents - but after a long moment's assessment, she realised that in spite of fur flying and claws slashing, nobody was getting hurt.

She shoved upright and circumnavigated the room, removing their empty glasses and draining her own. After another second's consideration, Aislinn dragged on her wolf form and leapt into the fray. Neither of the two males were expecting it though Flynn recovered the quickest, one large paw batting affectionately at her shoulder before he tumbled both wolves into a ball of fur and whiskers.

*Come to play?* Flynn's voice slid into her head along a path greased by years of practice.

*It seems better than running, for now,* she replied, the thoughts washing across her mind for Flynn to fish out. *Why should you two have all the fun?*

Flynn's rumbling laugh was very much audible, even as the three of them wrestled and romped across the floor. *It was either brawl or kill him; I figured you'd prefer this.*

Well, that answered the question of whether Tobias was included in the conversation or not. Aislinn caught Flynn's waving tail between her teeth and tugged him sideways into Tobias, bowling them both over and leaping on top. *You can't possibly hate him already - you don't even know him.*

*I hate everyone, Ash.*

Aislinn snorted at that - but really, why was she surprised? Flynn *did* hate everyone; those who earnt his trust and friendship had to do so the hard way. Still… *It took me four years before I had any inkling you liked me at all.*

*Let's hope T-fuzz is a faster learner, then.*

*T-fuzz?* Aislinn choked and found herself suddenly pinned by giant paws, Tobias' lips stretched back from lupine teeth. Laughter overcame her and she dropped her wolf form, reaching up to stroke both hands down the sides of his head. Like this, it was easy; even with the palpable tension between Alpha and Sabre and the insistent burn of the battle blood in her veins, Aislinn hadn't felt so relaxed in weeks. If only she had the luxury to continue this way, to sort out the curious blend of butterscotch and cloves that had taken root in her soul and put the pieces of herself back together at her own leisure.

"Ash?" Tobias shimmered into human form above her, one hand thumping down on the mat either side of her head. She winced and he moved immediately, rolling to one side and lowering onto his elbow. "What is it?"

Aislinn stared up at the roof for a long moment, then began talking. As Flynn curled up on her opposite side in his tiger form, she told them both about what had happened inside the barn, from the moment she'd left Tobias and Zeke by Old Tom's homestead until Flynn had returned from his thwarted pursuit of their enemy. The words shook her, body and soul - and barely was she part way through when Tobias wriggled closer, fitting his body against hers the way it seemed made to do, providing comfort with his presence. Flynn stretched full length on her other side, his feline face tucked into the crook of her neck and one giant, striped paw resting on her arm. For those few minutes, transitional episodes were forgotten and mutual dislikes pushed aside as the two men did what Aislinn realised she'd needed from the very beginning: listened to her talk without interruption, without judgement, without offering advice or opinions or potential solutions.

"Olaf will die for what he's done," Tobias said when she'd finished. His voice was cool and soft but vibrated in such a way that Aislinn knew he was keeping hold on his temper for her sake.

Flynn rumbled in his chest, a deep sound somewhere between a growl and a grunt. *On that, we're in agreement.*

Tobias' lips quirked, his face tender as he reached down to trace the curve of Aislinn's cheek with one finger. "Most important of all, though, is whatever *you* need."

"I don't know - but the two of you are a damned good start," Aislinn admitted. "And the pack… I owe Zeke, too."

"You owe none of us," Tobias returned evenly. "For better or worse, we run together."

Aislinn smiled at that and couldn't resist adding; "Except Jax."

"Jax belongs to you now," Tobias shrugged. "He made a good choice, and while we're all together, allegiances are no more and no less than family ties."

*And who do you belong to?* Flynn asked, raising his head to regard Tobias from glittering amber eyes.

Tobias frowned. "There's an obvious answer to that question but I'm sensing you've got more to say."

Flynn rolled his feline shoulders in a shrug that rippled the fur all the way down his spine. *You don't seriously think Andre's going to ignore what happened in that tumbledown old building, do you? He'll be sticking his nose in as soon as he can - and you're technically under his authority.* Flynn yawned, displaying a mouth full of impressive teeth. *What will you do if he orders you to do something you don't like? Say, for example, separating from Ash?*

"He wouldn't," Aislinn denied, eyes wide. "He bound us together for transitional purposes. That makes no sense."

*I might remind you that he bound us together for transitional purposes too, then didn't even blink at the thought of sending you away and leaving me unattended, which could have resulted in the deaths of hundreds of Kin.* Flynn humphed in disgust. *Your father does things that suit his own agenda, Ash, you know that. The hypothetical situation is irrelevant - I want to know whether T-Fuzz has the backbone to actually dig in when it counts.*

*"T-Fuzz?"* Tobias repeated incredulously. He frowned at Flynn and Aislinn laid a warning hand on his chest. After a long, glaring moment, he said; "Is there really no other damper as strong as Ash? Not that I'm asking for either of us to be reassigned, but was there really no-one else once she came back here?"

*No,* said Flynn, *There wasn't. Dampers are rare, too rare - and it doesn't normally matter so much, but for those like us? Ash is literally it.*

"He's right," Aislinn agreed, pressing the heels of her palms into her eye sockets. "I'm going to assume Dad decided you weren't much of a risk, seeing as it's been a good four months since the last episode."

*But, as Olaf's fucking taser proved, I'm not entirely out of the woods. Also, if T-Fuzz's energy is determined to rub me the wrong way, it looks like I'm about to take a giant step back into caveman territory.*

"Separating us was a stupid risk for Dad to take," Aislinn agreed quietly. Very, very slowly, she raised one hand and eyeballed Tobias. "And you haven't answered his question."

"After what our two fathers put us through, I didn't think an answer was necessary," Tobias returned, his voice equally as soft. "I know I deserve the smack down for the way I treated you before, Ash - but we cleared that air, didn't we?"

Aislinn rolled upright, bracing one hand behind her as she pushed to her feet. "Forgive me for wanting a verbal confirmation."

"Dammit, Ash," he growled, following her into the kitchen. "You really want to fight about this?"

"No, I really *don't* want to fight about this - or anything else." Aislinn yanked open the fridge and dragged out the remains of the casserole they'd shared earlier. "But you seem to like making it easy."

Tobias spluttered indignantly whilst she dug out a spoon and started eating the casserole cold. His mobile face worked through a varying range of emotions before he finally said; "No."

She blinked. "No?"

"I'm not letting you create an argument just because you're feeling vulnerable," he elaborated. "It's not going to happen."

Aislinn slammed the spoon down. "I am *not -*"

Tobias vaulted over the bench, landing neatly in Aislinn's personal space. She retreated but he crowded her backwards until she bumped against the fridge, heart hammering. "Yes," he growled, "You are. And we're both worth more than that." He thrust his hands into her unbound hair, the golden starbursts in his eyes blazing as he dragged Aislinn closer and kissed her.

Tobias' lips were soft but his body edged in steel, his teeth scraping across her flesh as he tilted her head for better access. This was not the kiss of a patient man who knew she'd been hurt and was waiting for her to recover; this was the kiss of an Alpha making a very clear point. Aislinn raised her hands to shove Tobias away but instead found them twining around his neck, her blood roaring as the vast energy inside her answered the call of his. Nobody else made her feel this way, breathless and tingling with an electricity that had nothing to do with the battle blood still coursing through her veins. Tobias growled and she growled right back; one of his hands swept down the curves of her body, caressing her breast and hip before brazenly locking onto one buttock and moulding Aislinn's pelvis against his.

*You know,* said Flynn casually, *I'm right here.*

Tobias broke the kiss long enough to rumble; "Then go somewhere else."

The tigerkin made a startled sound and Aislinn laughed, dropping her forehead against Tobias' thundering pulse but making no move to disconnect them otherwise. "Why does the very idea of this with anyone else freak me out but with you it's okay?"

*Really? You're **really** asking that?*

Aislinn twisted to see where Flynn stood in the lounge, tail swishing slowly from side to side. "What am I missing?"

*Hah! No way, princess - you need to work that out for yourself.*

"For once, I'm inclined to agree with the kitty," Tobias drawled, his hold on Aislinn loosening ever so slightly. "Some things are more fun when you discover them on your own."

Aislinn glowered at both men, but neither relented. Eventually she poked Tobias' sternum. "I guess I owe you an apology."

"I guess I'll accept it, then." He offered a very masculine grin. "Unless you want me to make my point all over again."

*I swear to Solaeden I'll vomit on your bed if you do,* Flynn growled.

Aislinn pressed a kiss to Tobias' throat and then moved back to the bench, reclaiming her spoon and the casserole. "Either of you hungry? Because I'm totally going to finish this otherwise."

"I'll make a sandwich," Tobias murmured.

*I ate earlier.*

"Your losses." She dug back into the casserole, pointedly ignoring Flynn's fake gagging. As soon as the spoon scraped the bottom of the dish, she looked over at Tobias, half way through his sandwich and then at Flynn, who seemed to have decided the arm of the couch was a good place to scratch the itch on his flank. "All right, I'm going for that run. Who's coming?"

# Two

A hot shower at maximum pressure did little to soothe Tobias' aching muscles. He rested his forehead against the glass and stayed under the spray until the water began to turn cold, whereupon he flicked the tap off and stepped out to meet his own haggard gaze in the mirror.

They'd run all night long and for most of the morning, circling and circling the outer reaches of pack land while Aislinn tried to work off the battle blood. Several times she'd stopped to examine seemingly trivial items which had suddenly become fascinating and, finally, she'd ended up having an argument with herself that had resulted in both Flynn and Tobias having to hold her down while she screamed and thrashed - and promptly passed out in the middle of the bush.

Tobias scrubbed himself with a towel and shook out his hair. A few hours' sleep curled up against Aislinn had been like paradise and he could have done with more, but it was already mid-afternoon and duty called. He dragged on a pair of torn denim shorts and a khaki t-shirt, picturing Ash as she'd been when he left; tangled in the sheets with her wine-tinted brown hair spread gloriously over the pillow. Olaf had come far too close to her the day before and he'd be damned if he let it happen again.

When he eased open the bathroom door and made his way into the hall, Tobias wasn't surprised to see Flynn still curled up in front of Aislinn's door in tiger form. Seemingly immune to the need for a bed, the tigerkin had dropped there when they'd finally tucked Ash's unconscious body into bed and vowed to stay until she woke. Tobias was, however, surprised to see the distinct black fur of Jaxon's gargantuan wolf form not only also asleep on the floor but actually curled up against the tiger for warmth. He must've returned from his patrol - a duty he'd re-accepted only after Aislinn okayed it - while

Tobias had been in the shower. Shiny-eyed zealot, Zeke had called him, and it seemed he was right. Tobias sighed. There was no way out of the house without either stepping on or kicking one of them, and though the idea of tromping on Flynn's face held a certain appeal, he settled for clearing his throat instead.

*I'm awake, asshole.* Flynn raised his head to yawn impressively. *You stomp around like a fairy elephant.*

Tobias chose to ignore that, instead poking Jaxon in the haunches with a toe until the wolf raised his head. "You boys enjoying your cheeky afternoon snuggle?"

"Shhhh," Jaxon melted into human form and yanked Tobias further away from the bedroom door. "Don't wake her."

"She's basically unconscious," Flynn said, resuming his own human form - such as it was - and stretching languorously. "Fire breathing dragons playing death metal wouldn't wake her right now."

Tobias looked to Jaxon, whose green eyes were clear and brighter than they had been in a week. "Did Sarah and the pups get the all-clear from Jem?"

"Pretty much." He held out both arms and turned them back and forth. "The serum wore off pretty quickly seeing as they spread it between the three of us. Jem's still not sure if it'll have a lasting effect on Ma's baby so she's staying over a couple of nights to keep a closer eye on things." Jaxon chewed the inside of his cheek for a minute, then said; "You go and do what you need to. I'll watch over Ash - Jem said she'd sleep for ages."

"Hmmmm." Tobias glanced back at the closed door and then turned to Flynn, trying to make his expression as neutral as possible. "You've got more experience with transition than I do. Is it safe to leave her and go about my business?"

"Like I already said, Ash is basically unconscious. Even if we both had a transitional episode simultaneously, she'd be unlikely to wake until long after everyone else was dead." The tigerkin's eyes glittered. "Don't worry. If Jaxzilla's willing to guard our princess, I'll come hold your little Alpha hand while she sleeps."

"Ash said our energies were rubbing off on each other and causing you to backslide," Tobias reminded him.

"Yeah, but I'm also the only Kin besides Ash who stands a chance of handling your ass if you lose it, T-Fuzz."

"T-Fuzz?" Jaxon echoed.

Tobias waved him off. "Forget you even heard that."

Flynn's elfin face creased with an evil grin that revealed all four of his ridiculously pointed fangs. "Well? You up for this or not?"

No, Tobias thought, he really wasn't in the mood for the tigerkin but there was little choice otherwise. "Fine. Come on." He moved to the stairs, pausing at the top to look back at Jaxon. "She wakes, you call me. Got it?"

"Got it." Jaxon waved a dismissal, returned to his wolf form and settled down in front of Aislinn's door.

*Let's go, sweet cheeks,* Flynn called from the bottom of the stairs.

Tobias rolled his eyes and descended to the kitchen. "Do you ever spend more than five minutes in human form?"

*Not if I can help it.*

"Somehow, I'm not surprised," Tobias muttered, yanking the front door open and stepping outside. He was immediately struck by a strong gust of wind and held up one hand to shelter his face. "Ash was right; looks like we're in for a storm."

*It'll be a welcome change from this gods-forsaken heat.* Flynn paused on the front porch, turning his nose into the wind. *I smell lightning.*

"Yeah. You haven't seen anything until you've seen a proper summer thunderstorm," Tobias replied. He looked out across the common lawns, where Bill and Rory Deepwater were directing a small group of pack members in a hand to hand combat training session. "What are you planning to do while you're here?"

*Aside from following you around and making your life miserable?*

"Aside from that." Tobias walked to the far end of the porch and jumped off, jogging across the common lawn in the direction of the den.

Flynn kept easy pace alongside, his long tiger's legs making it seem little more than a swift walk. *I haven't thought about it. I knew Ash needed me, so I came.*

"I see." Tobias considered what he knew of their relationship and the way Flynn looked at Aislinn. "Who needs who, exactly?"

The moment they were in the trees, the tigerkin tackled Tobias flat to the ground, claws unsheathing just enough to prick the skin of his shoulders. *Whatever you think you know, you don't.*

"Oh?" Tobias bared his teeth. "I know you're in love with her."

He'd been expecting a roar, a swipe, a fight - instead, Flynn merely backed off and said; *Fuck you.*

"Bit of a thorn in your paw?" Tobias sat up, rubbing the back of his head and grimacing as he came away with a handful of dried leaves and twigs. When Flynn didn't answer, he got to his feet and continued to the den, aware of the tiger following silently behind.

Zeke was inside with Dominic, their heads bent over the scarred old table by the fire pit. He looked up as Tobias entered, his usually easy grin decidedly tense. "Yo, dude. Glad you're here. Look at this, will you?"

"What is it?" Tobias poured himself a glass of iced water from a nearby jug and joined his second at the table, staring down at the map which had, the last time he'd seen it, been nailed to the wall. "More attacks."

Zeke nodded, jabbing a long finger at each of the pins. "I'm going to say these were organised before the Heliope-Flints were spotted because they all follow the old pattern - except this one."

"Hmmmm." Tobias inspected the pin in question, then turned to the seemingly empty doorway of the cave. "Kitty, you got a minute?"

"Kit - shit a brick," Zeke stood abruptly as Flynn appeared out of the underbrush, head low and eyes narrowed as he entered the den.

*You rang?*

"I did. Dom, Flynn. Kitty, this is Dominic." Undaunted by the very real threat present in Flynn's tone - and the swearing as his voice echoed inside both Zeke and Dominic's heads as well - Tobias pointed at the map. "Is this the direction you chased Olaf yesterday?"

With a long suffering sigh, Flynn shimmered into human form and bent over the table, the stripes etched into his skin stretching with the movement. After a long moment he put one finger down and said; "Is this the barn?"

"Yeah."

The finger moved north west. "This is the way… down this road. Tasered here…" the tigerkin's frown deepened, finger still moving. "And this is the attack that's out of pattern. Where is that?"

It was Zeke, his voice very soft, who said; "You can't read?"

"Not really," Flynn shook his head, seemingly unbothered by the idea. "I'm a street rat, Goldenrod - no one to teach us little old orphans how to shit, let alone read. Ash tried once or twice and I can make out some basic letters, but neither of us had the patience to keep it up. I get by."

"How?" Dominic asked, jaw dropped.

Flynn picked up Zeke's phone from the table and swiped the screen open, jabbing the icon for contacts and then waving a revelatory hand at the list of names and their matching photographs. "Everything important has a picture next to it. I want Ash? I get my phone, I press her face, she answers. Failing that, I shout until she rocks the fuck up." The tigerkin shook himself and prodded again at the map. "Now, where is this?"

"A quoll community about an hour from where you said you were tasered," Zeke supplied. "Small enough not to even really have a name."

Flynn grunted. "Any survivors?"

"No. It was called in by the mail service early this morning." Zeke's face was drawn. "I'm assuming the bearkin stopped for supplies."

"Or medicine." Flynn caught his lower lip beneath a wickedly curved incisor and looked at Tobias. "You might've hit Olaf harder than we thought if he's willing to risk leaving a trail."

"You think he's holed up close by?"

"It's possible. I mean, he's too smart for anything permanent but an interim camp? Sure. Although, he still wants Ash, so he's not going to go stupid far." Flynn clicked his tongue in thought, then spread a hand over the north-western part of the map. "This looks like a whole lot of fuck all. Rough country?"

"Yeah, very rough country with plenty of places for a group of bearkin to hide." Tobias frowned. "If I was Olaf, I'd withdraw a little to lick my wounds and formulate a new strategy."

Flynn rumbled his agreement. "Olaf's smart, but not even he would've counted on three midforms - and Ash being able to break his creepy mind hold. How does she do that, anyway?"

Tobias shrugged, unwilling to give up what little he knew on the subject, but aware the Sabre would smell a lie. "Not even Ash knows for sure."

"Well, we better find out because having her psychically crippled on a regular basis isn't going to go in our favour." Flynn frowned. "Want to draw straws on who brings it up?"

"I'll do it," Tobias answered. Wondering if his answer had been too quick, he added, "She seems reasonably comfortable talking to me so far."

The tigerkin nodded, poured himself a glass of iced water and drank it in several large gulps. "Fine by me."

"No pithy retort? I'm almost disappointed." Tobias crossed both arms over his chest. "Better be careful or we might mistake you for friendly."

Flynn smiled, displaying all of his impressive teeth, and made a rude gesture with one hand. "Don't worry, fluffpup, all truces are temporary. I'll be back to pissing on your breakfast in no time."

Tobias rolled his eyes, biting back the urge to smile as Flynn's off-kilter sense of humour reminded him of Aislinn. Dismissing the tigerkin with an equally rude gesture of his own, he turned back to Zeke. "Keep patrols running but focus particularly on the north-western edge of pack land. If Olaf launches a frontal assault, he's likely to come from there."

"You don't think he'll go 'round?" Zeke asked, tapping the lower half of the map.

"Not at this stage," Tobias returned. "Olaf would be a fool to think we'd overlook this ambush, so it's only fair to assume he's running low on time. When he's well enough, he'll come straight in - if he's coming at all."

"You got it," Zeke nodded. "I'll redraw the patrol routes to suit. Would you also drop by the training ring and offer some macho Alpha words or something? Sessions have started but after the Heliope-Flint incident the pack are a little nervous."

"Sure, I'll head up now." Tobias pushed off the table and glanced towards Flynn, who had once again returned to his tiger form. "Up for a little stop-off?"

*Because I love people so much,* he growled, padding towards the entrance. Half out in the sun, the tiger stopped. *Thanks for letting me into your den. The honour is noted.* With a flick of his striped tail, Flynn disappeared into the undergrowth.

"Mother Moon, that guy is weird," Dominic muttered, staring after the tiger. "How can something so big and so orange be so invisible?"

"Nature's little joke, I guess," Zeke snorted. "Do you have copies of the patrol routes handy?"

"Back at my place," Dominic answered. "Want me to fetch them?"

Zeke's eyes glimmered. "Depends. Is Deanna cooking tonight?"

"Chicken cacciatore," Dominic nodded and pulled out his phone. "I'll let her know you're joining us." He gave Tobias a long look. "And I'll have her do extra so it can be sent your way."

Tobias rubbed self-consciously at the back of his head. "I *can* cook, you know."

Dominic merely raised a perfect brow. "I was at your house only a few days ago and I've seen the contents of your pantry. Given you now have, what - three? Four? Kin in residence, there's no way you can feed everyone. Deanna's well aware that your role as Alpha takes away from the time you'll have to prepare a multitude of ham and cheese sandwiches, so she won't mind doing her bit to help out."

"Bam!" Zeke laughed, rocking back on his heels. "Oh, man, he got you good there."

"Fine," Tobias relented with a shake of his head. "Pass on my thanks, will you?"

Dominic raised his phone, where he was tapping out a message with swift precision. "Already done."

Tobias left the den with a half smile on his face. As he drew level with the waterhole, he spied Flynn sunning on a rock nearby. Though the tiger's eyes were closed, one ear swivelled in Tobias' direction as he approached.

"I see you found the best spot already." Tobias dropped down beside the tigerkin, who grunted noncommittally in response. "Look, man… I know we're not likely to get along straight away - if ever - but my comment about your feelings towards Ash was out of line. For the sake of the pack and the situation we're in, I wanted to say I was sorry."

Flynn remained silent and unmoving, without even the flicker of a whisker to show he'd heard. Tobias sat quietly on the rock for a few minutes, staring out at the horizon which was starting to turn pink with the first few rays of sunset. As he made to stand, Flynn's striped tail laid gently across his arm. *That's the first time since joining the Council's fucking crusade that anybody who wasn't Ash has offered me a sincere apology.*

"Really?"

The tigerkin wheezed a laugh. *I'm sure it's no surprise to discover I'm not everybody's idea of a good time, T-Fuzz.*

"Ash likes you," Tobias pointed out, unable to quite keep the disbelief from his tone.

*Not at first,* Flynn chuckled, *and only because I'm about as opposite to you as it's possible to get.*

Tobias frowned at that, picking up a pebble and tossing it into the waterhole where the ripples expanded slowly and inexorably outwards. "Are you saying she befriended you to spite me?"

*I'm saying she befriended me to stop thinking about you. From the day I met her, all Ash ever talked about was how fucking fabulous you were and how she was just biding her time until she could go back home - and I swear, that freaking weird-ass pendant with your hair in it? Beyond creepy.* Flynn's chest rose and fell in a sigh. *I didn't want a damned thing to do with her. She was clean and privileged and entirely too sassy. But she bought food for the cubs who couldn't always feed themselves and the more I got to know her... Ash has an inner darkness. Something that's fierce and deep and a little bit gritty that drew me in spite of my intentions otherwise.*

"Why tell me this?" Tobias asked, part intrigued and part confused.

*Because you were right - I'm in love with her.* Flynn raised his head and stared out over the lake, feline ears flickering. *I realised it the day she ran away, when Andre told her you were never coming to Ireland. Ash was ranting about how much she hated you and I was so fucking sick of Tobias this and Tobias that, so I kissed her for some peace and quiet - but it was like a spark to kindling. I couldn't stop, she couldn't stop and before I knew it we were bedridden for three days.*

Tobias growled deep in his chest but the sound didn't carry any real anger and Flynn's whuffing laughter said he was well aware of that fact. So he picked up another rock, palmed and tossed it. "What changed?"

*I eventually realised that while I was hopelessly in love with Ash, she didn't feel the same. Oh, she cared, and if I pushed, she'd probably have mated with me - and then one day, when she finally saw you again, we'd be in a hell of a lot more trouble than we are right now. I needed Aislinn Redding when I'd never needed anyone, ever; and she didn't need me at all.* Flynn lowered his head back onto his paws, tail flicking. *So I broke it off, told her we'd be better as friends. I never revealed how I really felt because I'd rather be a part of her life this way than not at all - which would've been the upshot in the long run.*

*No matter how she feels about me, or you, for that matter, I can't stop my heart from beating out her name… but I can do the right thing and let her go where she belongs.*

"You saw what she hasn't," Tobias murmured, feeling a pang of pity for the tigerkin.

*That you're her heartmate? Yeah - and it fucking sucks, by the way.* Flynn's claws shot out of their sheaths, digging into the rock beneath. *Of all the Kin in the world to be mystically fated for one another, it has to be her, and someone who's not me. Anyway, just… go easy on her.*

"Or you'll kill me?"

*And pick up where I left off.* Flynn looked Tobias directly in the eye, his face tranquil as he said; *Transition made things interesting for both of us. Relationship or not, Ash and I have been sleeping together on and off for the better part of eight years. That stopped with Olaf - and now, because I respect Ash, for you - but if you so much as wag a tail hair out of line I will tear out your throat and keep her for myself.*

Once again Tobias tried to be angry but the emotion simply refused to surface. In fact, every word the tiger spoke only engendered respect and Tobias found himself admitting, "I wasn't kind to Ash when she arrived. I thought she was mated to somebody else and I destroyed the torc in a transitional rage."

*An understandable reaction for a heartmate to have. She's yours, and you're hers, in a fucked up way that's both awesome and awful.*

"You know, if you keep being nice to me I might think you've become possessed by evil spirits or something." Tobias offered a lopsided grin and to his surprise, Flynn's tongue lolled out of his mouth in silent laughter.

*Don't worry, T-Fuzz - like I promised in the den, all truces are temporary. I'll be back to hating you in less than ten minutes.*

Tobias reached into his pocket and dug out his phone. "Well then, let me make the most of that time and show you a little something I'm trying to organise. If we can stand each other long enough to work together, we might just pull off a miracle."

*******

Aislinn woke to the undeniably raucous sound of a kookaburra laughing. She made to roll out of bed and throw something but her body refused to co-operate, leaving her to languish somewhere between asleep and awake while the damned awful bird koo-kooed and kaa-kaaed as it pleased, a notion which did nothing to improve her temper.

After considerable effort, she managed to pry one eye open and roll it towards the luminous green numbers on Tobias' bedside clock. 6.12am - why was it still so dark? Determined to surface now, she forced her second eye open and spent the next few minutes staring at the ominous black clouds boiling outside the window. A storm, then. No wonder the kookaburras were laughing; they loved the rain and often serenaded it in.

Muscles stiff from misuse and too much sleep twinged as Aislinn rolled her head in the other direction, coming face to face with Tobias. He lay on his side, one leg slung protectively over both of hers - that would account for their being numb, she supposed - and his rhythmic breathing stirring her hair. Soft brown lashes rested on full cheekbones and the jaw he so loved to grind his teeth with was relaxed in slumber. Unable to resist the temptation, Aislinn reached out to run her fingers through the leading edge of Tobias' golden brown hair, which was in sore need of a trim, or a brush, or both. With the kookaburra at last silent and her body still too heavy to roust, Aislinn contented herself with teasing tangles out of Tobias' fringe and thinking back to the boy she'd known in her youth; how he was, and yet was not, this incredibly sensitive, complex man now lying on the bed beside her.

Flynn had described Tobias as wholesome and while he'd been mostly kidding, it was true that Tobias was certainly more noble than Aislinn herself had become. They'd healed the space between them but... was there really more to it, or would the fascination of Tobias Greenwood simply wear off over time, no more than a childhood longing for a past well and truly done with?

Aislinn's body said no, her skin tingling with delight where it absorbed his warmth. As though he, too, felt that same connection, Tobias' lashes lifted and he stared out from steely blue eyes, the golden starbursts in the centre almost glowing in the dim light. There was such intensity in his expression that Aislinn felt a shiver trek down her spine - no, there was nothing about Tobias Greenwood that was going to wear off. In fact, the longer she spent with him, the more she *wanted* to spend with him; and it wasn't baking cookies or going on long walks that her body had in mind.

Aislinn blushed and made to retract her hand but Tobias was faster, curling his fingers around hers. "Stay," he whispered, his voice throaty from sleep.

She fell still, powerless to resist that deep, soft voice and the eyes which stripped her to the very depths of her soul. Impulse seized and though she was sure she'd regret it, Aislinn whispered, "What do you see?"

"I see *you*," Tobias replied. "Wild, free, perfect -"

Aislinn sensed the hesitation and in spite of the way her stomach flip flopped, raised an eyebrow. "And?"

He closed his eyes for a moment, chest expanding rapidly. "Not sure you want to hear the last part."

She choked a bit at that, tugging her hand abruptly backward and fighting the sting of hurt. "Okay."

"No, Ash -" Tobias cut off with a muffled curse and rose up on one elbow, turning her chin towards him with a gentle hand. "I just don't want to frighten you."

"Say it," she demanded, feeling unaccountably raw for a woman who'd just been wondering if there was anything to feel at all.

Tobias' thumb feathered across her cheek and his jaw flexed in a way that said he very much doubted the wisdom of acceding to her request. Slowly, he lowered his head, lips drifting lazily over Aislinn's temple, up to her forehead, over her eyelids and down her cheeks. And then, his lips brushing against her own, Tobias breathed, "Mine."

Aislinn couldn't help it - she bridged the minuscule gap between them, seeking more of his warmth, more of the strength Tobias exuded without conscious thought. Her heart thumped unevenly in her chest as he responded, applying just the right amount of pressure with his kiss to entice rather than intimidate. She smoothed a trembling hand across the line of his hips - causing Tobias to immediately freeze in place, eyes wide. Their gazes firmly interlocked, Aislinn felt her way slowly up his body, tracing sculpted obliques and a sun-bronzed chest, lingering just long enough over the pulse in his throat to elicit a shiver. Swallowing her fluttering nerves, Aislinn curled her fingers into the hair at the back of Tobias' neck, nipping gently at his lower lip before whispering, "Mine."

With that one simple word, all bets were quite suddenly off. Tobias made a strangled sound somewhere between a groan and a growl, clenching his fist in the sheets to bundle Aislinn closer. His lips slanted over hers, his tongue testing the curve of her pointed canines before sweeping inside her mouth to ignite a fire inside them both. The arm which had pulled her close slid down Aislinn's spine, pressing her body against his one vertebrae at a time, fingers kneading and smoothing the muscles in her back. The thick length of Tobias' erection pressed into her leg and though the touch of his hands was electric, Aislinn's heart jerked out of rhythm and her breath ended on a gasp.

"Hey," Tobias rolled his hips away, putting a safe distance between their lower halves while pressing gentle kisses to her face. "It's fine, Ash. You're fine."

"I'm sorry," she whispered, feeling alternately frustrated and pathetic. "It just-"

"Stop apologising to me," he growled, poking her firmly in the shoulder. "It's not necessary. Whatever you need from me, you get - or not, as the case may be."

"We can't go on like this forever," Aislinn grumbled, flopping down backwards on the bed and staring up at the roof. "It's ridiculous. I don't want Olaf to control me like this."

"I know," Tobias said gently, tracing the curve of her ribs. "But you also have to cut yourself some slack, Ash. If I could stop my body reacting, I would. I can't, but I *can* exercise my legendary patience and give you whatever time and space you need. Even," he added, cutting her off before she spoke, "If that's forever."

"You've said that before but seriously, Tobias, what sort of life is that?"

He raised a self-deprecating brow. "One where I get very well acquainted with my favourite hand, I'd imagine."

Aislinn snorted a laugh in spite of herself, thumping him in the chest with a clenched fist. "Classy."

"Practical," Tobias corrected, his face stretching into a broad grin that stole the air from her lungs. "And polite."

She covered her face with her hands and growled into her palms. "It's still stupid."

"Do you know," Tobias said, his fingers doodling absently on her skin, "that every time I touch you, it takes a little bit longer before you freak out?"

Slowly, Aislinn lowered her hands. "Really?"

"Sure - and even now, your freaking out isn't really freaking out," Tobias continued, his finger making idle progress northward.

She rolled her eyes down, where the back of Tobias' hand was brushing the underside of one breast. "Well… you're not Olaf. Contrary to the evidence, I do actually like it when you touch me."

"That's a good start." Tobias rumbled deep in his throat, rolling his hand to cup the full weight of one breast. "Mother Moon but I've been dreaming about these."

"What? Really?"

"You have no idea." Tobias lowered his head and began trailing soft butterfly kisses down the length of one of Aislinn's scars. Her breathing quickened as he crested the curve of her breast, pausing to scrape his teeth ever so gently over the sensitive flesh. He made to release her, then, but she buried one hand in his hair and arched her back in silent demand. Smiling against her skin, Tobias drew his tongue across her nipple and then sucked the peak into his mouth.

Stars sparkled across Aislinn's vision and she exhaled on a whimper, slave to a pleasure unlike anything she'd ever experienced before. It seemed impossible - she was no stranger to bedroom play - but when Tobias moved to pay the same gentle, reverent attention to her other breast, Aislinn thought she might very well die from the sensation alone. And then he was back at her mouth as he kissed her long and slow, the scent of butterscotch and cream filling her blood with champagne.

"How did you do that?" Aislinn panted as Tobias drew back to nibble a path along her jaw and down the side of her throat.

"Do what?" Strong teeth fastened over the join between neck and shoulder and bit down hard enough to send shocks of electric pleasure straight to Aislinn's core.

She fisted both hands in his hair, all but levitating off the bed. "Mother Moon, *Tobias*!"

He raised his head, the golden starbursts in his eyes blazing. "Did I hurt you?"

"No," she managed, chest heaving. "It's just - don't you feel it?"

"You're going to need to be more specific."

Of course she was. Aislinn dug her heels into the mattress and rolled, flipping Tobias onto his back. She gave him no time to prepare, lunging straight for the join between neck and shoulder and biting down hard. He gave a strangled gasp and for a moment Aislinn worried she'd been too rough, but his body twitched beneath her and strong hands yanked her hips against his. The weight of Tobias' erection pressed into her stomach but she chose to ignore it, releasing her teeth to lick over the bite mark in gentle apology. Tobias growled, his body singing with tension as he buried his face in her hair. "Solaeden save us, Ash - what *was* that?"

"I don't know." She pulled back to look into his face. Red-tinted brown hair tumbled around them in waves, blocking out the room and creating an intimate reality where there was only Aislinn and Tobias. "Did I hurt you?"

Tobias barked a startled laugh. "No. In fact, feel free to bite me as much as you like - just be ready for what happens when you do." He blinked downwards, where her scarred breasts were plumped rather magnificently against his chest. "I really like these. Really, *really* like them."

"They're too big."

"Impossible. They're perfect and they're mine and I won't hear a word against the most amazing gift I've ever been given," he said loftily, blue and gold gaze drinking her in. "If I could fall into that cleavage, I would."

"I'm glad you're impressed," Aislinn replied drily, shifting her hips against his. "Freaking out now, by the way."

"Oh, shit." Tobias released her at once, easing his body aside to give her some air. "Sorry, Ash - I wasn't thinking."

"It's fine," she said, the panic receding to more manageable proportions. "What do you think that was?"

Tobias tucked one hand behind his head, the other idly toying with a lock of her hair as he considered. "Intense?"

She crinkled her nose. "Helpful."

"You did say that transition can make things more interesting," he began but Aislinn was already shaking her head.

"Not like that. Stamina, enthusiasm, creativity - sure. But that? I've never felt anything like it," She murmured, then blushed at Tobias' scandalised expression. "I suppose you really don't want to know."

"Considering your previous practice buddy is currently a thorn in my side? Not really," he admitted. "But I'm adult enough to understand that it's only natural."

"Speaking of Flynn, where is he? How long was I asleep?" Aislinn looked out the window, where roiling grey clouds still hung low on the horizon. "That storm's not far away now, surely."

"Flynn said he had something to do and would be back soon." Tobias shrugged. "I didn't see much point in trying to convince him otherwise. As for your nap, I'd say it's been about fifteen hours."

"Fifteen hours," Aislinn repeated, massaging her temples. "That's an awful long time for you two not to kill each other."

Tobias spluttered indignantly, snatching the pillow from beneath his head and throwing it at her. "I'll have you know I'm completely innocent."

Aislinn dodged the pillow and waved an admonitory finger. "Your lies smell like sour whiskey, Tobias Greenwood."

He huffed good-naturedly and rolled out of bed. "Believe what you want, Aislinn Redding, but we managed just fine without you."

She sampled the air, surprised to find he was telling the truth - though it was obvious from the edge to Tobias' voice that it hadn't all been smooth sailing. With a quirk of her lips, she said, "What now?"

"I've got something to show you." With a secretive smile, he headed for the door. Aislinn waited until Tobias' back was turned and then grabbed the pillow from the floor, spun and hurled it at him, wincing as the motion pulled at her scarred flesh. The pillow hit Tobias square in the back of the head and he growled, glancing over his shoulder with a wicked gleam in his eye. "Don't think I've forgotten, Ash; ten minutes to do whatever I like once I catch you." And with that, he opened the door to reveal Jaxon curled up in the hall in his wolf form.

"Jax? What in Solaeden's name are you doing down there?" Aislinn demanded as the wolfkin raised his shaggy head. He might be short and stocky as a man, but as a wolf he was easily the size of a pony, if not a small horse.

Jaxon got to his feet, floorboards creaking as he shook out his long, black fur before shimmering back into human form. "Two things," he said. "First off, I swore to you. I owe you mine and my family's lives so get used to having me follow you around. I'm you're new favourite haemorrhoid."

"I... okay," Aislinn flicked a look at Tobias, who was now leaning on the door frame looking amused. "This is what you wanted to show me?"

"Yup."

Feeling completely baffled, Aislinn said, "I really don't need a door guard."

"No," Tobias agreed. "He insisted."

"You're my Den Mother," Jaxon added, thumping his fist in emphasis. "It's my job to protect you, even if you think you don't need it."

Aislinn stared between the two wolves, finally settling on Tobias. "You couldn't handle this on your own?"

He shrugged, looking even more amused. "Jax isn't my pack, remember?"

"Right. Okay," Aislinn looked back to Jaxon, feeling strangely light headed. She'd been a Den Mother for years, but had never thought about forming a pack of her own - now it seemed to be standing in front of her. Or sleeping on the floor, to be more accurate, which was just ridiculous. She chewed her lip a minute. "As much as I appreciate the gesture, wouldn't you be happier in the guest room?"

"Is it far?"

"Jaxon Heliope-Flint, you cannot seriously expect to sleep outside my bedroom door from now until the end of time," Aislinn snapped. "There are three empty bedrooms in this house! For the love of the gods, pick one."

Her self-appointed haemorrhoid straightened, green eyes gleaming. "Yes, Den Mother."

"And the second thing?" Tobias drawled, his tone thick with laughter. Aislinn glared but anything pithy she might've been thinking disappeared with the next words that came out of Jaxon's mouth.

"I was at Grandma Redding's with Mum today and there was a call from Andre. He's coming here, with Rupert."

# Three

Tobias held up a hand to shield his face from the punishing wind, keeping his head down as he followed Aislinn across the common lawns towards Grandma Redding's. His skin felt too hot after his shower, and the pancakes Jaxon had reheated sat like a lump of lead in his gut.

Mother Moon, their parents were coming back - would arrive tomorrow morning, in fact, if Jaxon was correct. Judging from the tense set of Aislinn's shoulders as she drew up in the shelter of Grandma's front porch, she felt no better about the impending arrival than he did.

Tobias jogged the last few steps to her side, instinctively stepping into the path of the wind. She'd chosen to wear a soft, wraparound dress in a deep shade of teal that hugged her curves and bought out the colour in her eyes and while it was incredible, the wind whipped her skirts up around her hips and tore mercilessly at her long hair. In fact, if not for the gold belt she'd fastened around her waist, Tobias was willing to wager the dress would have come completely undone and left her in no more than her underwear - not that he would have complained, of course.

"We need to wait for Flynn," she said, her voice snatched away by the wind. As Tobias edged closer, his broad shoulders taking the brunt of the near-gale so that her hair wasn't quite so wild about her face, she gave him a sharp look. "Not made of glass, you know."

"I've never thought you were," he answered equably. "You are, however, small enough to be blown clean off your feet."

Aislinn opened her mouth with what would likely have been a scathing retort, but Flynn chose that moment to come jogging around the side of the house in tiger form. *Morning, lovers.*

"Where've you been?" Ash hissed, mounting the steps and nudging the door open.

*So sour.* Flynn followed her into the house, shaking a great cloud of dust out of his fur. *Can you taste the storm coming? It's going to be big.*

Tobias stared up at the grey sky for a long moment, his stomach knotting even further. He had no weather sense to speak of but still he shivered, shoving into the house and tugging the door shut behind him. "I hate to agree with the kitty, but it doesn't look good."

"Aislinn?" Grandma's voice preceded her into the living room, where she stopped still in shock as Flynn walked right up to her, melting into human form as he went.

"Den Mother Redding," he purred, his Irish accent thick and rolling. "It is my greatest pleasure to make your acquaintance. My name is Flynn."

"Oh." Grandma Redding swallowed in a rare show of surprise as Flynn bent his lanky frame over her hand and rubbed his cheek against her palm. "Aislinn's told me a lot about you - except, perhaps, that you were visiting."

"I'm afraid I neglected to call ahead," Flynn purred smoothly, turning to wave an elegant hand in Aislinn's direction. "She needed me. I came."

As the tigerkin straightened, Tobias noticed he had a small black pouch hanging from the d-ring on his studded leather collar. "What's that?"

"What I went looking for, T-Fuzz." Flynn unclipped the pouch and rummaged inside, withdrawing something glittery and pink. "Here."

"My phone," Aislinn gasped, eyes bright as the tigerkin tossed it her way. "How did you get it?"

"It was surprisingly easy." Flynn shrugged, sounding almost disappointed. "Jacques was dumb enough to tell me your father had it. I went to steal it but your mother was home. She just… gave it to me."

"She *gave* it to you?" Aislinn's jaw dropped and she stared down at the phone as though it might suddenly explode. "Why would she do that?"

"Seems like she's on your side, as much as she can be," Flynn answered. "She opened the door with the phone in her hand, gave it to me along with a wad of cash, and said 'I can only buy you a couple of hours, tiger. Make it count.' Then she closed the door in my face."

Aislinn looked down at the darkened screen of her phone and then back up. "Why didn't you tell me before?"

"And then admit I hid the fucking thing outside that old barn and couldn't find it when I went back?" Flynn snorted inelegantly. "Don't be daft, Ash."

She ran her thumb over the dark screen and then, without warning, Aislinn collapsed onto the couch, hugging the phone to her chest while she howled with laughter. Grinning broadly, Flynn threw his naked body down on the couch beside her and laid his head in her lap. Tobias narrowed his eyes as she began to run her fingers through the tigerkin's satiny hair with the air of a long term habit. "You're a jerk, Flynn, you know that?"

He purred and rubbed against her leg. "You're welcome."

"What about the GPS? The minute you turn that thing on, Andre will know you have it," Tobias pointed out, his voice edged with a growl.

"How stupid do you think I am, T-Fuzz? I had that little issue fixed years ago - but I also got a friend to check it over before I left Ireland. That phone is cleaner than my asshole."

"That's a lot of fuss for a phone, young man." Grandma crossed both arms over her chest. "And a lot of things that don't add up."

"Flynn is the rogue Kin agent Andre neglected to tell you about." Tobias knew he was flexing his hands like claws, but he couldn't seem to stop. "If you knew who it was, you might've told Ash and she'd have gone looking."

"*You're* the rogue?" Grandma demanded. "Why?"

"Because some asshole of a bearkin tried to murder the only person I ever cared about, and when she didn't bounce back like the toy she's meant to be, her father decided to brush the whole thing under the rug." Flynn's fury was a palpable force that Tobias wrapped around himself like a cloak, allowing the sharp scent of cloves to invade his nostrils and give light to the fire of his own anger. His gaze locked with Flynn's as the tigerkin continued, "I tried to intervene and they threw me out like so much unwanted trash, then shipped Ash across oceans with the conceited belief they could stop me from trying to find her."

Grandma's face creased in thought, and she appraised Flynn with new eyes. "You were willing to throw away everything to make sure she was safe?"

"Of course. She's my pack, as you wolves would say." Flynn rolled his eyes up to look at Aislinn. "Don't let that go to your head, princess."

Tobias' fists clenched as her face softened and she leant over to press a sisterly kiss to Flynn's smooth cheek. "I'll try."

"All right," Grandma conceded, "I'm willing to accept that. It's a rare thing to - Tobias? Are you all right?"

"I'm fine," Tobias snapped, but even he could hear that his voice was oddly strangled. His skin itched and he took a half step back, shaking his head to clear it as fur crept across the flesh of his arms. "I need to... I can..."

"Focus on Ash," Flynn said suddenly, his voice sharp. "Focus on her scent. Imprint her face on your heart and soul - that way when you lose your mind, you'll instinctively seek her out."

Imprint her face on his heart and soul? As if it wasn't already. Tobias hunched in on himself with a growl, his body contorting beneath the confines of his clothing. "I've got it."

"You really don't," Flynn replied airily.

He looked up to disagree and his eyes locked with Aislinn's - but not before drifting over the other male whose head still lay in her lap. Something snapped and Tobias roared, the sound of his voice shaking the house so hard the pictures rattled. Fog crept in at the corners of his vision, his nose wrinkling as he drew a deep breath and got a second lungful of cloves and coffee. Tiger. He would have that tiger, he would tear it to shreds - *No.* He took another step back, half turning as if to make for the door, but his legs wouldn't go. Bones cracked and fur sprouted as, one slow moment at a time, Tobias lost his inner struggle and his midform emerged.

"Mother Moon," Grandma whispered, then froze with her hand partway to her mouth as he turned his shaggy head in her direction.

Dinner. No, not dinner. Den Mother? No, no. Far too weak to be *his* Den Mother. A challenge, then? A challenge to his Alpha position?

"Tobias."

Who was that? The red fog that clouded his vision revealed little more than silhouettes, but he could smell and hear someone approaching. The scent of honeysuckle and vanilla teased his delicate nose and he drew it deep into his lungs. Mate. His mate. The thought had the fog clearing just enough that he could see her face, eyes clear and hair tumbling around her face in gorgeous disarray. He wanted to bury himself in it. In *her*. She extended her hands, palms upwards, and he immediately bent to place his furred snout against her skin, his tongue edging out to taste her soft warmth. His mate. His heart. His soul. *His*.

Gentle fingers danced across his muzzle and threaded into the fur either side of his face, and he rumbled in appreciation. He edged closer, needing more of her, and began to rub his head against her neck and shoulder. Her scent was everywhere, sweet and soothing, her fingers were combing through his fur. This was what he needed; to be near her. And now that he was - Tobias grunted as cool energy washed over him in a rush, taking his legs from beneath him. His body shrank and slumped and the next he knew, he was kneeling on the floor of Grandma Redding's lounge room with Aislinn supporting his weight.

"Easy, tig -" She cut off with a low curse, taking a hasty breath and tightening her grip when he groaned and tried to move. "I've got you, Tobias. Breathe it out."

He couldn't even be annoyed that she'd been about to call him tiger; with the cool shadows still smothering his spirit, all Tobias could do was hang from Aislinn's arms like a limp rag. "Dammit. I thought I had it."

"The problem is that you're still fighting," Flynn said from the couch. Tobias half turned to see the tigerkin starfished on his back, one leg propped on the arm rest and the other hanging lazily off the side as he watched the tableau with open amusement. "That's like falling into the bath and telling the water it's not allowed to get you wet."

"Fuck you," he snarled, temper flaring - and then gasped as Aislinn smoothed her hands over his back, easing out the transitional echoes like wrinkles from a handkerchief.

"You okay?" She whispered, her lips near his ear.

"Yeah." Tobias shot another glance towards the couch, and the wickedly grinning oaf atop it. "Still fuck you, though."

"I am naked, so I can see why you'd be tempted," Flynn answered, twisting his hips back and forth so that his cock slapped around like a fish on dry land. "Sexy, right?"

"That is quite enough," Grandma Redding snapped, covering her eyes with one hand. "This is my house, young man. Behave."

"Sorry, Den Mother," Flynn replied, and though he didn't sound the least bit contrite, he shimmered back to tiger form and assumed a far less provocative position on the couch. *I don't have any clothes so it's fur or dick, I'm afraid.*

"Fur," said Tobias and Grandma in unison.

Aislinn rolled her eyes. "However crude the delivery, Flynn's point stands. You can't fight this energy, Tobias - it's part of you. The only way to win is to accept it."

"I don't know how," he mumbled, lifting his head to pin her with a stark expression.

"Probably because you're a control freak," Aislinn teased, stroking one hand along his cheek. "You need to let go and embrace your wild side."

"Solaeden save us," Grandma muttered. "Tobias, wild? We're doomed."

*Hah! Told you he was too wholesome.*

"Ignore the peanut gallery," Aislinn instructed, her hand clenching on his tightening jaw. "Your energy is strong and will only grow stronger as you gain momentum. Transition - particularly for males - is like peeling an onion. Every layer is trickier than the first and if you don't handle things very carefully, everyone cries." She paused, leaning in to feather her lips across his furrowed brows and leaving a tingling heat in their wake. "We also haven't seen the emergence of your other powers yet."

"Other powers?" Tobias flinched, his heart stuttering in his chest. "Like what?"

*My telepathic chit chat… Aislinn's shadows.* Flynn yawned lazily. *That sort of power.*

"I… but…"

"It's okay, Tobias," Aislinn murmured, brushing his hair back from his face. He lent into the gesture, craving her comfort. "We'll handle it when it happens."

"Much as this conversation is enlightening, I have things to do. Your fathers are bringing quite the entourage and I need to organise food and accommodation for everyone before they arrive," Grandma said briskly. "So, my dear - what do you want?"

"To ask about Dad." Aislinn helped Tobias to his feet and then slid under his arm, her body fitting against his like a jigsaw. "Why is he coming? Who is he bringing? What does he want?"

Grandma pursed her lips. "Andre's coming because of Olaf. As soon as he made an appearance in person, the High Council decided to move in. Considering your father's got his own agenda to protect, he volunteered to take the matter in hand personally."

"So the goal is to apprehend Olaf whilst still hiding the pack from the broader eye of the Council," Aislinn nodded. "That's pretty much what I expected. And his entourage?"

"That, I cannot tell you much about, I'm afraid. Three full teams - one staying with the Cartwright foxkin, one with the Grayden horsekin, one here. I don't know who they are," Grandma added, holding up a cautionary finger, "So don't ask. Then there's your mother, Rupert and Stephanie."

Aislinn's body went stiff and Tobias slid an arm around her waist in silent support. "What is it?"

She grimaced. "Just a feeling. Flynn, what do you think our odds are?"

*Of Andre trying to fuck us over somehow? About one hundred and fifty per cent,* he answered. *Grandma would be a nice ace in the hole - if she likes me enough.*

"If I like you well enough for what, tigerkin?" Grandma gave Flynn an assessing once over. "Whilst I'm grateful for your support of Aislinn, it takes more than a wiggle of the hips to impress me."

Flynn's eyes narrowed and Aislinn abruptly stepped between them, leaving Tobias to sway unsteadily for a moment before his legs decided to work. "Flynn's saved my life more times than I can count."

"He's also a fugitive," Grandma Redding replied, propping one hand on her hip. "If I offer him sanctuary, I put our pack firmly between Flynn and the law."

Tobias drew in a sharp breath. "Joanne, think. Ash and Flynn have a contract clause citing that the punishment of one is dealt equally to both. If you let Andre arrest Flynn, then Ash goes to prison, too."

"Then he best make himself scarce before Andre arrives," Grandma said firmly. "In light of past history, I won't reveal his presence but to protect a rogue? I have a pack to think of, Tobias - and so do you."

"You granted me sanctuary without a thought," Aislinn snapped. "This shouldn't be any different."

"I'm sorry, my dear, but it is. Flynn isn't my grand-daughter, merely a vagabond known for flouting the rules at his whim." Grandma sighed and shook her head. "You don't even know if your father *will* move to arrest him. Have a little faith."

Aislinn growled low in her throat. "Faith? I've never put stock in faith before, and I'm not about to start now. We need -"

*Save it,* Flynn cut in, his voice soft. *She's right, Ash. I'm just one tigerkin.*

"You're *my* tigerkin, and you damned well know it." Aislinn squared her shoulders. "Flynn and I are blood bonded. You disavow him, you disavow me too."

Grandma Redding's jaw dropped, the shock on her face echoing that which shook Tobias to the core of his soul. "A blood bond? Are you mad?"

"Debatable, but that doesn't change the fact that Flynn is mine, and I'll do whatever is necessary to protect him." Aislinn's jaw clenched, her eyes trained so intently on her grandmother that Tobias knew his horror had shown on his face. "I love you, Grandma, but this is wrong and you know it. Not long ago, you told me you wanted to fight Dad but now, at the first opportunity, you're balking."

"I'm doing nothing of the sort," Grandma hissed, hands clenching into fists. "All I need is -"

"Save it," Aislinn interrupted, making a cutting motion with one hand. "I'm not interested. Flynn and I will stay for now, but if Dad makes a single move out of line tomorrow, I will leave pack land so fast you'll be choking on the dust."

Tobias rumbled deep in his chest. "You won't go alone."

"You do that, you leave us wide open to the bearkin," Grandma whispered, her eyes wide.

Aislinn gave a tight nod of acknowledgement. "I know."

*Ash.* Flynn's tail lashed the side of the couch. *I didn't come here to fuck these people's lives up.*

"No, you came here for me, and I will honour that commitment until my dying breath." Aislinn thumped a fist against her chest. "Think about that from your lofty position on the fence, Grandma. Neutrality's a nice concept but in my experience, it you stay up there forever you'll lose both sides."

*******

Ignoring the shock on her grandmother's face, Aislinn stalked out the front door and into the searing heat of the afternoon. She called her wolf form, uncaring that the lovely teal dress would likely disappear on the wings of the lashing wind, and launched herself across the common lawn. Part of her wondered if it was cowardly to run, but her grandmother's dissemination felt all too close to the betrayal she'd experienced when her father had uttered the word 'compromised' and she didn't have the strength to face that scenario all over again.

The common lawn flew by beneath her paws and Aislinn lowered her head, shooting into the scrub and turning away from the path to the den. She didn't want to face anyone right now - she needed the silence of her own heartbeat and the peace of the bush. Following a road paved only by memory, she ducked under logs, danced through bracken and circled boulders, allowing the wild joy of movement to wash away her anxiety.

All too soon she scented water and a moment later, Aislinn wriggled through some particularly thick scrub and emerged into open air. The clearing was screened on one side by the undergrowth she'd just braved, and on the other side, by the rough arms of a cliff. An offshoot of the river which fuelled the waterhole trickled out of the rock at Aislinn's eye height, and had carved a thin bed between pebbles on the way to the edge of the cliff.

She padded over to lap a few mouthfuls of water from the little creek and flopped down on her belly, crossing her paws under her chin. The bushes behind her rustled but Aislinn didn't look around. She knew before his scent reached her that it would be Tobias, his long, sandy brown fur whispering as he padded across the clearing to flop down beside her. His wolf form was beautiful; every long line of his body, from deep chest to fluffy tail, made her tingle in a way nobody else - not even Flynn - ever had. The irony being, thanks to Olaf, that something which should have made her toes curl in delight was now terrifying.

As though he knew the direction her thoughts had taken, Tobias leant over to rub his nose along her jaw line. She rolled sideways so that their bodies touched, savouring the way his butterscotch and cream scent curled through the clearing. With the cliff sheltering them from the wind and the overbearing sun dampened by the rapidly approaching storm, there was nothing to distract her from the way her body softened with sudden awareness. She shifted slightly, pushing the sensations from her mind. They were relaxing, just like they always used to, taking comfort in each other's presence without needing the added weight of words. She was certainly not, in any way shape or form, recalling how expertly Tobias had moulded her curves or how delicious his lips felt against her tortured flesh. Or his kiss - no, Aislinn told herself, she wasn't thinking about that either. She was enjoying the peace and quiet of the bush, dammit.

Tobias rolled abruptly to his feet, shaking the sand from his fur as he padded over to the creek. Shimmering into human form, he dug in the undergrowth at the base of the cliff and withdrew an oiled canvas, unrolling it to reveal a cluster of what at first appeared to be spare parts. Aislinn's eyes widened as he began rigging up a temporary shower to the place where the spring flowed out of the cliff wall.

"I figured this is why you came here," he said without turning, his fingers busy making the final adjustments to the rudimentary shower head.

*Not entirely,* Aislinn thought - but it was as good a reason as any.

Tobias flicked a glance her way as he tugged the fastenings to ensure the shower was stable. "How did you know we still had it?"

Looks like they weren't going to avoid a conversation after all. Not nearly as irritated as she thought she'd be, Aislinn returned to her human form and pushed upright, dusting sandy hands on her thighs. "I didn't. I just figured it'd come in handy with all the training you guys do in the den. Keeping it makes sense."

"It was one of your better ideas," he agreed, dropping his hands with a grin.

"All of my ideas are good, you just never wanted to admit it," Aislinn replied, stepping around him to adjust the angle of the spray. The water was icy as it slicked her skin and she gasped, her chest tightening in an all too familiar vice.

Olaf, here, now? So soon? Her knees buckled as a wave of pain overtook her body but Tobias was there, catching her before she hit the ground. He went to his knees in the water's fine spray, drawing her into his lap and cradling her against the warmth of his chest. "Fight, Ash. *Fight.*"

She turned her head into the hollow of his neck, taking Tobias' scent deep into her lungs. Her hands moved of their own accord, one twining in his hair and the other splaying over his thundering heart. Tobias locked her body against his, kneading her back and murmuring soft encouragements. Warmth and life poured out through his fingers, a welcome heat that rushed to strengthen Aislinn's flagging reserves.

Recalling his story about the previous attack, she focussed her attention on the Mark which blazed with icy fury at her hip. Surely it had to be the source of Olaf's connection? Coating her essence in Tobias' heat, Aislinn clenched her teeth and flexed her mental muscles. It was a clumsy movement, but the icy choke hold slipped nonetheless. Buoyed by her success, Aislinn gathered as much of Tobias' wild energy as she could, using the skills she'd accrued as a damper to surround Olaf's icy energy in a shimmering net of crackling heat and light. When her net was in place, she tightened it, strangling the searing cold until it stuttered and cut out.

Very suddenly, it was just herself and Tobias alone in the outdoor shower, pleasantly cool water tumbling over their heads. Aislinn tightened her hands in his hair, leaning up to rub her forehead against his own. "We did it," she whispered. "He's gone."

Tobias' comforting rumble turned into a growl and he lowered his head, teasing her mouth with his own until it opened in invitation. The last of Olaf's influence dissipated as Aislinn leant into the kiss, her own chest rumbling as she flicked her tongue across Tobias' teeth. He whimpered into her mouth, his tongue invading with a hunger that bordered on desperation. One hand crept up to cradle her head and the other tightened around her waist, as though he would meld them together into one being. Aislinn waited for her panic to stir but it remained silent, leaving her gloriously trapped in a maelstrom of delicious sensation.

Tobias drew back to scatter kisses across her face. "Are you all right?"

"Yeah. I… What did we do?"

He arched a brow. "You need a lesson?"

"No," Aislinn flicked his chin playfully. "I *meant*, how did we get rid of Olaf?"

"I don't know. I was hoping you'd be able to tell me." His chuckle was bedroom rich and rolled down her spine. "It seems to have something to do with both of us; you used my energy last time, too."

Aislinn frowned, trying to sort through her rush of memories. "Agreed, but there's obviously more to it than simply seeing you or having you nearby. It was as though you gave me part of yourself to weaponise."

"I wanted to help." His forehead bumped against hers and she caught the flash of fangs. "I wanted to reach inside you and throw him out. I wanted my scent all over you, inside you -"

"It's all right," Aislinn murmured as he cut off, biting his lip. "I'm not afraid of you."

"I want him gone," Tobias whispered, the gold in his eyes blazing bright. "I want him gone forever and I want to make love to you the way it should have been from the beginning."

Aislinn swallowed heavily and his gaze, suddenly predatory, tracked the motion. "Tobias…"

"Relax." He smiled and kissed her softly on the cheek. "I won't lie about wanting you, but you get to make the call, Ash. I said it before and I'll say it again - whenever you're ready, I'll be right here."

The simple tenderness of his truth bloomed within Aislinn's heart even as the towering masculinity of his presence stoked a fire deep in her belly she had feared was totally extinguished. She dug her fingers into the base of his jaw, tilting his head to brush her lips against his. "Touch me."

Tobias froze. With her body already cradled in his lap there could be no mistaking the meaning of that request. His expression was alternately fierce and anxious and for a wild moment Aislinn wished she could capture that image and breathe it in again at a later date. Then one of his hands settled on her knee and all other thoughts fled as Tobias rumbled; "Are you sure?"

Aislinn laid her hand atop his, tugged it a couple inches higher. "Very sure."

His fingers flexed and then relaxed. Slowly, with her hand still resting atop his, Tobias began to caress her thigh. He moved carefully, no doubt catching the way her heart thumped unevenly in spite of her brave words, employing a silken touch which smoothed over her scars without any real hint of a destination. He hummed deep in his chest, a tuneless, almost purring sound which vibrated against Aislinn's shoulder and sent tingles of electricity up and down her spine.

Tobias caught her lips with his once more; soft and enticing. His kiss was like a drug, too much too soon and yet the moment he broke away, not nearly enough. Aislinn gasped as he nibbled on her jaw, tilting her head back to give him access to her throat. Sharp teeth scraped over her pulse, sending delicious shocks of electricity straight into her veins. And while Tobias' mouth made slow, erotic progress down her neck, he shifted his body so that his hand, still shrouded by hers, had an easier path up the expanse of her thigh.

"Stop me," he murmured, nipping at her collarbone. His fingers found the crease of her leg, stroked gentle, tingling circles around the jutting edge of her hip bone.

Aislinn tightened her grip on his hand and Tobias obligingly made to halt his languorous caresses. "I don't want you to stop," she whispered, guiding him down the curve of her pelvis. "I want you to kiss me like you mean it."

Tobias' breath expelled in a rush as she urged his hand ever lower, their joined fingers brushing the outermost edges of Aislinn's most sensitive place. In that electric moment he took her lips with his, tongue sweeping into her mouth while he drew his other arm further around her body, palming her breast with exquisite tenderness. She gasped into his mouth, one hand showing him how best to touch her whilst the other drifted across his lap to brush the hard length of his erection.

Nerves skittered through her belly and Aislinn's breath shuddered in her lungs but Tobias' touch was leashed lightning, his solid strength a balm to the rift in her soul. His fingers stilled, waiting; his mouth gentled, sensing her discomfort and offering the chance to pull away. Gathering the final shreds of her fading courage, Aislinn opened her hand wide and ever so gently feathered the flat of her palm up the warm velvet of his shaft, allowing the soft skin to slowly slide across her flesh. Her entire focus narrowed to the singular sensation of voluntarily touching Tobias, acknowledging it as *Tobias*, not the harbinger of fear or suffering which haunted her nightmares.

His breathing was well and truly ragged by the time she withdrew her hand, and when he spoke, his voice was a husky rasp. "Thank Solaeden I'm already in a cold shower."

Aislinn gave a shaky laugh. "Trying to wash me off already?"

"Never." Tobias threaded one arm beneath her knees and stood, cradling her against his chest for a long moment before he let her slide down to her feet. "Are you still okay?"

"Yeah." She nodded, stepping into his embrace. Tobias immediately shifted his lower body so the hard length of him pointed elsewhere, allowing her the sanctuary of his arms without further distress. Aislinn laid her cheek against his thundering heart, touched by the tenderness that was an inherent part of his personality. "I don't see the other room any more. I don't hear the sounds or feel those phantom claws and teeth. It's progress, it's just… slow."

"You really relived that every time?" Tobias' voice was aghast.

"In the beginning? Sure. Every time I closed my eyes, every time someone touched me, every time I heard a male voice - particularly at the hospital, surrounded by so many unfamiliar people." She shivered. "It was like a nightmare I couldn't wake up from."

Tobias tightened one arm across her back, his free hand stroking her hair. "I'm sorry it happened, Ash."

"So am I," she murmured, forcing her lungs to expand to full capacity. "I hope Regina's all right, too. Don't forget the attack was never meant for me in the first place - I'm just collateral."

"You're anything but," Tobias growled, his fingertips digging into her ribs. Aislinn fidgeted in warning and he immediately relaxed. "Sorry."

"It's fine," she returned, spreading one hand over his muscled abdomen and watching the water collect in the curves of her fingers. "I don't think I could do this with anyone else but for some reason you're mostly safe."

"I'm glad to hear that," Tobias chuckled. "I try to be generous where I can, but the idea of sharing you lacks a certain appeal."

She snorted. "I've noticed."

"Finally." A blinding smile lit his face for a fraction of a moment, then faded. "As for Regina, I'm sure they've got her well guarded."

"I hope so." Aislinn turned her face into his sternum and pressed a gentle kiss to the tanned flesh there. "Remind me to ask Dad about that before I disembowel him."

Tobias laughed aloud. "I'll try."

*You guys all right out there?* Flynn's voice was thready, a sign he wasn't particularly close by.

Aislinn stepped out of the water and called her wolf form, shaking the moisture from her fur. *We're fine. What's the matter?*

Flynn's reply was slow in coming but when it did, his mental voice was coloured with relief. *The storm front's hit the lower farms and is headed this way. Wind and rain and thu-* the sky cracked with a sound like a cannon firing and Aislinn shook herself again as rain pelted her back.

*Thunder?* Tobias' voice, warm and soft inside her mind courtesy of Flynn's psychic connection to them both.

*No shit, T-Fuzz. A couple of the mamas are freaking out - Achilles and three other young pups are out wandering. I've started tracking from here, but I figured if you two pitch in we've got more noses to the ground. This storm is going to fucking suck, I can feel it in my whiskers.*

*We're on it.* Aislinn looked over her shoulder at Tobias, now also in his wolf form, who nodded. *Wait - how do you know all this?*

*I'm with Zeke,* Flynn replied. *I like Zeke.*

*You can't have him, he's mine,* Tobias growled, his nose bumping Aislinn's hindquarters as they wriggled through the thick scrub. *Find your own second.*

*You know what they say, little Alpha; what's mine is mine and what's yours is also mine,* Flynn shot back, his voice even threadier than before. *Does he mind if his ears get nibbled? I like a bit of nibbling.*

*We're losing you - I'll howl if we find the kids,* Aislinn said, and received a faint mental nudge in return before the tigerkin's presence faded completely.

As they moved out of the sheltering arms of the cliff the wind became a lashing beast, tossing the trees back and forth and driving sharp raindrops before it. Thunder rumbled and growled almost continuously and the midday sky was so overcast as to be almost black. Aislinn laid her ears flat against her skull as lightning flashed overhead, followed quickly by a resounding crack that announced it had grounded nearby. The longer they took to find Achilles and his friends the more difficult the task would become, with the wind and rain working to erase any trace of their passage. She shimmered back to human form in the relative shelter of a hanging tea tree and turned to Tobias.

"You lead - I don't know the best places to play and hide any more," she all but shouted. Tobias nodded and bumped his head on her leg. Aislinn returned to her wolf body as lightning flashed again and with a synchronicity born of a lifetime's worth of practice, the two wolves plunged into the bush.

# Four

Tobias led Aislinn through the rain-lashed bush, all his senses on high alert. They crossed hollows and ducked beneath the sprawling canopies of low-hanging trees, constantly checking for any sign of the pups while thunder growled above and lightning hung so thick in the air that his skin crawled. Their lupine bodies moved as a single unit, energy shimmering between them with every electric brush of fur. Where one stepped, the other instinctively knew to follow, where one jumped the other was right behind. He could feel the growing heartmate connection like a living thing inside him and knew Ash felt it too, though she'd yet to realise what it actually was.

Tobias longed to tell her, the need to tip his heart right out of his mouth almost overwhelming - but he couldn't. *Wouldn't.* A simple mating was one thing, but a heartmate? It was a one-time deal, a soul deep connection between two Kin that bound them irrevocably until death and, if legend was to be believed, beyond. It was heat, light, sex and love, a connection rare and sacred enough to trump even the highest authorities, being an intimate blessing from the twin gods themselves. Two halves of a whole, destined from birth to complete the other, two energies that drew each other like the halves of a magnet. And though Tobias knew his heart had beat for Aislinn since the day he'd first drawn breath, she wasn't nearly so aware. To drop such a bomb on her so soon after her ordeal would be unfair… not to mention, he was male enough to admit he relished the idea of her coming to him, eyes wide and lips wet with sudden, sensual understanding.

Lightning struck close enough that the ground shuddered and Tobias lowered his shoulder, shoving Aislinn out of the way of a falling branch. He circled back to sniff at the singed wood, turning his eyes to the canopy above. The gums were tall, providing some protection from the weather but that also made them ideal targets for Mother Nature's fury.

*Any luck?* Flynn's voice broke into his reverie, still thready with distance.

*Not yet.* Aislinn's mental tone was filled with worry. *We've covered barely a quarter of the pack's territory and the storm is getting worse by the moment.*

*Told you it was going to be shitty*, Flynn replied. *Zeke's spread the other boys out but we're moving pretty slowly and with all the noise, it'll be impossible to hear the pups. I can't even call them out - I tried.*

Tobias had no idea what Flynn was talking about but Aislinn was nodding, even though the other male couldn't see her. *We need to put ourselves in their skins for a moment. Tobias? You know them best.*

Lightning slammed off to the left and Tobias staggered, shaking his head as the static charge seemed to crawl beneath his skin and lodge there. Red fog crept into the edges of his vision and he stopped in the lee of a boulder to scrub at his face with one soggy paw. Aislinn followed without prompting, smoothing her head along his jaw as her softer energy quieted the transitional surge. *Achilles,* he said at last, rubbing his own head against hers. *He'll have Rex with him - those two are never far apart - and most likely Rose and Connor Brexton. They follow Achilles everywhere.*

*It's good if they're together.* Aislinn bumped her shoulder to his, and Tobias knew she was remembering a time when they'd also run around creating mischief and making their adults worry. *A group is harder to conceal.*

*We've checked most of the places I'd expect them to - wait.* Tobias raised his head, snorting rain out of his nose. *There's an old lean-to behind the burnt shack. Sarah told Achilles off a couple weeks ago for going there; it's well within pack land but fairly tumbledown and she worried it wasn't safe. Achilles came to me looking for an Alpha's reassurance - Sarah was being overprotective and I think she knew it, but that didn't stop her giving him an earful.*

*I don't recall her being like that,* Aislinn's voice carried her frown. *We got up to all sorts of things far worse than playing in a lean-to, and she barely batted an eyelash.*

*Sarah took Draco's death really hard,* Tobias murmured. *She's never been the same since.*

Flynn's voice was unexpectedly respectful. *No parent should have to bury a child. Where's the lean-to?*

*Not far,* Aislinn answered. *Zeke can lead you, provided you stop nibbling his ears long enough.*

*Of course I can; we both know I'm the poster boy for self control.* Flynn's voice was deadpan but Tobias was a long-time friend of sarcasm and knew it when he heard it. The tigerkin's voice was stronger now, an indication the other male was getting closer. *Zeke says we'll meet you there.*

Once more alone in his own head, Tobias gave himself a shake and set off in the direction of the burnt shack. Lightning continued to strike all around them, splitting trees and echoing like cannon fire off the cliffs. Though the ground shook and the raindrops bordered on painful, Ash looked completely at ease, utterly fearless - which she was, unless Olaf was involved. Tobias hated what the bearkin had done, hated even more that he hadn't been there like his instincts kept insisting he should have. Most of all, he hated how the attack had stolen the light from her eyes and left her a vulnerable shell. He felt a surge of jealous rage directed entirely at Flynn - for almost a decade, the tigerkin had known and loved that wildfire inside of Aislinn which Tobias had always treasured. The only positive was that Flynn, like Tobias, had made it clear he'd do whatever it took to bring that glimmer back to her eye permanently.

Aislinn dropped slightly behind, her shoulder brushing his hindquarters. Tobias understood immediately, skirting ahead to the base of a sheer incline higher than either of them could jump by themselves. He braced himself and a moment later, Aislinn's paws were pressing into his shoulders as she bounced off him much like a trampoline, scrabbling momentarily before disappearing over the lip of the rock.

Tobias circled back a few paces, put on a burst of speed and leapt, his own claws scrabbling against the rain-slickened stone. At the peak of his upward momentum, teeth sank into the ruff at the base of his neck and with a single heave that belied her preternatural strength, Aislinn hauled him up beside her.

Or at least; that's how it had worked when they were younger. Now, his weight - or her strength - was greater than it had been back then, and they tumbled across the bracken in a confused mess of legs and fur. Tobias ended up flat on his back, vulnerable belly exposed to the storm above, with Aislinn's slighter body smack atop his. She huffed a lupine laugh, nipping affectionately at his jaw and setting such a fire in his loins that Tobias knew if he didn't lie very, very still, he'd lose his mind and pounce on her like some sort of ravenous beast. Which, at this particular moment, every red-hot nerve ending insisted that he was.

As usual, she seemed completely oblivious, batting playfully at his nose with a paw before extricating herself from the unplanned mess of limbs. Worried she'd glance south and see that his body was very much betraying him - again - Tobias rolled swiftly upright and took a moment to shake himself thoroughly. The rain was still beating down, negating any real good he'd do with the gesture, but it bought a few precious seconds to rebuild some semblance of equilibrium.

*We're almost there.* Flynn's voice, far stronger now.

*So are we,* Aislinn answered, raising her head to the wind and rain. *I can see the roof of the shack in the distance.*

Lightning crashed in punctuation to her words and though it should have cooled the fire raging inside Tobias, the howling in his soul only intensified. Gritting his teeth and aware he was growling well beyond his ability to control, he once again took the lead. The going was far easier here, the ground flatter and the trees further apart, so he poured on his preternatural speed in a vain attempt to slough off some of the wild energy flaying his senses.

*I can sense them,* Flynn's excited voice broke through Tobias' inner struggle. *Looks like you were right, T-Fuzz.*

*Don't go barging in - they're not used to tigers,* Aislinn warned. *Wait for me.*

*Us,* Tobias corrected.

*For the love of - all right, us.* Her eye roll was present in every syllable, and when Tobias glanced over his shoulder, it was to see Aislinn's top lip curled back from her teeth. *Children are lost in the bush, but by all means, let's argue about pronouns.*

His growl hitched up a notch, reacting to the spike in his temper. Tobias' skin crawled, every single follicle of his fur standing on end as he struggled to contain the cyclone inside of him.

*Cut her some slack,* Flynn's voice was intense enough that Tobias knew he was being addressed privately. *She doesn't know what you know.*

*Fuck off.*

Flynn chuckled. *Feeling the edge, T-Fuzz?*

*Since when do you care what I feel?*

*Since you might frighten the cubs,* Flynn returned, the laughter disappearing from his tone. *Either curb it, or I'll tell Ash to flip your switch.*

Knowing the tigerkin was right and hating him all the more for it, Tobias drew a deep, rain-filled breath. *I've got it.*

*Good.* The tiger's voice took on a slight echo as he re-introduced Ash to the conversation. *You're closer, you'll get there first.*

*All right. Anything we need to know before we arrive?*

*Fucking hell, Ash, I'm not a fucking magician,* Flynn snapped. A heartbeat passed, then another. *Four of 'em, huddled together, is all I got. The weather's your enemy here, not imaginary bad guys.*

Aislinn grunted. *It pays to be careful. See you soon.*

*Of course.*

A sensation not unlike the rubbing of fur punctuated the tigerkin's departure, and a moment later Tobias and Aislinn emerged into an overgrown yard. The lean-to was literally that; once some sort of feed shelter for cattle with three rickety walls and a rusty piece of corrugated iron on top. He followed Aislinn around the leading edge of the structure, immediately grateful for the surcease in rain the dented roof allowed - even if it meant the downpour was a near-deafening echo to the thunder that rolled almost continuously overhead. Ash was already in human form, crouching to hold out her arms to the four bedraggled, cowering wolf pups in the back corner.

The largest pup, a sweet black male with a distinctive white patch over half his face, came rushing forward first, his body flashing human a millisecond before he hit Aislinn hard in the chest. "Ash!" Achilles cried. "You came."

"Sure did," Aislinn smiled down at him and then out at the rest of the pups. "Come on now, I won't bite."

Tobias shifted into human form beside her, ducking his head to avoid hitting the lowered roof. The sight of someone more familiar bought the other three forward - and to his surprise, even the two pups who'd never met Aislinn crowded into her gentle embrace.

"You're hurt." Rose Brexton, a pale-skinned child with curly strawberry hair and an army of freckles, reached out to brush a finger down one of Aislinn's scars.

Tobias heard Ash's breath catch but when she spoke, her voice was even. "Yes, sweet heart."

Rose's brow furrowed, her nine year old mind trying to grasp the extent of the injuries. "You must be very brave."

"I try to be." Aislinn answered with the simple honesty that had always been at her core. "It's tricky sometimes."

"Don't worry," Rose smiled, and it transformed her face into nothing short of angelic. "Tobias will look after you. He's our Alpha, you know - mama always says he'll keep us safe."

"Ash can keep Tobias safe, too," Achilles said stoutly, his piercing green eyes bright in the gloom. "I watched her kill bears all by herself."

Tobias winced at the older boy's revelation but the other young children only rounded their eyes in awe. Rose reached up to touch another scar, this one along the base of Aislinn's throat. "When I'm bigger, I want to be as brave as you."

Aislinn made a strangled noise which was almost stolen by the thunder, and squeezed all four kids tight. "Thank you, Rose."

Tobias felt his heart clench as they melted beneath her easy, open affection. He'd first thought her a stranger but he'd been wrong; his Ash was there. Trapped inside, perhaps, but clawing through the demons one inch at a time. Tobias cleared his throat and stepped forward. "We need to get you all home. Your mothers are worried."

Connor and Rex flinched deeper into Aislinn's arms. Achilles said; "There's too much light and noise."

At that moment lightning flashed, thunder roared and the bush shuddered under the impact. The children squeaked in chorus and Aislinn peppered their anxious faces with soothing kisses, murmuring soft reassurances. Tobias turned his gaze outward, nostrils curling as he caught the scent of burning wood. Not good. If the bush caught alight, the entire pack would be in danger.

*We're here,* Flynn's voice rang clear as a bell in Tobias' mind and a moment later, the tigerkin came padding gracefully out of the trees, his exotic black and orange stripes somehow blending perfectly with the earthy tones of the Australian bush. Zeke trotted quietly by the tiger's side, his white-blond fur soaked dark by the pouring rain.

"There really *is* a tiger!" Connor howled in delight, clapping his tiny hands.

Flynn paced slowly under the shelter. *Want to pet me?*

Without waiting for an answer, he lowered his great head and rubbed against Connor's chest like a house cat. Tobias felt a strange sensation steal over him, a soft, almost-there susurration which raised goose bumps on his arms. A second later, Flynn dropped lazily onto the floor and all four children returned to wolf form so they could squeeze as close to the tiger as possible. In the time it took for Tobias to blink, Flynn had curled protectively around their tiny bodies, purring loudly enough to be heard even over the thunder.

"Hot damn," Zeke announced, thumping his head on the low roof as he stepped inside. "Was this always so small?"

"Yeah." Tobias couldn't quite swallow his grin. "You're just a bigger idiot now than when you were last here."

Zeke growled low in his throat, rubbing at his bruised skull. "Good call on this place - I'd never have thought of it."

"It's too dangerous to take the kids out in all that lightning," Aislinn announced, sauntering over to join them. "Flynn's volunteered to stay with them until the storm blows over."

Tobias glanced over her shoulder to where Flynn, still purring, was calmly adjusting furry little bodies until they were pressed more closely against his side. "Are they *asleep*?"

"Shhh. Almost - let him work," Aislinn replied. Reading his expression, she smiled. "Flynn's secondary ability is… interesting. Remember that old tale about the fairy boy who could charm rats with his pipe? It works a little like that. Wild animals are drawn to Flynn subconsciously and when he wills it, he can talk with them and even influence their actions. It works less with Kin, seeing as we're only part wild, but children? They love him unconditionally."

"That's what he meant before when he said he couldn't call them out," Tobias guessed.

Aislinn nodded. "He's lulling them to sleep until the storm clears. They'll be safe here."

"Someone needs to reassure their mothers," Tobias returned. "I'm also worried about the lightning setting the bush on fire."

"In all this rain?" Aislinn frowned out at the bush as though expecting it to suddenly combust. "Surely not."

"It's been a dry summer," Tobias replied. "Can't you smell the singed wood in the air? If the rain lessens off, we could be in trouble."

"Wasn't any lightning over near the settlement," Zeke said, squinting up at the greyed sky outside. "It was all near you guys. Almost like it was following you."

"Stalker lightning? You never did like storms," Tobias teased.

Zeke thumped him on the arm. "I still don't, you giant ass. I will say, though, that there are enough of us to report back, check the bush *and* look after the pups until this blows over."

"I was thinking similar," Tobias murmured, brows furrowing as he glanced back at Flynn. The pups were all breathing smoothly and he didn't need to go closer to know they slept peacefully. Flynn's soft purring had abated but rather than his own eyes being closed, they were fixed pointedly on Tobias.

*Don't trust me with your young, T-Fuzz?*

"You've given me no reason to distrust you," Tobias allowed, "but I'm Alpha here. These pups are my responsibility."

Flynn drew back his lips in a silent snarl and Tobias followed suit. He'd barely taken half a step forward when Aislinn placed one hand on his wrist and held the other towards Flynn. "Stop it, both of you."

Her voice was sharp enough that Flynn immediately subsided. Tobias, feeling a little like he'd been caught with one hand in the cookie jar, set his jaw. "I wasn't trying to-"

"Yes, you were," she interrupted, glaring at each of them in turn. "I trust Flynn with my life; he stays, end of story. Zeke, return to the pack and tell them the kids are safe and will be home when the storm's blown out. Come back yourself or send Jax in your place."

"Jax is on patrol," Zeke demurred. "I'll come myself."

"Whatever," Aislinn waved a negligent hand. "Tobias and I will make sure the lightning hasn't struck anything important."

*Only his brain,* Flynn said.

Aislinn levelled a finger at him. "Shut up, or I cut that tongue right out of your head."

Flynn rumbled, the sound carrying a distinctly sensual edge. *Try it, princess. You know I like it rough.*

Aislinn replied, Tobias knew she did, but the visceral rage clamouring inside his head was too strong for him to hear. His heart thundered in his chest and it was as though the storm itself crackled through his veins, urging him to peel Flynn's pelt off his body and hang it on the wall. Rather than give in to the impulse - it would, after all, frighten the children - Tobias stalked out into the rain.

The cool water hit his skin with painful force, each droplet increasing Tobias' agitation. Flynn *knew* what Aislinn was to him, and still the damned asshole was pushing. Clawed hands curled into fists, the pain a welcome distraction. He wanted to fight the rage, to push the energy away like he'd always tried to do but Aislinn's reminders rang in his head. If he wanted to win, he had to make peace with this new, wilder side of himself. The question was, how?

Aislinn's voice sounded behind him and Tobias paused, turning back the way he'd come. She stood framed in the entrance of the lean-to, long hair plastered to her body with a creative precision any artist would envy. Though a good fifteen paces stood between them, every curve and hollow stood out in sharp relief and Tobias' gut clenched as his eyes tracked down her body and back up again. Mother Moon, she was perfect.

He'd taken one step forwards when a curious tingling overtook him, sweeping from his toes all the way to the top of his head. Drawn by some instinct he didn't understand, Tobias turned his face skyward and had a split second's horrified realisation before the lightning struck, coursing white-hot through his veins. It tore him apart, crackling and leaping and rending, causing an agony unlike anything he'd ever known - until Tobias collapsed on the ground, no longer able to feel anything at all.

* * * * * * * *

The lightning receded as swiftly as it came, leaving Aislinn staring at Tobias' smoking body on the ground. No sooner had she blinked than she was dropping to her knees at his side, searching desperately for a pulse while her mind lurched into motion. What had happened? He'd been in a clear space, but Tobias wasn't so tall that the lightning should have sought him out - not when he was naked and there were plenty of better conductors around.

A sob of relief slipped free as her questing fingers found a strong, steady heartbeat. "He's alive," she breathed, dropping her head on his chest. "Mother Moon, he's alive."

"Fuck, Ash, that was stupid," Zeke growled, crouching beside her. "What if there was a secondary strike?"

"Then we'd have fried together," Aislinn snapped, leaning back so she could check Tobias more thoroughly. She'd never seen a lightning strike but instinct said he should be burnt, broken and bloodied - or some combination thereof - but no matter how she looked, he bore no outward signs of his ordeal. Except… "Do you see that?"

Zeke leant closer, but dared not touch. "Electricity is jumping all over his body."

"Yeah." Aislinn watched the white-blue sparks arc over Tobias' skin as if they belonged there, her heart lurching uncertainly in her chest. "You said earlier the storm moved, the lightning displaying a pattern. Almost like it was following him."

"Babe… are you saying this is something to do with Tobias being an Alpha?" Zeke's voice flattened in disbelief. "I think you *both* need the medic."

"I know it sounds weird, but think for a moment. Tobias was restless during the storm and you said yourself there was no lightning anywhere else." Aislinn chewed her lower lip. "What if that's because he was attracting it?"

"You're talking about magic, Ash. That's just…" Zeke trailed off and shook his head.

Aislinn bent almost double, listening to Tobias' breathing. "Call it what you want, but we both know what we saw."

"Shit a brick," Zeke all-but shouted, his agitation echoed by a low growl of thunder. "Are you trying to tell me Tobias is a wolfkin lightning rod?"

She straightened and raised an eyebrow. "I might remind you that I can turn into smoke in the dark, big brother. That's not exactly normal."

The endearment and the cool facts did exactly as she hoped; they caused Zeke to reel his panic back in and take a deep breath. "He should be dead," the second allowed, nodding. "And he's not. But if you're right and all that power's now in Tobias' body, why aren't you getting zapped?"

Aislinn splayed her fingers over Tobias' tanned chest, watching the sparks arc over her flesh and back into his. "It won't hurt me because of my damper nature. I'm immune to stuff like this - but it might very well hurt you, so don't touch."

"Wouldn't we be safer if you drain him?" Zeke asked at last.

"Hard to say," Aislinn returned. "Getting rid of the lightning reduces the immediate risk, but it might also tempt another strike. I need him out of the storm before I try it."

"We need my mother."

"Yeah." Aislinn frowned, reaching out to smooth down Tobias' hair. "Considering the electric charge, I think you should do a quick check of the area, then return to Flynn and the pups. I'll take Tobias to your mother."

Zeke grunted, his face tight with concern. "I guess so. No sense risking electrocution for the sake of my pride."

"Exactly." Aislinn scooped Tobias into her embrace and stood. His legs and arms were so long they dangled well past her knees but the preternatural strength afforded to her body was more than enough to handle the extra bulk. "I don't think there'll be much more lighting now, but wait until the storm has passed completely before you risk the pups."

"Yeah, don't worry, gorgeous - Flynn and I'll keep 'em safe." He began to turn, hesitated. "Take care of him, Ash. He's the heart of all of us."

Aislinn stared down into Tobias' face, serene and almost boyish in unconsciousness, and felt something squeeze deep inside her chest. "I know."

She waited until Zeke had ducked under the protection of the lean-to, then lowered her face against the rain and jogged into the bush. Bare feet were nowhere near as reliable as paws and Tobias' bulk blocked her view of the immediate terrain but she refused to let that sway her, pushing the minor hurt of scratching branches and sharp rocks into the same place she kept the constant aching pain of her scars.

A journey of fifteen minutes in wolf form took more than double that in human form, but at last Aislinn staggered out of the trees and onto the softer, more cultivated grasses that most of the pack's housing was built on. Rain still fell but with nothing like the fury of earlier, and the thunder had long since ceased rumbling. Still, without the cubs' successful return, their mothers would be looking to Grandma Redding for reassurance - and Jemima, as the pack medic, would be on hand in case either parents or children, when they came home, needed her attention.

With a final glance down at Tobias' still face, Aislinn sighed and moved towards her grandmother's house. She approached from the back, where a wide, covered decking gave way to a sliding door with a dog flap. Praying it was unlocked - and it was - Aislinn used her elbow to nudge the door open and stepped into the laundry. Water, mud and blood sluiced down her legs to pool on the floor, rapidly turning the white tiles a sickly shade of brown. Ignoring the mess, she began to cross the laundry when the door to the interior of the house burst open. A wild-eyed Grandma Redding took in the scene with a gasp. "What in Solaeden's name happened?"

"The pups are fine," Aislinn said without preamble. "Zeke and Flynn are with them. Is Jemima here?"

"Yes." Jemima's voice, followed by her capable hands tugging Grandma's sleeve. "What's wrong?"

Aislinn shoved past her grandmother and into the kitchen. "Tobias was struck by lightning. I can't find any outward sign of injury, but I don't want to take any chances."

"Lay him down somewhere," Jemima said at once, snatching her medical bag from the counter.

"My room." Aislinn moved into the lounge and paused as Sarah Heliope-Flint stood from the couch. By her side was an equally anxious Emma Brexton, whose freckled face and strawberry ringlets matched her daughter's.

Sarah swallowed heavily, her gaze flicking between Tobias' unconscious body and Aislinn's face. "The pups..."

"The pups are fine," Aislinn soothed, forcing herself to smile. "They didn't see the lightning strike and are warm, dry and comfortable. I know it's hard to relax but the storm is almost done - they'll be back soon, I promise."

Emma hesitated, but Sarah laid a gentling hand on the other woman's forearm. "Thank you."

Aislinn nodded and continued up the stairs to her childhood bedroom, where Jemima was already unpacking her medical bag on the battered desk. Aislinn carefully laid Tobias on the double bed, astonished at the way his frame dominated a space where they'd once both fitted with room to spare. Even unconscious he radiated power, the indefinable strength of an Alpha male far stronger than it had been that morning.

"My instruments aren't functioning properly." Jemima frowned, tapping the screen of a portable scanner. "There's some sort of interference."

"Oh - wait." Aislinn laid her hands on Tobias' broad chest and sent her soothing shadows through his body. A grim smile curved her lips as the blue sparks beneath his skin faded. "Try now."

"Much better." Jemima stepped to the bedside, running her scanner over Tobias' inert body and reading the results with her brows drawn into a pretty frown. "Hmmm."

"What?"

"He seems to be in complete health - apart from his brain. Nothing wrong," Jemima added quickly, holding up a hand when Aislinn drew a sharp breath. "What I mean to say is that there's an abnormally high level of activity going on up there."

"Transition," Aislinn nodded, relieved to have Jemima's official agreement. "I figured that was why he's still unconscious - the body's way of keeping him under wraps while the mind acclimates to the new abilities."

"Have you seen something like this before?" Jemima's voice was full of professional curiosity.

"Not really - but when I transitioned, I was sick for a week, then unconscious for a week, then sick another week." It'd been a living hell that Flynn had nursed her through, never leaving her side for an instant. Aislinn shook off the memories and forced a tiny smile for Jemima. "I have a personal theory that the stronger the energy, the harder the body has to work to adapt."

Jemima nodded, her dark curls bouncing. "That makes sense. This," she hefted the scanner, "Isn't as complex as the units in a Kin hospital, but it states his energy is off the chart."

"I figured." Aislinn's smile grew. "Flynn and I are the same for those handheld units. They just don't have a broad enough scope."

Another clipped nod. "Energies this large are so rare as to be almost non-existent, or at least, they are in my experience."

"Rare," Aislinn conceded. "Not non-existent."

Professional curiosity again sparked, but Jemima didn't pursue the topic. Instead, she turned her eyes on the unconscious male sprawled across Aislinn's bed. "You're going to be a more accurate judge of what Tobias needs than I - without any physical symptoms, I must defer to your skills as a damper."

"Rest," Aislinn returned immediately. "He can stay here until he wakes naturally."

"How long, do you think?" Jemima was quick to pounce, then qualified, "In case I ever come across something like this again."

Ash wrinkled her nose in thought. "Given that he's male and they transition gradually, I'd say he'll recover from the initial shock within a few hours. As for how long it'll take for the ability to fully integrate, well…" she lifted one shoulder in a shrug. "How long is a piece of string? Until Tobias turns thirty and the energy settles in for good, he's going to be stuck with all sorts of random shit."

"I suppose there's something to be said for a woman's ability to do it all in one go, isn't there?" Jemima offered a smile, already packing instruments back into her bag. "Much better than having the process dragged out over several years."

Given how terribly ill she'd been during her own transition, Aislinn begged to differ - but Jemima wasn't Alpha and couldn't scent a lie, so she simply smiled and said; "Yeah. Lucky us."

The medic clipped her bag shut and gave Aislinn a quick once over. "Your wounds are healing already. I'll head back downstairs to wait for the pups."

"Thanks." Aislinn waited for Jemima to leave, then went straight to the mirror. Sure enough, several of her larger scars had split during the journey and her entire body was coated in blood, mud and leaf matter.

Great.

Making a face at her ridiculous reflection, Aislinn crossed to the bathroom and showered, wrapping a towel around her body before returning to the bedroom and staring down at Tobias. It was only as she examined the sculpted musculature of his naked body that she realised she, too, had been completely naked in front of all the women down below, brutal scars on perfect display.

She forced herself in front of the mirror again, dropping the towel to examine the body which had mocked her for months. Aislinn purposefully filled her lungs, the movement thrusting her breasts forward and rolling back her shoulders. The scars were as vivid and pink as the first time she'd seen them, the slashing claw marks and round puncture wounds telling no less of a horrifying story. But… for the first time, those outer wounds didn't echo inside her heart or pinch the bright fire of her soul. She stared at each and every scar, even daring to raise a hand to trace a few with the pads of her fingers. She'd survived. All that pain, all that horror and she'd made it out - not a victim, but a blade ready to be honed.

Blinking back sudden tears, Aislinn rummaged in her dresser for a clean, if ancient, soft pair of cotton panties and a tank. Her actual clothes were at Tobias' house but she'd be damned if she was leaving his side until he woke, meaning the remnants of her teenage wardrobe would have to do. Locating a brush, she tugged it through her thick hair and let it fall where it wished, then crossed to the bed and tugged a blanket over Tobias' damp skin. A primal part of her saw the way his chest was painted with blood - her blood - and preened. For him, for *them*, she would gladly bleed. And if it meant Tobias woke up with her scent deeply entrenched in his pores, well then, who was she to complain?

The ghost of a smile on her lips, Aislinn sat down at her desk. She didn't wait well - always too wired - but she'd learnt to curb her inner restlessness when the occasion called for it. Her body might not be able to run but her thoughts certainly could, and for now, it would be enough. With a final, lingering glance at the Alpha sleeping on her bed, she tugged a notepad out of the top drawer and began to write.

# Five

Tobias sat up with a gasp, hands going instinctively to his chest. A pale yellow blanket fell around his waist in a heap, leaving him free to explore the unusual combination of grit and mud streaked across his body - interspersed with deeper red smears of what was undeniably blood.

"Don't worry, the blood's mine." Aislinn's voice, husky and low, drew his attention upward.

"I'm dead," Tobias rasped, eyes bugging out of his head. She was even now rising from her desk, hips swaying as she crossed to sit beside him on the bed. Apart from a pair of blue cotton panties that were probably meant to be sedate, Aislinn's legs were bare. Her top half was partly covered by a thin tank in a slightly darker shade of the same blue that exposed several inches of abdomen and skimmed low across full breasts. Soft, curling waves tumbled over her shoulders, the red-tinted brown almost glowing. He swallowed. "I have to be, if you're dressed like that."

"In my pyjamas? Silly," Aislinn leant forward to brush the hair back from his forehead, the crisscross of her scarring an intricate lacework that stretched and warped as she moved. "This was all I had left in the wardrobe after I took my things to your house. I haven't worn these clothes since I was fourteen."

"You fit them better than you used to," Tobias managed. He was rewarded with a deep blush and a playful flick on the nose. "So, I'm not dead. Is it my birthday, then?" Her blush blossomed into a laugh, throaty and sensual and so very real Tobias was forced to concede that he was most definitely alive. "What happened?"

Aislinn didn't even pretend to not know what he was talking about. "Transition."

"*Transition?*" He sat up suddenly straighter. "What the fuck?"

"I know it sounds weird." Her lips quirked at the edges and she drew his hand into hers. "But it looks like electricity thinks you're sexy."

"Ash," Tobias wanted to squeeze his eyes shut but couldn't look away from the gentle patterns she was tracing on his palm with a fingertip. "I don't know a damned thing about transition other than what you've told me. Please, before I lose my mind, will you explain?"

"All right." Aislinn shifted closer so that she had a better grip on his hand. "Transition is basically a second kind of puberty, where the full strength of an alpha's energy is revealed. For females, it's a one-hit, full throttle event. For males, it's a slow peeling of layers, like a pass the parcel at a kid's party. The stronger the alpha, the more layers there are to peel, and if you're really lucky there are a couple of bonus prizes inside."

"Extra powers, you mean." Tobias' breath hitched as her fingers tickled their way onto the inside of his wrist. "Like your shadows."

"Yes. I've been told it's a genetic anomaly; whether a flaw or a gift depends on your point of view." Aislinn filled her cheeks with air and blew out slowly. "One percent of all alphas carry the genetic anomaly. One percent of those pass it on, and one percent of *those* actually develop it."

"That would be…" Tobias tried to do the maths, failed. "Only a handful worldwide."

"Something like that." Aislinn smiled, feathering her fingers over his skin in such a way that he felt it deep in his gut. "The anomaly means we have too much alpha energy; so much that the animal half of our souls is present even in our human skin. Some of us develop powers that border on mystical. Flynn's telepathy, your lightning, my shadows…"

"And Olaf's psychic swordplay."

"Yes." She nodded, her fingers going still for a long moment. "There are other rumours about those like us; mostly hearsay. Longer lifespan than normal Kin, immunity to certain diseases, unable to mate by choice - nothing less than a heartmate connection will do. The list goes on and on. Extra abilities come in singular for most, but are double-faceted for the strongest of us."

Tobias swallowed, trying to calm his racing heart and focus on her words. "Double-faceted?"

"Sure. My shadow ability is, in simple terms, like covering myself in a blanket of darkness. The flip of that is I can reverse that blanket onto another, or an object." She smiled, teasing her fingertips up to the inner flesh of his elbow and then back down again. "For Flynn, it's the ability to talk to those of us in animal form, the back side of which allows him to call actual animals. Simplified again, of course, but you get the idea."

"So I can attract lightning - and what?"

"I don't know." Aislinn shook her head. "I've been considering this while you were sleeping; at no point after the strike did you release any form of electric energy. I think your body was collecting power for whatever the main facet of your talent will be. It wasn't the lightning that was important, as much as the energy itself."

Tobias frowned. "How can you be so sure?"

"You're proving it right now." Her fingers stilled their dance across his arm. "See?"

Tobias drew in a gasp as Aislinn lifted her hand, tilting his palm. Tiny sparks of blue energy flickered beneath his skin, following the intricate pattern she'd been tracing over and over again. "Solaeden save me, what is *that*?"

"Kinetic energy." Aislinn laid her palm flat over his and Tobias felt the cool, soothing balm of her damper powers settle over his soul. "Generated, in this case, by our bodies rubbing together."

"Like static electricity?"

"Exactly. And what is lightning if not the highest form of static electricity?" Aislinn's lips stretched into a slow smile. "Lady Lunaida's way of connecting the sky to the earth."

"Holy shit," Tobias breathed, flopping back on the bed to stare at the roof. It was as familiar as his own roof, covered with glow in the dark stars they'd stuck on as children, private constellations known only to the two of them. "Holy fucking shit."

"Relax." Aislinn climbed over the top of him, straddling Tobias' blanket-covered thighs to begin a soft, soothing massage of his blood-stained chest. "I don't think you're going to start brewing storms wherever you go. The lightning was just pure, unlucky chance. And no, before you say it, I don't think you're going to be a permanent risk. When you learn to control your energy, this should settle too."

"I guess I have to believe you."

"Would it make you feel better if I told you that when Flynn began transition, he had wild animals climbing him all the time?" Aislinn's lips quirked in memory. "Birds, insects, cats - a snake, once. It was hilarious and he hated it."

Tobias closed his eyes, luxuriating in the feel of her hands on his skin. "I don't want to think about that damned tiger while you're sitting on top of me. Not even a little bit."

"Really?" Her fingers dug in, the slight pain only heightening his awareness of her body. "Are you… jealous? Of *Flynn*?"

"Very. Flynn oozes dirty, sweaty sex like donuts ooze sugar. He's so classically bad boy he might as well be on a movie poster." Tobias forced his eyes open. "How can I ever compare to that? The guy wears a studded collar, for Solaeden's sake!"

Aislinn raised her hands to her face and it took him a moment to realise that, behind her palms, she was laughing. "Tobias Greenwood, you are the most monumental idiot in the history of monumental idiots. Don't you *know* how sexy you are?"

Unsure whether to blush or frown, Tobias managed; "Clearly not."

She slithered up his body to take his mouth in a kiss so filled with heat and light it stole the very breath from Tobias' lungs. "Should I tell you why Flynn and I broke up? Why we'll never, ever work?"

Tobias wasn't entirely sure he wanted to know, but it seemed like she'd answer either way. "Why?"

His voice was husky with ill-hidden desire and Aislinn's answering chuckle rolled all the way down to his suddenly rock hard erection. She leant closer, nipping his lips, breathing the words into his mouth. "Because he wasn't you."

Tobias' heart stopped. For a fraction of a second he was certain he was going to die, so pure and deep was the fist squeezing his soul. Then he inhaled, a great, shuddering breath, and dragged her close with shaking hands. Aislinn's lips met his with equal urgency, a desperate clashing of tongues and teeth, her fingers clawing at his chest as Tobias sat up, one hand fisting in her hair and the other so tight around her waist that if it had been anyone else, he'd have worried they might break.

He knew he should go gently but his control was well and truly shredded by her confession. Aislinn groaned as he tore away from her mouth, trailing kisses along her jaw until he reached her fluttering pulse. Tobias scraped his teeth across her jugular and was rewarded with a gasp, a jerk that was part pleasure and part panic.

Snapping to his senses, Tobias wrenched backwards. "Sorry," he managed, his heart thundering beneath her hands. "I shouldn't have done that."

"No - it's not your fault. Dammit, Tobias, I almost lost you," she growled, eyes brimming with unshed tears. "I saw that lighting burn you up and I thought that was it. All those opportunities wasted, all those years turned to ash in less than the time it took for my heart to stop. I don't want to waste another moment, not now, not ever, and *he's* still got a grip on me!"

Aislinn thumped her fists on his chest in emphasis, the blow hard enough to make Tobias wheeze for air. She immediately soothed her hands over the hurt, murmuring wordless apologies and completely oblivious to the fire those feathering caresses ignited deep inside. Gritting his teeth so hard his jaw hurt, Tobias forced himself to hold her softly. "I'm sorry I frightened you, but I'm alive and well. We have time for this, okay? We have time."

She caught her lip between her teeth, biting down to hide the way it trembled. He leant in slowly, brushing soft kisses over the corners of her mouth until Aislinn relaxed. "I don't think I've ever been so frustrated or terrified in my entire life as I am when I'm with you," she admitted.

The comment drew a laugh from deep in his chest and Tobias drew back to see the familiar twinkle returned to her eyes. "Feeling's mutual and always has been. Now, do you want to explain to me why I'm covered in your blood?"

"Nothing major." She blushed when he raised an eyebrow, dropping her gaze to the now-crusted blood on his front. "Some of my scars split open when I carried you back here."

"By yourself?"

Aislinn looked out the window, where the sky was a significantly paler shade of grey than it had been when he'd last seen it. "You make it sound like you don't think I could've."

"It's not that," Tobias snorted. "You're the strongest woman I've ever known, inside and out. If anyone can carry my foolish hide, it'd be you - Lunaida knows you've done it before. What I meant was, why aren't Flynn and Zeke and the pups with you?"

"Oh! I didn't know if you'd attract more lightning so I told the boys to guard the pups until the storm blew over." She looked back at him and blinked, reading something deep in his eyes that Tobias tried desperately to bury. "You didn't hurt them."

His fingers tightened on her shoulders. There was little use denying the fear now that she'd seen it, so Tobias merely nodded. "Thank the Lady for that."

A tiny smile quirked the corners of her lips, then faded as Aislinn looked back at his muddy, bloodied chest. "I'm worried about what happens when Dad gets here. I'm finally starting to find my feet and some inner part of me is sure he's going to ruin it."

Tobias braced both hands behind him on the bed, looking her up and down. Tousled and slightly flushed, the blanket pooled between them while she sat cradled in his lap, Aislinn looked like she'd walked straight out of the dreams he'd been having for nigh on a decade. He ached to peel those tiny pyjamas off her, to have her writhing with pleasure, gasping his name. But it would, like so many other things in his life, have to wait. Tobias took a deep breath and said; "Andre doesn't own you, Ash. You're a Den Mother well out of transition - independent in every sense of the word. Forget for a moment the trauma you went through and remember who you are."

Aislinn wrapped her arms around herself and squeezed, blue green eyes huge in her pale face. "I've made peace with the outer damage -"

"Really? When?"

"While you were sleeping." She glanced at the mirror and then back at him, her smile tentative. "I realised after I carried you home that scarred or not, in pain or not, I did what had to be done. And I have to be prepared for the possibility that these," she waved a hand at the network of vivid scars over her body, "Might never heal." Aislinn's fists clenched for a fraction of a moment at that possibility, then relaxed. She traced a finger over one particularly vivid slash mark. "I think I'll call this one Deklyn."

"My middle name?" Tobias laughed, running a finger down Deklyn's thick, ridged backbone. "Surely you've got better taste than that."

She raised a single brow. "I suppose you do?"

"Of course." Tobias slid his finger sideways, tracing a smaller, rounded wound. "Judith."

"Judith?" Aislinn looked appalled. "Solaeden save us, next thing I know you'll be plastering me with names like Herb and Madge."

"What can I say?" He spread his hands, grinning wide. "It's a talent."

"Hah! You are definitely *not* naming our children," Aislinn snorted, eyes twinkling as she rose from the bed and threw a towel at him. "Here, go and shower. Maybe you can think of something more inventive while you're scrubbing all that mud off."

The towel wrapped haphazardly around Tobias' face and shoulders and he let it, wondering from behind the safety of the fluffy fabric if Aislinn even realised what she'd said. When he gathered the courage to yank the towel off she was back at her desk, humming under her breath and scribbling furiously on a dog-eared notepad. No, she'd not noticed the involuntary slip of the tongue, a continuation of years-old banter that had taken on a sudden and more dramatic meaning. Not sure whether to be relieved or annoyed, Tobias balled the towel in his fist and went looking for the bathroom.

*******

Aislinn waited for the door to snick shut behind Tobias, and another few heartbeats for the bathroom door, and then another few again for the shower to start. Then, and only then, did she drop her head into her hands.

"You are definitely not naming our children?" She repeated, shaking her head and setting unruly masses of hair tumbling over her shoulders. "Bloody hell, Ash, where did *that* come from?"

Of course, there was no answer - the voices which had been a smooth, silky by-product of the battle blood had long since faded, leaving her alone in her own mind. Aislinn tore off the pages of the notepad she'd written on and began folding them as small as possible. She was stressed about her father arriving in the morning, that much was true, and had been shaken by the lightning's relentless fury. But to say something like *that* to a man as intense as Tobias Greenwood? Insanity.

When Tobias walked back into the room with his towel slung low around hips she'd seen but were suddenly all the more enticing for being hidden, Aislinn made sure not to let her composure slip. "I'm pretty sure I hear Zeke's voice downstairs. Want to go meet the cubs?"

He ran a hand through damp hair, chewing the inside of his lip. "Is it safe?"

"With me around?" Aislinn gave him her best smile, dialled up to full wattage. "Definitely."

"It's beautiful," Tobias said after a long moment, reaching out to trace the curve of her cheekbone, "But it doesn't reach your eyes."

"Oh."

His fingers spread, cupping her jaw. "Are you really so worried about our fathers coming home?"

"Our fathers?" Aislinn considered the question, tested the truth of her answer. If she lied, he'd scent it. She swallowed, hoped for the best and said; "Yeah. I guess so."

"We're together now - there's nothing either of them can do about it." Tobias stepped closer, filling her personal space with tanned skin, male heat and the smooth scent of butterscotch and cream. His fingers slid down Aislinn's neck, drawing a line of goose bumps over her scarred skin. "I want to lick every single one of these."

"What?"

"I have a list of things in my head that I want to do with you when I get a chance." Tobias continued his single minded progress down her throat. "I'm adding 'lick Edith' to it."

"*Edith?*" Aislinn choked, slapping at his hand. "You can't be serious."

"Beryl?"

"Tobias!" She shoved him hard enough to earn a laugh - and then paused. "Were you trying to distract me?"

"Yes and no," he shrugged, his eyes still tracing the scars etched across her shoulders. "It was more so a statement of my foremost thoughts with bonus distraction potential." Blinking rapidly, the mask of sensuality fell away and Tobias offered a boyishly charming grin.

"Think how hard our fathers have worked to keep us apart and yet here we are, rubbing all over one another like out of control teenagers."

"Amusing as that is, they won't go so easily into the dark." Aislinn crossed her arms over her chest, aware it plumped her breasts up like some sort of proverbial feast and not caring. "Don't underestimate them, Tobias. You don't know what they're like anymore."

"No, but they don't know what I'm like, either." Tobias' face grew cold, filled with a fury unlike anything Aislinn had ever seen. "I'll kill anyone who tries to take you away again."

It was a silly thing, but her heart warmed at the display. She reached out to cup his cheek and stilled when Tobias closed his sharp teeth over the inside of her wrist. Her heart thumped unevenly as his elongated canines pricked her flesh, his eyes riveted firmly on her face. Testing who, exactly? She flexed beneath his mouth, pressing her flesh firmer against his lips. "Harder."

Tobias growled and complied, scraping his teeth across her skin and causing a shiver to roll down Aislinn's spine. She let out a groan, hugging her chest with her free arm in a vain attempt to ease the ache building there. His tongue flicked gently over her skin before he pressed the tiniest of kisses to her wrist. "Dammit, Ash," he complained, voice husky. "Don't do that to me."

Her eyes dropped to the ill-concealed bulge in his towel and she grinned. "You brought it on yourself, biting down on a woman like that. What else did you expect?"

"Either complete terror or a solid slap," he admitted, the corners of his mouth twitching. "But I couldn't help myself."

"A slap? Please, if I was going to hit you, I'd do it properly." Aislinn strode to the wardrobe and yanked out a faded pair of denim shorts. "Here. Pretty sure these are yours."

"Thanks." He caught the shorts mid-throw, dropping the towel to tug them on. Aislinn kept her eyes firmly on his face, not sure what would happen if she dared acknowledge anything lower. "I stashed them here a few months ago, just in case."

"In my room?"

He paused and Aislinn was surprised to see a dusting of pink spread over Tobias' cheeks. "I missed you."

"Hopeless."

"You know it." Tobias grinned as he strode to the door and yanked it open. "After you?"

The lounge was in chaos. Aislinn paused at the bottom of the stairs, watching as Sarah Heliope-Flint rained kisses on a delighted Rex and a stoic Achilles. Emma Brexton hovered nervously by a reclined armchair where Jemima was checking over little Connor, his older sister waiting nearby.

Flynn, lounging in human form on one of the couches, rolled to his feet the moment he spotted Aislinn, brows furrowed as he stalked across the room. She stepped into his embrace, wrapping her arms tightly around the tigerkin's wiry body and laying her head against his sternum. Flynn's arms locked over her spine, his cheek rubbing against her hair while he purred. Aislinn stroked her hands down his back, soft, soothing motions with the flat of her palms, allowing the barest trickle of shadows to leak into his flesh. The tigerkin wasn't used to crowded places and loud noises, didn't enjoy being caged inside buildings for long periods of time in his human body. He'd never admit it aloud, but it was why he'd come straight to her for comfort, his need for physical contact the only way to reassure the wild panic in his spirit.

"You did good," she murmured against his skin, the words so soft none but the two of them would be able to hear.

"I know." His lofty response was filled with Flynn's particular brand of humour - and a silent signal that he'd received what he needed from her.

Aislinn drew back enough to poke him firmly in the ribs. "Egotistical jerk."

"Snob." Flynn's amber eyes glittered with humour. After a long moment, he glanced up at Tobias from beneath long, black lashes. "He hasn't tried to kill me yet. I'm disappointed."

"I reassured him." Aislinn looked to where Tobias stood, talking quietly with Zeke. "And he was worried about the pups."

"I give it an hour," Flynn predicted, "before I get under his skin again."

"Are you *trying* to piss him off?"

"Of course. How will he learn to get a handle on his instincts if nobody's testing them?" Flynn's smile was slow and wicked. "T-Fuzz can't go around blowing his stack every time someone looks at you. I figure I'm ideally placed to taunt him best."

Aislinn sucked on her teeth for a long moment. "It's a dangerous game."

"Just the way I like it." Flynn lowered his head, soft lips tickling her ear. "Did you tell him we only hiccupped a few days before your… bear encounter?"

"No - and don't you dare," Aislinn hissed, slapping the tigerkin lightly on the arm. "I mean it."

"As my lady commands." Flynn straightened. His face was still twisted with a wicked bedroom smile, but Aislinn knew he'd keep his word. The lapse in their measured distance from one another was a regular occurrence but it had been, like so many other things, before Olaf had waded into her life and shredded it. However, for the first time since waking up in a hospital bed without even her dignity for company, the nightmarish sheen that Olaf's attack had layered over her previous sexual encounters had lifted, giving Aislinn back her pleasant memories and reminding her that sex itself wasn't her enemy, only a cruel bearkin without limits. She knew enough from her torturous counselling sessions that such a distinction was paramount to her recovery, so she drew memories of Flynn's naked body close, wrapping herself in the recollection of the soft, sensual purr that was for her and her alone. She had no doubt that Tobias was her future - he was in her blood, a thumping pulse in her spirit - but Flynn was her past, the harsh exterior disguising a gentle lover who'd teased her with tenderness as often as he'd challenged her with raw, unbridled passion.

She brushed a finger over the soft skin of his forearm, aware of the tigerkin's laser focus on her face. "Thank you," she murmured, the words so quiet as to be no more than a breath, "for showing me how to love."

Flynn stiffened beneath her fingers and Aislinn wondered if she'd pushed him too far. Sex and laughs were one thing, but her tiger didn't like to be vulnerable and liked even less to discuss his - or anyone else's - innermost heart. A curiously wistful expression flickered over his face, quickly hidden. "It was my honour." Amber eyes glinted. "And my pleasure."

Aislinn laughed at that, the sound attracting a smouldering look from Tobias which she deflected with a wink. That quickly, it was done, a pressure she hadn't known she bore easing from her heart. She hugged Flynn fiercely, then leant back to look up at his elfin face. "The kids behaved themselves, I assume?"

"Of course." Flynn shrugged. "They slept and then I let them go human to catch a ride home."

She reached up to tug the studded collar around his neck. "Such a soft touch."

Flynn didn't answer - they both knew that where children were concerned, it was the truth. He did, however, step back as Grandma Redding bustled up.

"Don't leave," she reached out as if to touch the tigerkin's arm and then hesitated. "Please."

"*Please*?" Flynn's eyebrows shot up. "Did that hurt?"

Grandma Redding's eyes narrowed. "You're in my house, young man."

Flynn's grin was no less wicked, despite the obvious reprimand. "I beg your forgiveness, Den Mother. Would you like to spank me?"

"Stop it," Aislinn growled. Flynn subsided at once, a clear statement of whose authority he would accept. She sighed and turned back to her grandmother. "I'm not interested in fighting right now. Whatever you have to say, make it quick."

Grandma took Aislinn's hands in her own, raising them to kiss her knuckles. "I came to apologise. You were right; I've sat on the fence too long. When your grandfather died, I let your father take most of the burden of leadership off my shoulders."

"You don't need to explain," Aislinn murmured gently. "It's okay to hurt."

"Perhaps, but there's a difference between pain and cowardice." Grandma grimaced, shaking her head. "After he died, I - oh, Ash, your father looks just like him."

"You couldn't fight him because he reminded you so strongly of Grandpa."

"Yes, but he's grown out of hand." Grandma's jaw hardened and she looked up at Flynn. "I'm still the senior authority in this pack, no matter my son's position on the Council. You rescued those children without thought for your own safety - I grant you sanctuary and my full support."

Aislinn gasped and alongside her, Flynn went still. Sanctuary meant he was accepted, from here on out, as a fully fledged member of the pack and could come and go as he pleased. He swallowed. "I'm not worth going to war over."

"You are Aislinn's and therefore you are mine," Grandma returned firmly. "I should've gone to war for her and Tobias long ago. Consider this merely an extension of that sentiment."

Tears blurred Aislinn's vision and before she could reach for her grandmother, Flynn tugged them both into a rough, three-way embrace. His almost bottomless energy slipped the leash for a fraction of a moment and Grandma's breath caught as raw, primal power sizzled over them, no doubt putting every well-honed sense she had into overdrive. The sensation disappeared as quickly as it had come and after a final, proprietary squeeze, Flynn allowed the older woman to escape. "Thank you, Den Mother. I accept."

Grandma stared at the tigerkin in shock. "What *are* you?"

Flynn preened, every inch of him pure feline. "One of a fucking kind."

"Stop it," Aislinn elbowed him lightly.

"What? It's true." His arm, still lazy around her ribs, began tracing slow circles as it drifted lower. "How long do you think it'll take T-Fuzz to-"

"Enough, kitty cat." Tobias' firm voice - though Aislinn could have sworn it held laughter, of all things - was quite suddenly in her ear. "Keep your hands to yourself."

Aislinn blinked rapidly as Tobias' arm snaked around her waist, pinning Flynn's wrist between their two bodies. "I'm not a bone to be fought over."

"We're not fighting," the two men said in unison. Aislinn startled - and when she saw Grandma's eyes widen in sudden comprehension, she knew something was afoot.

"What's going on?" She tried to turn but in a curious continuation of their sudden and inexplicable desire to cooperate, both Tobias and Flynn tightened their grip on her body. "Grandma!"

"Don't appeal to me - they're your boys," Grandma's tone was dry. "I'd advise you to keep them under wraps when your father arrives, but I feel that's probably going to fall on deaf ears."

"I'm not leaving Ash without support," Tobias growled. "We're not children to be contained."

"No, you're both hot, macho alphas," Zeke's laughing voice preceded him into their little circle. "Not that it matters; even I can see Ash's got you both by the balls." The second brushed damp golden curls off his face and offered a flourishing bow. "My queen."

Aislinn rolled her eyes. "Fuck's sake, now all I need is Jax volunteering to be my new floor rug and this farce will be complete."

"Watch your language," Grandma snapped.

"She's right though, G-ma." Zeke snorted a laugh, sapphire eyes sparkling with mischief as he looked Aislinn up and down. "Be careful what you wish for, your royal highness, because Jax would do exactly that if you asked him to. He's yours now; hook, line and stubborn-ass sinker."

"Mother Moon." Aislinn rubbed her hands over her face, sagging back into Flynn and Tobias' combined embrace - until she realised what she was doing and forced herself upright. "I need to get out of here before you all drive me crazy." She glanced at the two men behind her. "And someone needs to tell me what's going on."

Tobias and Flynn shared a loaded glance before Tobias finally said; "Not here."

"Later?"

He met her stare with his own. "I promise."

Aislinn narrowed her eyes. "I'm going to hold you to that."

"You should," Grandma agreed with a nod. "But for now, go home and rest. Andre and the rest of his entourage will be here early tomorrow."

Deciding not to comment on the implication that Tobias' home was now hers, Aislinn nodded. "I need ice cream. Lots of ice cream."

"You ate it all during the battle blood withdrawal," Tobias rumbled.

Zeke produced a phone from the pocket of his shorts. "I'll text Sens; she won't mind sharing." He frowned at the screen. "Huh. Weird."

Aislinn leant forward. "What?"

"It's dead." Zeke held the phone out so they could see the black screen. "I was using it a minute ago and the battery was fine."

"Use my phone," Grandma offered. "It's in the kitchen."

Zeke tugged at his hair and then shrugged, slipping the phone back into his pocket. "Sure. Thanks."

Aislinn tried to move and this time, both Tobias and Flynn released her. "Where did the others go?"

"I saw them out - kids were all clear, not a scratch on them," Zeke returned. "Ma will make sure they get home and rest."

"Good. They've had enough of an ordeal already." She kissed her grandmother on the cheek and smiled. "I'll see you in the morning, then?"

Grandma nodded, squeezing Aislinn's shoulder. "I'll be here."

"I'll meet you guys on the lawn," Zeke promised, dashing towards the kitchen. "Won't be a moment."

The sky had considerably lightened by the time they all stepped outside, the rain replaced by a cloying humidity that covered Aislinn's skin in a thin sheen of sweat. The common lawn was wet underfoot, the moisture a cool, soothing contrast to the stickiness already pasting her thick hair to her back. A feminine voice called her name and she looked up to see Sienna jogging across the damp lawn, wearing skin tight hot pants and a matching black sports bra. Flynn whistled low and long between his teeth.

"No," said Tobias. "Don't even think about it."

"That's my sister," Zeke added, face red as he came barrelling across the lawn to join them.

Flynn merely raised a brow and looked at Aislinn. "Really?"

"Really." She prodded him in the ribs. "Play nice."

The tigerkin rumbled a deep, sensual purr. "Oh, I intend to."

"Ash, I-" Sienna cut off as she caught sight of Flynn, pausing in her loping gait to freeze like a rabbit in a spotlight. "Holy shit, you weren't joking."

Aislinn grinned. "Nope."

"About what?" All three males, this time, each wearing varying degrees of suspicion on their faces.

"Uh uh - girl secrets." She glanced at her friend. "What's up, Sens?"

"I got Zeke's message about ice cream, and figured you were about." Sienna inspected her nails for a long moment. "We need to talk about the training - everyone is scared."

"Scared?" Tobias frowned. "Is it -"

"Bill and Rory are great," Sienna reassured, her smile quick, "But the bearkin are the proverbial monsters under the bed. So many of our soldiers died at the peace summit that it's hard to imagine how we could ever beat them."

Aislinn nodded. "I know the feeling. That's what the training's for, though."

"I know, it's just - ugh, I'm not saying this right." Sienna buried a petite hand in her perfect curls and tugged. "Ever since I woke up this morning, there's been this ache in my head. Like a bee buzzing between my ears." She grimaced. "I look at the other pack members and it's like they're bees too, all buzzing at the top of their voices. I know this sounds crazy, but it's a sad buzz; like they all need hugs and blanket forts. Only... how do I make a blanket fort for the entire pack?"

Tobias and Zeke's mouths dropped open and they stared at Sienna as though they'd never seen her before. Finally Zeke recovered enough to ask, "Do I need to get our mother, little sister-wolf?"

"I don't know." Sienna frowned. "Maybe I'm going crazy."

"No, I don't think so." Aislinn tapped her chin in thought. "Flynn, would you mind giving Sens a once over for me?"

In less than the time it took to blink, the tigerkin had Sienna crushed to his chest, his face buried in the curve of her neck while her feet dangled a couple of feet off the ground. Zeke made a strangled sound but Aislinn stilled him with a splayed hand.

"Ash," Tobias, while more reserved, also quivered with tension. "Now would be a good time to explain."

"Just wait, and watch. Trust me."

"Healer," Flynn said suddenly, his rumbling voice closer to a real purr than Aislinn had heard in months. "Emotional sentience."

Of course. Sienna was so sensitive, so intrinsically wound into the lives of her people - and had earnt Aislinn's trust in mere moments in the dim lighting of the clothes boutique not so very long ago. "Active?"

"Waking." Flynn set a shell-shocked Sienna back on the ground but kept her close, smoothing his hands almost absently up and down her arms. "Hence the headache. By tomorrow morning, she'll be all systems go."

"Um, hi," Sienna squeaked, her eyes wide. "You're very close and very naked."

Flynn lowered his lashes halfway, his expression one of pure male arrogance. "Nudity is an accepted part of Kin life, cupcake. Why does it bother you?"

"Nudity doesn't bother me," Sienna managed breathlessly. "But yours is far too personal."

He pushed further into Sienna's space. "You're sensing the feral temperament inside me. It's intimidating. What else?"

"Nothing."

"Liar." The tigerkin ran a finger along the shoulder strap of her sports bra. "I can smell it."

Sienna frowned. "Get away from me, you perverted brute."

"Ah." Flynn's lips twisted into a toothy grin. "Make me."

"I don't know -"

"You do."

Sienna's lips drew back in a snarl and her hand moved like liquid silver. "Back off."

Flynn's lashes barely fluttered as he released her arms and took as much of a backwards step as her vicious grip on his genitals allowed. "Damn, Ash - she's just like you. Knows how to lead a man around by his balls."

Sienna blushed and retracted her hand at once.

"You're a menace," Aislinn laughed, jogging forward to elbow him out of the way. "Good job, Sens."

"What in the world was all that about?" Sienna asked, her brow wrinkling in confusion.

"Flynn's ability to connect with the animalistic parts of us allows him to scent certain energies." Aislinn patted her friend on the shoulder. "You've got some healing talent - not like a medic, more like a counsellor. It's how you sensed the underlying emotional current of the pack."

"I did?"

"You did," Aislinn nodded. "And just now, when Flynn pushed until you lashed out? You might have thought you were going for his pride but you weren't. Look."

Sienna glanced to where Flynn now stood on one leg, shaking the other out like a wet dog. "What did I do?"

"Chi point," Flynn grunted. "We have 'em different to the humans but we have 'em - and you have a radar that knows exactly where they are. You turned off my left leg, pretty kitten."

"I'm a wolf," Sienna retorted instinctively. Then she looked up at Aislinn. "I really did that?"

"You did. And now that we know the pack's problem, we can work to fix it. But first, reassure your brother before he bursts."

Sienna, eyes still moon-wide, tottered over to Zeke and pressed both hands to his chest. "Brother? I'm okay. No need to shed blood today."

"Good." With what had to be a colossal effort, Zeke forced a smile onto his face. "Get your dick hand off me, Sens."

She stroked both hands tauntingly across his chest. "Which one was it? I can't remember."

"Dammit, Sienna," Zeke growled, but his face fractured with amusement and he tugged her close.

Tobias sidled up to Aislinn. "You sure?"

"Flynn's never wrong."

"But Sens is a fashion designer," he returned, the blue of his eyes almost grey in the gloomy afternoon.

"Yes - a profession that allows her to help people in a creative, but also very elemental way." Aislinn narrowed her eyes, picking out individual beads of moisture on the lawn and counting them, using the menial task as a way to focus her thoughts. "Natural abilities like this come out in response to the energies of the alphas around them. Healers and dampers and those who sense weather are not usually alphas themselves, but Kin who respond to the needs of their pack."

Tobias sighed. "You're saying this is all brought on by my transition."

"Not necessarily." She shook her head. "You're a strong energy but so am I, and so is Flynn. Any or all of us could've set Sienna off - but, Tobias, it would've happened eventually anyway."

"Right." Tobias rolled his shoulders, the muscles shifting across his bare chest. "For all I'm Alpha here, I feel like I'm flying blind."

"Your knowledge has been stifled." Aislinn tilted her head and a small, wicked smile tugged her lips. "Lucky for the rest of us, mine hasn't."

He considered that in silence and then, so slowly she'd have missed it if she hadn't been watching, nodded. "First thing we need to do is reassure the pack."

"I know exactly what they need." Aislinn took a step back, reaching deep inside herself to the place where her wolf form slept. She called that energy, let it rise halfway through her spirit, and settled it there. Fur bled over her skin, the ancient pyjamas stretching and then shredding as she gained height and breadth. Her legs reshaped, became lupine. Claws shot out from the ends of her fingers and toes. Fur coated her body, hung in silken tufts from her tail. Her vision changed as her eyes spread apart, making room for the wolf's long snout, black nose and sharp teeth.

Aislinn stepped away from her shredded clothing and gave her midform a solid shake. She didn't need the enhanced hearing of her pointed lupine ears to tell her that every single member of the pack was glued to their windows. The minute someone had spotted their alpha standing on the lawn - probably Barbara Forthrite and her thousand cats - they'd have called someone, the messages filtering onward until everyone was now looking, waiting, hoping.

"Ash?" Tobias' voice was low and cautious.

*Should I let him in on the secret?* Flynn stood barely ten paces away, also in his midform. His striped fur shimmered in the dull afternoon light, amber eyes glittering as he tilted his feline head to the side. His tiger's muzzle didn't have the same reach as hers but his teeth were longer, sharper. His claws were just as deadly, his muscles just as, if not more powerful. A good opponent.

Aislinn smiled, drawing her lips back from her teeth. *Bring him into the conversation.*

*T-Fuzz? Now's a good time to put on your fur coat. Wouldn't want anyone to see you pissing yourself.*

Tobias startled, then snorted. "What's the plan? Fight each other until you're both bloody?"

*All of us. Show of strength to bolster the pack.*

"Wait… you want us all to spar? Here and now?" Tobias looked around at the houses, at Zeke and Sienna, and then back up at Flynn. "Are you nuts?"

*Actually, it's my idea - and it won't be sparring. It'll be fighting. Down, dirty, no rules fighting.* Aislinn bent almost double to sniff at his face, then let her lupine tongue lick a long trail up the side of Tobias' head. *You trust me?*

"Always."

Flynn's laugh resounded inside her mind, echoed by a huffing rumble from his feline throat. *Then either put your big boy pants on or fuck off.*

"I can't control my midform," Tobias returned, setting his feet. "I can't summon it on demand."

*Is that a problem?* Aislinn asked, putting every ounce of her considerably mischievous spirit into the question.

As she'd hoped, Tobias' face split into a feral grin. "Hell, no. Tiger, I'm coming for you."

*I'm not going anywhere, little puppy.* Flynn spread his clawed arms in welcome. *Come get some.*

# Six

Flynn went down with a grunt that was far less satisfying than it should have been. Eager to remedy that discrepancy, Tobias dropped heavily onto the tigerkin's ribs and grinned at the wheezing sound that followed. Clawed hands dug into his shoulders and he felt the first trickle of blood as Flynn bucked him off. He crashed, rolled, pushed to his feet and spat out a mouthful of dirt, lowering his shoulder as the tigerkin came flying towards him. He could've gone wolf; Zeke already had and was rolling in a yelping, golden blur across the lawn with his jaws snapping near Aislinn's throat. But Tobias stayed human, trusting his solid musculature as Flynn's freight train tackle threw them both backwards.

*Let it out, T-Fuzz.* The tiger's voice was thready with laughter as he drove Tobias spine first into the dirt. *Show your people what you've got.*

"Not angry enough," Tobias ground out, slamming his knee into the tigerkin's kidney. Flynn took the blow with only the barest of flinches, took, too, the solid right elbow to the jaw - though this one with enough of a grunt that Tobias knew he'd hit home.

*You don't need to be angry.*

"I don't want to hurt anyone."

*These wolves are scared; they need to see your strength. Tumbling with you in the dirt will reinforce the bonds of pack and reassure your people in a way words can't.*

"I can do that in my skin," Tobias grumbled, slamming the heels of both palms into orange furred shoulders.

*It won't have the same effect. Don't worry, we won't let you hurt them.* Flynn reared up, claws out - and then disappeared with a roar as a snarling black bullet slammed into his chest.

Tobias rolled to his feet in time to see Jaxon, wearing his pony-sized wolf form, sink his teeth into the tigerkin's shoulder. Flynn curled his clawed hands into the wolfkin's fur and tugged, only to be hit from the other side by a smaller black streak - Dominic. The two wolves were howling with feral excitement, the sound echoed by Flynn's deeper, feline rumble. For a moment it appeared the tigerkin would gain the upper hand, then Zeke's pale blonde body thumped, paws-first, into Flynn's chest and he dropped like a stone.

Which just left Aislinn. Tobias began to turn but he was too slow, her knee connecting with his back even as her hand twisted in his hair. She slammed him chest first to the ground, landing squarely on his buttocks. Her clawed fist slammed into the earth beside his head, showering his face with dirt and seconds later, a hot breath shot down his ear.

*Come on,* she murmured, and even though Tobias knew Flynn was listening in, it felt like an intimate invitation that reached deep inside his soul and tugged. Fur immediately sprouted along his arms and over his chest, his body reacting to her call without his conscious thought. Tobias rolled onto his back, staring into Aislinn's face while his own elongated, his bones reshaping into his midform. She whuffed in approval, snapping her teeth playfully near his snout. *There you are.*

A howl announced the arrival of Zeke, his golden-furred body a pale blur in the overcast afternoon as he tackled Aislinn from behind, slamming them both down on Tobias' chest in a messy tangle of limbs. The pile quickly enlarged as other wolves followed, pack members who'd exited their homes seeking contact with their Alpha. Underneath the magnificent pile up, Tobias' heart squeezed with gratitude. *They came.*

*They came,* Flynn agreed, his voice lighter than Tobias had ever heard it, *And they're still coming, T-Fuzz. Time to show them a good time.*

Tobias shivered, a familiar red fog creeping in at the edges of his vision. *I'm losing it.*

*I've got you.* Aislinn's teeth sunk into his bicep and with them, her cooling shadows. *I'll keep you from homicide, I promise.*

He could only trust that she was right, his body already moving by itself as the melee progressed, a howling, furry mess of violence and delight. Tobias found himself perpetually suspended between the all-consuming fog and the soothing cool of Aislinn's damper energy, individual faces blurring into a hum of movement which consumed him whole.

After what seemed forever - and judging from the way the sun hung low and watery in the sky, could very well have been - Tobias' vision gained a stunning clarity. He was lying flat on his back, blinking up at the clouds as Aislinn soothed his midform away, her human hands cool and soft against his heaving chest. "You okay?"

"Yeah." Tobias brushed tangled hair back from her mud-spattered brow. "Beautiful."

"Sweaty," she rebutted, but he was gratified to see her colour deepen with a blush. Tobias turned his head to the side, spotting several other pack members also sprawled naked in the churned up grass. Following his gaze, Aislinn smiled. "They're all exhausted. Some surface injuries, nothing serious. Scrapes and bruises."

"Good." He swallowed around his dry throat. "I feel like I've been hit by a bus."

"How much do you remember?"

"Not much." He shook his head. "Enough to know I didn't try to kill anyone, but if you weren't there, I probably would have."

"That's why I *am* here," she returned, eyes twinkling. When Tobias merely waited, her smile broadened and she crouched by his side. "Flynn got you a good right hook in the jaw at one point. You dislocated his shoulder for it."

"Hah." The glee slithering through his system was immature, but he didn't care in the slightest. "Does he need a medic?"

Aislinn shook her head. "He put it back himself. Any bruising will heal overnight."

"Overnight?"

"Yeah." She smiled, but there was something flat about it. "Genetic anomaly, remember? We heal faster than everyone else."

Except, of course, the injuries Olaf had inflicted. Tobias ran a finger down the length of one scar. "Don't worry. We'll kill Olaf and then Englebert will be gone for good."

"*Englebert*?" Aislinn demanded, her face a delightful mixture of irritation and amusement. "It's like you're doing it on purpose."

Tobias schooled his expression into a facade of innocence. "I would never."

"Of course not," she chuckled. "Well, I think we've done all we can out here, and I for one could use a shower."

"Me too." Tobias forced his aching body upright and bit back a groan. "Did it work?"

Aislinn looked first at the pack members who were still sprawled on the grass, then up at the silent circle of houses. "It's probably too early to tell, but I think so. If nothing else, it's helped vent some frustration."

Tobias followed her gaze and nodded. "Where's Flynn?"

"With Sienna," Aislinn answered, then snorted at the look on his face. "Nothing like that. She muttered something about ramen for dinner and he offered to help."

"He *cooks*?" Tobias frowned, trying to imagine the tall, elfin tigerkin in a kitchen.

"He's actually pretty good," Aislinn answered, pushing to her feet and dusting both hands on her thighs. "Flynn cared for a bunch of orphaned street kids for years without assistance. If there's one thing he's skilled at, it's disguising vegetables."

"Orphaned street kids? Where was the Kin High Council?"

"Focussing on the bigger picture," Aislinn rolled her eyes. "The war with the bearkin is more vicious overseas, even if it's still mostly kept quiet. Attacks like what we saw in Gerup, or what happened to the marsupial burrow? They're almost normal across the ocean, and they don't discriminate over who's left behind."

"But… children?"

"Unfortunately, age means nothing." Aislinn's face suffused with an old anger. "All societies have their flaws, and ours is no exception. When I first met Flynn, he and a couple of the older orphans had marshalled their group into some semblance of a pack, and worked together to protect and raise them as such. Even now, Flynn's still caring for his group, who in turn reach out to others - after we appealed to the Council for assistance and were told nothing could be spared from the defence lines."

Tobias felt a part of his soul freeze at that soft declaration. How could anyone justify abandoning the needy, much less children? He cleared his throat but his voice was still rough when he said; "How does Flynn help them?"

"Our job is dangerous, so he earns a fair wage from the Council. The entire thing goes into an account one of his older street pals,

Melchior, has access to. He uses it to rent a house, and together they feed, clothe and care for any orphans they can find." Aislinn stared off at the horizon, as though she could cross the vast distance with her thoughts alone. "It's not enough but it makes a difference."

"And you?"

"I pay for Flynn and I to live." She flicked a glance Tobias' way, face expressionless. "Nobody else knows."

"I won't tell," he promised.

Aislinn nodded and turned away, leaving Tobias to stare at her grass-stained, mud spattered behind as she waltzed up the steps to his sprawling home and slipped inside. He followed, kicking the door shut and wrapping both arms around her from behind, her damp hair cool against his cheek.

"Tobias?"

"Thank you," he murmured, closing his eyes and nuzzling at her hair. "For what you gave to the pack."

She twisted to stare up at him, her blue-green eyes shimmering with all the hidden depths of the ocean. "A roll in the grass?"

"Empathy," he corrected, nipping at her cheek. "And a little piece of yourself."

"Oh." She was still for a moment, the hard lines of her body relaxing against his until it was impossible to tell where Tobias ended and Aislinn began. "It's funny, you know. The life I had with you, and the life I had with Flynn, feel like polar opposites. If someone had asked me, even a month ago, if you'd both be standing in front of me today.... I'd have said it was impossible."

"Nothing is impossible," he returned, tightening his arms.

"So it seems." She laid her head on his shoulder, her smile crooked. "Now I not only have you both here, but I have to work out how all our lives mesh together."

Tobias shifted one hand to brush at the furrow forming between her brows. "We have time."

"We don't," she refuted, biting her lip. "Once Dad gets here, every single word and action will be analysed."

"We'll find a way. Kitty and I can play nice if we need to."

"That's a relief. I'd hate to be banging your heads together every two seconds."

"I thought you'd be impressed." He bent down to speak against her throat. "He drives me insane, but he's smarter than he likes to let on."

Her chuckle reverberated through Tobias like a soft rumble of thunder. "I know."

There was a sharp rap at the door and he stepped backwards with a sigh. "I better go and shower."

"What happened to ladies first?"

"Are you kidding me?" Tobias shook his head, heading for the stairs. "No way am I letting Sienna see me with a raging hard-on."

"Huh?" She glanced down and raised an eyebrow. "Really?"

He shrugged, offering a lopsided grin. "I'm naked, you're naked, we're all hyped up and sweaty and dirty and -"

"Mother Moon, get that thing out of here," Aislinn laughed, shooing him towards the second floor. "It's twitching with every word."

"What can I say? He likes what he sees." Tobias winked, her laughter following him all the way to the bathroom - and the very cold shower waiting for him.

*******

Aislinn counted to five before she pulled open the door and smiled. "Come on in."

Sienna smiled back and skipped across the threshold, eyes sparkling in a face that, like Aislinn's, still bore evidence of the all-out brawl they'd incited on the common lawn. Flynn followed, laden with several canvas shopping bags that he hefted effortlessly onto the bench.

"Where's T-Fuzz?" The tigerkin asked, crossing the two steps between them to drag Aislinn into a full bodied hug.

"In the shower." She smoothed her hands up and down his spine as he buried his face in her hair. "A cold shower, in case you were wondering."

Flynn rumbled a laugh, tilting his head so his words slipped into her ears alone. "I wasn't wondering - my nose works just fine. He's all over you."

"And now, so are you."

His amusement became a sly purr. "Not sorry."

"Rogue." Aislinn stepped back to find Sienna staring at them - at Flynn, rather - and smiled.

The younger woman caught her eye and blushed, returning to her task of unpacking the groceries. "Do you like ramen?"

"Who doesn't?" Aislinn sauntered to the bench to help. Flynn trailed along behind, taking a hunk of her hair in his hands and beginning to untangle the knots.

Sienna's eyes tracked the movement and a moment later, Flynn said, "Want me to do your hair instead?"

"What?" She blinked in surprise and blushed. "Oh, I - I'm sorry. I didn't mean to stare."

"I'm used to it," Flynn shrugged. "I need to touch. I can't help it. Other people think it's weird; Ash lets it go."

"So it's not -" Sienna cut off and blushed as Flynn at last looked up.

"Sexual? Not unless you want it to be, pretty puppy."

Sienna laughed, the sound tinted with nerves. "You'd eat me up and spit me out."

"Oh, but it'd be fun," Flynn purred, his accent thickening as his voice dropped into bedroom range.

"No thank you." Sienna sniffed and tossed her golden curls. "I don't need Ash's sloppy seconds."

The tiger looked immediately scandalised as Aislinn burst out laughing. "Oh Sens, that was perfect."

"No offence," Sienna giggled. "I'm still recovering from the last man I had in my sights."

Aislinn felt a twinge of guilt at that admission but the gaze Sienna turned on her was clear and forgiving and she couldn't help but smile in response. "I'm lucky to have a friend like you."

Sienna blushed prettily and handed Aislinn a bag of carrots. "Then you won't mind attending to these. I need batons."

"Batons it is." Aislinn washed her hands and rummaged through Tobias' kitchen drawers until she found a peeler. Flynn humphed, muttered something about precocious women and disappeared into the downstairs bathroom. When the door was closed and Aislinn could hear the water running, she flicked Sienna a more serious look. "How does the pack feel now?"

"Better." Sienna smiled brightly. "I'm still not sure I entirely understand what Big, Bad and Delicious was trying to tell me, though. What on earth is emotional sentience?"

Aislinn dumped a pile of carrot peelings into the bin and paused, her nose crinkling in thought. "I guess the best way to describe it would be a form of intuition."

"Like knowing when it's going to rain?"

"A little, but instead of sensing weather patterns, you sense emotional undercurrents."

Sienna chewed her lip a moment and Aislinn returned to the bench, giving the younger woman time to corral her thoughts. Several carrots later, Sienna said; "People talk to me. They often trust me with secrets and then later don't know why they did it."

"I know the feeling - and I'll bet you never break a confidence, right?"

"Of course not," Sienna gasped. "I'd never do such a thing."

"Exactly. The chi point you isolated on Flynn is an extension of your intuition, too. Even healers have the potential for a martial ability," Aislinn chuckled, then dumped the pile of carrot batons into a pot by the stove.

"I suppose being able to sense chi points would allow me to block off pain receptors or cause unconsciousness if a patient required it," Sienna mused.

"Yes," Aislinn agreed, allowing respect to colour her voice. "You're a quick study, Sens."

"My mother's a medic."

"We don't have any intuitive healers here, though." Aislinn smiled. "Don't downplay your strengths."

"Why not? If I walked around with my head up my backside all day, nobody would want to talk to me." Sienna's smile was brilliant and brief. "In my experience, the more unique someone becomes, the more normal they wish to be, and the harder they work to appear that way. You do it - all that mucking about, the cajoling and joking and cleverly hidden innuendo. It makes people forget how deadly you are."

Aislinn allowed her grin to go wolf-wide, showing off pointed canines. "You got me."

"And Tobias," Sienna continued. "He seems calm and easygoing on the surface but underneath, he's strong as a mountain and has an intractable will. Lots of people assume he's a pushover and then get a nasty surprise."

"Hah!" Aislinn snorted, shoulders shaking with laughter. "You know us all so well - which I should expect from someone with your ability, I suppose."

"Hmmm." Sienna tilted her head, considering. "I think I'd like to hone this sense - is there somewhere I can go to learn?"

"Not that I know of," Aislinn shook her head. "It's not really a rare ability but seems to differ from one Kin to another. Flynn knows an awful lot about both chi and pressure points, if you're game to ask - and I'd hazard a guess that the more attention you pay to yourself, the more you'll learn."

A thumping on the stairs announced Tobias' return, his body clad in a pair of faded red shorts and a charcoal t-shirt, hair damp and unruly. "It feels much better to be clean," he announced, yanking a bottle of water from the fridge and drinking directly from it.

Dragging her eyes away from a body she very much wanted to bite, Aislinn turned to Sienna. "You want the next shower?"

"I'll wait for Flynn - my stuff is in the downstairs bathroom anyway. You go." Sienna watched Tobias with eyes narrowed in contemplation. "Besides, I need a quick word with our Alpha before everyone else gets here."

"Sure." Aislinn paused partway to the stairs. "Everyone else?"

"It's the last Friday of the month," Tobias said, capping the water and dropping the bottle back into the fridge. "Pot luck dinner night." Catching her astonished expression, he smiled. "You're not the only one who has ideas, you know."

Aislinn flipped him a rude gesture and then disappeared up the stairs and into the ensuite. It was heaven to wash the sweat and grime away, to relax - even briefly - into the soft confines of a fluffy towel. She returned to Tobias' room and donned a soft pair of harem pants in dark green, and a white tank with a maroon lace overlay that hugged her like a second skin. She made a face at the half-inch of creamy flesh visible between her top and bottoms, where Olaf's Mark could clearly be seen. Jagged-edged and carrying hints of cruelty and temper in the design, those thick, dark lines spread further than her combined hands would be able to cover; made as big as possible to enhance the message Olaf had intended to send with her dead body.

But she'd lived.

Ironic that in escaping Olaf, she'd tied his hands. He could send no more grisly 'messages' while she lived, turning the Mark into a shackle - and it wasn't shackling her, but a sociopath who believed it his right to defile and murder Kin women. A sociopath she'd denied and would continue to deny, not just for her own sake but for the sake of all those women who had gone before her and had their lights so brutally extinguished.

Aislinn resettled her clothes and picked up a brush, working out the tangles in her hair and tying it back from her face with a soft green scarf whose tiny silver bells matched those on the waistband of her pants. They jingled softly when she moved, a delicate, sensory invitation to life and joy - and a deliberate reminder to surround herself in those things as often as possible.

Giving herself a final once over in the mirror, she bared her teeth in approval of the woman who stared back. Not broken; forged. And when she and Olaf at last met in that final confrontation, Aislinn vowed it would not be the light from her eyes that faded. It would be his.

********

The soft jingling of bells drew Tobias' attention away from the drink in his hands. Aislinn stood at the base of the stairs, a combination of flared hips, narrow waist and full breasts that sucker-punched him in the gut every time he looked anew.

"You're drooling," Zeke murmured, reaching out to flick at Tobias' glass.

He fumbled the drink, managed to keep it from spilling by the skin of his teeth. "I am not."

"Zeke!" Aislinn swept across the room to fold the other male into a hug.

"Hello, beautiful." Zeke pulled back to tug gently on the scarf in Aislinn's hair. "Pot luck dinner just got much more appealing."

"Don't think you can win me over with that charm," Aislinn chuckled, twisting away. "Did you bring anything good to eat?"

Tucking long arms behind his head, Zeke did his best to look mysterious. "You'll have to wait and see."

Dominic strolled in then, freshly showered and with a covered dish he took to the kitchen bench, adding to the one Zeke had contributed only minutes before. The classically handsome wolfkin smiled in greeting even as he moved to fetch an empty glass. "Anyone else need a drink?"

"I do," Aislinn raised a hand.

"And me," Sienna's voice trailed out of the bathroom.

"Me too." Flynn rolled out of the guest bedroom, a borrowed pair of shorts barely clinging to his narrow hips.

Tobias shot a glance at Zeke. "Well, they fit."

"Barely." Zeke's eyebrow arched. "Hard to believe anyone's actually that thin - you should've seen Ma's jaw drop when I asked her if she had any of my old clothes still lying around."

"I guess we're lucky she did," Tobias chuckled, watching as the tigerkin flowed gracefully into the kitchen to help Dominic mix the drinks. "You know, for a feral creature, he's surprisingly domesticated."

"I can hear you, T-Fuzz," Flynn said calmly, shaking ice into four glasses.

Tobias' grin widened. "I was counting on it."

The door slammed open at that moment and Jaxon stomped in with a face like a thundercloud and several cartons of ice cream balanced precariously in one hand. "Dessert," he announced tersely.

Aislinn leapt forward to catch two of the three cartons as they toppled forward. "Geez, Jax! Watch it."

"Sorry." His face softened and he deposited his remaining carton on the bench, returning to take Aislinn's. "I've been running for hours, then Sens sent me to get ice cream. I'm tired."

Aislinn smoothed her hand up the stocky wolfkin's bicep and ruffled his almost non-existent hair. "Why did you cut your hair so short? You look like a thug."

"I've tried telling him that," Sienna snorted, emerging from the bathroom in a sweet blue sundress the exact colour of her eyes. "He never listens."

Jaxon's eyes widened as both women descended on him, pulling at his clothes and chattering merrily about how they could 'fix' his look.

"Think they'll thaw him out?" Zeke murmured.

Tobias shrugged, the barest rolling of his shoulders. "Hard to tell. If anyone can do it, Ash can."

"Damned straight." His second's eyes darkened in appreciation. "She's as smart as she is sexy, and she's as sexy as she is deadly. Jax has no chance."

Tobias drew back his teeth in a mock snarl. "You hitting on my woman?"

"At least you admit it now," Zeke returned. "Don't worry, I'm not going to cut your lunch. There's not enough trees in the bush to survive you being separated from Ash a second time."

Tobias growled and thumped him hard in the shoulder but Zeke only laughed. "I should throw your sorry ass outside."

"You'll do no such thing," Aislinn scolded, stomping over with both hands on her hips. "I don't know what's so funny, but Sienna's dishing up. Wash your hands and get up to the table."

Tobias - and everyone else in the room - did exactly what they were told before anybody realised what had happened. A couple of astonished glances crossed the table and then Flynn said; "You get used to it," and everyone broke out laughing.

*Pack*, Tobias thought as Sienna began plunking dishes onto the table. *Family*. Even Flynn's jagged edges fit the mould, having spent so long in Aislinn's company he knew her rhythms and therefore, the rhythms of everyone else.

"Serve yourselves," Sienna instructed, passing out empty plates and bowls. "Whoever makes the biggest mess does the dishes."

The meal passed in a warm blur of food and laughter and Tobias wrapped the sensations around himself, almost unable to believe that they'd been at each other's throats less than a week ago. When the mains were finished, Jaxon served out copious amounts of ice cream, baring his teeth at anyone who looked like they might have refused, while Dominic made a round of alcoholic hot chocolates.

"We're just missing Rory," Aislinn sighed, her eyes closed in bliss as she savoured the taste of her triple chocolate ice cream.

"He's still on patrol." Zeke glanced at the clock. "I'll trade with him in a few hours, then greet our esteemed guests early in the morning."

"Lucky you," Aislinn murmured, her smile sardonic. She glanced at Flynn. "I wonder who they'll bring with them."

"Grandma said three full teams." The tigerkin leant back in his chair, balancing the furniture precariously on two legs. "I wouldn't be surprised if they drag the rest of our squad into this."

Dominic's brow furrowed. "Why?"

"Why not?" Flynn chuckled. "All bets are off if you're trying to separate the prodigal daughter from her feral street rat."

********

There was a short silence, where the pack exchanged quizzical looks. Sienna said; "Maybe you should fill us in on a little backstory?"

Aislinn glanced at her tiger and shrugged. "Flynn and I already had a bond before we started working for the Council. They put us together under the condition that Flynn's mistakes come out of both our hides, and vice versa."

"Before you were his damper, or after?" Tobias asked.

"Both." Aislinn stirred her hot chocolate, the spoon tinkling against the sides of the cup. "They probably intended it to fracture us, but it only made us a tighter team."

"Trying to drive a wedge between us would be like trying to separate T-Fuzz and his glamazon," Flynn nodded towards Tobias and Zeke. "Some things are just set in stone."

Dominic frowned. "That sounds like gross misconduct on behalf of the Council. Wouldn't Andre put a stop to it?"

Aislinn's fingers tightened around her mug. "It's very hard for me to talk without bias, but Dad blames himself for the peace summit massacre that almost destroyed the pack."

Jaxon's brow furrowed, his eyes dark with an old pain. "That was eight years ago."

"Does that make the pain of losing people we cared about any less?" When nobody had an answer for that, she sighed and tipped her head back to stare at the exposed beams in the ceiling. "Right or wrong, Dad's spent the better part of the last eight years seeking to make amends for his perceived mistakes and running into one dead end after another."

Flynn growled deep in his chest. "Then the murders started."

"Yes." Aislinn gestured down at herself, the damage clear for all to see. "I wasn't the first victim, you all know that. At least thirty-seven other women went before me. What I haven't mentioned is that each one had a name stapled to their bodies after they died - the name of an allied Kin who was at the peace summit."

Aislinn watched in silence while faces around the table paled. Sienna mouthed 'stapled' over and over, as though to make the idea less grotesque. Tobias cleared his throat. "All the same name?"

"No," Flynn shook his head, "Each name was that of a Kin who had a personal link to the dead women, be it pack connection, family or otherwise."

"Personal taunts," Zeke mused, his sapphire eyes glittering with rage. "And Olaf all-but admitting to involvement in the bombing. He makes a new wound and simultaneously rips the scab off an old one."

"Exactly - the situation was driving my father to distraction even before I ended up involved," Aislinn growled, clenching her hands into fists. "As soon as I was compromised, I became nothing more than evidence. A body to be prodded, poked and questioned in the vain hope that the bearkin had revealed something of their plans."

Zeke choked. "Andre wouldn't."

"He would and he did," Flynn snarled. "Why do you think we tore the fucking hospital room to pieces? There was no healing there, only an endless line of assholes forcing Ash to relive her ordeal."

That particular revelation settled like a stone in the sudden silence of the room. Sienna, eyes doe-wide, said; "But why would Andre send you home if he was so determined to get information?"

"Because I didn't leave him any choice," Aislinn said quietly. "I couldn't take any more blood samples, skin scrapings, or DNA tests. I couldn't stand one more internal examination, psych evaluation, lie detector test or interrogation. No more sedations, no more pithy excuses, skittering glances or haughty scientists with cameras and notebooks. I couldn't stand being cuffed to the bed in case I developed some sort of Stockholm syndrome. I couldn't handle the whispers, the looks, the lack of friendly faces. The shame." She paused, tears trickling down her cheeks. "When one of the doctors answered an emergency call, he left his kit behind. I swiped a pressure injector - it was a pain in the ass, too, because I couldn't summon the shadows or shift into my other forms. But I managed it."

"I got tired of being told Ash was in isolation for her own safety, so I broke into the medical facility where they were keeping her," Flynn snarled, his voice barely human. "Nobody recovers properly like that - you need your people. When I got into the room, she'd emptied the injector into one orderly and was in the process of strangling another with his own stethoscope."

"Once the nurse passed out, I begged Flynn to help me escape," Aislinn said quietly. "He broke the chains holding me down and together we set about destroying as much of the facility as possible on our way out."

"Unfortunately for Andre, they'd requisitioned a wing beneath an actual Kin hospital so even though security eventually turned up and tranqed us both, there was no hiding what had happened." Flynn's lips peeled back from his teeth in a feral grin. "Andre was hauled before the High Council and made to explain himself."

"The Council eventually decided that I was deemed too dangerous to be around people," Aislinn continued, her smile rueful. "Funny, that - a trained assassin, actually dangerous? Who'd have thought?"

Flynn snorted a laugh but the rest of the table remained silent, their expressions somewhere between horror and awe. "I demanded they release Ash to me, but as you can imagine, it was an unpopular theory. Andre managed to salvage the situation by suggesting that, as per the psych evaluation, Ash be sent back here to recover in peace and quiet."

"Which carries the added benefit of keeping her away from the Council, whilst still being under Andre's influence," Dominic said quietly.

"Yup." Flynn raised his mug to the wolfkin in salute. "Considering I'm a threat to Andre's influence, they reassigned my stripy ass and shipped the princess back here without my knowledge."

Jaxon's green eyes narrowed. "How did you find her, then?"

Amber eyes glittered. "Ash is mine - my pack, my blood, my life. All I have. Nothing and nobody could keep me away from her."

Tobias slammed his fist onto the table and the lights in the house flickered and went out, plunging everyone into a darkness so complete Aislinn's heart leapt to her throat. An instant later they stuttered back on, revealing Tobias sitting in the wreckage of his smashed mug, shards of porcelain embedded in his wrist.

"Fuck," Zeke glanced over his shoulder and then back again. "Did he do that?"

Dominic pulled out his phone and grimaced. "Looks like it. My phone's dead, too."

"Hey." Aislinn leant towards the quivering Alpha, her voice pitched low. "It's okay."

He turned to look at her, the golden starbursts in his eyes bright with emotion. "I'm sorry."

For letting her leave. For not following. For judging her, for treating her the way he had when she'd returned. Aislinn read it all and more in those eyes, in the hard, grief-stricken lines of his face. "It's not your fault."

Tobias growled, but allowed her to take his hands and slowly unfurl his fingers. Sienna appeared with a pair of tweezers and the rest of the table sat in silence as Aislinn carefully removed the shards of porcelain from his flesh.

"I should probably point out," Flynn said, his tone clearly reluctant, "That she couldn't shift, couldn't fade out, was handcuffed to a bed and still kicked serious ass."

Zeke sniggered at that and a moment later Dominic tried to muffle a guffaw behind his hand. Flynn's razor of a smile was betrayed by the amusement glittering in his gaze and Sienna, petite fingers delicate across her lips, giggled. Even Jaxon huffed a quiet laugh. Tobias blinked, very slowly, and though his eyes never left Aislinn's face, one corner of his mouth twitched. "That doesn't surprise me in the slightest, kitty cat."

Relief bubbled in her chest at the easing tension and Aislinn flicked a glance at Flynn. "I never said thank you."

"It wasn't necessary." He shrugged, an easy rolling of shoulders that disguised his innermost feelings. "You thanked me enough by fighting."

Aislinn nodded. "I have no plans to do anything else, but we can't overlook the important facts: my father wields a lot of political power, has considerable influence and is unlikely to let familial ties stand in the way of getting what he wants."

"Vengeance," Zeke muttered.

"Vengeance," Aislinn agreed, her fingers tightening on Tobias' arm. "Cold, vicious, bloody vengeance - and that's not necessarily limited to the bears."

# Seven

The pack stayed well into the night, with Zeke tagging Rory in on his way out. Sienna and Aislinn spent a great deal of the time curled in an oversized armchair with their heads bent over each other's phones, looking at photographs and learning about the twelve years they'd spent apart.

Tobias watched from his position against the kitchen bench, bar for a small break to spar with Flynn and Jaxon when they asked. When Rory approached, his quiet voice delivering a steady report about the border patrol, Tobias tried to pay attention - but as soon as he heard the all-clear, he grunted and sank back into the recesses of his own mind, the hubbub of conversation passing by unnoticed.

"Wallowing doesn't suit you," murmured a soft voice by his elbow.

"Sienna?" Tobias blinked in surprise. "I thought -"

"She went to the toilet," Sienna cut him off, her blue eyes gentle. "Rory whispered that you were a world away."

"The borders are clear," Tobias muttered, brows drawn.

Sienna laid a hand on his arm. "He also ordered three large pizzas with a side of fuzzy slippers and you didn't even blink."

"Oh." Tobias winced. "I just... Lord and Lady, Sens. What they did to her. If the Council had decided to press charges, or if the situation had gone on too long, or if Ash wasn't so damned strong... We could've lost her."

"We could have - we didn't," Sienna said, quiet and firm. "But you know what? Indulging in your own self-pity *is* a sure way to lose her. For good."

He blinked. "What?"

"This whole scenario? It's not about you." Sienna bared her teeth, face set. "Don't make Ash feel guilty for things beyond her control."

"I'm not-"

"You are. Whether you intend it or not, you *are*." Sienna's voice, still calm and quiet, was like a whip to his soul. "Olaf tried to take everything; every little bit of her. Ash chose to share some of that with us - not to weigh you down, but because she trusts us to lighten her burden. Hold out a hand, Tobias. Give something back."

He swallowed, considered the words and pulled Sienna into a fierce, tight embrace. "You're right. Thank you."

She prodded him in the ribs until he let go. "Good, because I'd have hated breaking your legs for ruining this."

A laugh, sharp but real, bubbled out of his throat. Aislinn walked back into the room at that moment, her startled gaze going to his face. Now that he was paying attention, Tobias could see nerves that hadn't been there before, an uncertainty in those blue-green eyes. He pushed off the bench and strolled towards her, one hand in his pocket, the other outstretched to tuck her against his ribs. "Do I get to see your pictures too?"

"What?" She blinked, slender fingers tightening around the glittery case protecting her phone.

Tobias offered a crooked smile. "Is it against the rules?"

"Of course not." Aislinn shook herself and headed towards the couch. "Come on then."

A few moments later Tobias was seated, Aislinn beside him with her feet curled beneath her. She unlocked her phone and he watched her cheeks darken as the screen revealed an ancient picture of the two of them, lying on their backs on the common lawn while sunlight played over their laughing faces.

"I remember this," Tobias murmured, his fingers hovering above the glass. "We'd just come back from the orchard. You convinced me to steal apples straight off the tree."

A flash of blue-green beneath long, long lashes. "That's right."

"You were twelve," he said quietly, smiling down at the screen. "Skin and bone and fire and mischief - but too short to reach the apples."

"I was going to climb but you were worried about getting caught, so you shook the tree and they all fell out." Her face softened and she tapped on her picture gallery, then offered him the phone. "Here."

Hoping the slight tremor in his hand wasn't as obvious to Aislinn as it was to his own eyes, Tobias accepted the slim device and replaced it with his own. How long they spent, talking and comparing pictures, he couldn't say - except that when he looked up next, the lights were dimmed and everyone, even Flynn, had disappeared. Leaving Aislinn to yawn and stretch, Tobias wandered into the kitchen for a glass of water and found a hastily scrawled note. "Ash?"

"Hmm?" She appeared at his side, brushing his arm as she leant over to look at the note. And laughed. "Flynn."

"Why did he draw a dick and balls on a sticky note and leave it on the bench?"

"Because he's illiterate," Aislinn said. When that clearly didn't explain anything, she pointed again at the note. "See how the penis is ejaculating?"

"Bit hard to miss."

"It means he's gone." Aislinn grinned. "As in, out. For the whole night, judging from the size of that sperm cloud."

Tobias rolled his eyes. "You couldn't just teach him to write 'back later'?"

"He's stubborn - and nobody else sees a message here, just a crude picture from someone notoriously immature." She screwed up the note and dumped it in the bin. "I tried to teach him a couple of times but we're both too hard headed. Flynn will learn when he's ready."

"So you baby him?" Tobias asked, brows drawing together in a frown.

"I understand him," Aislinn corrected. "He leans on me, yes, but I also lean on him. You'll work it out as things go on."

There didn't seem much else to say to that, so he didn't bother, glancing instead at the clock. "It's three in the morning. Tired?"

"Yes and no. Not sure I can sleep but we should probably try." Aislinn ran both hands across her face and then blinked. "Why are you smiling like you just got the last cookie in the jar?"

Tobias grinned. "Because that's how I feel. Come on - if you're not tired, I want to show you something."

Eyes narrowed, she nevertheless allowed him to take her hand and lead the way outside onto the back deck. Stars winked on and off overhead, the last of the storm's moisture giving an otherwise dry summer night the fresh tang of forming dew. Tobias reached the far side of the raised decking and sat on the edge, leaning back on his palms to stare up at the partly clouded moon. After a moment's hesitation, Aislinn dropped down beside him.

"We're here to stare at the sky?" The skepticism was so thick in her voice that Tobias bit his lip to keep from laughing aloud.

"Do you think she's really up there?" He asked. "Lady Lunaida, I mean."

"Mother Moon," Aislinn murmured. "The female half of the whole, the first Kin to achieve a heartmate bond and generally accepted lunar deity of our species." Her head tilted to one side, red-tinted brown hair the colour of deep shadows in the night. "I don't know. I like to think so."

"And Solaeden?"

"Well, the Sun is her other half - if Lunaida's up there, then so is he," she returned, slowly leaning back on her hands in a feminine mirror of Tobias' own posture. "They're eternally bound; where one goes, the other follows. Heart to heart, souls entwined, the darkness and the light."

"Strong alone, invincible together."

"I fail to believe you bought me out here at three in the morning for a philosophical discussion." Aislinn's voice turned dry and she raised an eyebrow.

Tobias stared down at her, the soft lights from the house casting the planes of her face in light and shade. Shadows moved beneath her skin, blurring her edges as though, if he blinked too long, she might fade away. "I have something for you." Tobias reached under the edge of the decking and withdrew the square golden box he'd stashed earlier in the day. His fingers curled around the edges for a moment and then, with a deep breath, he reached over and placed it in her lap. "Here."

Aislinn blinked, sitting up straight to catch the box before it slid off her knees. "What is it?"

"Open it and find out."

She lifted the box, hesitated. "Your heart is going a million miles an hour."

"When you open it, you'll understand why."

Aislinn narrowed her eyes and for a moment Tobias feared she'd demand something from him that he wasn't able to properly articulate -

but then she settled herself more comfortably on the edge of the decking, rested the box on her thighs and carefully prised the lid off.

The thick cardboard was lined with black velvet, a perfect frame to highlight the torc within. At first glance it was no more than a simple twist of precious metals, four lengths of yellow and rose gold twined around one another to form the whole. Thinner at the back where the clasp was hidden, the torc broadened until it was three fingers thick by the time it reached the front, where the twisting yellow and rose broadened to show off the intricate carvings etched into each individual strand of metal.

Aislinn's breath came out on a gasp as she traced her fingertips over the beautiful craftsmanship. "Tobias?"

Still not trusting his voice, he leant over and pulled the torc free, flipping it in the palm of his hand so that she could see the almost invisible seam of the compartment at the back. Torc, and locket - just like the old one had been. A soft press of his thumb in the right place and it sprang open, revealing the contents.

Aislinn drew the pieces out with shaking hands. First, the letter and lock of his hair that had always been worn against her skin. Then, a second lock of hair - black, shimmering even in the depths of the night, with a small piece of paper wrapped around it, secured in place by a delicately braided piece of twine.

"Flynn," she breathed, tugging the bow on the twine to unroll the paper. In shaky, malformed letters, Tobias read: *i gcónaí agus go deo.*

"What does it say?" He dared to ask, voice quaking in his throat. "He wouldn't tell me."

"It's Gaelic," Aislinn answered, her voice thick with emotion. "It means 'always and forever'."

Tobias blinked. "Flynn speaks Gaelic?"

"It was his first language," she whispered, nodding. After a long moment, Aislinn fingered the braided threads, a combination of amber and teal which Flynn had also wound around the lock of his hair - provided to Tobias, along with the note, a bare twelve hours after he'd requested it outside the den what seemed an eternity ago. "He used to make these for the kids he cared for. I teased him mercilessly for months about how deft he was with his fingers, braiding together loose threads from clothes, rugs, rope - you name it. Then he made me one and I wore it every day until it frayed to nothing." She swallowed heavily. "Amber for his eyes, teal for mine."

"So he *is* soft at heart," Tobias murmured, his attention still on the small note. The letters were wobbly but clear, an indication of care and painstaking concentration. "How long would it have taken to write that?"

Aislinn shook her head, carefully rolling the note and re-wrapping it around the lock of midnight hair. "Probably half the night, a voice activated internet search, several tantrums and an almost infinite amount of previous attempts."

Carefully setting Flynn's lock of hair in the box beside Tobias', Aislinn withdrew the final scrap of paper and unfolded it. She read through once, blinked, then bit down on her lip and read through again. Tobias watched her eyes move, heard the words he'd written aloud in his head.

*Dear Ash,*

*You took a piece of me with you when you left. Then when you came back, I broke a piece of you I had no right to touch and in doing so, a piece of us.*

*It wasn't until I held your letter in my hands that I realised you were never really gone. Every time I closed my eyes I saw your smile. Every silent room held echoes of your laughter and every ray of sunshine bathed me in your warmth. You were always with me and I was always with you - we just didn't know it.*

*If you look inward, you'll find me waiting there for you, the other half of your soul as you are mine. Now that we're together again I will let nothing, nobody - not death, not the gods, not the Council - come between us. You are inside of my heart, my blood, the very air I breathe, and I will lay down my life to keep it that way.*

*I might have been a colossal ass but I hope you'll accept this paltry attempt at an apology, even if I'm not sure I deserve your forgiveness. I asked Flynn to help me out because I know he shares a part of you as well, is bound into your essence forevermore. I wanted you to have us both where we belong - against your skin, every day, from now until eternity.*

*Always yours,*
*Tobias.*

Watching the tears that slipped down Aislinn's cheeks was enough to put Tobias' heart in his mouth and he bit down on his tongue lest he confess the heartmate connection between them. He'd hinted at it in his letter, even discussed it with Flynn when the other male delivered his contribution for the torc.

"Let her come to you," the tigerkin had grunted, pain flickering in the depths of his amber eyes. "Don't pressure her now, when she's finally starting to come back together."

It was good advice but it was almost impossible to follow as Aislinn, fingers trembling, carefully began packing her precious things back inside the torc. When she slid the compartment closed, listening to the snick of metal against metal as it locked, Tobias held his breath, wondering if she'd figured it out - but she just shook her head, staring down at the jewellery with a bemused expression. "How did you manage this?"

"Sienna designed it," Tobias said, brushing a finger along the torc's edge. Swallowing the lump in his throat, he added; "It would normally take months to have it made but she's got connections. The yellow gold is your original torc, melted down and reforged. It wasn't enough, so I chose rose gold because I know it's your favourite."

Aislinn nodded, turning the torc over in her hands. "I don't know what to say, Tobias."

"Say you forgive me," he murmured, daring to slip the necklace from her hands. She made no move to stop him as he thumbed open the catch. "It's fused with the same alloy as your old torc, so it'll shift with you, accommodate whatever size or shape you take. And after I explained what happened to the old one, Sienna ensured the jeweller reinforced it so that was unlikely to happen again."

The hint of a smile tugged at Aislinn's lips and she bared her throat. Tobias slipped the torc around her neck, brushing the silken fall of her hair aside so that he could fasten the clasp; a special design that would not be undone by accident. As he withdrew, the sparkle of the diamond Sienna had cleverly worked into the torc caught his eye, glittering like one of the stars above. It was a heartfire diamond, Flynn had said - a rare gem that held hints of amber and gold in its cold, white depths.

Feeling the weight of Aislinn's silence heavily in his heart, Tobias brushed a finger over the burning stone and made to stand. She snatched his hands as he rose, her eyes lined with glittering tears. "I forgive you."

********

It was more than a piece of jewellery. More than an apology. It was a piece of Tobias' heart, carved out, sculpted, and offered in a velvet-lined box. A piece he'd even shared with Sienna and Flynn to make sure it was perfect. The torc should have weighed a tonne, with the sheer amount of gold and the treasures it contained, but such was the magic of the unusual technology that it was almost weightless, a warm comfort around Aislinn's throat that felt immediately as familiar as it was alien. The old torc had been flat, this one was thick and ropy. The old torc had been plain, bar for the diamond; this one was elegant, intricate. Aislinn was sure could stare at it for years and never discover all the secrets, in the same way that no matter how much she thought she knew Tobias Greenwood, he continued to surprise her.

The single tear that escaped at her declaration of forgiveness rolled unhindered down his cheek to plop, warm and wet, on the back of her wrist. As it soaked into her skin Aislinn felt a curious warmth steal through her, sealing up wounds and smoothing out wrinkles she'd carried for too long. Tobias was healing her, by word and deed and the unspoken trust that she would return to who she was before. No, Aislinn corrected - someone different, someone who could accept her scars and find a place in her heart for two different men in two different ways.

Tobias' tacit acceptance of Flynn and the complicated role he played in her life was perhaps the greatest gift of all. It would have torn her asunder if the two of them had grown to hate each other - and though neither would have ever asked her to choose between them, Aislinn knew in her heart of hearts it would have come to that in the end. Instead, they'd chosen each other; a former lover turned brother bowing to the man who'd had her heart in a stranglehold from the moment she first drew a breath.

She'd seen his face, known Tobias hadn't truly expected forgiveness. He'd torn his chest wide open anyway and that understanding twisted something deep inside her, causing a sweet pleasure-pain that lit a fire where before, there had been only ashes.

Aislinn released his hands, saw them tense as though he'd have caught at her but made a conscious effort not to. She drew her fingers across his tanned forearms, darkened to a deep shade of honey in the dim lighting. Tobias remained still as she stroked her way up his biceps, over his collarbones, up the pillar of his throat and along his jaw. They stared at each other for a frozen moment in time before Aislinn tugged and he moved, slow and fluid, to meet her halfway.

She brushed her lips against his and a very real spark arced between them, brilliant and blue-white in the night. Tobias swore and tried to pull back but Aislinn held firm, pressing soft, light kisses to the corners of his mouth. Electricity tingled between them, effervescent as bubbles and warm as the spring sun's first rays. When it became clear there were to be no further light shows Tobias relaxed, the tension draining out of his body to be replaced by a strong, masculine sensuality.

He opened his mouth, a soft groan escaping as Aislinn took the invitation and swept her tongue inside to tease his, winding her hands in the unruly golden-brown hair she adored so much. When he still didn't move, she leant back enough to nip at his nose and whispered, "I'm not made of glass, Tobias. I won't break."

"I don't want to-"

"Take advantage of me?"

He drew a deep, shuddering breath. "You're in heat."

"I know." She'd figured it out earlier, while laughing with Sienna on the couch. The earlier signs of the hormonal surge were always harder for her to notice than they were for anyone else, but when simply looking at Tobias sent fire racing through her veins - even though he'd been clearly brooding and was oblivious - and every other male who walked into the house blinked rapidly and gave her an odd look, Aislinn had realised what was going on.

Tobias blinked, looking adorably confused. "I didn't know how to tell you. I'm sorry if I -"

"What? Let me kiss you under the stars?" Her lip quirked at that, and Aislinn leant forward to bump her head against his. "At least I know why you and Flynn pulled the caveman trick on me at Grandma's."

He had the grace to blush. "We didn't want you to feel pressured after... you know."

She knew. She also knew he didn't want to ruin the magic of the night by saying Olaf's name out loud, but the time had come for that particular wound to close. Aislinn smiled and said, "Being in heat doesn't rob me of my sense of reason. It just makes me smell different."

It would also, if she didn't quench the hormones eventually, drive her into a chaotic rage of thoughts and feelings, her scent increasing in potency until she addled the brain of every unmated male within sniffing distance - but right now, in the early stages, it was only a gentle enhancement to what she already felt. And every single part of her, hormonal or otherwise, felt like a piece of Tobias.

"You don't smell different," Tobias demurred. "Just… more inviting."

"Are you blushing?" Aislinn asked, examining his face. "You are!"

"I'm trying not to throw you on the ground and leap on top of you," he growled, pulling out of her arms. "Your scent is like a drug and I'm not sure I'm strong enough to resist."

No, not after everything that had passed between them since they'd stepped outside. Aislinn watched Tobias walk across the narrow stretch of lawn and disappear into the trees beyond, hands shoved deep in his pockets. Protecting her - but she didn't want to be protected. She was through with hiding, through with throwing up shields and excuses. Particularly where he was concerned.

Dissolving into shadow, Aislinn streamed into the trees, circling around and ahead of Tobias while he stomped through the bush. He came to a halt in what was less of a clearing and more of a gap between two giant eucalypts, chest heaving in a way that told Aislinn he was trying to regain some sense of composure. She rematerialised at the base of one of the trees and launched across the open space, tumbling them both onto the ground.

He grunted in surprise as they rolled beneath the boughs of a low-hanging tea tree to end up resting in the intimate, cave-like space beside the trunk. Tobias reached to shove her off his chest but Aislinn lowered her weight with a thump, snatching his wrists and slamming them into the soft earth.

"No more running," she growled, and kissed him with everything she had.

Tobias froze, his shuddering inhalation taking Aislinn's scent deep into those powerful lungs. She held firm for a moment, driving home the point that she was strong enough to restrain him if she so chose, then let go. Part of her feared he'd try and throw her off again but Tobias only dragged her closer, one hand clenching in the lace of her tank and the other splayed across the base of her spine. His kiss was hot and melting, his tongue a brand against her own. In less than a minute their breath came in gasps, the need for each other perilously close to outweighing the need for air. She wriggled against him and Tobias groaned, fingertips digging into her flesh in a slipping of his normal control that sent tingles down Aislinn's spine. It was good, but it wasn't enough - she wanted him unleashed.

Breaking the kiss, Aislinn nipped his nose and sat up, claws slicing out of the ends of her fingers. Tobias' eyes went wide as she carved up his t-shirt with several swift, precise strokes and then swept the remains of the fabric onto the ground.

"I seem to be making a habit of this," she murmured, leaning down to press a kiss to the hollow of his throat. "I hope that wasn't a favourite."

"I don't remember," he managed, voice hoarse as her mouth moved across the broad, golden expanse of his chest. When her teeth scraped over one flat nipple, he gasped and shuddered. "Scratch that; I don't care."

"Good." Raking her nails down his pectorals, Aislinn kissed her way back to Tobias' sternum and began making her way downward. He swore as she reached the waistband of his shorts, trailing her fingers across the sensitive flesh near his hips.

"Ash," he warned, then cut off as she raised her head and fixed him with a glare.

"What?"

Tobias swallowed. "Are you sure?"

"Yes." She closed her teeth over the curve of his hip and bit, none too gently.

"Fuck!" He arched into her bite, hands fisting in the dirt. "Ash!"

She laughed, licking away the twin dots of blood her sharpened canines had drawn free. "You taste good."

"You're trying to kill me," he accused, eyes going wide as she reached for the fastening of his shorts. "You really are."

"Oh, no." Aislinn favoured Tobias with her most wicked grin as she undid his shorts and, finding his body an irritating weight she had no inclination to move, simply bunched her muscles and tore them in two. Staring down at the velvet and steel of his erection, she murmured, "I have no intention of wasting you on death."

Silence met that statement and she flicked a look up from beneath lowered lashes to find Tobias' cheeks flagged red and his eyes glittering with heat. Aislinn sank down between his knees and blew a long, soft breath along the inside of one muscular thigh, followed by the other. He twitched, breath hitching, but made no move to stop her as she followed her breath with her mouth, kissing and nipping her way up one leg whilst she smoothed her palm along the other.

"Ash-" she never found out what he'd been about to say because her hand closed around the thick, warm length of him, followed swiftly by her tongue and then, a moment later, the rest of her mouth. Tobias swore, his hands scrabbling in the earth as she employed long, gentle licks and the barest scrape of teeth that had his hips arching after barely a minute.

"Not yet, not yet," Aislinn chuckled, leaning backward with a final flick of her tongue. She blew a soft breath across the broad, flat head and smiled at his groan, then began the long, languorous journey up his body. Aislinn had barely made it halfway when Tobias' hands wrapped around her ribs and he dragged her upward, depositing her on his thighs as he sat up, drawing the soft lace tank over her head in one swift movement.

"You," he ground out, flinging the top to one side and then following it with her bra, "Have no idea what you're getting yourself into."

Aislinn's lips curved as her breasts - too big for a warrior but plenty perfect for Tobias' large hands - fell heavily into his palms. The hitch in his breathing was there, the tone of his voice frayed but still Tobias clung to his self-control, the construct of stubborn strength he wrapped around himself. His blue eyes were almost indigo in the dark, the golden starbursts in the centre glimmering to her wolfkin night vision. They were focussed wholly on her face as Tobias ran both thumbs over her nipples, watching closely for any sign she might break and change her mind.

Not this time, Aislinn swore silently. Never again.

She arched into his touch and he lowered his head, nuzzling the creamy swells - and then flicked out his tongue to trace the long, ridged line of a scar. "I told you I was going to lick these," he growled, repeating the motion until Aislinn jerked in his hands. "Every. Single. One."

"I don't think I'm that patient," she gasped, twining her fingers in his hair as Tobias sucked one of her nipples into his mouth. His hands may have been gentle but his mouth was firm; teeth scraping gently in time with the rhythm of his tongue and the deep, pulling motion of his throat. Aislinn squirmed in his embrace and Tobias, always knowing what she wanted, what she *needed*, moved his mouth to her other breast and repeated his claiming. Her fingers clenched in his hair hard enough that it had to hurt but he made no complaint; tugging her hips against his abdomen with one hand so that the steel and velvet weight of his erection was pressed against her core, gloriously hot even through the layers of her clothing.

"Tobias," she managed, tugging imperiously at his hair. His mouth had stopped moving at the contact as though he was so stunned by the sensation it was impossible to do anything else. "*Tobias.*"

"Sweet mercy," he breathed - and then sank his teeth into the side of her breast, a bite as proprietary as the one she'd laid on his hip earlier. Hard enough to pierce skin and draw blood; a final test of her nightmares.

But there were no nightmares here, not with Tobias. Only the decadent sin of his mouth on her body as she arched into the bite, cradling his head until he groaned, sucked once and then leant back to lick the blood away. Strong hands moved from her breasts to her ribs, moulding the muscles in her back before settling on her hips, thumbs curling into the waistband of her pants.

When Tobias raised his head she took his mouth with greedy, hungry kisses designed to whip him into a frenzy. Hot, possessive kisses that told him she wasn't letting go, wasn't backing down. Soft, sweet, nibbling kisses that told him how much it meant that he was here, accepting her as she was, scars and all. With a final, hard press of her lips to his, Aislinn rose on her knees to wriggle out of her softly jingling pants and plain cotton underwear.

Tobias' hands began to tremble as he helped her with the task and by the time she settled in his lap he was shaking in earnest. Aislinn stared into his too-wide eyes, brushing the pad of her thumb over one cheek. "What's wrong?"

"Nothing," he managed, his throat thick with emotion. "I just - I've spent so long imagining this I'd started to think it'd never happen."

Aislinn's heart squeezed and she leant forward to brush a tender kiss across his lower lip. "Well, it is, so you have about three seconds to get your mind around the reality of it."

Tobias blinked and then laughed, a throaty, sensual sound that tightened something in Aislinn's gut even as he tightened his arms around her body. They'd been naked before and they'd been intimate before, at least so far as Aislinn's baggage had allowed. But nothing had prepared her for this moment, here and now, where electricity zinged up and down her spine as they sat chest to chest, stomach to stomach, his arms heated steel around her body and his heart thundering in time with her own. He tilted his head, expression uncertain in a way that made her breath hitch. "I don't want to hurt you."

"You won't." Smiling with her whole heart, Aislinn placed both palms on his shoulders and pushed. "Trust me."

Tobias reclined slowly, one liquid inch at a time, until her forearms were braced on his shoulders and her fingertips trailing in the dirt beside his head. He loosened his grip when she shifted her weight, rising up above him just far enough to tease the broad, flat head of his erection with her soft folds and draw a gasp from them both. Bracing her palms in the dirt, she drew back to stare into those blue and gold eyes, trusting he'd find the balm to his doubts in the depths of her gaze.

The moment his expression softened, Aislinn settled her entrance against the head of his erection and began to bear down slowly. The burn of her body stretching was an ecstasy unto itself; the thickness of Tobias almost more than she could stand and yet, at that very same time, nowhere near enough. She let him fill her, his warmth and life brightening the darkened corners of her spirit. When he was buried to the hilt, his eyes locked with hers, Aislinn knew there was no going back. Not now, not ever.

"No more waiting," she whispered, leaning down to brush her words across his lips. "Give me everything."

"Always." His voice was hoarse with strain and she knew it was only Tobias' incredible strength of will that kept him still and patient. "Always."

She nipped his nose. "Now."

He tightened his grip on her hips and Aislinn began to move, a slow, languorous ride that gave her body time to adjust, allowed her to find a rhythm that suited them both. When she began to pick up the pace, Tobias tilted his pelvis and Aislinn cried out as he arrowed deeper than before. Lost in the incredible sensation, her rhythm faltered - but Tobias was there, slipping his leash at last to take the reins. The pace he set went swiftly from erotic torment to blistering firestorm and Aislinn thought she might die from the sheer pleasure of it, her breath catching in her lungs as Tobias drove deeper and deeper inside her.

Breath mingled, lips tangled, tongues and teeth clashing in furious desperation as their bodies fused ever more tightly together. Pleasure built in an ever-expanding wave, tightening and loosening her muscles simultaneously. Aislinn screamed as the orgasm took her over and Tobias captured her mouth with his, pushing her through wave after wave of searing ecstasy until he gave one last, almighty thrust and shouted his own release down her throat.

Aislinn tasted salt and realised she was crying; she leant back long enough to see that Tobias, too, had a face wet with tears. Then he caged her cheeks with his palms and dragged her down for a soul-rending kiss, his heart thundering in time with her own.

"I think I've died," she managed when he released her at last.

Tobias' chest rumbled with laughter and Aislinn felt the vibration deep inside her, their bodies still connected on the most intimate of levels. He tucked her face into the curve of his neck, fingers tangling in her hair. "That's my line."

Aislinn nipped at the sweaty skin of his throat and Tobias laughed again, tightening his grip as though he would indeed melt their bodies together. The pithy comment she'd been about to make died on her tongue and she swallowed, throat suddenly dry. "We really did that."

Tobias stroked a hand over her hair, his rumbled assent filled with a healthy dose of male satisfaction. "We really did."

"What does that make us now?" She raised her head, seeking the answer in the depths of his eyes.

"Satisfied?"

Aislinn nudged him in the ribs with her knee. "Not what I meant and you know it."

Tobias opened his mouth, shut it, opened it again. And somehow, when he answered, Aislinn knew it wasn't what he'd originally intended to say. "We're exactly what we always were."

Her brows furrowed but she couldn't fault the answer; his scent rang with truth. "And what's that?"

"Each other's." His lips curled, mischief dancing in those gold and blue eyes. As Tobias had known it would, the ambiguous answer drew a growl from her throat and Aislinn thumped her fists against his chest.

"Asshole."

"Troublemaker."

"Me?" Her eyes widened. "Never."

He laughed at that and drew her close for another searing kiss which wiped away the rest of the world. "Always."

# Eight

Tobias opened his eyes to waving tea tree and the shimmer of early morning sunlight. Aislinn was a warm weight atop his chest, her hair spread across one shoulder and her fingers curled around his neck. Their legs twined together in the dirt and though his body had slid out of hers in sleep, Tobias had enough of Aislinn's bites and scratches over his flesh to prove that the previous night had, indeed, been real.

He tightened his grip - of course he was still holding her, it was in his blood and bones to do so - moulding one hand against her buttock and the other across the back of her shoulders, revelling in the silken feel of her hair. Aislinn might not have recognised the heartmate bond, but she'd pushed through the depths of her own personal hell to reach out for *him*, Tobias Deklyn Greenwood.

To say it was more than he'd dared to dream was the single greatest understatement of his life.

Yes, he'd have preferred she realised they were mated and yes, he'd fought every instinct he possessed not to tell her - but that would come. By accepting the torc and then by accepting his body inside of hers, Aislinn had set them on a road that could only end with the two of them bound together forever. Tobias shifted the hand on her buttock to glance down at Olaf's mark, thick and jagged and very black in dawn's first light. *That* was something they were going to have to deal with somehow and if he was being honest, he had no idea; save for rending Olaf limb from limb. Certainly the most preferable option but Tobias was no fool to think the bearkin Ursar would go gently into the long night. No, Olaf Gruybere had fought long and hard and dirty to get where he was. Unseating his head from his shoulders would be no simple task.

Aislinn stirred, then, banishing the dark thoughts from Tobias' mind by the simple expedient of raising her head. Sleep tousled hair fell thick around her face, dusted with a faint layer of freckles and home to the brilliant, blue-green eyes he adored. She blinked at him once, twice… and then blushed an adorable shade of deep red.

Tobias lifted a hand to cup her cheek, feathering his thumb over the sweep of one cheekbone. "Good morning."

"Good morning." She leant into the caress and he couldn't stop the rumble in his chest, nor the twitch of his cock against her leg. Now it was Tobias' turn to blush but Aislinn laughed, turning her head to stare at the body part in question. "Good morning to you, too."

"Sorry," he muttered.

"For what?" She turned back, eyes sparkling with mischief. "For paying me a compliment? Or is it your morning pee erection?"

Tobias spluttered in astonishment and Aislinn laughed again, the sound crisp and clear in the privacy of their tea tree hideaway. He tried to regroup, failed as his body clenched in response to her laughter, and finally said; "Not my morning pee erection."

She hummed deep in her throat, her expression turning wicked. "Excellent."

Embarrassment turned to something hotter as Aislinn lowered her head, brushing warm lips across his chest. As her mouth made slow, inexorable progress up the column of his throat, Tobias managed; "We don't have much time before we need to be at Grandma's."

"Well then," she said against his lips, "You'd better put your back into it, hadn't you?"

The heady scent of Aislinn's arousal was more than he could bear and Tobias caught her mouth in a scalding kiss, his heart picking up speed. "Dammit, Ash," he whispered, nipping at her lower lip. "What are you doing to me?"

"Turning you bad," she replied without remorse. "But you're right - as tempting as it is to indulge in you all day, I'm starving. I need crumpets."

Tobias groaned in erotic disappointment as she lifted herself off him, rolling to her side in the dirt. "I don't know if I've got crumpets."

"Don't tell me that," Aislinn groused, pillowing her head on his shoulder and doodling idle patterns on his chest. "Looks like we charged you up good with our shenanigans earlier."

He looked down to see sparks of blue light following the path of her finger. "Is that going to happen every time some wicked harlot comes along and distracts me?"

Tobias' heart threatened to break the land-speed record as Aislinn drew her lips back from her teeth and growled in the base of her throat, a dangerous sound which promised only death for those foolish enough to ignore it. "I am the only wicked harlot allowed in your life, Tobias Greenwood."

"Possessive," he replied, not bothering to hide his delight at her reaction. Wrapping a hand in her hair, Tobias tugged until Aislinn bent close enough for him to speak against her lips. "You know full well I've never wanted anyone else."

"Good." She rose onto one elbow and frowned down at his chest. "I should probably soothe this out of you, but it's fascinating. I wonder what it's for?"

"No offence, but I'm not particularly interested in finding out with our parents due sometime in the next couple of hours," Tobias replied. He dropped his head back to the earth. "Hello, sir, welcome home. Good to see you after twelve long years. Oh, these blue lights? That's because I made wild and passionate love to your daughter this morning. Yes, we managed to generate enough static electricity to turn my body into a walking strobe light. Isn't it pretty?"

Aislinn's laugh was long and low. "You wouldn't."

"Definitely not, but *you* would," he muttered, lips twitching. "I'd put nothing past you, Aislinn mischief-is-my-middle-name Redding."

She snorted, flattening her palm across his chest. "It'd almost be worth it, just to see the look on his face."

"No, thank you," Tobias growled. "Banish it, please."

Cool, soothing energy washed over him. "There. All gone."

"Then why are you still laughing?"

She pressed a searing kiss to his lips and then rolled upright. "I'm wondering how you're going to explain all those bite marks."

Tobias narrowed his eyes and reached for her, but Aislinn faded into the shadows with a wicked laugh. "Just for that," he announced, getting to his feet and dusting dirt and leaf litter from his skin, "I'm telling everyone you did it."

The woman who materialised on the opposite side of their little clearing was part smoke, part wild thing, all delicious curves. Aislinn winked and said, "I should hope so."

"Troublemaker." He bent to gather his clothes and was suddenly reminded they were in shreds. Tobias snorted, scooping up the tattered pieces of fabric and brandishing them in Aislinn's direction. "I'm going to run out at this rate."

Her eyes tracked a scorching path down his naked body and back again. "Not sorry."

"Why am I not surprised?" He gathered Aislinn's clothes and held them out. "You want these on?"

"Nah," she took the bunched garments with a wink. "It wouldn't be fair to make you go naked on your own."

The sun had barely topped the horizon when they slipped back across the lawn and into Tobias' kitchen. The house was quiet, the curtains still drawn, though a quick glance at the bench revealed someone had cleaned up the remains of last night's party. Aislinn's nose twitched and she mouthed 'Jaxon,' pointing upstairs.

Tobias nodded; the other wolfkin's scent was all over the kitchen and somehow, Flynn didn't strike him as the cleaning type. He dumped his ruined clothes in the bin and they crept up the stairs, Aislinn's eyes dancing with laughter as she glanced down the landing towards the room Jaxon had appropriated as his own. After placing a finger over her lips, she shooed Tobias towards the shower and he went gladly, well aware of the sweat and grit coating his skin.

"Do you think we woke him?" Tobias asked as she closed the ensuite door behind them.

Aislinn met his eyes in the mirror and shook her head. "No, I don't think so. You're pretty quiet for a fairy elephant."

He flipped her off, half listening to her humming as she started the shower. "You did quite a number on me, young lady." Indeed, the man in the mirror wore Tobias' face but that was about where the resemblance ended. Smeared in dirt and grass and gods-knew what else, he bore several long scratches courtesy of Aislinn's nails and more than one clearly visible bite mark. The one she'd laid on him first, just above the swell of his left hip, bore two small bruises where her canines had sunk deep enough to draw blood.

A warmth at his back was the only warning Tobias had before Aislinn's palms smoothed across his chest and then swept lower. His breath caught as she cupped him, pressing generous breasts into his back and nudging her pelvis against his butt. "Stop admiring yourself in the mirror and get into the shower so I can admire you instead."

He turned in the circle of her arms, already hardening against her body. "Admire what? I'm filthy."

"I like filthy."

"We're short on time," Tobias reminded her - but nevertheless allowed Aislinn to tug him into the shower, the hot water so blissful that he sighed. "What about breakfast?"

She hooked her arms around his neck and jumped, locking both legs at the small of Tobias' back. "I'm breakfast."

He opened his mouth to argue - why, he wasn't quite sure - but Aislinn twisted her hips and impaled herself on him in one swift, smooth movement that almost buckled his knees. "Fuck!"

"Yes," Aislinn agreed, her body already seeking a rhythm. "Right now."

"Dammit Ash," he pinned her against the wall, one hand braced on the tiles while the other angled her for better penetration. "You're a demon."

She leant forward to nip his nose, her body still working against his in spite of the tight confines in which he'd squashed her. "You like it."

"I love it." Tobias stole her mouth in a kiss, pulling out almost all the way before he thrust back in deep and slow, drawing a long moan from Aislinn that set every single one of his nerve endings on fire. He kept that torturous pace going, ignoring the way she clawed at his back in an attempt to speed him up, laughing when she tried to use the wall as leverage to grind harder against him. When he could no longer stand the exquisitely drawn out sensations, Tobias nibbled his way down Aislinn's neck, drew her nipple into his mouth and sucked as hard as he could.

She shattered with his name on her lips and Tobias gloried in the sound, picking up the pace at last, surging into her while she rode wave after wave of pleasure. His name became a desperate plea in her throat, a panting mantra as the faster pace wound Aislinn tight all over again. Her fingers dug into his shoulders and Tobias raised his head from her breasts, looked her right in the eye and took them both over the edge.

Aislinn shuddered around him as eternity swept around them, water poured over them, lightning coursed through them. He clung to her, to the exquisite tempest between them, until the last wracking shudder left his body and reality seeped back in. When she lowered her legs and reached for the wash cloth, Tobias stood and let her wash him, then returned the favour.

They stepped out of the shower as one and he towelled them both dry, catching Aislinn up against his chest with the fluffy length. He lowered his lips to hers, brushed against them once and whispered; "Next time, we're going to do that my way."

"Oh?"

"Yeah. Long, slow, and in my fucking bed." He deliberately let a healthy dose of alpha energy slip through and saw Aislinn's eyes spark with delight.

"I'm going to hold you to that."

Tobias dropped the towel, nipped her nose, and growled deep in his chest. "Am I lit up like a Christmas tree again?"

Aislinn wiped a hand down his collarbone, leaving soothing shadows in her wake. "Not anymore."

"Good. Let's go get some breakfast."

********

Flynn was waiting in the kitchen, curled up in front of the large windows in his tiger form. Bright amber eyes swept open as Aislinn reached the bottom of the stairs and his whiskers twitched in amusement.

*Well, well. You don't look like you slept very much.*

"And I suppose you did?"

*Like a baby, actually.* Flynn purred, stretching his legs and displaying wicked looking claws in the process. *Although Sienna wasn't impressed to wake and find a tiger at the foot of her bed.*

Aislinn choked a laugh that had Tobias pausing on his way to the fridge. "Do I want to know?"

"Flynn decided to warm Sienna's bed."

*Not like that!* The tigerkin's voice echoed in her mind as he broadened his range to include Tobias. *Fucking hell Ash, give me a little bit of credit.*

Tobias relaxed and finished crossing the kitchen, yanking the fridge open to rummage inside. "Looks like Jax loves his Den Mother. I see crumpets."

"Remind me to knight him," Aislinn returned fervently.

Flynn stood and yawned. *This isn't the dark ages, you know. You can't do that.*

"He's my pack, isn't he? I can do what I damned well please - and if Jax provided crumpets, he's definitely my knight in black furry armour." She reached under the bench and pulled out the toaster, watching in open delight as Tobias stacked it full of crumpets and pressed the lever. "Sir Jaxon Heliope-Flint, fetcher of perfect breakfasts."

"There's creamed honey in the cupboard, too," Jaxon's voice preceded him down the stairs, his green eyes glittering with amusement. "I assume that's still your favourite?"

"Tobias, you're dumped," Aislinn announced, skipping around the bench to wrap Jaxon in a fierce hug. "You didn't provide me with crumpets."

"I screwed you three ways from Sunday and you're ousting me because I didn't have a well stocked pantry?" Tobias clutched at his chest. "That shit is cold, princess."

"Actually, I believe *I* screwed *you* three ways from Sunday," Aislinn replied primly. Jaxon choked and she leant back to pat him on the cheek. "Don't bother acting innocent, Jax, you would've scented it on us by now."

"Well yeah, but I didn't think you'd come out and bloody well announce it," Jaxon managed, his cheeks flushing beneath her touch.

Aislinn shrugged. "My father's also not going to expect me to be wearing a corset that shoves my scarred titties up in his face this morning - but we can't all win at life, now, can we?"

Jaxon choked again, turning his gaze very pointedly to the ceiling. "I honest to Lunaida didn't notice."

"Stop lying out your ass and tell me how bad I stink of Tobias." Aislinn prodded Jaxon in the ribs while Tobias sniggered from the other side of the kitchen. "I don't want Dad figuring anything out before I'm ready for him to know."

Jaxon closed his eyes and inhaled deeply, considering. "I can scent the difference because I've been around to compare but I don't think Andre will notice. It's no worse than you used to stink of each other."

"What's *that* supposed to mean?" Tobias caught the crumpets as they shot up out of the toaster and began lathering them with butter and creamed honey.

"When we were younger," Jaxon said, speaking as though to someone incredibly dense, "You two always had your scents mixed. Either one of you always smelled like the other. Always."

Aislinn blinked. "But we never…"

"I know," Jaxon returned, his arms tightening around her waist. "Doesn't change the fact that Tobias had your scent all over him for a good few months after you were gone."

"Huh." Tobias rounded the bench to hand Aislinn a plate of crumpets, which she wiggled away from Jaxon to accept. "I never realised."

The stocky wolfkin rolled his eyes. "You were too busy crying into your breakfast cereal."

Tobias blushed and Aislinn snorted a laugh around the decadent delight of her creamed honey. When she'd finished, swallowing with an appreciative hum, she said: "So you're telling me Dad won't pick anything up?"

"I don't think so." Jaxon shook his head. "I mean, maybe under normal circumstances he might but you're forgetting that you also still stink of bear, which is going to do a fair job of covering up anything else."

"I never thought I'd say this, but thank the Lady for that," Aislinn muttered, shoving the rest of a crumpet into her mouth and chewing industriously.

Flynn padded up to Tobias, who was now cooking his own crumpets, and sniffed loudly. *You smell of butterscotch and cream and vanilla - your scent, and hers. Very obviously hers.*

Jaxon crossed to the Alpha's other side and leant in close enough to fill his lungs with Tobias' scent. "You smell like you again. Andre's never scented you any other way - he won't notice a difference."

Aislinn frowned when Tobias accepted that announcement as though it made complete sense. At what point was it commonly recognised that Tobias' scent, when no longer mixed with hers, was abnormal? And how was it that, mind blowing sex aside, she felt more relaxed and at home this morning than she had in well over a decade? Her fingers reached of their own accord for the torc around her neck, playing over the woven strands of metal. It was almost the opposite of her old torc but the meditative motion worked nonetheless, her fingertips finding soothing hollows and etchings as though they'd always known where to look. She glanced up from under her lashes and caught Tobias watching her, the golden starbursts in his eyes dark and intense. He knew something, she realised - something she'd missed.

Aislinn narrowed her eyes and bit into her next crumpet with enough enthusiasm that Tobias chuckled as he looked away to attend his own breakfast. Whatever it was he knew, she intended to find out - but Tobias had a mile-wide stubborn streak and if he hadn't already divulged the information, it was because he wanted her to figure it out herself.

*Stumped?* Flynn rubbed against her legs like a kitten, his weight such that he almost knocked her over.

Aislinn crouched beside him, the exotic cloves and coffee of his scent wrapping her in a familiar warmth. "Yeah. What am I missing?"

*Like I said the first night I was here - there ain't no way in hell I'm telling you that.*

"Flynn," she hissed, tugging at the fur in his armpit. "I will shave you while you're sleeping."

*Kinky,* Flynn's chest rumbled with laughter. *Bored with T-Fuzz already?*

Aislinn paused, weighing the unusual edge to his words, and teetered on a painful knife's edge. Lowering her voice until it was no more than a breath, she murmured; "Are you... okay with this?"

*No,* the tigerkin answered, his words reaching deep inside and shaking her soul. *I've never been okay with it. But I've learnt to live with it.*

"What're you not saying?"

Flynn was silent for a long moment and when he turned to look at her, his eyes were bright with emotion. *If you have any love for me at all, Ash, don't ask me that fucking question.*

"But we -" she paused, shook her head. "You were the one who broke it off."

*Yeah.* He leant closer, rubbing his head under her chin in the way he did when he desperately needed comfort. *I did.*

There was nothing more to be said to that, so she threw her arms around Flynn's neck and buried her face in his fur. When the rock in her throat loosened just enough, she whispered; "I'm sorry."

Flynn twisted his head to lick at her face with a rough tongue. *I'm not. I got to thoroughly debauch you while the ever wholesome T-Fuzz was deciding which hand to use to sate his frustration.*

Her heart eased a little, and she leant back to offer a trembling smile. "You're a rogue, you know that?"

*Of course. Now if you don't mind, you've put honey in my fucking fur.*

Laughing, Aislinn pressed a kiss to Flynn's cheek and let go, collecting her plate from where it sat on the floor and jamming the last crumpet in her mouth as she stood. "We need a plan."

"It's only a visit, Ash." Tobias reached out to take her empty plate, dumping it in the sink. "What do we need to plan for?"

She smoothed her hands over the frayed denim mini skirt she'd teamed with her corset and frowned. "First and foremost, we need to work out why Dad and Rupert are even coming here in the first place."

"To sort out the Olaf threat," Jaxon supplied immediately. "He can't ignore the bears now that their General has made an appearance."

"I've been thinking about that," Aislinn said, leaning back against the bench. "It doesn't make complete sense. The High Council would have ordered someone to take care of this, sure - but to risk one of their own members coming in person? No way. That's what cannon fodder is for."

*The asshole's also spent twelve years keeping you two apart. Now, my interfering ass aside, he's thrown you back together and risked his entire career. Nobody is that stupid.*

"Maybe he's assuming we'll hate each other after all his meddling?" Tobias offered.

"I'm sure he hoped it would buy him some time," Aislinn allowed. Her lips compressed as she recalled the animosity her altered scent had caused. "Flynn has a point, though. There's more going on and until we work it out, Dad cannot know that Tobias and I are… complicated."

"Agreed." Tobias jerked his chin at Flynn. "I also think we should keep the kitty cat here under wraps until it suits us."

*I'll keep a watch from outside - but if you need me, I'm going in.*

"Fine. I want you nearby, too." Aislinn levelled a finger at Jaxon. "If you're next on patrol, swap with someone."

Jaxon's chest puffed with pride but none of it was evident in his voice as he said; "No need. Dominic is following after Zeke this morning."

"Should I ask one of the others to provide extra backup?" Tobias tilted his head, brows furrowed. "Apart from Zeke."

"No," Aislinn shook her head. "They belong to you and thereby to Dad. I'm independent, so Flynn and Jax aren't under his direct authority."

Tobias shook his head. "I still can't believe he made you swear out."

*It was one of the conditions of her contract. That way if we screwed up, none of it could come back to bite Andre.*

"Son of a slug," Jaxon murmured.

Aislinn shrugged. "I survived. And I wasn't packless - I had Flynn." She reached out to scratch between the tiger's ears. "It's ancient history now, anyway. The point is, Flynn's a Sabre in his own right and Jax is sworn to me. Dad can't influence them, or hold their fates over your head."

Tobias looked like he wanted to protest but subsided with a grunt. "Anything else?"

"Hmmmm." She chewed on the inside of her lip a moment, glancing up at the clock. "Not that I can think of. We better get a move on."

*I'll stay in tiger form so I can talk to you if need be,* Flynn said, following her to the door. *Jax, with me.*

Aislinn wandered onto the porch as Jaxon shifted into his wolf form and slipped into the bush with Flynn on his heels. Tobias blew out a long, slow breath, leaning on the banister to watch them go. "You really think we can pull this off?"

"What? Annoying our collective parental group? I know very well we can."

"No." He ran a hand through unruly hair. "Pretending not to be… us."

Aislinn moved to stand beside him, leaning her head on his shoulder. "For now, we don't have a choice."

********

Grandma Redding pulled the door open before Tobias had a chance to knock, her face stern. "What have you done?"

"I don't know," he answered, bracing for a possible cuff over the head. "Should I know?"

"She's talking about the brawl yesterday." Aislinn strode past him into the lounge, tossing her head. "You know very well what we did, Grandma. It was necessary and, if the packed lawn out there is anything to go by, it worked."

"If you say so." Grandma's voice was clipped as she stepped back to let Tobias inside the house. It was barely 8am but the temperature was already well up, promising a return to the scorching weather which was a trademark of the Australian summer. Grandma Redding positioned herself beneath the slowly spinning ceiling fan and crossed her arms. "I've been fielding nothing but phone calls ever since."

"Let me guess - Barbara Forthrite." Aislinn's eyes glittered as she looked back over her shoulder at her grandmother. "I have better things to do than worry about that meddlesome old biddy. For instance, did you know Sienna has emotional intuition?"

Grandma startled at that and Tobias had the immense satisfaction of watching the older woman scrabble for her composure. "No."

"Well, she does." Aislinn turned and flopped herself onto one of the couches, the relaxed display at odds with the tension Tobias could see behind her eyes. "She said the pack were uncertain, so I decided to reassure them."

"I've had six pack members approach me this morning already, thanking us for our efforts," Tobias rumbled, dropping down beside her and stretching one arm along the back of the chair. "They'll fight better now."

Aislinn nodded in agreement, shifting her body to lay across his lap, her head pillowed on his opposite shoulder and legs thrown casually over the arm of the couch. The result was an astonishing amount of her plump breasts being waved constantly under Tobias' nose and enough leg draped across the couch to make him pant like a dog. He traced the smooth line of one calf with his eyes as Aislinn said; "The bearkin are frightening but we showed off three midforms and a solid group of warriors who will go to the mat to defend their people."

"Well, I suppose I should be thanking you both, then." Grandma pursed her lips and looked up at the clock. "Zeke went to meet our guests at the burnt shack - I expect they'll arrive any minute now. Tobias, would you organise some refreshments whilst I have a quick word with Aislinn?"

"Yes, Den Mother." Tobias slipped out from beneath Ash and strode into the kitchen, flicking on the kettle as he moved to pull a handful of mugs out of the top cupboard.

It was no big deal for a grandmother to speak with her grand-daughter in private but he strained his ears nonetheless, hefting the sugar bowl in one hand whilst digging in the kitchen drawers for a teaspoon with the other. Grandma Redding, predictably, was smart enough to keep her voice low and Tobias could hear no more than the buzz of voices from the other room.

Fine. If it was important, Ash would tell him later. Tobias hummed softly as he spread the mugs out and arranged tea, coffee and hot chocolate where guests would easily spot them. While the kettle boiled, he opened the fridge to retrieve a platter of fruit, a jug of milk and a plate of scones. After fetching jam, cream, a stack of plates and some knives, Tobias made Aislinn her customary hot chocolate, a coffee for himself and returned to the lounge.

Aislinn leapt up as he returned, accepting her drink with a murmur of thanks. She took a sip and beamed up at him, her smile so bright it was like a fist to the gut. "You remembered."

"Two chocolate, one sugar, two thirds water, one third milk," he recited dutifully, then smiled. "How could I forget?"

"I don't suppose," Grandma drawled, "You remembered mine."

Tobias blinked innocently. "I'm afraid not, Den Mother. My apologies."

"Of course." She snorted a laugh. "If you'll excuse me, I'll go and make it myself."

Tobias waited until Grandma had left and then used his free arm to tug Aislinn close, bending to bury his face in the long, luscious waves of her hair. "I hate this already."

"Relax. Nobody said we can't be friendly - just no pashing while they're watching." She took his hand and lowered it to her right hip, where part of Olaf's jagged black Marking was visible above the waistband of her skirt. "This is the true enemy, remember?"

"I haven't forgotten." Tobias drew back just far enough to catch her blue-green gaze with his. "I will point out, however, that your attempt to make a statement for our incoming guests is very distracting. You look good enough to eat."

Aislinn blushed and opened her mouth but a loud rap at the door made them both jump. Tobias pressed a gentle kiss to her forehead, set down his coffee and went to open the door.

"We made it! Record time, too." Zeke's amiable grin faded and his nostrils flared as he stepped into the doorway. Shock lit his sapphire eyes as he scented Aislinn on his Alpha's skin and his next words were so low as to be almost inaudible. "Shit, dude, *now*? Talk about timing."

"Go to Ash," Tobias hissed, not inclined to talk when he'd already spotted a group of silhouettes at the bottom of the stairs behind Zeke. His second glanced across the room and nodded imperceptibly, moving swiftly away.

Seconds later a small, fine-boned woman threw herself across the threshold and into Tobias' arms, causing him to stagger backwards in surprise. "Tobias Greenwood, *look* at you!"

"Hi Mum," Tobias spoke down into a mess of short black hair, his heart warming in spite of the situation.

Stephanie Greenwood pulled back to look up at her son, her hazel eyes filled with tears. "You've grown so much!" Curls flew about her face as she embraced him again, her bright yellow sundress flaring out behind her.

"Steph, get a move on." Rupert Greenwood pushed his wife and son aside and stepped into the house, his enormous shoulders barely fitting through the doorway.

Feeling suddenly young, Tobias mumbled; "Hi Dad."

"Hello, son. She's right, it *is* good to see you again." Rupert grinned. "And you've definitely grown."

Tobias was shocked to discover he looked down on his father by several inches, a fact that eight years of communication via the Internet had been unable to convey. What Rupert lacked in height, however, he more than made up for in bulk. Muscles bulged in every available space, tanned skin accentuating blue eyes and a sprinkling of dirty blonde hair which he kept so short as to be almost bald. Tobias freed one arm to clasp hands with his father, tensing in order to survive the crushing handshake which was Rupert's signature. "Good to see you too."

"It's been too long." Stephanie's voice was muffled by Tobias' t-shirt and he gently peeled her away, smiling down into her flushed face. "Oh, by the Lady Lunaida, you're so handsome!"

"You see me every week onscreen, little mother. You know what I look like." When it became apparent his mother wasn't going to let go, he added; "I'm glad to see you but I must greet our other guests."

"Oh, fine. Where's Joanne? In the kitchen, I'll bet." Stephanie waved Tobias back to the door, where a tall man hovered just inside.

He watched his mother leave, then turned and extended his arm to the Redding Pack Alpha. "Hello, Andre."

"Tobias." Andre nodded, stepping in to complete the shake. Six foot four and slender with brown eyes and grey-streaked brown hair, twelve years away had not been kind to Andre Redding. His face was drawn and his eyes flickered around the room incessantly, as though unable to perceive there would be somewhere devoid of any kind of threat.

Tobias forced his expression to remain calm, open. "Welcome home, sir."

"Good to be back," Andre said. He spotted Aislinn and walked away without as much as a backward glance.

"I'm so sorry, Tobias. He's been like that ever since the attack."

"Don't worry about it." Tobias' lips curved as he bent to embrace the tiny woman in a sleek grey pantsuit. Marguerite Redding's long red hair was straight and glossy, her green eyes burning with the same inner fire that lit Aislinn's. "It's good to see you."

"How is she?" Marguerite whispered.

Tobias considered for a moment and decided on the truth. "Better, but not healed."

"She'll be better for having you with her." Marguerite squeezed tighter, setting her lips against the shell of his ear. "Did Flynn-"

"He's here," Tobias murmured. "Hiding, for now. Does Andre know?"

"No, but he'd be a fool not to suspect." Marguerite's voice was full of regret. "I should have done more to help her."

It was true, but Tobias found it difficult to be angry with the sweet hearted woman, regardless of the fact that it had been Marguerite's idea to take Aislinn to Ireland in the first place. He gave her a final squeeze and leant back, making eye contact so she knew he was serious. "You did what you could. Now it's up to us."

Marguerite nodded, fingers clenching briefly on his arm before she crossed the room to her daughter. Tobias watched the two of them embrace, both women's arms locking almost desperately tight around the other. Andre curled his lip and turned towards Grandma Redding, his face a thundercloud and his hands clenched to fists. Stifling a growl, Tobias began moving towards his heartmate but was stopped by an imperious tug on the sleeve of his t-shirt.

"You must be Tobias Greenwood, apprentice Alpha to Andre, am I correct?"

"Pardon?" Tobias turned in astonishment to discover a fifth person in the doorway. The man was short, approximately Aislinn's height, with unruly black and grey hair. His yellow eyes were fixed on Tobias' face with unnerving intensity. *Apprentice* Alpha?

"Are you not Tobias Greenwood?" the man repeated, smoothing both hands over his tweed waistcoat.

"I am. And you are?"

"Professor Percival Postlethwaite, head of the paranormal research wing under the Kin High Council," the man announced, his nose lifting into the air as he spoke. He made a little waving gesture and a reedy man with thick black glasses and dirty blonde hair stepped into view. "This is my assistant, Gerard Montrose. He'll be accompanying me for the duration of our stay." The professor sniffed, his round face pinched in distaste as he surveyed the room. "I assumed you had heard of me until I actually arrived in this backwater community. I'm surprised to note that you have electricity, much less brick and mortar housing."

"Pleased to meet you," Tobias managed, not sure whether to laugh or toss the pompous asshat out the door immediately.

"I should think the proper term would be 'privileged to meet you' but I suppose pleased will do. Oh no, don't be ridiculous," Percival stepped away from Tobias' outstretched hand as though it were leprous. "What an odious trait you lupines have."

"I gather you're not wolfkin, then," Tobias returned, retracting his hand.

"Of course not! Owlkin, if you must know." He sniffed again, then flicked a glance at Gerard. "And a rat. A lab rat."

Tobias clenched his teeth in an effort to keep from snarling. "And why are you here, Professor?"

"Are you stupid as well as ill-mannered? I'm leading the team of researchers who are working to cure Miss Redding, of course."

"I see you've met the Professor," Rupert interrupted, pushing his bulk into their personal space. "Try not to kill him, will you? Come on, Percy. Let's get you a cup of tea."

"How many times do I have to tell you - it's *Professor* Postlethwaite to you, General!" Percival hugged his briefcase to his chest as Rupert propelled him in the other direction at high speed, Gerard trailing quietly along behind.

Tobias watched as Stephanie took the Professor's arm and led him into the kitchen. "I don't like him."

"Nobody does," Rupert laughed. "I survive the urge to eat him by calling him Percy. Really gets on his nerves."

In spite of everything he wanted to say to his father, Tobias grinned. "I'll remember that."

# Nine

Surrounded by a sea of familiar faces, Aislinn felt like she was drowning. "I need to kill something."

Zeke chuckled as though she was joking, but revealed he knew her better than that by flattening one long, slender hand across the small of her back in preparation for a full-body grab. "Remind me never to piss you off, gorgeous."

"As if you could." Smiling, she rose on tiptoe to press a friendly kiss to his jaw.

"Miss Redding? Is that you?" Professor Percival Postlethwaite shoved his way through the throng, eyes narrowed as he gave Aislinn a critical once-over. "I trust you are not making much progress with your recovery."

"And why would you think that, Percy?" Aislinn asked. "I was doing perfectly fine until your pudgy face appeared - now I have the uncanny urge to vomit."

Percy clicked his tongue in officious reprimand. "This is no time for jokes. If you were recovering as anticipated, it wouldn't have been necessary for me to trek down to this horrific place. You don't look at all different."

Aislinn barked a sharp laugh. "I find that hard to believe, considering the last time I saw you I was sedated and cuffed to a hospital bed."

"A necessary precaution given your state of mental imbalance at the time." The Professor raked a scathing gaze across first Aislinn, then Zeke, and sniffed. "Whilst the doctors recommended this course of action, I have to wonder at their decision. Now that I've seen this wretched settlement for myself, I wouldn't be surprised if you have, in fact, worsened. Does anyone here own a pair of shoes?" Percy tapped his patent leather dress shoes together as though it would magically alter the footwear - or lack thereof - of everyone else in the pack.

"I beg your pardon, Professor, but I must protest." Marguerite stepped out of the crowd, her face creased in a delicate frown. "I realise you are used to a certain level of comfort but this place is our home."

"Ah, Mrs. Redding," Percy looked relieved to see Marguerite's pale suit and black pumps. "Perhaps you can talk some sense into these young people about the proper etiquette for greeting men of my status. The manners of these bumpkins leave something to be desired, I'm afraid."

"In my experience, what you offer to others is what you get in return," Marguerite replied, her smile tight.

"Is something wrong?" Tobias' voice was edged with a growl as he appeared by Aislinn's other side.

"Not at all. Professor Postlethwaite was just going into the kitchen to check his notes," Marguerite said, her voice a whip of disapproval.

"What a magnificent suggestion." Percy hoisted his briefcase as though it were a shield. "Come along, Gerard. My tea won't make itself."

"Yes, Professor." Gerard trailed along behind, hands shoved in the pockets of his overlarge pants.

Zeke growled low in his throat as the door to the kitchen swung closed. "That dude is seriously up himself."

"You don't know the half of it," Aislinn muttered, fisting both hands on her hips. "Why is he here, Mum?"

"Council's orders." Marguerite sighed, flipping hair out of her face with elegant fingers. "You know your father, dear. Deliberately vague."

"You didn't think to ask?" Aislinn growled low in her throat. "If that lice-infested excuse for a scientist thinks he's getting his hands on me again, I'll rip his balls -"

"There's to be a welcome home picnic and dance on the common lawn tonight," Zeke interrupted, stepping partly in front of Aislinn. "Sarah's organising the celebrations as we speak."

Marguerite lit up at once. "Oh, really? I haven't seen her in such a long time! Perhaps Steph and I can give her a hand once this is finished."

"I'm sure she'd love to see you, mama wolf," Zeke answered, a smile in his voice. "Especially seeing as she's pregnant again."

"How wonderful! I must tell Steph," Marguerite clapped her hands in delight and slipped away in search of her friend.

"I thought you didn't want to piss me off?" Aislinn asked, watching her mother retreat.

Zeke chuckled again. "You're not pissed off, babe. If you were, I'd be six inches shorter where it counts."

"Mother Moon, you boys are all the same." Aislinn flicked a glance toward the window, where the sun was well and truly up. "If I'd known Percy was coming, I'd have made a few phone calls and had the plane hijacked."

Tobias cleared his throat. "I'm going to go out on a limb and assume that was a joke."

"Really?" Aislinn gave them a smile with a razor's edge. "Wait until you spend more time with the guy."

Tobias opened his mouth to reply but a sharp clap rang out and Andre's loud voice cut through the hubbub. "All right, everyone, let's take a seat."

"Come on." Tobias took Aislinn's hand and dragged her over to one of the couches, Zeke close behind. She sank down between them, one of their thighs pressed to each of hers.

Andre paced into the centre of the room and slipped his hands into the pockets of his tailored trousers. "There are two reasons for us being here, both as important as each other. First of all is the matter of the anti-shifting serum which the bearkin used on Aislinn."

"They also had it during the attack on the Heliope-Flints."

Andre inclined his head in Grandma's direction. "Yes, I received that report, thank you. As you know, the bears have a limited supply of the serum and a shelf life within which it must be used. The Council's science team theorises this is likely to make the bearkin… generous with its application."

"Makes sense," Tobias rumbled. "May as well cause as much havoc as possible before it expires."

"Something like that." Andre's lips pressed together in a thin line and there was a feral glint in the gaze he turned on his daughter. "How much do the boys know about Regina Aircombe?"

"Everything relevant to the situation."

"Good." Andre adjusted the sleeves of his business shirt, his permanent frown deepening. "Despite my assurances that Regina was safest within my custody, the Council moved her to a different safe house shortly after you left Ireland."

Proof of the blow to her father's reputation when the imprisonment of his own daughter had been so publicly revealed. Rather than feeling a sense of satisfaction, Aislinn studied his drawn expression and bit her lip. "What happened?"

"Four days ago, bearkin infiltrated the new safe house and Regina was murdered."

"No!" Aislinn cried. She'd almost given her life to keep Regina safe - but more than that, the bearkin had been a friend. Shrinking into the collective warmth of Tobias and Zeke, she buried her face in her hands. "Mother Moon, why weren't they watching her?"

"They were," Andre said, his voice rough. "It wasn't enough."

"Did the bears -" Aislinn broke off, throat closing over.

"No. Her throat was slit but it was an otherwise clean death."

*Princess?* Flynn's voice, gentle in a way he reserved only for her. *What's wrong?*

She couldn't talk to him in human form, and he knew it - but a moment later Aislinn felt a curious tingling in her chest and knew Flynn had connected through their blood bond.

*I thought we agreed it was too dangerous to talk like this,* she snapped. *The last time nearly killed you.*

*That was three years ago. I'm stronger now, and at this very moment, the more immediate danger is me smashing this window and tearing out the throat of every fucking person in that room.* Flynn gathered himself, a sensation Aislinn wouldn't normally be able to feel but for the sacred connection between them - fuelled by the raw power of her tigerkin's very life force. *Now spill.*

Knowing full well it was useless railing once he'd made up his mind, Aislinn determined to keep the conversation as short as possible. *Regina's dead.*

*Fuck.*

*They slit her throat.* She forced another breath. *No rape, though.*

*Sounds like they were acting on desperation rather than being demonstrative,* the tigerkin mused. *Particularly if it was a stealth job. You okay?*

*Angry.*

Feline laughter warmed her mind. *Good. I'm here if you need me to tear heads off.*

*If you don't back out to a standard telepathic connection, you won't be strong enough to tear toilet paper, let alone heads from necks.* Forcing her mind to calm, Aislinn lowered her hands and steadied her breathing. *Stay close so you can listen in, but no smashing windows unless I ask.*

*No promises,* he grunted, dissatisfaction evident in his tone - but his touch became less intense, a sign Flynn had cut back on his energy output and was once again safe. *Shout if you need me.*

"You okay?" Tobias murmured, squeezing her shoulder.

"Yeah." Aislinn nodded, her eyes firm on her father's face. "What else is there?"

Andre examined the worn carpet for a long minute before meeting Aislinn's gaze. "At the time of her death, Regina had not, as yet, passed the formula on to us."

"What?" She blinked in surprise. "Why not?"

"Her demands were substantial."

"Substantial?" Aislinn screwed up her face in disbelief. "To my knowledge, she only wanted clemency, extraction of her allies and protection against the rest of the bear nation. What changed?"

"Nothing," Andre ground out, his tone making it clear she was revealing knowledge of things above her pay grade. "The surgical removal of Regina's rebel co-conspirators from hostile territory was a big risk, with little perceived gain. We have no way of confirming their location or loyalty."

"Little perceived gain?" Aislinn echoed, her jaw dropping. "How about their *lives*?"

Her father shrugged. "They're bears."

"How dare you," she hissed. Claws sliced from her hands and Tobias barely caught her as she lunged at Andre, now half-hidden behind Rupert. "A life is a life! No one is more or less valuable than another. If you bunch of bigoted, addle-brained asshats bothered to spend more than a minute slumming it with your own people, maybe you'd see that."

"Regardless of your personal thoughts, the Council's decision is final." Andre waved Rupert aside and continued as though discussing the weather. "Regina used her final moments to inform our soldiers that she'd passed a copy of the formula on for safekeeping."

"A backup plan." Aislinn's heart warmed at the thought of her friend fighting to the bitter end. "But how would the bearkin know about it? Unless… shit. It was a set-up."

"Yes. The attack occurred minutes before a change of guard and the autopsy report says Regina's wound was a surgical strike rather than an act of haste and fury." Rupert sucked on his teeth a long moment. "My personal theory is they were hoping to record her verbalising the formula aloud but we've no proof one way or another. Either way, they secreted a listening device on her body which wasn't discovered until some time after her death."

"Meaning the bears heard everything until that point," Aislinn mused. "Did Regina say who she gave the formula to?"

Andre nodded curtly. "Of course. She said she gave the formula to you."

Aislinn's mouth dropped open, her stomach hollowing out. "She *what?*"

"She was very clear upon her deathbed that you were the one. We have it on record from the guard who found her as well as the audio surveillance equipment that was inside the safe house."

"And the bearkin heard every word." Aislinn's heart lurched unsteadily. "Olaf said he had questions for me. He must've meant the formula."

"Yes." Another curt nod. "I'm thankful you were able to escape; it means you can give the formula to us instead."

"Your concern for my welfare is overwhelming."

He didn't flinch from the warning in her tone. "You're an agent of the highest calibre. There is little capable of causing you harm."

"Excuse me?" Aislinn sat up straight on the edge of the couch, one hand braced on each of Zeke and Tobias' thighs while rage tore through her body.

*Fucking useless fucking assholes!*

*Don't you dare,* Aislinn hissed, her mental voice a whip. *If anyone kills them, it'll be me. Now get out of my head, and stay. Outside.*

*Your anger is riling me up. I need you.*

*As soon as this is over, I'll stroke you as much as you want.* Channelling her anger until it was sharp as any blade, Aislinn bared her teeth at her father. "Insinuate that I invited Olaf's attack one more time and I don't care who you are, I'll tear out your throat. If I had the formula, I'd have given it to you already."

Andre's face darkened but Rupert stepped forward, laying a restraining hand on her father's arm. "We had to ask."

"Except you didn't ask," Tobias growled, his leg like a rock beneath Aislinn's hand. "You accused - as though Ash is some sort of traitor."

Rupert flinched as though struck. "Now come on, son, be fair -"

"Fair? *Fair*?" Tobias leant forward, bracing both forearms on his knees, Aislinn's hand safely ensconced within the curve of his body. "You accuse her of treason after she put her life on the line to defend our people and you're asking *me* to be fair?"

Andre's eyes flashed. "We're only doing what we must to protect the pack."

"From who? *Aislinn*?" Tobias surged to his feet, Alpha energy pouring off him in silent waves. When he spoke again, raw power slunk through every syllable. "How is it protecting the pack when you'd throw one of your own to the enemy?"

"She's not part of the pack."

A low, rumbling moan shook the house and all the lights went out. The effect was lessened by the fact that it was daylight, but Grandma had drawn the curtains to ensure privacy and in the wake of the blackout, the room stood in dim and unearthly silence.

"Shit," Zeke breathed.

Tobias began to grow, bones stretching and cracking, his clothes - for the second time in less than twelve hours - falling in tatters to the floor. Stephanie Greenwood gasped, one hand pressed to her mouth as her son's body contorted, his emerging midform a glorious blend of power and fury. Even Andre and Rupert, who'd seen many a midform in their day, took half a step back when Tobias lowered his lupine head and roared in unmitigated rage.

Aislinn pushed to her feet, deliberately turning her back on her father and Rupert as she stepped in front of Tobias. "Stop. They're not worth it."

"Aislinn!" Marguerite's voice, caught somewhere between terror and reprimand.

*Let him kill them. I've almost got line of sight through the window; it'll be the best show I've had in months.*

"If you want to live, Mum," Aislinn said equably, not tearing her gaze from Tobias' blue and gold one, "I'd shut up."

Her mother's mouth clicked closed and Flynn's manic laughter echoed in her mind. She ignored both, extending a hand towards the transitional Alpha in front of her. Tobias dipped his head, weaving back and forth like a snake about to strike - and though he lacked the ability to speak in midform, the glance he flicked over her shoulder said more than enough.

"I can't let you eat them," Aislinn said, her tone chiding and her hand steady in the air between them. "You'd get terrible indigestion."

In a movement she'd seen from Flynn countless times in the past, Tobias' ears flickered, then he tilted his head to the side and rubbed his cheek over her palm.

"That's better." She smiled slowly, raising her other hand to run her fingers through that gorgeous, sandy brown fur. "You're a handsome one, aren't you?"

He rumbled deep in his chest, eyes slitting in pleasure as she continued to stroke his face, reaching up to scratch behind those large, pointed ears. Aislinn dared a half step forward and, when he made no protest, walked into his embrace, spreading her palms across his muscular chest. The body he curved around hers, for all it was twice its normal size and covered in thick fur, was familiar.

"Hush now," she crooned as his strong arms wound around her waist. "I've got you."

Tobias burrowed into her hair, his wolfish snout digging through the silken layers until his breath was hot against her neck. Aislinn hummed gently, feeding her cooling shadows into his body while he drew his long, rough tongue over the thumping vein in her neck.

Something twitched against her leg.

"No, hot stuff." She lowered her voice so only he could hear. "Not here."

He whuffed in her ear, a sound that made it clear he didn't care at all where they were, and nipped her neck hard enough to leave a mark. Aislinn hissed, letting some of her own dominant energy out. "Stop that."

Tobias rumbled in delight, his clawed hands beginning to slither down her spine and his pelvis tilting to fit against hers. Gasping with effort, Aislinn abandoned her attempts at subtlety and shoved Tobias' power back into his body, praying he wouldn't pass out from the shock. She caught him as he sagged, fur receding and bones shrinking in a mind boggling rush.

"Ash?" His voice was croaky, his legs wobbly.

"I'm here." She discreetly checked Tobias' body to make sure his arousal had been doused as swiftly as his Alpha energy. "I've got you."

"Did I kill anyone?"

"No, but they'd have deserved it if you did." She slid an arm beneath Tobias' shoulder and raised her voice. "It's safe now. He's contained."

"Excellent." Grandma Redding stalked across the room and slapped Andre hard. "If you ever speak about my grand-daughter that way again, I will eviscerate you myself. Is that clear?"

Stunned, Andre took a half step back. "Mother-"

"*Den* Mother," Grandma corrected. "Is. That. Clear?"

"Yes, Den Mother."

Stephanie let out a jagged sob, racing across the room to throw her arms around Tobias' neck. "Oh, my baby boy. You're so *strong*."

"How strong?" Rupert directed the question at Aislinn, inspecting his son and then the still darkened house. "Have you measured him?"

"I tried; Tobias blew the lid off the basic instruments we have here. I don't know if anyone can exceed Flynn, but he's got the potential to exceed me." Aislinn swept an assessing look over her lover's naked body. "Although if you know what's good for you, Tobias Greenwood, you won't dare."

Tobias huffed a laugh. "I think you'll find we'll be exactly the same level once this is over."

"What makes you say that?"

Blue and gold eyes caught hers, flickering with hidden amusement. "Just a hunch."

"So a strong midform," Rupert said, tapping one finger on his opposite arm. "What else?"

In quiet, precise words, Aislinn told them about the lightning strike, tensing in preparation for Stephanie's second hugging attack when she described how Tobias had been consumed by electricity. "I've been waiting for the second half of the power to become clear," she said, helping Tobias support his frantic mother, "And we've just seen it."

Rupert turned his eyes toward the darkened lights. "The blackout?"

"Check your phones," Aislinn invited. Everyone did as instructed, making noises of alarm and disbelief as every electronic device upon their person proved dead. "Electromagnetic pulse."

"Electro-what?" Zeke's brow furrowed. "Wait… an EMP blast?"

"Exactly." Aislinn reached out a hand to pat an astonished Tobias on the cheek. "He absorbs electricity - kinetic energy, static electricity, even lightning which, I might add, is a form of electromagnetic energy all by itself. I've not tested the theory but I'd wager the more Tobias absorbs, the bigger the EMP blast he can emit. The blackout happened because he drew extra electricity from the house to expend on the pulse."

Tobias stared first at Aislinn and then down at his body, to which his mother still stubbornly clung. "Well, shit."

"Can he expend the electricity too? Put it back where it came from?" Rupert asked.

"If you're asking about lightning from his fingertips, I think you're pushing the boundaries a little," Aislinn snorted. "This isn't a sci-fi film."

"I shocked you last night," Tobias put in, straightening slowly to his full height.

Aislinn bit her tongue to keep from laughing. "A couple of times, if I remember correctly." His eyes went wide as he understood the implication and she saw the faint dusting of a blush on his cheeks. "Any build-up of static electricity causes a spark to be emitted. My best guess would be that if your body can conduct and absorb electricity, you might be able to close a connection and form a loop but I don't think you'd be able to magically reactivate your father's phone - if that's what you're getting at, Rupert?"

"It was," the General replied, staring mournfully down at his phone. "With any luck it's a fried battery and not more permanent damage."

Andre stepped forward. "Tobias. You will submit yourself to a medical facility for proper testing as soon as possible."

"Why, so you can draft him into service now that I'm no use to you?" Aislinn shook her head. "He hasn't broken any laws. You can't force him to do anything."

"I'm the senior member of this pack -"

"Actually," Grandma Redding interrupted, "*I* am the senior member of this pack, and the choice to undergo further testing will be Tobias' own."

"Mother - Den Mother." Andre tugged on his shirt sleeves and cleared his throat. "With all due respect, this is not a matter to be summarily dismissed. We've now got a transitional Alpha of incalculable strength to deal with."

"Fortunately, we also have a damper of equally incalculable strength," Grandma replied. "Now, if you'd like to return to the topic of the most unfortunate Regina and her formula - without accusing my grand-daughter of treason - I'd be most grateful. I need a cup of tea and your endless windbagging is preventing me from getting it."

Andre ground his teeth together for a long moment, then turned to Aislinn and grunted; "I'd like permission to search your things."

"Why?" Aislinn rubbed at her forehead. "Surely if Regina had hidden the formula in my stuff, it'd be back in Ireland."

"No. We searched your personal belongings in Ireland but found nothing. The formula has to be here."

Aislinn's jaw dropped. "You searched my room without asking?"

"The entire house - as is well within the Council's jurisdiction," Andre confirmed. "There was no need to ask due to the delicate nature of your medical condition."

"Despite your constant attempts to prove otherwise, I've never been delicate," Aislinn growled. "I don't have anything to hide, but I'm still a person. You should have called."

Andre's nostrils flared and she knew he'd avoided speaking to her on purpose. "There was no time; we came here as soon as we realised the formula must be with you. We need to look through your things at once."

"No."

"Aislinn, please." Rupert's face was sympathetic, his hands held out in placation. "Help us help others. No disrespect was intended."

"No disrespect?" Aislinn barked a sharp, bitter laugh. "Cut the act. I've seen it enough times to know it's fake." When Rupert made to respond, she a raised hand. "Search my things if you want, but I didn't bring anything other than my clothes. Unless you know how to hide a complex scientific formula in a bikini?"

"Perhaps Ash is simply the key to the location of the formula." Tobias tightened the arm he had draped over her shoulders. "Regina trusted her above all others."

Aislinn took a deep breath and tried to think of Regina, a woman she'd known only a short time but who had depthless wells of courage and a mind like a blade. "Tobias has a point. If you show me Regina's notes, I might be able to see something."

"We didn't bring them," Andre answered, his face shuttered. "You don't have the clearance."

Aislinn threw her hands up with a snarl. "Helpful."

"Is my word not enough?" Her father asked, raising a brow. "She says you have it and for now, it's the best lead we've got. The formula cannot return to bearkin hands."

"I'm not sure we should have it, either," Aislinn muttered under her breath. "Why would Regina give it to me, of all people?"

"Think about it - you were protecting her and you were also her friend," Zeke said quietly. "Nobody could keep that formula safe like you could."

"I still say I don't have it."

"Prove it," Andre challenged.

"Whatever. I already said you can look through my stuff," Aislinn sighed. "Are we done here? I'm hungry."

"There's one other item on the agenda." Andre hesitated, then pursed his lips to let out a shrill whistle.

"Lord and Lady." Aislinn rolled her eyes as Professor Percival Postlethwaite blustered into the room. "This gets better and better."

"Councillor, I must protest. I'm not a dog to be whistled for when you - arrrrgh!" Percy cut off with a shriek, throwing both hands over his face.

"Professor?" Andre's face was mystified.

"Are you all *heathens*? That cretin is naked!" Percy shrieked, flapping one elbow in Tobias' direction.

"Dammit, Postlethwaite, we're Kin. Naked is normal," Rupert growled - but stomped over to the stairs, where a cupboard revealed a stack of towels.

"I won't have it!" Percy stamped a foot, his voice muffled behind his palms. "It's uncivilised!"

Tobias caught the towel his father threw and, with an amused glint in his eye, wrapped it around his hips. "All right, Percy, I'm covered. No need to feel inadequate any more."

Zeke guffawed, turning away to hide his face as the Professor peeped out from a crack between his fingers. "I'll have you know, you *barbarian*, that I didn't feel the slightest need to check your levels of adequacy."

"Shame," Aislinn replied, patting the towel over Tobias' crotch. "Now you'll just have to imagine it instead."

Percy shrieked and covered his face again. "What sort of people," he cried, "Go around letting other people caress their genitalia in *public*?"

There was a moment's silence at that, into which Aislinn said; "Ones who enjoy pissing you off?"

Percy drew a breath, no doubt for some scathing retort, but Andre dropped a warning hand on one tweed-coated shoulder. "Professor, pull yourself together. This behaviour is most unseemly."

"Of course, Councillor." Percy lowered his hands and straightened his ridiculous suit. "My sincere apologies."

"Accepted. Now, if you will?"

"Ahem. Yes. The other matter to be discussed is the unfortunate effects the bearkin attack have had on Miss Redding." Percy waved a finger in Aislinn's direction without actually looking at her and, thereby, at Tobias' half naked body. "As we are all aware, she was subjected to a humiliating experience which has left her branded with the personal mark of one Olaf Gruybere, General of the enemy militia."

"Don't forget powerful Ursar, all around asshole and monster under the High Council's bed," Aislinn said dryly, rolling her eyes.

"Ursar?" Percy narrowed his eyes. "Yes, that does make sense - I had theorised such a thing, in fact. Gerard!"

The weedy looking Kin appeared from the direction of the kitchen, adjusting his glasses as he crossed the room to hand Percy a sheaf of papers. "Here you are, Professor."

"Thank you. Now, where was I?" Percy began shuffling through his papers with the air of a man looking for something, but Aislinn had been privy to this particular scene before.

"I believe you just finished telling everyone how pathetic I am, Percy." Aislinn smiled to show all her teeth. "I must say, I've missed being knocked down to size in such a spectacular fashion."

Percy ceased his shuffling and gave her a venomous look over the top of his glasses. "As I was saying, Miss Redding's situation is unique in that Olaf has been able to prevent her body healing itself properly, resulting in the grotesque disfigurement we see before us now. I -" the Professor cut off as Tobias' fingers wrapped around his throat and hoisted him into the air.

"If I hear the words *grotesque disfigurement* out of your mouth again, it will be the last two words you ever say," Tobias snarled, his knuckles white. "In fact, let's go one step further. Tell her how beautiful she is."

The Professor wheezed a garbled jumble of half words, papers scattering as Tobias shook him like a doll. Aislinn stepped to her lover's side and laid a gentle hand on his arm. "Stop it."

"No. He doesn't get to talk to you like that." Tobias shot a glance at Andre. "And you shouldn't let him. *Sir.*"

Andre narrowed his eyes at the honorary spoken as an insult, but he reached out a hand and plucked Percy from Tobias' grasp. Instead of releasing the owlkin, he shook him harder and said; "I'm waiting."

"My… apologies," Percy gasped, clawing at his collar. "You are indeed… most beautiful, Miss Redding."

Andre dropped Percy to the floor with a loud thump and toed the other man with his patent leather shoe. "I'm disappointed in you, Professor."

The Professor wheezed and coughed for a moment, his eyes wild as he looked from Tobias to Andre and back again. "I meant no disrespect," he said at last, scrambling to his feet. "I am used to a laboratory, not a lounge."

"Talk," Andre said. "While you still can."

"I was going to ask if Miss Redding had any further information about her circumstances to add to my summary of events?"

Aislinn considered her answer and finally decided the truth could do no harm. "Olaf can reach out psychically through the Mark and attack both body and mind. The power is like a great vice around my chest, squeezing the life out of me. When we fought in Old Tom's Hollow,

Olaf intimated that he originally intended to kill me this way but I was able to stop him."

"Remarkable," Percival murmured. "What is your professional opinion on this particular skill set?"

"Olaf's a powerful enough Ursar to have permanent access to this perverse psychic ability and my survival has allowed him the unique opportunity to hone it. That said, he's not omnipotent - there's a delay between episodes which leads me to believe he needs time to recharge." She tilted her head, considering. "In theory, I should be able to use my skills as a damper to thwart him but so far the attacks have robbed me of conscious thought."

Percy's keen gaze drifted to her hip, where parts of the Mark were visible between corset and mini skirt. "Given this connection seems to follow some of the rules of a normal Marking, I'd assume that your death frees him to pass the curse onto another. By the same token, it would stand to reason that Olaf's death would also free you from his influence."

"Too bad he's proven difficult to kill."

"Professor, you said you had an alternative solution to offer," Andre prompted. "Is it still viable in light of this new information?"

"I believe so." Percy tapped a finger against his chin. "My first thought was to surgically remove the flesh bearing Olaf's Marking to see if that would negate his influence. However, given that the ties seem to be rooted in a combination of Ursar powers and our sacred Marking ceremony, I doubt it would work."

Aislinn spread a protective hand over her hip. "That, and I'm not keen on being more chopped up than I am already."

"I rather thought you might say that, Miss Redding, though I'd urge you to reconsider." Percy's lips pursed. "The scientific benefits of studying your Marked skin could benefit countless Kin in the future."

"I fail to see how, given Olaf's a one man show."

Percy shrugged, clearly expecting that very response. "My other solution revolves around the ethereal nature of your predicament. The basis of the Kin mating process is one of mutual acceptance – each party receives a Mark from the other, voluntarily tying them together. In this instance, Miss Redding was the only one to receive the Mark and it was bestowed against her will. There is a chance that if the proper mating ceremony were undertaken, it would overwrite that which Olaf has put in place."

Silence gripped the room for all of five seconds before a babble of voices erupted. Beneath the ocean of sound, Aislinn's jaw dropped as her mind grasped the true implications of the theory.

*Holy shit,* Flynn whispered, his mental tone tickling her inner ear. *What the fuck is wrong with this guy? You okay, Princess?*

*I don't know.*

A low growl, which she thought was mental until Tobias' head shot up. *I'm going to gut this motherfucker and roll in his entrails.*

*You can't,* Aislinn hissed desperately. *It's all just words right now - I can refuse. If you bust through that window, we're in all sorts of deep shit.*

*I should be in there.* Flynn's rage was a living thing inside of her, carrying an air of desperation that Aislinn knew meant his need for tactile reassurance was overcoming his rational mind. *I can feel your pain through the blood bond.*

*Flynn, stop. Think. Dad's been deliberately trying to antagonise me from the moment he walked through the door, and yeah, I'm pissed - but I'm biting my tongue because the second I retaliate, I violate the laws of sanctuary and give him full leave to arrest me.* Aislinn ground her teeth together, fighting to keep her voice calm. *If you come roaring in, you give him exactly what he wants. And if we have to fight our way out of here, who's going to protect the pack from Olaf?*

*Fuck me, but I hate it when you're sensible.*

*I know. I'll also add that this is the third time in fifteen minutes you've used the blood bond to forge a telepathic link we know isn't healthy. Are you even standing right now?*

Silence. Then, *Jaxzilla is here with me. I'll be fine.*

*Dammit, Flynn! I can hear the exhaustion in your voice.*

*All right,* he relented. *I'm pulling out.*

"Please! I am not finished," The Professor's reedy voice wavered as he struggled to be heard. "As we have confirmed this morning, Olaf is an Ursar of formidable strength. I believe it will take a partner of significant power to eliminate the current branding. The other key element to this plan is that Miss Redding must be more than a participant - she must be actively willing to proceed or she will be unable to place a Mark of her own. I believe it is *her* Marking which will be the most important aspect of this cleansing ritual."

"What about Tobias? He's an Alpha," Grandma pointed out.

"Tobias Greenwood is in the middle of transition," Percy answered, waving a hand in dismissal. "His Alpha powers are unpredictable at best and while we have proof that he's strong, if he cannot control the energy - as, indeed, he cannot - then he is not a wise choice. I wouldn't recommend a transitional male under any circumstance, be it Mr. Greenwood or otherwise."

"That's not a problem. I can list any number of powerful and eligible Alphas." Andre pulled his phone out of his pocket - and frowned to note that it was still dead, thanks to Tobias' earlier outburst.

"All right, stop," Aislinn growled. "If you think you can line a bunch of males up and have me pick whoever has the best pedigree, you've got rocks in your head. This isn't the Middle Ages."

"I think you need to reel that attitude in." Andre's nostrils flared in disapproval. "Professor Postlethwaite is offering you a very reasonable and attainable solution."

Black humour welled and she barked a sharp laugh. "I know you're eager to get rid of the stink, but using sex to bind me to a stranger? That's pushing it, even for you."

"Aislinn, please," Marguerite begged. "We had no idea what the solution was before Percy arrived."

"Didn't you?" Aislinn pinned her father with a glare. "There are a lot of Alphas in this room right now - not like Mum, with her poor, normal nose. You can't lie your way out this time."

"Andre? Don't tell me - did you know about this?" When Andre remained stoically silent, Marguerite gasped in horror. "How *could* you? She's our daughter!"

"She *was* our daughter. Now look at her! Ruined by a fucking bearkin, after all I did to -" Andre cut off with a snarl.

"After all you did to what?" Aislinn stepped into the silence, lifting her chin. "After all you did to keep Tobias and I apart, so you could hide the pack from the Council's attention? After all you did to turn me into a perfect soldier, so you could go about seeking your own personal revenge? After all you did to lock me up in that hospital, where none of my family or friends could get in to see me, so that the doctors and scientists could dissect me like an experiment gone wrong? After all you did to send me home so that the people I once called family could put me in a gilded cage, waiting upon your *convenience*?"

"No." Marguerite stared at her husband in horror. "Tell me it isn't true."

Andre's jaw clenched but he remained silent.

"I would've been the perfect instrument of your revenge," Aislinn whispered, tears of rage gathering in the corners of her eyes. "All you needed was a way to keep me on a leash which only you had the power to tug. And *you*," she turned her scathing gaze on Rupert, who had the grace to flinch. "Complicit in every single aspect of it. You both disgust me."

Grandma's voice was soft and filled with recrimination. "This isn't how we treat our pack."

"Oh," Aislinn said, her voice a sinister thread of sound. "But I'm not pack. Remember?"

Tobias snatched her hand and spun her to face him. "You're *my* pack."

"And mine," Zeke followed up swiftly.

"And mine," Grandma declared.

"Mine," Marguerite agreed, rushing to wrap her arms around Aislinn. "My daughter, my beautiful, strong daughter. Always."

Whilst the reality was, in fact, the opposite, Aislinn appreciated the sentiment. She folded her mother's shuddering frame close and dropped a kiss on her hair. "Don't cry, Mama."

"Rupert?" Stephanie took a tentative step towards her husband, reached for him, stopped. "What's going on?"

Grandma Redding swivelled her eyes to the General. "Yes, Rupert. Explain yourself to your wife and son - and that's an order."

"The Council slapped down a conscription order after the peace summit bombing," Rupert said slowly. "When Andre took the job as Councillor, we knew he'd be expected to cough up more warriors."

"You got an extension," Stephanie waved that knowledge off as though shooing a fly.

"Yes. Four years. But we were decimated by the bombing." Rupert shook his head. "Aside from Aislinn, who was already in Ireland, the only youth of appropriate age were the five boys who remained behind." He nodded at Tobias and Zeke. "We put everyone into farm work and deliberately stifled their knowledge of the outside world. The vast majority of international Kin think Australia's populated by a bunch of yokels, so we played on it. Tobias and the others were trained in secret so that the pack had some protection, and we forwarded the Council forged proof of our sub-par youth. By the time the four years was up, I was the only pack member who qualified for service, so I went to Ireland as our representative."

Stephanie blinked. "But Tobias…"

"I lied," Rupert said shortly. "I told you he didn't want to go, and I told him Aislinn didn't want to muck around with a simple farm boy. I said she'd moved on, become cultured the way Marguerite always wanted."

Marguerite gasped in shock, shaking her head in instinctive denial. "I only wanted a chance for Aislinn to see the world and decide for herself!"

"It was a fool's dream, but it worked to our advantage. If Aislinn and Tobias were ever reunited, the Council would discover our ruse and not only would Andre be ousted, but the pack either conscripted in entirety or dissolved." He passed a hand over his face, expression grim. "So we did what we had to, in order to make sure they were kept separate. When Aislinn transitioned - by the Gods, she was our salvation. A powerful Den Mother and a damper to boot, with the added benefit of controlling Flynn. The Council were only too happy to bargain away the debt in exchange for her services."

"You sold her like cattle," Marguerite rasped, her face white. "For what? Your pride?"

Rupert sighed. "We hoped she'd mate and forget Australia, forget the family she left behind. Once Aislinn re-signed voluntarily, the pack would've been able to commission her to remove the bearkin who'd been responsible for the bombing. The ones we know of, at any rate."

"Once the war was ended," Andre said at last, his voice strained, "Conscription would end, too. Our dead could be permanently laid to rest and the pack free to pursue a future."

"With a group of five strapping young men safe at home to seed the next generation," Grandma Redding finished, shaking her head. "That's as bad as the bearkin. You bring shame to your names."

"It doesn't matter now," Andre growled, burying his head in his hands. "The minute Aislinn was branded, she was considered too dangerous to be used offensively. There's no way to know Olaf isn't influencing her thoughts and actions through the Mark, like a sleeper agent. Worse, if her psyche was fractured by the trauma, she could turn rogue whilst out on a mission."

"Rogue?" Aislinn loosed a wild cackle, tempered only when Zeke gripped her arm in warning. "If I truly went rogue, you'd already be dead."

"I tried to tell the Council exactly that," Rupert replied, surprising her, "But they wanted you contained for the greater good."

"Lock me up and throw away the key, huh?" She didn't bother to hide her bitterness. "Thanks for all the hard work, see you next lifetime."

Rupert looked distinctly uncomfortable, but nodded. "We managed to talk them out of straight imprisonment and into the hospital instead, but then Flynn busted in and you both wrecked the place - and took out a good number of security guards dressed as doctors, too."

"Why was there no punishment?" Tobias frowned. "You're describing a Council who are merciless; that doesn't seem the type of government to let Aislinn go."

"They're not, but the hospital incident was well publicised and the Council didn't like the way the media painted them. They were quick to sanction our request for Ash's return to Australia because it softened their public image." Rupert shrugged. "It wasn't ideal, but Andre and I figured years of bad blood, on top of the scent of bear, would keep you all distracted long enough for us to find a more permanent solution."

Andre stepped forward. "We didn't think Olaf would follow you to Australia but it doesn't matter - with the Professor's assistance, you'll be free to return to your life."

"And become your weapon?" Aislinn's voice burnt in her throat like the bile which threatened to overwhelm her. "That's not freedom; it's not even the illusion of freedom. It's a trap."

Andre flinched. "I just want my daughter back."

"I'm right here!" Aislinn screamed, slamming a fist against her chest. "Open your eyes, Dad; this is what you wrought with all your scheming."

"You're being unreasonable."

She flicked her fingers and they turned into claws. "I'll show you unreasonable."

"Enough." Grandma stepped between them, her eyes intent on Rupert and Andre. "As your Den Mother, I command both of you into wolf form. Patrol our borders while I decide how best to handle the shitstorm you've dumped us in." Grandma Redding strode to the door and tugged it open. "Do not return until you're summoned."

Rupert shimmered into his wolf form; a dirty blonde wolf surprisingly slender in contrast to the General's meaty human frame. He trotted to the door, sat and waited.

"Mother," Andre whispered, his eyes wide. "The Council -"

"I will deal with the Council," Grandma Redding snapped. "Now get out or I'll have Tobias throw you out."

"Yes, Den Mother." Swallowing heavily, Andre shimmered into a charcoal and brown wolf. With his second on his tail, the two slunk outside and off into the bush.

Grandma closed the door and leant against it. "Zeke, the Professor and his assistant are staying with your mother. Would you kindly escort him to his accommodation? We don't need anything more from him today."

"If I may, Den Mother," Percy began.

"You may not," Grandma Redding snapped. "You've been privy to some very delicate information just now, Professor. I should think, if I were you, I'd keep my mouth shut."

Professor Postlethwaite shifted from foot to foot, then finally said; "I don't recall hearing anything more than hearsay that cannot be proven. In fact, the journey here has so exhausted me that the entire discussion is decidedly foggy."

"I'm glad to hear that." Grandma smiled tightly. "Zeke?"

"Yes, Den Mother." Zeke strode towards the back door and Percy, to his credit, did no more than incline his head politely to Grandma Redding and trail along after, Gerard on his heels.

"Are you sure they'll keep their mouths shut?" Tobias asked once the door slammed behind them.

"The phones are dead," Grandma returned, "Leaving no way for anything damning to be recorded as evidence. Even if the Professor was foolish enough to think about it, there's enough of you here to impart the fear of Solaeden into him."

"Gods above." Aislinn sank to her knees on the floor, her claws returning to human hands so that she could rub at her face. "What now?"

Grandma dropped to a crouch in front of her, brushing the hair from her brow with a weathered hand. "First, Tobias is going to fetch the tigerkin I know full well is sniffing around outside, while I make you a cup of tea to settle your stomach. Then we're going to see about fixing the mess your fathers have made."

# Ten

When Tobias yanked open Grandma's front door, Flynn was already on the doorstep, his tiger's tail lashing impatiently. He shoved into the house and disappeared in a matter of moments with Jaxon's massive wolf form hard on his heels.

Safe in the knowledge that they'd support Ash for the moment, Tobias jogged across the common lawn to his house, waving to Bill Deepwater and his latest batch of trainees as he went. As soon as he had the front door closed behind him, he threw his towel aside and raced upstairs.

It took less than five minutes to dress and rummage in the top drawer of his bedside table for Aislinn's phone - after first poking his own to make sure he wasn't going to accidentally fry the device while transporting it. Tobias was just about to close the drawer when he spotted a blood-stained strip of paper up the back. Grinning, he tucked it inside Aislinn's glittery phone cover and slid both devices into his pocket. He ran a hand through his perpetually tangled hair to settle it and, after a quick glance in the mirror to confirm he looked slightly less like he'd just been mugged, jogged back down the stairs and out the door.

He kept his pace brisk as he passed back over the lawn, waving at his packmates a second time before slipping back through Grandma Redding's front door. He found Aislinn in the kitchen, Flynn sprawled naked on the floor beside her in human form. His long arms were tight around her waist, his head in her lap, eyes squeezed shut. Judging from the way Stephanie and Marguerite were chatting idly with Grandma Redding over tea, the scene was a familiar one to them - but Tobias couldn't help but stare.

Aislinn met his gaze and bit her lip, one hand tangled in Flynn's hair and the other moving to her torc in an unconscious gesture for reassurance. Realising she thought he was jealous, Tobias dug a blazing grin from the depths of his heart and indulged in a very male sense of satisfaction as she blushed.

Jaxon stomped in through the second entrance at that very moment and didn't stop until he was directly in Tobias' line of sight. "We're going to need more chairs."

Taking the command as a request, Tobias nodded. In a matter of minutes, they'd replaced Grandma's too-small kitchen table with a low, wide coffee table and encircled it with enough chairs to seat everyone plus Zeke, who arrived in enough time to snag the last scone.

Flynn had begun to mutter under his breath in a melodic language Tobias assumed to be Gaelic. It fit somehow with the tigerkin's elfin face, his fairytale build. Though the words were beautiful, there was a haunted quality to his tone and Aislinn's brow creased with concern as she listened.

"Hey," she murmured, her fingers gentle in hair like liquid night. "Stop it. You're free now. Free."

The tigerkin repeated himself and burrowed impossibly closer. Driven by an instinct he didn't entirely understand, Tobias dropped into the empty chair on Aislinn's other side. Tugging it close enough that their knees brushed, he laid his hand against Flynn's arm. "We've got you, kitty cat."

Expecting a clawed response, Tobias was surprised when the tigerkin caught his hand in a crushing grip and dragged it to his face, his soft, rhythmic breathing tickling the back of Tobias' wrist. Flynn didn't speak - but he also didn't let go, and when Tobias met Aislinn's gaze, it was soft with gratitude.

"Now that we're all here, let's not waste time." Grandma steepled her fingers beneath her chin and swept the room with a cool gaze. "How big of a threat is the Professor?"

"That depends on what he decides to do next." Marguerite's crisp, cool tone betrayed her legal background. "If Percy were to approach the High Council with what he heard today, particularly because there's no proof, he'd be up on charges for breaching pack confidence laws."

"Ma said something similar." Zeke finished the last of his scone and wiped his hand on his shorts. "As soon as Percy realised she's as posh as he wants to be, he told her everything and demanded advice."

"I assume she advised him to keep his baseless theories to himself," Marguerite returned.

Zeke's wolfish grin was accompanied by a nod. "And quickly prescribed him a sleeping draught for his obvious stress. Still, whether he's got proof or not, I wouldn't trust that shady little owlkin as far as I could throw him."

"Neither would I." Aislinn's voice was colder than Tobias had ever heard it. She ran her fingers continuously through Flynn's hair, her face thoughtful. "It'd be safer to kill him now and be done with it."

Tobias's jaw dropped but neither Marguerite nor Stephanie so much as batted an eyelash. His mother inspected her nails and, in a voice much like she'd use to discuss a new pair of shoes, said; "Are you well enough?"

"For *Percy?*" Aislinn snorted. "Don't insult me."

Stephanie shrugged. "I only have the official reports."

"Written by dicks," Flynn grunted, his eyes still closed where he lay across Aislinn's knees. "She's running at about eighty percent."

"Eighty?" Steph sat up straighter. "That's a huge improvement. Mental stability?"

"All but solid."

"Excuse me, are we actually talking about murder?" Zeke broke in, his face white. "Over morning tea?"

"No," Aislinn's blue-green eyes were steady as she met Zeke's. "It's not murder. The correct word is assassination."

"It's also a bad idea - tempting though it may be." Marguerite sighed, picking up her china cup and sipping with one pinkie extended. "The Professor's disappearance would be enough to garner Council attention and I know your father did wrong, but we're the ones who will suffer if an investigation uncovers his treachery."

Aislinn slumped sideways into Tobias, the picture of dejection. "Fine. Percy lives - but only as long as he keeps his nosy little beak to himself."

Marguerite narrowed her eyes, considered. "Agreed. If he moves on you overtly, you have enough grounds beneath the laws of sanctuary to dispose of him without question."

Aislinn's lips twisted into what could only be described as an evil grin. "Excellent."

"Solaeden's asshole, what do you people *do* in Ireland?" Jaxon demanded.

"I'm a lawyer," Marguerite responded primly. "I represent the pack and I also have a private practise. Stephanie works in logistics, with a specialisation in… procurement of goods."

"Flynn and Ash are the Council's pet assassins, with the rest of their team providing support," Stephanie added. "They were well and truly pissed when the bearkin put a hold on their personal agenda."

"I fucking hate those Council fuckers," Flynn growled, his breath hot on the back of Tobias' wrist. "One day I'm going to eat them."

"Shh." Aislinn tapped him gently on the cheek in reprimand but her lips were twitching in amusement. She twisted her head to look up at Tobias. "You're not bothered by any of this."

"Why would I be?" He raised an eyebrow. "We need every edge we can get. Olaf's running around out there with seasoned soldiers and this morning I got a note from Barbara Forthrite complaining that the training schedule cut into her crochet time."

"Ash thought you'd be pissed," said Flynn lightly, his eyes still closed. "We had bets."

Tobias cupped Aislinn's chin, feathering his thumb across her cheek. "You're not the only badass around, you know. Just last month I babysat for Sarah and Brian for an entire night - and I had all the kids in bed on time."

Laughter bubbled out of Aislinn's throat and her eyes danced. "Well then," she chuckled, "I think we know which of us is the crazier."

"If I may be so bold as to bring this meeting back on track," Grandma interrupted firmly, "Now that Percy's off grooming his feathers, I feel we should be discussing our first and largest threat."

Marguerite's face fell. "Andre and Rupert."

"Whilst my son and his second have caused us significant trouble, they're contained for the moment." Grandma's jaw tightened, her next words coming out through gritted teeth. "I've neglected my duties for too long. That ends now."

"Don't blame yourself, Joanne." Stephanie laid a comforting hand over Grandma's. "We were all fooled. As long as we work together from now on, it won't happen again."

"Agreed - and our first step should be addressing the bearkin situation." Aislinn drummed her fingers on Flynn's shoulder, then looked up at Stephanie. "Who else did you bring?"

"Two full teams; one each for Joseph at the horsekin herds and Carrie-Anne at the foxkin earth. They have their own people on hand but Andre and Rupert figured a little extra muscle wouldn't go astray. As for us, the remainder of your team are due to come here after they drop off the others." Stephanie pursed her lips. "Rupert intended to send Jacques after Flynn but he's already here, so I suppose that's unnecessary. Percy and Gerard took the remaining two seats in the party at the last moment."

"Jacques," Flynn snorted, at last deigning to crack one amber eye, "Would never be able to catch me."

Stephanie merely smiled. "I know, but he's mighty pissed you trussed him up like a roast pork and left him inside the roof cavity."

Both amber eyes opened. "He deserved it."

"And the apple you shoved in his mouth?"

"I didn't want him to starve."

Stephanie bit her lip in an attempt to maintain her serious expression. "It was half rotten."

Flynn's smile was slow and wicked. "Matches his soul."

"Bearkin," Grandma said, raising her voice to be heard over the sniggers pervading the room. "Stay on track."

"Right. The easiest way forward from here is to reach out for assistance," Aislinn muttered, brow furrowing. "I need my phone."

"Here," Tobias fished it out of his pocket and slid it into her hands. "I forgot."

"You're an angel," Aislinn declared, flipping the cover open. "Now all I need is - oh, very good, Tobias Greenwood." She tugged free the bloodied scrap of paper and grinned. "Very good indeed."

"What is it?" Jaxon asked, frowning.

"Steve's phone number."

"Steve? Crocodile Steve?" Zeke asked, sitting up very straight.

"Yes, crocodile Steve. Also known as Joseph's private muscle, got his finger in all the pies Steve. Now quiet while I'm working," Aislinn instructed.

The room complied and for a few minutes, there was only the insistent tapping of her fingers on the screen as she typed and sent several messages.  Tobias heard the incoming jingle of at least two responses before she'd finished writing and, moments later, felt his heart skip as she laughed low in her throat.

"I know that laugh." Flynn lifted his head. "It means game on."

"Steve's going to set up a meeting with Joseph and Carrie-Anne for us," Aislinn announced. "Likely tomorrow morning. He'll get back to me later with details."

"And?"

"Jacques and the others will be here in about thirty minutes, and they're none too pleased I demanded they report directly to me." Aislinn sniggered. "They'll get over it."

"You mean Jacques will." Flynn stretched and yawned as though waking up from a nap. "The others won't care - fuck, Kaira will be celebrating."

Aislinn nodded. "That Jacques didn't argue means he knows I'm reinstated."

"Conditionally," Tobias reminded her.

"It doesn't matter." Marguerite straightened in her chair, smoothing out invisible creases in the trousers of her suit. "Even a conditional reinstatement returns Aislinn her rank. She's in charge of her team unless that status is revoked completely."

"Which only the Council can do," Stephanie finished, nodding. "Shame Andre's gone camping for a couple of days, right?" Silence. "Ash?"

Tobias twisted in his chair and Flynn's head shot up, both their attentions on Aislinn. She'd gone rigid, knuckles white around her phone and her other hand clenched tightly into a fist. Her breathing was silent but shallow, blue-green eyes unfocussed. Tobias pressed the back of his hand against her hip at the same time as Flynn laid long fingers on her forehead.

"Olaf," they said in unison.

Aislinn's Mark was so cold it burned Tobias' hand but he didn't remove it, rather slid up against her as though he could combat Olaf's hold with his body heat alone. "Help me," he said to Flynn.

The tigerkin didn't argue. While Tobias wrapped his free arm around Aislinn's shoulders, Flynn braced himself on her thighs and laid his ear against her heart. "Too fast."

"Ash," Tobias murmured, setting his lips to her ear. "Come back to us."

She wheezed a breath and Flynn rumbled in encouragement. Tobias found himself echoing the sound, curving his body around hers until Aislinn had almost disappeared beneath the combined efforts of wolf and tiger. He reached for the strange pathway through which she'd drawn his energy last time - and came hard up against a solid wall.

"Fuck," he whispered. "Olaf's blocking us."

"Kiss her," Flynn growled. When Tobias blinked at him in surprise, the tigerkin snarled, "She needs an anchor, you fucking idiot. Either you do it or I will."

Painfully conscious that both his mother and Aislinn's - and her grandmother - were watching, Tobias muttered; "You better be right," and lowered his lips to hers.

She was cold, rigid and unresponsive. The acrid scent of bearkin slithered into his nostrils; a weapon that stoked his wayward hormones. Tobias shook it off, searching through the muck of clashing scents until he found vanilla and honeysuckle with a hint of his own butterscotch. The transitional surge which had begun to trigger at Olaf's scent immediately calmed, his instincts recognising his heartmate and purring in response.

Whatever lingering awkwardness Tobias felt evaporated on that wave of warmth and he tightened his grip, tilting Aislinn's head as he pressed his mouth more firmly to hers. Her breath was cold where it mingled with his but he persisted, nipping at her lips, digging his fingers into her shoulder - anything that might breach the barrier Olaf had erected between them - and knew, as her heart faltered and her breathing shallowed, that it wasn't going to be enough.

********

Cold. Overwhelming, incredible cold. Aislinn was drowning in it, unable to tell up from down, inside from out. Her body was gone, her vision turned inwards and the only sound between her ears the roaring of her own blood.

Olaf was everywhere, his presence caging her spirit in a chamber of ice. She slammed her innermost self against those glittering, frigid walls but they were impossibly strong and all she succeeded in doing was rattling her brain inside her own head.

*Aislinn Redding.* His insidious voice whispered inside her mind, echoing with the screams of all the women who had gone before. *Sweet, soft, luscious Aislinn.*

*Hello, Olaf.* She allowed the growl in her voice to become more obvious as she searched her prison for a way out. There was none; the bearkin's influence was as vast and cold as the icy tundra he'd come from. *If this is how you treat all your dates, it's no wonder you're still single.*

Olaf's mental grip tightened, turning her breath to razors in her lungs. *Give me the formula and I'll make your death a swift one.*

A month ago, she'd have taken him up on the offer. Now, however, Aislinn had no intention of laying down her arms without a fight. *I don't have the formula.*

*Liar,* Olaf said silkily. *I have a most excellent recording of Regina's final moments, where she used her last, bubbling breaths to speak your name.*

*You're a real asshole, you know that?*

Olaf laughed again and Aislinn took advantage of his distraction, throwing herself against the icy walls with all her might. She bounced off again - but warmth filtered in, the barest breath of butterscotch tickling her lungs. Aislinn wrapped her cold, trembling fingers around that shining thread and held on.

*Asshole? I've been called far worse things.* His voice hardened. *Now, the formula.*

*No.*

The walls of her prison tightened again but with nowhere near the strength of before. *You would do well not to infuriate me, girl. I am your executioner and I say how long it takes for those eyes of yours to close.*

*Unfortunately for you, I've never been very good at following instruction.* Aislinn could feel the chinks in Olaf's armour now and began to press against them, feeling more of Tobias' warmth on the other side.

*What are you doing?* Olaf's energy shifted and one of the cracks in her prison sealed - but another widened in response, heat and light flowing in. *Where is that coming from?*

Aislinn struck, using her borrowed energy to slam into the walls of her prison again and again. Olaf's grip faltered and more of Tobias' strength flooded in, shouldering the bearkin aside until she could at last access her own talents. Cool, whispering shadows flooded her mind and she drew a deep breath, tearing the Ursar's claws from her soul one by one. *Time to go, twat waffle.*

*No!* Olaf tried to hold on, but his strength was nothing compared to the dual energy Aislinn now commanded. *I own you!*

*Nobody owns me,* she hissed, binding the other male in layer after layer of unforgiving black. *Least of all you.*

Olaf shrieked in rage, a sound neither human nor bear as Aislinn thrust him from her mind. As the tail end of his essence collapsed, she caught fragments of image and sensation; a bed, a hastily erected medical station, mouldy bread, a clear sky through a shattered window.

Then Aislinn was alone in her own mind again, the vast well of Tobias' power mingling with her cool, peaceful shadows. She could feel her fingers; tightly clenched in something silky-soft. Her back, pressed against the chair. A pain in one leg, a weight on her chest. Cloves and coffee and butterscotch and cream in her lungs and an insistent, drugging pressure against her lips.

Aislinn's eyes swept open as Tobias leant back from his kiss, his expression more desperate than she'd ever seen it. One hand trembled against her face, the other rigid on her shoulders. "Gone?"

"Yeah." She nodded, the movement drawing her attention downward - to a pair of amber tiger's eyes. Flynn, his head against her chest, monitoring her beating heart. He'd never admit to fear but she saw it in the haunted depths of his gaze, focussed with unwavering intensity on her face. "What happened?"

"The best weapon against sensory deprivation is touch," said Flynn, a thousand unspoken demons fluttering in his voice. "When pain didn't work, I told T-Fuzz to kiss you for all he was worth."

"Oh." Aislinn closed her eyes for a moment, feeling a sudden sweep of heat in her cheeks. "Please tell me we're all still dressed."

Tobias rumbled a self-conscious laugh. "Except for Flynn, who seems determined to be naked all the time."

"Grandma ushered your mother out," Flynn added. "Her screaming was fucking distracting."

Tobias and Aislinn shared a look of mutual astonishment and turned as one to find the kitchen empty, bar for a pale faced Jaxon by the door. "Nobody gets in until you're ready," he announced.

"Thanks, Jax." She turned back to Flynn. "How close?"

"Close," the tigerkin answered. "I could barely hear your heart inside your chest."

"Olaf wanted the formula," Aislinn mused. "He was desperate enough to come after me long range when he's not fully recovered from the encounter at Old Tom's Hollow."

"I'd say he's got the report that your father's in town with reinforcements." Flynn raised his head at last, bracing one hand on Aislinn's knee to push himself upright. "Sorry, by the way."

"For wha - shit!" Aislinn gasped as pain tore through her leg. She blinked back involuntary tears as Flynn retracted his claws and began licking her blood off his fingers. "How deep did you go?"

"As deep as I could without snapping your fucking thigh bone," he returned, lip curling. "You're too good at blocking the pain."

"Never thought I'd see the day when that was a bad thing," Aislinn snorted, spreading her hand over the deep puncture marks in the flesh of her thigh. The blood had already started to clot but that made it no less painful. "Funny how these will be gone in minutes but the ones Olaf left behind might never heal."

"He's getting stronger." Flynn's eyes narrowed until they were almost shut. "What if Percy's wrong and a transitional Alpha *would* work?"

Aislinn's jaw dropped. "What? You can't be serious."

"Why not?" Flynn asked quietly. "Would it really be so bad if it were one of us?"

"No, but think about what you're suggesting." She shivered. "I'm fairly sure Percy's wary of transition because the energy surges unpredictably, meaning that if we attempted the ceremony while one of your powers were low, it wouldn't work - but there's no way to judge when those surges or troughs occur."

Tobias blanched visibly. "You're saying we'd have to -"

"Fuck each other blind until we luck out and one of you ends up bound to me? Pretty much." She shook her head, tears blurring her vision. "Dammit, Flynn! How can you ask me to ruin the two people I care most about? How can you ask me to ruin myself like that?"

"I can't." Flynn slammed his clenched fists into the sink, denting the metal. "Fuck. Fucking *fuck*."

"If and when I ever mate, it will be for me, and no other reason," Aislinn whispered. "Olaf's already tried to ruin that once; I won't let him do it again."

Flynn muttered under his breath in Gaelic and waved an angry hand; the closest he'd get in a mood like this to declaring his own agreement.

"Olaf's getting stronger - you're right about that. But I'm not going to just lay down and die." Aislinn shuddered, part relief, part grief. "No matter what happens, I'm fighting him until the bitter end."

"We," said Tobias, his voice low and intense. "Together."

Flynn's eyes were wild when he turned to them, but he nodded. "Fuck me but I hate it when you're right."

# Eleven

A brief knock on the kitchen door echoed in the silence. Jaxon tugged it open a fraction, exchanged heated whispers with whoever was outside, and then stepped back enough to allow Zeke's head to appear. "Rory's out front, panting like a lunatic. We have guests at the burnt shack."

Aislinn's answering smile was wobbly but real. "Right on time."

"Tell Rory to keep them at the shack; we'll go up there." Tobias stood and tugged Aislinn up beside him. "I'm not letting anybody into pack territory that I've not vetted in person."

Zeke's sapphire eyes narrowed and he slipped fully into the room, taking in Aislinn's bloodied leg and pale face. "You want backup?"

"No," Tobias shook his head. "Hold the fort here. If things go sour I'll need you to formalise some sort of defence."

"Sure. You okay, little sister-wolf?"

"Nothing I can't handle," Aislinn returned. Flynn snorted and she cut him a glance. "I'm *fine*."

"I hate to agree with your stripy stalker, but you don't look so hot right now. Still, I'm going to pretend like I can't see your knees wobbling and move on." Zeke reached out to ruffle Aislinn's hair. "I know you've got a lot happening, but your mama needs you, too. Grandma took her upstairs for now."

Aislinn slid her arm around Tobias' waist and he tucked her into his warmth. "I'll talk to her at the picnic tonight."

The second's long, calloused fingers twined in her hair and tugged playfully. Tobias let out a low, warning growl and Zeke grinned. "Don't worry, your alpha-ness, I'm not cutting your lunch." He tucked his own golden curls behind his ear. "I'll run interference for you with Grandma and Marguerite until you're ready."

"Thanks, Zeke."

With a deliberately goading look in Tobias' direction, Zeke took Aislinn's free hand and lifted it to kiss her knuckles. "For you, gorgeous? The world is not enough."

"How," She chuckled, elbowing Tobias as he growled again, "Did I manage to surround myself with so many devilish men?"

"By being a devil yourself." Zeke winked, gave her fingers a squeeze, and was gone.

Aislinn shook her head, something in her expression sad. "I guess that's true enough."

"Don't." Tobias wrapped an arm around her shoulders. "You bring out the best in us."

"I hope you're right." She paused, then shrugged. "Let's head to the shack on foot. I'm not in the mood to be naked right now."

Flynn took a step away from the bench and shimmered into his tiger form. *Since I'm already naked, I think I'll wear my fur coat.*

The tiger slunk past Tobias, pushed the kitchen door open with his head and sauntered out. Aislinn and Jaxon were close behind, leaving Tobias to bring up the rear. By the time he tugged Grandma Redding's front door closed they were already running through the bush.

*Let me scope the lay of the land. Come in later, in case Jacques is planning something.*

"You still don't trust him, huh?" Aislinn's voice floated back to Tobias and he pushed hard to catch up.

*I don't trust anyone - but after what Jacques pulled? I trust him less than all the other fuckers I don't trust. Give me ten minutes.*

"Take Jaxon, at least," Aislinn said, her pace slowing until she stopped beneath the shade of a particularly fragrant eucalypt. "He can back Rory up."

Flynn's mental grunt was barely an echo but Jaxon picked up speed and the two disappeared into the bush ahead. Tobias was squinting after them when something dry and soft splatted into the side of his head. He wiped the clod of dirt away from his temple and glared at the woman who'd thrown it. "What?"

"Play with me."

He ducked the next flying piece of earth on instinct alone. "You want to play *now*?"

"Why not? Flynn said we have ten minutes."

"I thought you'd be ignoring his orders and charging in yourself," Tobias teased. "That's the girl I remember."

"That's what I'd like to do, but Flynn and I have been working together a long time and I trust him. After that run in with Olaf, he's trying to make sure my head's on straight." Aislinn's voice was full of laughter and she disappeared, her body dissolving into the shadow of the tree's branches. When it came again, it was directly in his ear. "I just had a near death experience. Celebrate life with me."

"What if I don't feel like it?" Tobias turned, but she was already gone.

The clump of dirt that hit the back of his head was a teasing reprimand. "Since when has that excuse ever worked on me?"

Since never. Tobias turned to find her standing in the shelter of a bottlebrush, lips curving as he dropped the gruff pretence she never bought. "Looks like someone needs a lesson in manners."

"Oh?" Challenge sparkled in her eyes. "You brave enough to teach me?"

"Maybe." He darted after her, unsurprised when Aislinn dissolved again. This time Tobias was prepared and when the shadows began to coalesce further to the south, he pounced, wrapping both arms around her waist. By the time she was fully formed, Tobias had lowered his shoulder and slammed her to the ground with enough force to knock the wind out of her lungs. "Surprise."

Aislinn's mouth dropped open. "You caught me."

"Yeah."

"Nobody's ever -" Her protest died as he lowered his head and nipped at her neck. "Twin gods, do that again."

He repeated the motion with a little more pressure and felt her shiver in response. "According to the rules of our bargain, I get ten minutes of your time to use however I wish."

"All right." Aislinn's cheeks burned red but she lifted her chin. "I'm counting."

Tobias shifted his weight, letting her take all of it without fear of crushing her beneath him. "Back there in the kitchen… I thought I was the one dying, having to watch your life seep out of you." Spreading a hand over her hip, he nuzzled at the vein in her throat. "I want to bite you hard enough to leave a mark. So hard that even death hesitates."

"You'd fight death for me?" Her smile was teasing. "I'm an assassin - death is my shadow."

Tobias growled, low and deep. "I just conquered your fucking shadow."

Aislinn's pulse jumped beneath his lips, her arousal scenting the air around them. "It bothers you, doesn't it? That Percy said you couldn't fix me."

"Of course it does."

She set trembling hands against his shoulders and pushed until they were face to face. "Tobias Greenwood, I could belt you. Honestly, I could."

Tobias stared down at her, spread out beneath him like a glorious sacrifice, and managed a heavy swallow. "I thought this was *my* ten minutes."

"It is." She raised her head to drop a tender kiss on his nose. "I've come to terms with the Olaf situation; don't let it poison you. I need you to help me out of the dark."

The stark vulnerability in her confession undid him. Tobias dropped gentle, sweet kisses on the corners of her mouth, spoke against the lush fullness of her lips. "I want a rematch, by the way."

She opened her mouth to protest and he claimed it, sweeping his tongue across her teeth and thrusting boldly inside. Tobias poured everything he was into that kiss, bracing his weight on one arm so that he could mould her curves with the other hand, settling the length of his erection in the juncture of her thighs.

"Tobias," Aislinn gasped, her hips shifting to press against him. "You're not serious."

"Deadly serious." He curled his fingers into the top of her corset, knuckles caressing the side of her breast. "I want a rematch - and I don't think ten minutes is going to be enough of a reward."

Laughter bubbled in her throat. "Oh?"

He raised an eyebrow and ground against her, turning her laugh into a gasp. "Were you expecting… something else?"

"Of course not." Aislinn's eyes rolled back in her head, lashes fluttering. "If you're looking for a bigger reward, the stakes will need to be raised."

"I'm listening."

"Catching me is too simple," Aislinn breathed. "I could've thrown you off just now, if I wanted. Get me to yield and you can have me to yourself for an entire night." Her eyes glittered in challenge. "However you like."

"Done." Tobias gave her a kiss as raw and wild as he could muster, then shoved upright. Aislinn's arms, still tight around his neck, meant she followed him to her feet, where she lifted her legs to wrap them around his waist. "Pretty sure our time's up, princess."

"Almost." Aislinn used her leverage on his waist to raise herself upward, all but thrusting her breasts into his face. Tobias couldn't help it; he buried himself in her cleavage even as he slid one hand up the back of her thigh, several of his fingers sliding sideways to tease the soft skin beneath her underwear. She clenched her fingers in his hair. "Do I get my bite before we go?"

"Yes." Tobias licked once, twice, then sunk his elongated canines into the creamy swell of her breast. She groaned, a breathy sound of ecstasy, and pushed her need-slick body harder against his fingers. It took every ounce of his considerable self control not to shred Aislinn's clothing off her body - but somehow Tobias managed, growling low in his throat as he drew his tongue across the puncture wounds on her skin. "No cheating," he whispered, kissing his way up her neck. "If I have to wait, so do you."

She yanked the neckline of his t-shirt aside and bit down hard on the muscle connecting neck and shoulder. Pleasure swamped him from the ground up, threatening to steal his legs from under him and covering his vision in sparkling stars. "*Ash!*"

"What? Just sharing." She spoke against his skin, her tongue a brand across the bite. "You were the one complaining about waiting."

She lowered her feet to the ground and they leant on each other for support. When he thought at last his voice would obey, Tobias said; "Another few seconds and you would've had me embarrassing myself in my shorts."

Aislinn chuckled deep in her throat, highly sensual and completely unrepentant. "That's what you get for indulging my biting fetish," she returned, drawing his hands over her hips, across her ribs and up between her breasts so she could kiss his knuckles. "Now, if you're not in desperate need of new underwear, I think we better keep moving."

"I'm not wearing any underwear," Tobias growled, reclaiming one of his hands to shove at the uncomfortable rigidity of his crotch. Catching the calculating gleam in Aislinn's eye as she followed the gesture, he turned her none too gently in the direction of the burnt shack. "Later, dammit."

She laughed, gave herself a shake and danced off into the bush, leaving Tobias to follow. They ran in silence, dodging trees and jumping low-lying scrub until the blackened trunks surrounding the shack rose like silent sentinels from the green and brown undergrowth. In silent accord they slowed, keeping to the cover of the trees as the shack itself came into view. Aislinn paused for a moment to listen, then leapt up the back steps and dematerialised, the shadowy interior of the tumbledown building perfect for her astonishing ability. Tobias ascended the stairs with painstaking care, his bare feet whispering across blackened floorboards. The three-room house was empty, but he found Flynn curled up on the front porch in his tiger form, tail flicking lazily back and forth in the sun.

*Good timing,* the tigerkin said, not bothering to open his eyes. *I saw Brayden overhead before, but he's gone now.* A black and orange ear flickered. *So far, everything seems legit.*

"Don't sound so disappointed."

*I can't help it; fighting's in my blood.* Flynn yawned widely. *Jaxzilla's watching the perimeter and your little Rormeister is leading our guests in.*

"While you bait the trap?"

*You're smarter than you look.*

"Thanks." Tobias leant carefully on the remains of the fire-blackened railing surrounding the verandah. "Are these Kin a threat?"

*We all are, T-Fuzz, and best you remember that - but most are loyal to Ash, if that's what you're asking.* Flynn rumbled deep in his chest, part purr, part growl, as a tall figure stepped out of the trees. *Oh look, meals on wheels.*

The newcomer was tall, just shy of six and a half feet by Tobias' estimate. Long black hair had been pulled into a ponytail at the base of his neck and striking golden eyes focussed on first Tobias and then Flynn with devastating intensity. He wore a black shirt, open at the collar and rolled up to the elbows, black jeans and black boots.

"Flynn." The man's French accent was unmistakable, his words coated in icy fury. "I should've known you'd be here."

*Fuck you too, Jacques,* Flynn responded, rolling half onto his back and waving one paw in the air. Tobias choked back a laugh as, despite the limitations of his animal form, the tigerkin flipped the other male off.

Jacques' very white skin coloured with anger and he began to stride across the clearing - only to leap back with a shout as Aislinn materialised in front of him. "That's far enough."

"Aislinn." Jacques' voice was like rough silk as he said her name and Tobias gripped the burnt banister a little harder. Vivid golden eyes swept her length before settling on her face. "You look better than when I last saw you."

"Not surprising, since the last time you saw me I was shredded into a million pieces," Aislinn returned evenly. She flicked a glance over her shoulder at Flynn. "You going to play nice?"

*No.*

"Jacques?"

"Absolutely not." The Frenchman crossed both arms over his chest. "He tied me up like an animal for the spit."

"Word is you deserved it." Aislinn waved a hand and Tobias stumped down the stairs, crossing the grass to her side. "This is Jacques Elegante, owlkin. For Jacques -" she raised her voice, "- and the rest of you, who I can hear crashing around back there like a bunch of novices, this is Tobias Greenwood."

The bush fell silent for a fraction of a second and then branches snapped, someone swore, and a group of Kin stumbled out of the bush.

"Greenwood?" A different male, his skin tanned golden and his eyes a bright hazel, was still buttoning a pair of jeans as he sauntered over. "As in, Rupert Greenwood?"

"He's my father," Tobias allowed, looking the rugged man up and down. Shorter than Tobias, perhaps slightly under six feet, the other male bore dirty blonde hair, a carefree smile and a glossy sheen to his skin which should've been illegal. "And you are?"

"Holy shit, Rupert has a *kid*?" The other man whistled, then stuck out his hand. "Brayden Maxwell. Eaglekin."

"Flynn said he spotted you overhead," Tobias returned, accepting the handshake and the smile that went with it.

"Daytime surveillance," Brayden agreed, thumping himself in the chest. "Jacques takes over when it gets dark." He thumped the Frenchman's chest in kind and Jacques bore it with a grunt, still glowering at Flynn beneath lowered brows.

"Ash!" A diminutive woman launched herself into Aislinn's embrace, laughing in delight. She had to be no more than five feet tall, Tobias decided, astonished that someone so petite should own so many tempting curves. The woman's skin was the colour of mocha and lit from within, an ambience which also leaked from enormous, almond shaped eyes of a deep brown. She wore tight black shorts which were more like underwear than outerwear, and a strappy black halter neck top held in place by a harness full of knives and not much else. Her hair fell long and straight to her waist and was cut blunt across her forehead in a style that reminded Tobias of Cleopatra - if the ancient Egyptian queen had possessed hair in shades of blue and purple, of course.

"Kaira," Aislinn spun her tiny friend around twice and then deposited her back on her booted feet. "Where are your spikes? I'm disappointed."

"I left them in my backpack," Kaira answered, her accent thick and exotic. "Didn't want them getting trashed in the wilderness."

"Tobias, this is Kaira Balcourte, lynxkin." Aislinn released the smaller woman with an affectionate ruffle of her astonishing hair. "And before you ask, yes - Balcourte as in Lord Balcourte, the French nobleman whose great grandfather so kindly allowed the High Council use of Bhaile Roinnte for their headquarters."

"A pleasure." Tobias accepted the elegant hand Kaira extended his way and shook firmly.

"Oh, my. Tell me there's more of you." Kaira used the handshake to draw herself into the circle of Tobias' arms, flattening her tiny, calloused hands over his chest. "Lady Lunaida above, you are *glorious*."

Tobias' jaw dropped but Aislinn, clearly used to her friend's behaviour, yanked Kaira backwards by a hank of cobalt hair. "There's four others for you to slobber on, Kai. That one's mine."

A short silence, then the final member of the group snorted. "I thought he smelt like you."

"Hard to tell with the bearkin scent now, isn't it?" Aislinn agreed. "This is Lena Skirit - catkin."

Lena shoved Kaira sideways and offered Tobias a warrior's firm handshake. Tall for a woman at just over six feet, Lena had a willowy frame and gorgeous skin the colour of darkest coffee. Her hair was a myriad of tiny braids that had been wound into an elaborate crown on her head and secured in place with a hairpin in the shape of a tiny dagger. She, too, wore combat shorts that looked to be painted on, the effect mitigated by a loose khaki t-shirt with a deep scoop neck that showed off small, pert breasts and an even smaller black bikini top. When she spoke, her voice was smooth and warm as honey. "Pleased to meet you."

"And you," Tobias returned.

Kaira peered around Jacques and raised her voice. "Hey asshole! You coming to say hello or what?"

*Depends if you're going to break pack law and try to arrest me,* Flynn's voice took on the slightly tinny quality it got when he'd spread his range to include everyone in the vicinity.

Kaira raised a perfect black brow. "Pack law?"

"Den Mother Redding has granted Flynn sanctuary," Aislinn explained. As soon as the words were out, the tigerkin rolled to his feet and padded across the grass to join the throng.

"Sanctuary!" Jacques blurted. "To a rogue?"

*I'm no more a rogue than you're Jack Frost and you fucking know it,* Flynn growled, lips drawing back from long teeth. *Or you would, if you didn't have your head jammed so far up the Council's ass.*

Jacques' mouth set into a thin line. "I am nowhere near the Council's ass, you flea-bitten cesspit of a creature."

*You say that but when Ash needed us you were fucking prolonging the -*

"You think I wanted to?" Jacques cut the tiger off, his voice vibrating with fury. "The Council were threatening to sideline the lot of us, you arrogant prick! How would we have been able to do anything then?"

Flynn shook himself thoroughly, unmoved by the other male's rage. *Do anything about what? You didn't visit Ash while she was locked up -*

"We weren't allowed-"

*- and I'll bet you did fuck-all to keep hold of Regina when we got shafted -*

"- you have *no* idea what I tried -"

*- shut the **fuck** up -*

"- you shut up, or I will stitch that grinning mouth closed -"

"ENOUGH!" Aislinn shoved between them and when man and tiger began pushing from either side, Tobias slid in behind her, their spines connecting as he turned to intercept Jacques while Aislinn dealt with Flynn.

"Get out of the way," the owlkin said quietly. "I don't want to hurt you."

"Aislinn said enough," Tobias rumbled.

Jacques didn't answer; he just threw a punch. Tobias caught the other's fist as it came through the air, sliding his fingers around the outstretched wrist and pivoting in place, aware that Aislinn's body moved in smooth mirror image to his. A moment later Jacques' body thumped heavily onto the ground, the air leaving his lungs in a great rush.

"Get him up," Aislinn snapped. Tobias bent to haul Jacques upright, lips curled back from his teeth in a warning snarl in case the other male decided to try anything cheeky. Tobias was perhaps an inch or so shorter than the Frenchman and Aislinn even shorter again, but she wasted no time in fisting a hand in Jacques' black ponytail and wrenching him out of Tobias' grip. When Tobias turned, she had Flynn by the scruff of the neck and was shaking both men like dolls. "Are you two done pissing on each other?"

Tobias couldn't help the amused expression that flitted across his face. "I remember your grandmother shaking us like that."

"The difference is that we were children and these idiots are supposed to be grown men - and don't try the transitional card on me, Flynn Tigerkin, don't you fucking dare."

Flynn, whose ears had indeed begun to perk, wilted like a sad kitten. *He started it.*

"Mongrel!" Jacques snapped, then followed up with a string of French vitriol.

Aislinn growled in frustration and smacked their heads together, the resulting crack echoing through the clearing and causing both men's eyes to cross. "What's done is done and I'm not interested in rehashing it. Anybody who's not willing to play nice can piss off back to the horsekin and sleep in their paddocks. Decide now." Silence greeted that statement. "Good. Now, as punishment for being *juveniles*," Another shake, "Both Flynn and Jacques will play at the picnic tonight."

"What?" Jacques spluttered. "You can't be serious."

Even Flynn looked stricken. *Ash -*

"No. You did the crime, you may both do the time. Tobias - does Rory still play bass guitar?" Aislinn glanced over at him and though her face was set with fury, those blue-green eyes danced with mischief.

Tobias dug his phone out of his pocket. "Yeah, though not so much since Leif died."

"Leif? Leif Deepwater?" Lena asked. When Aislinn nodded, she sighed. "He was a good kid. Played the guitar like a crazy man but had a heart of gold."

"You knew him?" Tobias asked, halfway through tapping out a message.

Lena nodded. "I'm older than the rest of you; Leif and I trained together when he first came to Ireland. We lost a good Kin and an extraordinary warrior, and I lost a friend."

"You'll like Rory then; he's Leif's younger brother," Tobias answered, finishing his message and sending it on. "Misses him like an amputated limb, though he won't admit it."

"Leif used to talk about him." Lena smiled faintly. "Maybe Rory and I should have a little chat."

"Go gently, if you do." Tobias glance downward as his phone vibrated. "Ash; Rory's in. He says he can access a drum set, too, if we have someone to use it?"

"I'll do it," Brayden volunteered. "I'm no expert but I can get by."

"Thank you, Brayden," Aislinn said sweetly. "I owe you a big, wet, sloppy kiss."

The eaglekin's sun-bronzed face brightened. "Can I choose where?"

"Only if I can bite it off afterwards," Aislinn returned - and chuckled when Brayden paled. She lifted the two males in her grip and gave them another shake. "Now, how about you two? Are you going to accept this graciously or am I going to start breaking bones?"

*I hate you,* Flynn declared, but there was no heat in it.

"Good. Jacques?"

The owlkin looked positively murderous for another long moment and then sighed. "Fine."

Aislinn dropped them both at once, staring down at the tangle of limbs with her fists on her hips. "I expect this to be the last time I hear about this argument. Got it?"

Jacques and Flynn, both looking suitably chastised, only nodded.

********

Aislinn was still grinding her teeth in frustration over the ridiculous egos of men several hours later when a small knock on Tobias' bedroom door interrupted her brooding. "Yeah?"

Sienna poked her head around the door. "Got a minute?"

"For you, always." Aislinn smiled and sat up as Sienna entered the room, closed the door behind her and dropped a burgundy tote at her feet. "What's up?"

"Now that we've got a live band, Grandma's upped the dress code to semi-formal for tonight. I figured you wouldn't have packed evening wear?" She grinned as Aislinn groaned and shook her head. "Lucky for you, then, that I've a mild talent for sewing."

"Oh?"

Sienna reached into the tote and drew out a dress. "This is a prototype I was working on for Ysera. It's almost done, and I think with a few adjustments it might just suit you."

"That? Suit *me*?" Aislinn stared down at the layers of chiffon with something akin to horror. "I'm covered in scars!"

"Scars you've been showing off for a couple of days now," Sienna said, bunching the fabric in her fists. The rich not-blue and not-green was a gorgeous colour and when it caught the light, Aislinn saw the fabric was shot through with a turquoise shimmer that made the dress come alive like a mermaid's scales. Sienna looked up from under her lashes, challenge sparkling in her sapphire eyes. "Don't you trust me?"

"Of course I do," Aislinn protested.

Which seemed to be how, five minutes later, she was stripped down to her panties while Sienna arranged layers and folds of the half-made dress across her body. "Hmm. Want a bra? I don't have anywhere near the assets you do - actually, you know what?" Petite hands hefted first one breast, then the other, as Sienna poked and prodded. "Yeah, I can build one in. That'll be pretty easy."

"Do you always manhandle your models?" Aislinn asked, amused in spite of herself.

Sienna straightened to cup her own tiny breasts, shoving them together in a vain attempt to create cleavage in the bodice of her sundress. "Yeah, because they're all me, usually. It'll be nice to work with someone who has curves."

"You're just lucky I don't mind you touching said curves," Aislinn chuckled, gripping the fabric where prompted while Sienna added some pins. "You really use yourself as the model?"

Sienna grunted in agreement, her head lost among swathes of skirt. "It's easier that way. Seriously, Ash, this ass of yours - I'm so jealous." The younger woman's face appeared, looking chagrined. "You're a busty, hourglass-shaped bombshell and I'm a twig."

Aislinn hesitated over her response, sensing a deep vulnerability in the other's words. After a moment, she dropped into a crouch and grabbed Sienna's hands in hers. "You're beautiful. Don't you see?"

"I'm pretty," Sienna corrected. "Cute, even. Men want someone with giant tits, sculpted butt cheeks and good meat on their bones. Like you."

"I..." Aislinn faltered. She'd never considered herself in much of a feminine light; she'd been a tomboy as a child and later, when she'd grown into her figure, Flynn had been the only one who seemed to pay attention. "That can't be right, Sens. You're a sparkling gemstone out here - I'm just a shadow."

Sienna's face flattened with dry humour. "Uh huh, that's why they're drooling all over you and don't even blink at me. Nice try."

"Nobody," Aislinn denied, "Is drooling on me."

"Not even Tobias?"

Aislinn rolled her eyes. "He's seeing me through rose-coloured glasses. We both know that."

"Gods above us, Ash - he's probably the only one of us who's seeing *straight*," Sienna laughed abruptly, then shook her head. "Fine, but I'm going to use the picnic to illustrate my point and once it's over, we'll have this chat again." Amusement turned to a frown as she checked her watch. "Now get that off so I can hit the sewing machine, or we'll run out of time."

Aislinn complied, handing the dress over and planting one hand on her hip. "What do your instincts say about a formal occasion when the bears could attack any minute?"

"It's a good thing," Sienna said, bundling her supplies back in her bag. "Having Andre and Rupert back here will boost morale."

"Hah!"

"They don't know him like you do." Sienna smiled to soften her words. "I'll be back in a few hours - no escaping."

"Fine," Aislinn agreed absently, chewing on one thumbnail as the other woman left. How could someone as elegant and beautiful as Sienna Smythe doubt her own appeal? What had happened in the pack since she'd been away? She reached for her clothes, eschewing the corset in favour of her favourite bra and a loose, flowing tank to match her denim mini. With no hair tie leaping to her immediate notice, she grabbed the sections of hair hanging down either side of her face and tied them in a knot at the back of her head, leaving the remainder to tumble freely down her back. Sliding her phone into her pocket, she wandered downstairs.

With the entire Redding pack rushing around like headless chickens in an attempt to set up for the banquet, Tobias' kitchen was empty when she arrived. Knowing they'd soon break for lunch - and that the boys, at least, would likely appear at this very bench - she rummaged in the fridge for bread and fillings and began making a stack of sandwiches.

The scars on her forearms seemed to stand out in stark relief as she worked, somehow more vividly purple than ever before. She stared down at the raised flesh and bright lines, her mind still trying to sort through the strange conversation she'd had with Sienna. The problem wasn't anything near as shallow as who was 'prettier', it was about self-confidence and value. Sienna's words had been light but the vulnerability and pain in her expression had been alarmingly real.

"Now that's a serious face if ever I saw one." Rory's soft, pensive voice preceded him into the room. He wore a pair of board shorts and nothing else, his blonde-tipped brown hair beaded with moisture. "Mooning over Tobias?"

Aislinn threw a piece of ham at him. Rory blinked as it slapped against his narrow chest and stuck there. "I do *not* moon. And if you're looking for his Alpha-ness, he's out hunting Andre and Rupert with Zeke."

"I wasn't looking for him." Rory peeled the ham off his chest, rolled it into a cigar shape and ate it. "I ran into Sienna on the way back from my swim and she said you were here."

Aislinn blinked. "You came looking for me?"

"Yeah." He nodded, looking so suddenly uncomfortable that she flashed him her most brilliant smile.

"Cool." Aislinn finished making the first sandwich and offered it to him. "Better than straight ham, you know."

"I like straight ham," Rory replied, but he took the offering with a hint of a smile.

They watched each other as he bit and chewed, the silence stretching until it creaked. Unsure what he needed, Aislinn decided to follow on with her previous train of thought. "What do you think of Sienna?"

"Huh?" Rory's face twisted momentarily with surprise before it smoothed out again, and Aislinn wondered how many of his emotions he hid that way. After a long moment, the slender wolfkin ventured, "Well, she's Sienna."

"That's it?"

"I'm not sure what you're asking."

She arched a brow. "You don't look at her and think… what if?"

"What if…" Rory's brow furrowed a moment and then comprehension dawned, his cheeks flagging pink. "Ew, Ash! She's like my sister."

"So am I."

The look he flashed over her was suddenly, incredibly male. "No way."

Filing that response away, she tilted her head. "You've really never looked at Sienna like that? Ever?" He shook his head with such desperation that in spite of herself, Aislinn bit back a laugh. "What about the others?"

Rory's eyes went wide. "Zeke would kill us."

Ah. Familiarity and older brothers. Aislinn gave a slow nod, her mind churning. "I see."

Puzzlement flashed over his features, then Rory squared his shoulders. "Why aren't you outside with the others?"

"I had some calls to make." She finished another sandwich and set it aside. "Trying to find out more about Regina's death. I'm not taking a single thing my father says as gospel until I've had an outside source confirm it."

Rory swallowed and though his expression remained calm, Aislinn knew they were finally getting to the heart of the matter. "Jacques and Lena said they knew Leif."

"I didn't know before they said it but it makes sense - they're close to his age."

"Or the age he would've been, if he were alive," Rory murmured, picking at the slice of cheese in his sandwich. "They said I look like him."

Aislinn leant against the bench and took a bite out of the next sandwich. "Really? Your hair colour's wrong. You're also too white and you have too many freckles."

"We have the same eyes." He lifted a hand self-consciously to his hair. "I dye my hair and keep it short because people used to tell me all the time I looked like Leif, no matter the fact that he was all big and muscly and tanned while I'm the opposite."

Dropping her sandwich, Aislinn rounded the bench so they were on the same side, propping one fist on her hip as she gave him a critical once over. Rory's soft almond and sage scent wrapped around her senses, his slender frame exuding a subtle sort of strength. He wasn't much taller than she and lacked the physical presence of Tobias - or any of the other men, come to think of it - but there was such gentle assurance about Rory Deepwater that Aislinn knew his slighter stature and boyish features were nowhere near the complete picture. Whilst he might have been slim, his muscles were finely honed from working the land and all the training he did, and the glitter of intelligence in his eyes made him far more a threat than he at first appeared.

Aware her answer was somehow incredibly important, Aislinn said, "You look like you, Rory."

"I try to." His hands clenched to fists, tendons straining. "But Leif is everywhere I go, in everything I do. I don't know how to let him go."

"Do you want to?"

"No." Rory spoke through gritted teeth. "But I can't move on if I don't. I can't be me if I'm living in his shadow, and having Jacques and Brayden at the house…"

"Why haven't you been to Grandma about this?" Aislinn murmured gently. "It's plain as the nose on my face that you've been letting this fester for years."

His shoulders hunched inward and his next words were barely a whisper. "I can't." Tortured eyes looked up, desperate hope deepening their brown to the colour of bitterest chocolate. "You're a Den Mother. You can help me."

"Me?" Aislinn sucked in a breath, the bench bumping her spine as she took an involuntary step backwards. "That's not a good idea."

"You have the energy - I know you do."

"I have too much of it." She pressed her lips into a thin line, her breath coming too fast. All Alphas and Den Mothers carried a heavy dose of charisma, a physically tangible force that drew others to them with the promise of safety, support and unconditional love. It had the power to heal broken hearts, mend tattered spirits and was the essence that bound a pack. Aislinn had learnt early on that she carried far too much; so much that everyone could feel it, so much it gave away her position on a mission and was a huge distraction to everyone around her when she wasn't. Most Den Mothers and Alphas were encouraged to spread their energy around, to sprinkle it through their packs like so much fairy dust. Aislinn - and, when his time had come, Flynn - had been taught to smother it, strangle it, draw it deep inside and lock it forever in a box. The edges peeped out, of course; no method was perfect, but it was a background hum most Kin overlooked entirely, the energy so well hidden that unless Aislinn revealed her Den Mother status, it was impossible to guess. Since Olaf's attack, she'd been even less inclined to slip her self-imposed leash; the idea of strangers staring at her slack jawed and dewy eyed was more than she could handle.

"Please," Rory whispered. "I don't trust anyone else."

A sharp spike of anger punctured Aislinn's bubble of nightmares. Grandma had admitted she'd been neglecting her duties, but this was inexcusable. "If I slip the locks on my energy, it's going to come pouring out in a tide."

She'd be naked. So, so naked.

Tears gathered in Rory's eyes but he nodded, biting his lower lip to stop it trembling. In that moment he didn't look like the grown man he was but the young boy she remembered, sensitive and deep with a huge heart; a heart that had been crushed by the death of the brother he'd worshipped like a hero.

"Solaeden save me," Aislinn whispered, shaking her head. Nobody had stood by these boys in her absence; nobody had nourished their souls or tended their hearts - and though she wasn't technically part of the pack anymore, she also knew she didn't have it in her to turn away. She'd never been a coward. "All right."

"No, I don't want you to hurt yoursel -" Rory cut off as she scooped him into her arms like a child and strode into the lounge. His body trembled with tension, his eyes wide as they sought hers. "Ash."

"Shhh." Aislinn plopped them both down onto the couch, curled their bodies together and settled his head over her heart. "Let's fight this battle as a team."

Rory bunched his fists in her top and for a moment Aislinn wondered if he was going to shove her away. But then he relaxed, his lashes fluttering closed as he snuggled into her like a puppy. She draped one arm along his spine and stroked his hair with the other hand, closing her eyes and sending the Twin Gods a prayer for a strength she wasn't sure she had. Reaching deep inside herself, she shattered the prison that kept her Den Mother energy contained.

Power roared out - pure, undiluted energy that expanded her starving veins and exploded from her pores. Rory gasped as it rolled him under, a palpable wave of purity and love and strength, that indefinable *something* that marked her beyond doubt as a caretaker of her people. Blinking back tears as a sense of rightness flooded her spirit, Aislinn laid her chin atop Rory's damp hair and began to hum, a tuneless, silly sound which nevertheless saw the wolfkin's breathing even out and a smile tug at the corners of his lips.

She was free now, wholly and completely without restraint, the way nature had intended. Too much Den Mother energy, too much damper energy, too much of a personality to squeeze into one body. Aislinn felt both heavy and weightless at the same time, drunk on her own senses whilst simultaneously more clear-headed than she'd been in years. It was perfect and terrifying all at once and though there'd been no sound to accompany the smashing of her internal vault, she knew without doubt that the ripples of the explosion would spread like wildfire through the surrounding area.

The door opened quietly behind her and a moment later, Jaxon crawled onto the couch on Aislinn's other side, drawn by the pack oath that bound them together. He folded his body around hers, chest rumbling in the wolf equivalent of a purr, and closed his eyes.

Flynn came next, his tiger form dropping away to reveal amber eyes shining with the vulnerability he hated to the very depths of his soul. He curled up on the floor and laid his head on her leg, uncaring that his arms also circled Rory and Jaxon in an effort to reach her.

Dominic arrived soon after, his skin smudged with grease and his hair stuck up in a disarray at complete odds with his persona. Aislinn wasn't sure what he'd been doing but she smiled nonetheless, continuing with her gentle humming and stroking of Rory's hair. Step by jerky step, Dominic rounded the couch and settled onto the floor beside Flynn, hooking one grease-stained hand around her ankle and resting his cheek on top of her arm.

This was, in essence, what she'd feared; but there was no going back now. The fact that Dominic had felt the energy surge when he was well and truly connected to the Redding pack and her father - and thereby, though not directly, to Tobias - only served as proof of the strength of her violent release. The most likely scenario was that Dominic had been working nearby and had caught the trailing edge of the blast, though it should have been deflected somewhat by his affiliation to a different pack. The only exception to that theory was if Tobias himself was susceptible to her energy, and through that, those closest to him - but how could he be? One wild night was enough for a scent transfer, but the sort of third hand energy pass-on Aislinn was considering was… well, pretty much impossible.

As though to deliberately refute her theories and shatter the fragile comforts she'd began to placate herself with, the door to the house slammed open and Zeke tumbled in, his head swinging wildly from side to side as though looking for a threat. Aislinn felt her heart stutter. Connected directly to Tobias' wild, raw energy, Zeke shouldn't have felt a thing from her, but the half-mad look in his sapphire eyes said otherwise.

If Zeke could feel it, then that meant - Aislinn swallowed her gasp, her fingers clenching momentarily in Rory's hair as the impossible became reality. Standing silhouetted in the doorway, rubbing one hand over his chest as though to ease an ache, was Tobias.

# Twelve

It was rude to stare, even at someone you'd known all your life - but Tobias couldn't help himself. No more than he could help rubbing the ache in his heart where Aislinn's energy, only minutes before, had punched a hole right through and lit him up like a Christmas tree. A moment later Zeke had staggered beside him and Tobias realised that somehow, the blast had affected his second as well. They'd both gasped "Aislinn," dragged each other upright and bolted home.

Drawn by an energy that grew in strength with each passing moment, Tobias followed Zeke to the couch. Aislinn was curled on the cushions with Rory in her lap, his head on her chest and his breathing even as though in sleep. She was humming softly, stroking his hair, with Jaxon, Dominic and Flynn draped over her like a living blanket - and Zeke, who squeezed onto the couch on Rory's opposite side, his long, slender arms snaking behind Aislinn's shoulder and his cheek resting on the arm she'd draped down Rory's spine.

Tobias' hands brushed warm skin as he bumped up against the back of the couch, Aislinn's thick, luscious hair caressing his arms. Drawn to her like a magnet, he began kneading her shoulders, the contact causing his gut to tighten and a low growl to echo in his throat.

What in the world was going on?

Apart from Aislinn using her Den Mother energy to bolster Rory, of course; that much Tobias *did* understand. He'd seen Grandma Redding do it - albeit to a lesser extent - on the odd occasion and had even tried somewhat unsuccessfully to do it himself. But the odd pain in his chest? And the fact that more people than Jaxon, the only one of them actually bound to Aislinn, had felt the energy and come running?

Without ceasing his firm massage of her shoulders and neck, Tobias twisted to look back at the door. It was still closed behind him, the veritable wellspring of energy that Aislinn had released likely no more than a background hum where those on the common lawn were concerned.

Tobias's breath caught in his lungs and he fought to swallow around a sudden thickening in his throat. It was the heartmate connection. It had to be. When Aislinn had done whatever it was she'd done to release all that energy - and twin gods, but it was a *lot* - the ripples had reached through Tobias to those closest to him, calling each and every one like moths to a flame.

The thumping ball of magma inside his chest jerked and Tobias gasped, pitching forward until his face was buried in Aislinn's hair, his fingers digging into her shoulders. "Ash, I can't breathe. You have to stop."

She blinked and looked up in surprise, her smooth hum fading. "What?"

"I… can't…" Tobias slithered down the back of the couch, his knees no longer holding his weight. He stared up at the roof, arms limp by his sides, and declared; "Fuck."

And then he fainted.

*******

"Tobias?" Aislinn reeled her energy back in, panic fluttering in her chest when she received no answer. Still tangled in her packmates, she did the next best thing she could think of. "Flynn!"

The tigerkin was up in an instant, disappearing around the back of the couch. "He's alive."

Aislinn breathed a sigh of relief as Zeke sat up, sapphire eyes bewildered. He ran a hand through his hair, then shook it wildly in an attempt to clear his head. "What happened?"

"Rory needed a little help." Aislinn pressed a soft kiss to the other man's forehead. "You in there, bud?"

Brown eyes flicked open. "Thank you."

"Welcome."

One by one the men extricated themselves from the tangle of limbs and after what felt like forever, Aislinn vaulted over the back of the couch to land beside Flynn and Tobias.

"He fainted, by the looks of it," Flynn said, amber eyes narrowed on Tobias' face. Indeed, the Alpha's chest rose and fell rhythmically, though one hand was still tangled in the fabric of his overly tight t-shirt. Sparks of blue light danced underneath sun-bronzed skin, so many that it seemed Tobias had a river of fireflies coursing through his veins. Flynn cocked his head as though the problem were prey to be stalked. "Energy overload."

Aislinn sat back with a frown. "That shouldn't be possible."

"Are you shitting me right now?" A perfect black brow flicked upward. "He's in flux and you were dialled up to full strength. I haven't felt that sort of pull since you transitioned."

She tried to wave that fact away, but her hand trembled. "We're blood bonded. You're more sensitive to it than you should be."

"Blood bonded?" Zeke's eyes widened but Flynn bared his teeth.

"Not today, Goldilocks."

"Look, full strength or not, this can't be me," She insisted. "Den Mother energy doesn't choke people. And even if it did, the idea is a moot one - Dom, Zeke and Tobias have no conscious link to me." All five men suddenly found somewhere else to look, Dominic even going so far as to shove his hands in his pockets and start whistling softly under his breath. Aislinn glared but not a single one of them would meet her gaze. "What am I missing?"

"That's a discussion you need to have with Tobias when he's up and about. In private," Zeke added, holding up a hand when she opened her mouth. "Right now, it might be a good idea to wake him up."

"Me?" Aislinn blinked down at the unconscious Alpha. "What makes you think *I* can wake him?"

Zeke shrugged. "Hunch."

Feeling uncharacteristically uncertain, she laid her hand flat on Tobias' chest. His eyes flew open on a gasp, his expression pure confusion as he tried to sit up. Aislinn leant into his chest, keeping him flat on the floor. "Breathe."

Tobias obeyed, the golden starbursts in his eyes glinting with an inner light as his gaze locked with her own. Confusion faded and he offered a megawatt smile. "Ash."

The way her name left his lips on an exhale had Aislinn's cheeks darkening with colour and set a couple of the others coughing - but when she whipped around, their faces were carefully blank.

She turned back to Tobias, noting the blue sparks were now darting frantically around beneath the surface of his skin. Leaving one hand on his chest and settling the other over his navel, Aislinn spread out her damper energy like a blanket.

The blue lights winked out one by one, leaving behind a wolfkin watching her with predatory focus. Suddenly very much aware of the ridged muscles under Tobias' t-shirt and the way his tanned skin gleamed in the sunlight, Aislinn cleared her throat and offered an encouraging smile. "Are you okay?"

"I think so." Tobias sat up and Aislinn crinkled her nose as she was assaulted with his scent; heady butterscotch with a hint of liquor and decadent lashings of cream. Who'd dialled it up to such epic proportions? Muscles shifted and bunched as he thrust both hands into his hair, met her gaze for a fraction of a second, then focussed over her shoulder. "Well?"

"Nothing," Zeke answered; too quickly. The second stalked into the kitchen and continued working on the sandwiches Aislinn had begun what felt like a lifetime ago. "Dom, how are the picnic preparations coming along?"

"Shit!" Dominic caught the sandwich Zeke lobbed his way and raced out the door.

Rory looked up at the clock. "I'm going to take a shower. Flynn and I are due to meet Jacques and Brayden for rehearsal at my place in half an hour."

"I'm going for a run," Flynn grunted. "I'll meet you there."

Rory nodded and walked into the bathroom without a backward glance. Flynn bent to rub his cheek swiftly and firmly against Aislinn's, pausing when she grabbed a hank of his silken hair. "Don't think I haven't noticed you all beating hasty retreats."

"Take it out of my hide later." Flynn winked, twisted out of her grip and jogged out the door.

She narrowed her eyes at the remaining men; Zeke gave her an unrepentant grin and Jaxon hauled her upright rather than answer the question in her gaze. He accepted the sandwich that flew his way and turned to Tobias. "I'm assuming you got hold of Andre and Rupert all right?"

"Yeah, they were doing a round of patrols." Tobias pushed to his feet with a grunt. "They're going to come in for the official part of the festivities, then go back out. Lena and Kaira will cover for the hour or so they're here."

"Just like that?"

"Yeah." Tobias rubbed at the back of his head and then shrugged. "I thought they'd be more pissed off, honestly."

"Probably saving it up to torture us later," Aislinn growled. "Did you tell them about the meeting tomorrow?"

"Of course," Tobias nodded, brows pinched. "They just asked me to pass on the details when I know them."

"Now I know they're *definitely* up to something," Aislinn declared. "That never happens."

Zeke snorted and handed Tobias a ham and cheese sandwich. "You sound a tad jaded, little-sister-mine."

Aislinn bared her teeth. "Oh, I'm very jaded - but not without reason."

"Can't argue with that, I guess." Zeke flicked a glance towards the bathroom, where the shower could clearly be heard running in the background. "Rory okay?"

"Yeah, I think so." Aislinn accepted a sandwich of her own and munched thoughtfully. "Lena and Jacques spoke with him about Leif. It stirred things up a little."

"They knew Leif? What about Draco?" Jaxon asked, eyes alight with hope.

"I don't know but you could ask them," she said. "They're all the right age."

"If they knew each other, how come they weren't at the summit?" Zeke asked curiously.

"That, I *can* answer - Jacques and Lena come from bigger groups of Kin who, unlike us, had more warriors on hand than the summit demanded. There was a ballot for who was allowed to attend and neither were picked." Aislinn finished the last of her sandwich and dusted both hands on her skirt. "Something that haunts them both, in its own way."

Jaxon nodded slowly, face speculative. "I'll go gently."

"Thanks."

"In the meantime, do you need me to hang around? Mum said she could use some help with the kids while Dad's still in Melbourne." Jaxon's face lit up as he spoke of his younger siblings.

"No, I'll be fine." She shot Tobias a look. "Unless anyone in particular wants to explain themselves?"

Tobias grunted low in his throat while the other two males looked innocent. "Nothing to explain."

"Liar." Aislinn turned her edged smile on Jaxon. "I'm meant to meet Sienna here but considering we're all playing mind games, I think it'd be better if I went to her instead."

"Sens is at my place," Zeke announced, eyes on his own sandwich. "Seeing as Mum's putting up Percy and Gerard."

"I'll show you where it is." Jaxon twined his fingers through Aislinn's and gave Tobias a hard look. "I know you've still got things to do."

The alpha blinked. "Well, yeah, but -"

Jaxon's look was searing this time, and Tobias fell silent, shoulders taut. When it became obvious he intended to maintain his stubborn silence, Jaxon shook his head. "You're worse than me. Come on, Ash - let's go before Achilles does something to make Mum blow a gasket."

"Wait." Aislinn twisted to look over her shoulder as Jaxon towed her to the door, his enormous hand tight around her smaller one. "Zeke - if Tobias looks like he's going to lose it, just howl and I'll come running."

"Er..." Sapphire eyes blinked rapidly. "Okay."

Tobias drew himself up. "I thought we were supposed to stay together."

"Yeah, and I thought we were done with secrets." She narrowed her eyes in warning. "I only just soothed your energy - the residual effects should last a while, if you're careful. Besides that, I'm annoyed with you."

Leaving Tobias looking decidedly maudlin, she allowed Jaxon to pull her out the door and across the lawn. Several pack members were hard at work setting up an impromptu dance floor and some packing crates which Aislinn assumed would eventually become a stage.

Jaxon hauled her halfway through the ruckus before he noticed her face. "What?"

"I feel like I should be... doing something."

"You had other stuff to do."

Aislinn glanced over one shoulder to where Frank Smythe hastily avoided her gaze. "Why do I feel like that's a convenient and bullshitty excuse?"

"You want the truth?" Jaxon shrugged. "Grandma said you're not allowed to help because you always get too distracted."

"Distracted? By what?"

"Everything." He shrugged again, green eyes glittering in the late afternoon light. "Remember that time we were supposed to be laying out morning tea and you started a scone fight?"

"We were eight!"

"All right, what about the time you helped Achilles set up a lemonade stand and then sprayed everyone with lemonade when they showed up? You were older then."

Aislinn bit her tongue to keep from laughing. "I was bored."

"Or that time you threw tomatoes through Tobias' window at three in the morning because he wouldn't wear the yellow bikini your Mum bought you that was too big?"

There was no way she could stop the smile now. "It went with his eyes; he would've looked fabulous."

"And only a few days ago, you and Zeke got drunk at breakfast and served us dick-shaped fruit."

"Okay, okay, I get it." Aislinn shot him a mischievous look from beneath her lashes. "Imagine what I can get up to now that I can melt into the shadows."

Jaxon's shoulders shook with laughter as he led her up the overgrown path of a dilapidated old cottage. "*Exactly* the reason nobody wanted to give you a job."

"Jerk," she teased, then looked up at the little house and paused. "Isn't this the Arthknott's place?"

"It was, once." Jaxon rapped on the peeling front door and then turned the handle. "It sat empty after they died at the peace summit… Now Zeke lives here."

"By himself?" Aislinn paused inside the door, eyebrows high. Zeke's house was a two bedroom affair with a shared dining, lounge and kitchen space. In contrast to the outside, the interior was in far better repair - though the tortoiseshell carpet had faded with time and the mission brown decor stood testament to the era in which the cottage had been built. "Wow."

"It's something, isn't it?" Sienna rose from the fold-down table where her sewing machine was set up. "Zeke and Ma don't get on so well; this was the best option. He's such a boy, though."

Aislinn took in the sunken couch covered in rumpled clothing and food wrappers and crinkled her nose. "*Such* a boy."

"Uh huh." Jaxon gave her a knowing look. "What's *your* house like, Ash?"

"Spotless," Aislinn returned, lifting her chin. "Kaira's the daughter of a very traditional French Lord and he pays for a housekeeper on her behalf."

The stocky wolfkin grinned. "I knew it." Jaxon drew Sienna close with an arm around her neck and used his free hand to muss her hair. "Turn my Den Mother into a princess, Sens?"

"Of course." Sienna favoured Jaxon with a smile that glittered like cut gemstones but he didn't seem to notice, leaning in to drop an absent peck on her cheek before doing the same to Aislinn and seeing himself out. Sienna jabbed an angry finger at the closed door. "See? Invisible."

"Weird," Aislinn agreed. "That smile was so bright even *I* wanted to take my clothes off."

Sienna snorted. "With that in mind, it's time to try the dress on - so strip."

"Really?" Aislinn groaned. "How did I let you talk me into this?"

"Zeke has booze. Fancy booze," Sienna offered. When Aislinn pursed her lips in mock thought, the younger woman laughed. "You undress; I'll make cocktails."

Two hours and several cosmopolitans later, Aislinn was pleasantly tipsy and considerably more relaxed. While Sienna fussed with her hair, she found herself relating the events of the afternoon, starting with Rory's sadness and going right through to Tobias' mysterious fainting attack. "They clearly know something," she finished, frowning. "The others, I mean. Something they're not telling me."

Sienna's hands hesitated in Aislinn's hair. "You didn't feel anything when Tobias burst in through the door?"

"Sens, I had my energy turned up to max; I felt a lot of things."

"Right, yeah, I know." Sienna clicked her tongue against her teeth. "About Tobias, I mean."

Aislinn tried to twist around but was locked in place by firm fingers against her scalp. "After Tobias woke up, he looked… different. If that's what you mean."

"Different how?"

"I don't know." She bit her lip, trying to mime Tobias' broad shoulders and narrow hips, his solid frame and sun-kissed skin. "More… more."

Sienna giggled. "Descriptive."

"He smelled better. Like something I wanted to eat. Or drink." Aislinn sighed. "Lady Lunaida, I shouldn't be telling you this! You love him, too."

"Oh, Ash." Sienna released her hair and came around in front, dropping into the rickety chair opposite. "I've realised I didn't love Tobias so much as the *idea* of Tobias." She twisted a glittery hairpin in delicate fingers. "I'm not a complete innocent - I've been with men before. Not many, mind you," she added quickly, blushing. "But enough to realise that I've had my fair share of jerks. And by picking Tobias - who, let's face it, is the most epic brother figure in my life aside from my actual brother - well, it's safe, you know?" Sienna's smile was tight. "Hard to get hurt again when the guy you love is in love with someone else and doesn't even know you exist."

Aislinn felt her heart twist. "You do know not all males are like that, right?"

"Of course, but… once bitten, twice shy, I guess." Sienna sighed. "Your arrival burst the bubble on the pack's insular lifestyle, made me realise we've been sitting here stagnating."

"Not entirely your fault."

"No, but we were comfortable in our ignorance, I think. I mean, I love my job but the boutique's small game. Agreeing to start that outreach refuge with you was a massive reminder that my ambitions - fashion, business, you name it - are bigger than what I've settled for so far." Sienna frowned down at her hands. "My blindfold's been torn off, professionally and personally - and suddenly I realise I want someone, *anyone*, who won't look at me like their little sister every time I open my mouth."

"There's nothing wrong with feeling that way." Aislinn tugged the hairpin from Sienna's grasp, replacing it with her cocktail glass. "The problem is that every eligible male in this pack is also basically related to you. And you're not eyeing them off as mating material either, right? You need someone who's going to appreciate you like a woman, and worship you in bed - even if it's a temporary arrangement."

Sienna choked on her cosmopolitan, turning a brilliant shade of red. "Why are you looking at me like that?"

"Because I happen to know someone who will worship you hella good." Aislinn winked. "He arrived a few hours ago, in fact."

"Ash! I don't want a pity screw!"

"Do I look like I'm arranging one?" Aislinn leant forward, bracing both hands on her knees. "Trust me this once, let me introduce you - an introduction, that's all - and I'll let you dress me however you want tonight. The whole nine yards, whatever you say, no arguments."

"Really?" Sienna blinked, embarrassment fading as she considered. "Promise?"

"Promise." Aislinn held out a hand, challenge ripe in her smile. "You get to princess me and in return, I swear to both the Lord and Lady up above that after tonight, those boys will *never* look at you like a little sister again. Except for Zeke, of course, because gross."

Sienna looked down at Aislinn's hand, licked her lips, then shook firmly. "Deal."

"Great." Aislinn waited for Sienna to stand but to her surprise, the younger woman set aside her glass and dropped to her knees on the floor. "What are you doing?"

"You've always been my friend, Ash. Even when I was just a chubby kid following you around, pretending to be grown up. And now - I want to see things, experience things. I want to grow and laugh and spread my wings." Sienna's voice trembled but she didn't drop her gaze. "The thing is, I'm not brave like you are; I can't do it alone. Can I... come with you?"

"To the picnic?"

"Anywhere. Everywhere." Sienna's eyes were shining. "I want to swear into your pack."

"My *pack*?" Aislinn sat bolt upright and would have withdrawn her hand on reflex if Sienna hadn't clenched tightly. "Solaeden save me, you're serious."

"Yes. You're an independent Den Mother and you have Jaxon now, too." Sienna swallowed. "Please."

Aislinn blinked rapidly, her throat thick. "I don't know if I'm the best role model - Jax was listing my qualifications outside and they weren't exactly glowing. You need to be sure."

"I'm sure." Sienna took a deep breath and reached for Aislinn's other hand, twining their fingers together. "I, Sienna Ellyse Smythe, hereby pledge my life to you, Den Mother Aislinn Jaide Redding, by the light of the Father Sun. I vow to walk in your shadow, defend your honour and give my life, should it be necessary, for the keeping of yours. I offer my strength, my will, my soul, into your keeping from now until the end of my days." She lifted her chin, baring her delicate throat. "For the pack."

Heart racing, Aislinn bent to place her teeth over Sienna's jugular and scraped the flesh ever so gently. "Welcome to the pack, Sienna Smythe. May time make me worthy of your choice."

Something 'clicked' into place, as it had when Jaxon had sworn his oath. Sienna let out a choked sob and threw her arms around Aislinn's neck, hugging her close. "Thank you."

"You're welcome - though I still say you don't know what you've gotten yourself into." Aislinn pressed a kiss to Sienna's cheek, watched as the younger woman leant back and wiped tears from her face. "You okay?"

"I need a drink," Sienna declared, then laughed shakily. "You want a double?"

Aislinn gave her new packmate a long look. "Considering I just promised to let you turn me into a pretty princess? Hell yes, I want a double."

Sienna stood and made her way into the kitchen, grinning wickedly. "You're the one with no idea what you're getting into - and neither does Tobias."

"Tobias," Aislinn repeated, frowning as she watched liquor splash into her glass. "Do you know what I'm missing there?"

"I do. He's waiting for you to figure it out."

"Figure out what?" Aislinn growled as Sienna added cranberry juice and a dash of lime. "What am I supposed to *feel*? What sort of connection is he expecting me to -" she broke off, the colour draining from her face. "No. Are you... are you saying we're *heartmates*?"

Soft footsteps through the lounge, a cool glass being pressed into her hand. "Yes."

"Shit. I - shit!" Aislinn shook her head, flattening a hand over her pounding heart. "But… heartmates are so rare as to be mythical."

Sienna scoffed low in her throat. "They're not as rare as a woman who can dissolve into shadows or a man who can absorb lightning. Heartmates might be rare, but I've done the maths on your skills, Ash. In a population of two and a half billion Kin worldwide, there's a potential maximum of twenty-something with additional powers like the ones you and Tobias have. *Potential* maximum - I bet the real numbers aren't that high. And the odds of you both being in the same country? Don't make me laugh." Golden curls flew as Sienna shook her head. "You two were built for each other - this is just the Gods' way of formalising it."

"Heartmates." Aislinn swallowed heavily. "Are you sure? Really, really sure?"

"Of course." Sienna's laugh was gentle. "It's been pretty obvious for a few days now."

"Really? Who else knows?"

"Um… everyone except you?" At Aislinn's look of complete horror, Sienna giggled. "Okay, okay. The boys plus Grandma have figured it out."

"Hence the scene in the kitchen earlier." Aislinn pinched the bridge of her nose. "Flynn, too?"

"Oh, yes. He was the first, I think - but I'm still learning to use my intuition, so that's mostly a guess."

Aislinn twisted her fingers in the loose robe Sienna had dragged out of Zeke's room and insisted she wear while they made final adjustments to her hair and makeup. "Why can't I feel it?"

"I think it's because of Olaf," Sienna said gently, tapping the cocktail glass until Aislinn sipped. "Makes sense his perverted Marking would prevent you feeling another connection - even if it's been there, unacknowledged, your whole life."

"So you're saying Tobias can feel it?" Aislinn swore as she recalled the way he'd been clutching his chest right before he fainted. "It was an energy overload. *My energy.* He couldn't process it or funnel it back because Olaf's got me in chains."

"It also explains why you saw and scented Tobias differently when you touched him," Sienna murmured softly, her hands slipping back into Aislinn's hair to pick up where she'd left off earlier. "Physical contact gives you a literal connection, allowing a temporary - though likely only partial - bridge."

"Shit." Aislinn blinked fuzzily into her cosmopolitan. She wasn't crying. Nope. She was just tipsy, that was all. "What do I do?"

"What you've always done," Sienna said lightly. "You knock his fucking socks off."

"Shit," Aislinn repeated, puzzle pieces dropping into place at long last. Tobias had known, that much was certain. He'd given her space to heal and come to the realisation herself - but thanks to Olaf's interference, she'd been oblivious to all the hints he'd dropped. And he'd dropped plenty, Aislinn realised, her cheeks heating as Sienna put the finishing touches on her hair. "Solaeden save me, I'm an idiot."

"Yes, but sit still or you'll be an idiot with messy lip gloss," Sienna muttered, ratting through her bag for said lip colour. Emerging triumphant, she applied the gloss with a firm hand and a single, squinted eye. "Good. Done. Now to get you dressed."

Aislinn allowed herself to be bullied into the bedroom, balking when she was handed a scrap of navy lace. "Really?"

"What? You can't wear normal underwear on a night like this," Sienna snorted. "They only took a few minutes to whip up and should fit you perfectly."

"What sort of underwear are *you* wearing?"

Sienna fisted a hand on her hip. "I recall someone promising not to argue."

"Ack!" Aislinn dropped her robe and stripped off her comfortable cotton panties, wriggling the delicate lace on over her hips. "Happy now?"

"Definitely." Sienna did a quick circle and then nodded. "Good fit. Comfy?"

"Actually… now that you mention it, yes. How'd you manage that?"

"Perseverance." An elegant golden eyebrow shot skyward. "I'm also a woman, and I hate getting a vagina wedgie as much as the next person. What good is sexy underwear if it's not comfy?"

Aislinn giggled. "I don't think I've ever loved you more than at this moment."

"Well now, that's saying something, isn't it?" Sienna laughed, trekking back to the lounge and returning with the completed dress. "Let's get this on, so you can help with mine."

After fifteen minutes of lacing, tying and giggling, Aislinn was firmly secured in her new dress. She had to admit it suited her perfectly, the colour an excellent complement for her eyes. When Sienna produced a pair of sparkly, strappy heels from a box under the bed, Aislinn didn't bother grimacing; she just put them on. They were, naturally, a perfect fit - procured through some sort of fashion designer magic, no doubt. With her hair and makeup immaculate, Aislinn looked like… well, like a princess. "Sens, it's beautiful. Thank you."

Now in a state of undress herself, Sienna winked. "I told you so."

"Hah!" Aislinn helped her friend into a short, sunset-coloured dress with a flirty skirt and zipped up the sides. "Strapless?"

"Considering I have basically no breasts, I may as well take advantage of it," Sienna chuckled. "No need for an uncomfortable bra, either. I just let them float free."

"I'm jealous," Aislinn replied, and meant it. "If I let mine float free at a dance I'd knock someone unconscious."

"I don't think Tobias would mind," Sienna returned, dragging out a pair of platformed stilettos the colour of ripe watermelon, with gold accents. She noticed Aislinn's look and grinned. "What? I'm short; I need all the help I can get."

Sienna slipped the shoes on and then tottered across the room with the air of confidence that only came to someone very familiar with their chosen type of footwear. She adjusted her blonde curls, swept on some smoky makeup with an ease that Aislinn envied and completed the outfit with simple gold jewellery. "You look amazing, Sens."

"Well, thanks. I've been saving this dress for a while now - figured tonight was as good a time as any to give it a whirl." She spun in place, setting the skirt whizzing cheerfully and baring an astonishing amount of slender leg. "It feels fun."

Smoothing down her dress with restless hands, Aislinn looked up at the clock. "What time are we meant to be there?"

"Oh, sort of now, I guess." Sienna moved to the window and flipped a corner of the curtain aside. "Tobias is out there - and so are the rest of the boys. We might as well join them."

"Why am I so damned nervous all of a sudden?"

Sienna took her hand and squeezed tightly. "Because you're normally kicking butt, rather than dressing as a princess? And because your heartmate is out there?"

"Thanks," Aislinn managed, licking suddenly dry lips. "What's your excuse?"

"You promised me a potential worshipping. Can you blame a girl for wondering?"

"Fair enough." Aislinn laughed - but didn't let go her friend's hand. "Together?"

Sienna nodded. "Let's go."

# Thirteen

Tobias looked up from his phone as fingers dug into his arm hard enough to bruise. "Zeke? What's wrong?"

"Did you see that?"

"See what?" Tobias slid his phone in his pocket and frowned at the throng. The common lawn was almost unrecognisable, soft grass covered by wooden panels and strings of fairy lights hanging from repurposed farming implements that had been shoved into the ground around the perimeter. To his right, several old crates had been bound together and topped with yet more panels to create a stage, upon which Jacques and Rory were muttering to each other as they tuned their guitars.

People were all over the dance floor, with more arriving every moment. It'd been some time - too long, Tobias thought - since all the pack had gathered in one place. The hum of conversation carried joy, and all around him people were smiling and laughing. He flicked a glance at his second, who wore an uncharacteristically serious expression, and said, "What? For Solaeden's sake, man, spit it out!"

"Sienna!"

With, finally, a little more direction, Tobias began scanning the crowd for Zeke's younger sister. He spotted her towards the back of the dance floor, partially obscured by Sarah Heliope-Flint as she chased little Juliet into the tangle of arms and legs. Sienna was breathtakingly beautiful, golden hair shining underneath the fairy lights and her petite frame clad in a scandalously short, strapless dress that highlighted her slim figure. "Holy shit, she looks incredible."

"I know." Zeke started forwards, leaving Tobias little option but to follow, seeing as his friend still had a strong grip on his arm. "When did she learn to look like that?"

"Like what?"

"Like someone's dessert!"

The crowd parted before them, revealing Jaxon and Dominic wearing equally star-stuck expressions as they stared at the slender creature who'd always been like a sister to them. Sienna was standing with Brayden, the eaglekin dressed immaculately in a pair of black trousers and a deep jade shirt which highlighted his yellow eyes. It was unbuttoned far enough to display a healthy dose of tanned chest and the muscles underneath, giving the formal attire a distinctly roguish cast. Brayden's lips were close to Sienna's ear as he spoke, his face lit with an inner joy that Tobias suspected was his natural demeanour. She nodded once, golden curls bouncing, and blushed a deep shade of crimson as Brayden pressed a kiss to the back of her knuckles and faded into the crowd, heading in the direction of the stage.

Zeke stomped over to Sienna with a face like a thundercloud. "What were you doing?"

"Doing?" Sienna turned a smile like crushed diamonds on her older brother. "Just talking to Brayden. Ash was kind enough to introduce us."

"Where. Is. Ash?"

"Getting us a couple of drinks, last I heard." Sapphire eyes narrowed to slits. "Is that a problem?"

Zeke exhaled sharply between his teeth. "You look -"

"Amazing," Dominic cut in, his gaze openly admiring.

"Gorgeous," Jaxon agreed.

"Well, thanks guys. I didn't think you'd ever notice." In the wake of four jaws dropping in astonishment, Sienna stepped into Zeke's embrace and slid her arms around his neck, drawing his head down until their golden curls mingled. She whispered something in his ear and pressed a kiss to his cheek, then gave Jaxon and Dominic a broad wink and disappeared into the crowd.

"Zeke?" Tobias waved a hand in front of sapphire eyes which were a mirror of Sienna's. "What did she say?"

"She's sworn to Aislinn," Zeke said, then swallowed heavily. "Then she reminded me that she's twenty-four years old, thank you very much, and I can mind my own fucking business or she'll burn my eyebrows off while I sleep."

"She swore to Ash?" Jaxon's eyebrows shot up and he whistled between his teeth. "I've got me a packmate, then."

"You do," Aislinn said from behind them, "And none of you will say a single word to Sienna about anything else, or I'll geld the lot of you."

Tobias turned and felt his heart seize in his chest. She wore a dress of deepest ocean, the colour somewhere between navy and teal, shot through with a brighter thread that shimmered like a mermaid's scales. Multi-layered skirts undulated in the light breeze, affording tantalising glimpses of her legs and the short under-skirt which hugged her thighs. A collection of delicate straps crossed her shoulders and chest, holding the twined fabric in place across her breasts and emphasising the lacework of her scars so that they appeared an elaborate part of the design. The torc shone bright at her throat, accented by glittering silver pins in her partially upswept hair. What remained free of the elegant pinning curled loosely down her back, brushing against her waist and absorbing the ambient light so that it glowed wine-red.

Sparks popped in his vision and Tobias realised he'd stopped breathing. He started again with a frantic inhalation, drowning in the decadent scent of vanilla and honeysuckle which clung to her skin. His chest ached, his fingers itched and yet he couldn't move, couldn't speak. Quite suddenly the charcoal suit pants he hadn't worn for almost five years and the equally elderly black shirt he'd dragged on for the occasion seemed nowhere near enough. They'd only been worn once before but he'd filled out since, his shoulders straining at the seams and the pants slicked to his backside and thighs. Standing in front of the woman who haunted his every moment, Tobias wished he'd gone shopping - though the gaze Aislinn raked across his body was far from disappointed. She paused bare moments from him, catching a handful of his hair and rubbing the strands between her fingers. "You brushed your hair." Her voice was honey, thick and rich, rolling across his skin and seeping into his pores. When he didn't immediately respond she turned her eyes to his, gut-punching him all over again with the sheer intensity in that blue-green gaze. "You okay?"

Somehow, he got his voice working, hoarse though it was. "I've died."

The smile which creased her features was like nothing he'd ever seen before and it stole his breath all over again. Aislinn's chuckle, low and throaty, vibrated in his bones. "You must have; I can't think of anything else momentous enough to get you to brush your hair."

Her fingers were still threaded through said hair but Tobias caught her hand and drew it down to nip at her fingers. "I did it for you."

It sounded silly out loud but her smile only widened. "Then why aren't you letting me play with it some more?"

"Because I might die all over again if you keep touching me," he managed, the words no more than a breathy exhalation. "Lord and Lady, Ash, you're so beautiful I can't believe you're real."

With her heels on, she was almost his eye level and it took less than a tilt of her head for their lips to brush, sending a jolt of electricity down his spine. "Does it feel real now?" Aislinn spoke against his lips, the touch of her skin such a sweet caress that Tobias could only nod. "If this is the reaction I get, I think I'll dress like this more often."

Tobias choked, searching frantically for something - anything - to help restore his equilibrium. "I thought you didn't want to chance people working things out."

"It's come to my attention," Aislinn murmured, her body now close enough that Tobias could feel her warmth seeping into him, "That everyone worth mentioning already knows."

"Not our fathers," he managed, knowing that if Aislinn accidentally gave things away in the heat of the moment, she'd regret it later.

But she smiled, walking the fingers of her free hand across his chest. "They're not here yet."

"Our mothers -"

She silenced him with a kiss, lips pressing firmly against his for a brief, scintillating moment. "Shut up, Tobias Greenwood. You're ruining the moment."

He shut up.

Someone sniggered and Tobias realised with a start that Zeke, Dominic and Jaxon were still with them, though they'd backed up half a pace and positioned their bodies in front of the dance floor, affording he and Aislinn a few moments of - albeit limited - privacy. If you didn't count the three of them staring and grinning like idiots, of course.

"Well?" Aislinn turned to face them, her spine now pressed against his side. "Do feel free to share the joke." They all affected innocent expressions and her grin turned feral. "Oh, don't worry; this time I know what it is - all of you realising what jerks you've been by ignoring an extraordinarily beautiful young woman. Now it's too late and you all miss out. Your loss, Brayden's gain."

Zeke blinked rapidly; Jaxon and Dominic shared astonished glances. Tobias rumbled a laugh, sliding his arm around Aislinn's waist. "You're mean."

"Yeah." She flicked a mischievous glance up at him from beneath criminally long lashes. "But only when it's deserved. Besides, Sienna's mine now. Mine to nurture and mine to protect. So when I say back off," she added, levelling a finger at Zeke, "I mean it."

"I just…" he stammered, choked, then wilted. "I don't want to see her hurt. Dammit, Ash, she's my sister."

"You don't want to see her hurt? Then don't treat her like a child," Aislinn said primly. "We're not humans, with their odd gender biases and funny social etiquette. Yes, Sienna is your sister and yes, you may love her and care for her but she's also an adult. She has hopes and dreams and a perfectly functional vagina that she's allowed to share at her whim."

"Arrrgh," Zeke slapped his hands over his face. "Why did you have to say that?"

"Because you're behaving like a Neanderthal," Aislinn snapped, slipping away from Tobias to prod the second in the chest. Her voice softened, and she nipped playfully at the back of Zeke's wrist. "I know you can do better, big brother. Don't hold her back; help her fly."

"Eagle reference *not* appreciated," Zeke muttered, but he was lowering his hands to reveal a wry smile. He flickered a glance towards the stage, where Brayden was now settling in behind the drum kit. "Is he… nice?"

"The nicest," Aislinn promised, patting Zeke's arm. "Sweet, gentle, a little cheeky, heart bigger than the moon - reminds me a lot of you."

Zeke grunted noncommittally but his eyes sparkled at the compliment. He glanced down after a moment and said; "You've been drinking my booze. I can smell it."

"Damned straight I drank your booze." Aislinn's grin was broad and unrepentant. "How else would Sienna manage to get me dressed up like this? Shame it wears off so fast; I was nervous as a mouse in a cat run when I stepped outside."

"Nervous?" Tobias' jaw dropped. "Why?"

Aislinn sent him a coy look but he knew her too well; vulnerability glittered in the depths of her eyes. "I wasn't sure what you'd think."

"What I'd -" he swallowed his response and shook his head, equally aware of the floored looks on the faces of the other men. "Ash, you're a killer. Surely you know that by now."

She frowned. "Of course I'm a killer. That's what an assassin - oh." A blush crept up her neck and over her cheeks. "Thanks."

Music blared out of the speaker system, a few tentative test riffs from Rory on his bass guitar which were quickly echoed by Jacques' electric. Once the two were satisfied, they launched into a familiar tune, joined by Brayden on the drums. Tobias watched as a tall, imposing figure of a man stepped onto the stage, silken black hair falling forward into his eyes. He wore tight jeans and a black t-shirt which had been splattered with bleach to mimic the spray of blood. Recognising the clothes as ones Zeke had worn as a lanky teen, Tobias squinted at the man approaching the microphone and spotted a familiar spiked collar around his neck. "Is that *Flynn*?"

"Looks different in clothes, doesn't he?" Aislinn chuckled. "Now get a load of this."

The tigerkin, looking more Bad Boy with a capital B than Tobias had seen thus far, snatched the microphone off the stand as though personally offended by it. Jacques and Rory switched their song to one of Tobias' - and therefore likely Aislinn's - favourites and a few beats later, Flynn began to sing.

It was… everything.

Tobias knew he would never in his life hear another voice like it; sweet, haunting, with delicious danger stalking every syllable. It struck a chord deep in his soul and judging by the murmurs of everyone else on the dance floor, he was not the only one.

"How?" He bent to press his lips to Aislinn's ear. "How is he doing that?"

"I don't know." Aislinn shook her head, eyes glistening as she watched the man onstage. "Sometimes I think it's got something to do with his ability to call animals, sometimes I think it's the gods' idea of a joke to put the voice of an angel into the body of a devil. It's probably both."

Tobias shook his head in quiet disbelief, watching as Flynn closed his eyes and gave himself over to the music. For the first song, people simply stared in spellbound silence but as the tigerkin continued flawlessly into another, there began to be movement on the dance floor. "Why does he hate it so much?" Tobias asked as Aislinn drew him into the crowd, coaxing his arms around her body.

"He doesn't hate singing; he used to sing the urchins to sleep all the time," Aislinn returned, smiling at the expression on his face. "What he hates is the attention it garners."

"Flynn, hating attention?" Tobias flicked a glance at the tigerkin, whose eyes were still squeezed shut as his mesmerising voice rolled out across the common lawn. "I don't believe it."

"Believe it." Aislinn fidgeted and then finally jabbed him in the ribs. "Are you *really* still such a terrible dancer?"

"I'm afraid so."

"How the hell did you woo unsuspecting women in the pubs and clubs? And don't bother telling me you didn't," she added, raising an eyebrow.

"You already know I did, so why would I bother lying?" Tobias snorted, slowing even further as he thought about it. "I never needed to dance. They just sort of… appeared."

Aislinn rolled her eyes. "I suppose you *are* pretty enough to draw attention but really, I can't believe they didn't make you work for it at least a little!"

"You make it sound like there was a horde," Tobias protested, unable to stop the heat creeping over his cheeks. "There was only a few, Ash. It got old pretty quickly when I realised none of them were ever going to be you."

He shouldn't have said that out loud but she didn't seem to mind. In fact, a gentle blush stole across her cheeks and for a few moments, they stood completely still, both as embarrassed as teenagers on a first date.

"Hey! You call that dancing?" Stephanie bumped into them from behind, her eyes alight with mischief. "Stop mooning and dance with her properly, Tobias."

"Sorry." He tugged Aislinn close again, the movements still frightfully awkward. Her toes clunked against his, her face twisting into a look of such complete resignation that Tobias couldn't help but laugh - and then, because it was so rare that he was able to surprise her with anything, he adjusted his grip and swept Aislinn through the crowd with a fluidity that had her gasping. "What I have discovered, though, is that fighting's an awful lot like dancing; and fighting I am *definitely* good at."

"Tobias!" Aislinn squealed in delight as he swept her feet out from under her - literally - caught her with a firm hand on the back of her neck and scooped her upright. "How many of those other women fell for this little trick of yours?"

"I haven't done this with anyone else," he answered, allowing a hint of fang to tint his smile. "They'd all run screaming if I told them a take-down is a lot like a tango."

"Not me."

"No," he agreed, brushing a thumb over her cheek. "Not you."

Aislinn's eyes were bright as Tobias drew her closer, their bodies moving in perfect synchronicity as he twisted less like a dancer and more like a martial artist. It worked - and being the consummate warrior that she was, Aislinn had no problem keeping up with him. In fact, her laughter only grew as they dipped and spun and ducked together. "It's like sparring! Only better."

"It came about by accident," Tobias admitted. "Zeke likes to play loud music while we train and after a while I realised they kind of went together. I've just never had a willing victim - I mean partner - before."

Tobias ducked the laughing elbow she swung his way, tightening his arm and dragging Aislinn against his chest. Flynn's voice slid smoothly sideways into a soft ballad, the instruments fading out until the tigerkin's crooning melody was the only thing breaking the softly approaching night. She stopped her playful struggle and Tobias' heart hitched, the rest of the world dropping away as Aislinn's hands linked around his neck, her body soft and forgiving against the hard lines of his.

Quite suddenly there was no today, no tomorrow; no bears, no war, no scars and no separation. There was only the two of them, foreheads touching, eyes shining and breath mingling in the golden light of the Australian sunset.

*******

When Flynn's voice faded and Aislinn surfaced from the hazy dream in which she'd found herself, her heart was thumping and her body incredibly sensitive. Tobias' hands felt like brands upon her skin, the heat of his presence a blanket she couldn't have escaped if she wanted to. She barely registered the stage clearing to make room for Andre and Rupert, who both gave quiet, short speeches before announcing dinner.

Tobias led her to the trestle table and Aislinn filled her plate mechanically, unable to look away from the play of fairy lights over bronze skin. The soft fall of his golden-brown hair called to her until Aislinn's fingers tightened around the edge of her plate in an effort not to indulge.

"Do you want to find somewhere quieter to sit and eat?" His voice was velvet in her ears, a throaty rumble unlike anything she'd yet heard. Startled by her body's response, Aislinn could barely nod her agreement. She was, she reflected, still in heat, the pressure building again already. A pressure that would need alleviating unless she wanted her father to notice and take it as some sort of unholy signal that Percy's ridiculous solution was the right one.

The thought poured ice over her dreamy thoughts, bringing Aislinn well and truly back to reality as she followed Tobias to a shadowy gap between two houses. He sat cross legged as the first strains of music broke out; no longer that of the band but a stereo system instead. Aislinn dropped down on the grass beside him and settled her plate in her lap. "Looks like the formal part of the evening is over."

"Most of the pack are either young or old enough to prefer an early bedtime," Tobias answered, his smile lopsided as he poked roast beef into a bread roll. He caught her raised eyebrow and paused. "What?"

"You literally have to make everything into a sandwich, don't you?"

"No, I - oh."

"It's okay," she said when he looked torn. "I won't tell."

"Thanks." Tobias grinned and continued cramming as much of his roast dinner as possible into the roll before squashing it firmly into shape and stuffing half of it into his mouth in one bite. Aislinn snorted a quiet laugh and began picking at her own meal, watching Tobias out of the corner of her eye while her face was tilted towards the rest of the pack. She thought the silence was companionable enough until he set aside his empty plate, captured her fingers in his and tugged gently. "Tell me."

"Tell you what?"

"What's causing that face." He inclined his head in her direction. "It's the thinking face - and not the fun thinking face, either; the pensive one."

"You have names for my faces?"

Tobias' expression took on a curious intensity that had her heart suddenly racing. "Of course I have names for all your faces. Now tell me what's on your mind."

"Tobias, I -"

"Miss Redding, how unusual to see you looking so very relaxed." Professor Postlethwaite's reedy voice preceded him out of the shadows to their left, where he had ostensibly been sheltering beneath the porch of the nearest house. He wore the same tweed on tweed suit as earlier, though he'd made the outfit more formal by adding a gold pocket watch on a chain and a bowler hat, which was currently clasped under one arm. The owlkin raked dirty golden eyes over Tobias and added; "Mister Greenwood. What a surprise."

"Your sarcasm needs work, Percy." Aislinn sighed, subtly disengaging her fingers from Tobias' and leaning back on one arm. "Won't you join us, since that's obviously the point?"

The Professor regarded the grass with a look so icily condescending it was a wonder the individual blades didn't break out in a sudden case of frost. After a long moment, he pulled a handkerchief out of his waistcoat pocket, spread it on the ground and sat with a grace that reminded Aislinn that, for all his faults, the Professor was still a predatory Kin.

"Thank you. I did indeed wish to speak with you, though I'd have preferred it be alone." Percy shot a second sharp look in Tobias' direction.

"It's a shame, isn't it," Tobias drawled, leaning back on his hands in a pose to mirror Aislinn's, "Realising we can't always have what we want."

The Professor tsked in the back of his throat, then turned to face Aislinn in summary dismissal of the alpha by her side. "I've come to discuss your treatment, Miss Redding. I should like to make a start as soon as possible."

"My *treatment*?"

Percy nodded, his eyes fever-bright. "Indeed. As it will be several days before we reach my laboratory, where work can begin in earnest, I should like to set up an interim schedule. I require high resolution images of your Marking and all relevant scarring as soon as possible; I had thought to arrange Gerard to take them tomorrow morning, when the light is best. I also need blood, urine, saliva and vaginal secretion samples from you on a regular basis - perhaps three times a day - which will allow me to assess how deeply the process has altered your cells since your return from Ireland and how quickly the bear's influence is spreading through your genes. Once we return to my facility, I shall compare the strength of your possession to known Alpha males on file and we can begin the selection process -"

"No." Aislinn's voice vibrated with enough menace that Percy ceased his zealous ramblings to blink at her in confusion.

"No? Is tomorrow morning too early a start?"

"No, as in, *no*. I will not provide pictures or samples, I will not look over potential candidates and I will certainly not be accompanying you to your research facility," she growled, making a cutting motion with her free hand. "No."

Shock turned Percy's face so comically still that for a sudden, insane moment, Aislinn wanted to laugh. Then his brow furrowed, fingers curling around the brim of his hat. "Surely there must be a misunderstanding; my project has already been approved."

"That's not how it sounded in Grandma's lounge earlier - it was put to me as a suggestion."

Percy waved that away. "A formality. The paperwork was completed and signed by your father before we even left Ireland."

A chill puckered Aislinn's skin. Yes, her father was more than capable of doing exactly what the Professor had said, signing away her rights as he'd done so many times - wait. She frowned, drew a careful breath into her lungs. Sorting through the pressing scents of the pack and their party, she focussed on the particular brand of earl grey associated with Percy. Her hackles smoothed as she found it edged with bitterness, as though someone had steeped the tea too long and bought the tannins to the surface.

Professor Percival Postlethwaite was lying.

Tilting her head to the side, Aislinn allowed her lips to quirk in a smile that was anything but friendly. "Was the paperwork formalised before or after Flynn and I wrecked the hospital?"

"I fail to see why that's important," Percy humphed. When she remained silent, he sighed. "Before. It hasn't been rescinded, however, and your father still agreed upon my inclusion in this little excursion. I feel the proof, as they say, is in the pudding."

"My father," Aislinn returned evenly, "Doesn't own me."

"If you're referring to the fact that he is no longer your Alpha, then yes, you are most correct." Percy adjusted his glasses, face schooled once more into professorly calm. "However, he *is* also the wolfkin representative to the Council and as such, retains a secondary authority over you."

She raised an eyebrow. "Done your homework, I see."

"Of course." A quick nod. "So, what time tomorrow -"

"I said no, Percy."

"Miss Redding, I thought we just established the sort of authority your father holds over you as a Councillor," Percy returned, his attempt at a chiding tone slipping beneath brisk impatience.

"We did," Aislinn nodded. "Go and get him to order me to do as you ask."

"I beg your pardon?" Percy's spine stiffened.

Aislinn sat up, dusting her palms against one another. "You heard me; go and get my father. I want to hear him request samples of my *vaginal secretions* with his own mouth."

"You want him to -" Percy plumped himself up in a credible human imitation of a flustered chicken, his face aghast. "What a preposterous thing to suggest."

"Is it?" Aislinn chuckled, deep and dark, reaching out to pick up the plastic knife from her discarded paper plate. "Did you know there are forty-seven different ways to remove a pair of testicles with plastic cutlery?"

Percy frowned down at the knife in question. "That is the most ridiculous fictional theorem I've ever heard."

"No more unbelievable than the threat of my father's authority when you don't actually have it," Aislinn returned, allowing death to stalk her words. "I can smell lies, little bird. So, whose theory would you like to test? Yours..." she flicked the knife through her fingers, "... or mine?"

Percy's face turned red as he watched the plastic knife move. "Do you have any idea what sort of a scientific opportunity this is? Think of all the Kin you could help with your sacrifice."

"Since I'm a unique and heretofore impossible case, the only Kin I can see benefitting from this opportunity is you, once you garner whatever accolades you've got stored in your imagination." Aislinn flipped the knife up in the air and caught it in a grip that was consummately professional. "I'm going to count to three, Perce. And in that time, you're either gone, or losing the ability to reproduce."

"How *dare* you." Percy turned to Tobias. "You there, apprentice. Do something."

Tobias stared back, his face implacable.

Aislinn bared her teeth. "One."

"This is unacceptable! I am the head of the Council's paranormal research branch," Percy expostulated, shaking a finger under Tobias' nose. "And I'm here by the grace of your senior Alpha. If I order it, you're honour-bound to hold Miss Redding down while I extract my samples."

Tobias' knuckles whitened but he didn't move from his relaxed position. "Two."

"*What?*" Percy leapt upright, snatching his handkerchief from the ground in panic. "She's counting, not you!"

"And I," Tobias murmured softly, "am hers."

Aislinn unfolded with a predator's fluidity. "Three, Percy."

With a speed astonishing for a man of his build, the owlkin disappeared across the common lawn, leaving a trail of reedy curses in his wake. Tobias' throaty chuckle wrapped Aislinn in a warm cloak and a moment later he, too, was on his feet, one arm draped around her shoulders. "Shame he didn't hang about. I was looking forward to your demonstration."

"Hmmm." Percy's words echoed through her head, over and over. Staring down at the knife in her hand, Aislinn squeezed it so tightly the plastic shattered, just like the illusions she'd allowed to cloak her in the last few days.

"Hey." Tobias' fingers were soft around hers as he prised them open, the remnants of the knife fluttering to the ground like confetti. "You know I'd never have let him go through with it, right? I just figured you'd prefer to defend yourself."

Aislinn glanced up at him, concern burning in his gold and blue eyes. "I'm not worried about Percy. I could take him with my eyes shut."

"Then what-"

"You're not mine." She swallowed the razors in her throat, forced the words out. "Not really. You belong to Andre and the Redding Pack."

His face stormed over immediately. "I belong to *you*."

"You might think so," Aislinn said softly. "But what Percy said was true; you're under the pack's banner. If my father ordered you to hold me down while Percy extracted those samples, you'd be bound by law to do so."

Tobias' arm turned to steel across her shoulders and after a moment's long, loaded silence, he dragged her back into the trees, his grip tightening until it felt more like a headlock than an embrace. When she opened her mouth to protest, he growled; "Quiet," with such trembling fury that Aislinn obeyed.

When they arrived at the watering hole, the still surface of the pool reflecting the rising moon, Tobias released his grip and stalked away from her, both hands shoved into the pockets of his pants. He swore as he went, kicking off his shoes and then tearing his shirt over his head, throwing it into the trees with sharp, angry movements. Aislinn watched in fascination as the peculiar magic of twilight made the muscles in his back gleam, his shoulders broad and strong as he wriggled tight pants down over his hips, revealing the luscious curve of a backside that took her breath away. After discarding said pants in similar fashion to the clothing that had gone before it, Tobias dove into the water with barely a ripple. He swam to the opposite side and back again, cresting the surface to stare up at Aislinn with blue and gold eyes that glittered in fury.

"Either take your dress off," he snarled, "or you're going in fully clothed."

Startled - and intrigued - Aislinn's hands moved to the straps of her dress. She began to slip them from her shoulders, cheeks heating as Tobias' gaze remained locked on her face. She hesitated and cleared her throat. "I don't know if I can get it off by myself."

The golden starbursts in his eyes flared brighter and a moment later, water sheeted off his magnificent body as Tobias hauled himself out of the pool and padded to her side. His fingers were deft as he found the hidden zipper and slid it down, his touch gentle in spite of the way his jaw was clenched so tightly the tendons stood out on his neck. Being undressed in such a manner was an intimacy Aislinn had never experienced and in spite of his obvious temper, she felt her thighs clench in sudden need.

Tobias' soft growl said he'd scented her body but he made no move to accept the silent invitation, continuing to peel and tug at the dress until it puddled on the ground at her feet. Aislinn heard the catch in his breath as he sighted her lacy underwear, his roughened fingers trailing across one hip - and then she gasped as Tobias swept her up in his arms.

"If I jump in that water," he said, the words clipped, "Are you going to lose your mind again?"

"I don't think so," Aislinn said quietly. "Not if it's with you."

Rather than assuaging his temper, she saw the fresh spark of anger in Tobias' eyes as he stepped backwards into the water. The cool liquid closed over their heads almost immediately but, as she'd theorised, Aislinn remained safe and sane in his steely grip. When they surfaced, the cool stone bordering the waterhole pressed into Aislinn's back and Tobias' chest shoved against her front. Clutching at his shoulders for balance, it was instinct to wrap her legs around his waist, his warmth steadying and unsettling all at the same time.

She was completely and utterly unprepared when his mouth descended on hers, his kiss violent and raw, his hands gripping the ledge on either side of her head. When Tobias at last broke away, it was to glare down at her from blazing eyes, his face set in an expression of incandescent fury - and hurt, Aislinn realised. She opened her mouth to speak, but he beat her to it.

"I've known you since the moment you first drew breath. I followed you from the moment I could walk. I bathed in your laughter, brushed away your tears. I fell in love with you under the stars, running through the trees, swimming in this very water, rolling on the grass. I loved you while we laughed, I loved you while we fought. I loved you while you grew and after you'd gone, that love tore a hole inside of me until I knew I'd never be complete without you." Tobias drew a deep breath, face set in harsh, implacable lines. "I hated you when you came back stinking of bear - because I loved you so much I thought I'd die if I didn't have you and I couldn't stand the thought of losing you to someone else. I loved you without your scars, I love you with them and I loved you when you couldn't love yourself. I loved you while I was inside you, I loved you while you slept. I am desperately, impossibly in love with you, Aislinn Jaide Redding, and I will continue to love you until the stars have burned clean through the sky and the heavens are crying for their loss. So don't ever - *ever* -" he thumped both fists against the rock, hard enough to send shards of stone flying free, "question my loyalty like that again. Because whatever you think I owe the pack, the Council, the fucking *world*, is nothing compared to what I feel for you. To what I would *do* for you. Do you understand?" He was breathing hard as he finished, tears mingling with water across the sculpted planes of his cheeks. Aislinn didn't need a mirror to know her own face was wet with emotion, her heart twisted fit to breaking point.

"I'm sorry, Tobias." And then, because she didn't know what else to say, "You're my heartmate; I would never hurt you on purpose. I -"

Tobias cut her off with another kiss, less violent but more passionate. His chest shuddered against hers and Aislinn realised with a shock that he was crying in earnest, tears slick against her face even as his body hardened. He broke the kiss on a sob. "You know."

"I know," she managed and he kissed her again, a frantic clash of lips and teeth and tongues that only served to back up the enormity of the emotion he'd just laid at her feet. "I'm sorry, Tobias. I am. But what he said -"

*"No."*

Aislinn paused, stared into the furious agony of his face, and let go her doubts. "I love you, too."

A strangled cry slipped his lips and Tobias released his grip on the ledge to wrap both arms around her body, one fist in her hair and the other broad and strong down the length of her spine. They slid under the water locked against one another, combined body heat overpowering the chill shock of being completely submerged. Tobias pushed them back up to the surface with a strong kick, a different kind of emotion playing across his face. "I need you. I need to be inside of you."

Unlocking her legs, Aislinn wriggled until the lace panties were in her hand and re-wrapped herself around his waist. "Do it."

"I -"

"I need you inside me, too." The sentence ended on a strangled shout as Tobias thrust his hips upward and buried himself to the hilt, catching at the edge of the pool with one hand whilst he kept the other locked around her waist. Aislinn tried to move against him but his grip was firm, his eyes serious. "What?"

"This isn't… I want…"

"Be tender later," she growled, desire a molten fist inside of her. "Make wild love to me *now*."

"We're making this a habit," Tobias muttered - but began moving nonetheless, deep, desperate strokes inside her body that had Aislinn biting her lip in an effort not to scream her ecstasy to the moon. They were both close to the edge already, the tendons standing out in Tobias' neck as he fought for control, his cock thickening inside her with every glorious stroke. Unable to deny herself the temptation of his flesh, Aislinn bit down on the curve of Tobias' shoulder. His muscles locked immediately, his release triggering her own - and as stars danced behind her eyes and Tobias emptied his body inside of hers, Aislinn surrendered her heart into his keeping.

# Fourteen

Tobias hauled them both out of the pool and flopped down on his back in the grass. Aislinn sprawled across his chest, resting her chin on crossed wrists while water dripped from her hair to run in rivulets over his skin. "You didn't try to bond us."

Tobias raised an eyebrow. "Aside from the fact that I was a two stroke wonder just now, do you really think I'd try something like that without asking? I love you, I don't own you."

Warmth bloomed in her blue-green gaze. "Say that again."

"I. Love. You." Propping a finger under her chin and tilting her head up, Tobias glared with everything in him, his alpha energy colliding with her own in a shower of sparks. "If and when we mate, it'll be by conscious choice. I won't take that from you - from us."

Aislinn bared her teeth, pretending to bite. Her breath raised goose bumps over his skin but Tobias refused to be distracted, shoving at her power with his own until she smiled. "All right, all right. Forgive me for being a little jumpy; it's been a long twelve years. I've got the bad habit of assuming everyone has an ulterior motive."

"That's because they probably do." Tobias gave her a smile that did nothing to disguise the rub against his pride. "Don't get me wrong, Ash - I want you. And this thing with Olaf, this hold he has on you? It terrifies me. If Professor Postlethwaite's transitional theory is valid, then we could be in very real trouble. The man might be a category nine asshole, but he seems dedicated to his science."

"Yes, but in this case, Percy doesn't have all the information - and I'm not about to give it to him, either." Aislinn's expression turned thoughtful. "A heartmate connection is the strongest bond Kin have. My gut says it'd overpower Olaf's one way Marking, transition or otherwise."

"Are you sure?"

"No." She smiled; a crooked smile that took twelve years off her face and sent Tobias straight back to his teenage fantasies. Just as quickly, it was gone, and he stared into the gaze of a woman who'd seen far too much. "I love you, Tobias, but I'm still broken. If we tried to mate and it didn't work, I don't know if I'd recover."

Trying to swallow around the knot of emotion in his throat proved all but impossible. Tobias settled instead for brushing Aislinn's damp hair back from her face with a trembling hand while he waited for his voice to return. "Is there some way we can look into it without alerting Percy?"

Aislinn leant into his caress, her lashes drifting closed. "I might be able to call in a few favours and get my hands on a more powerful measuring device. If we could track the surges in your power and map them out, we'd get a better idea of whether the mating would be viable."

"How soon can you make the call?" Tobias tried not to sound too eager, but judging from the twitch of Aislinn's lips, he'd failed spectacularly.

"After tomorrow's meeting; everyone will be too distracted to monitor my calls." She opened her eyes, vulnerability swirling in the blue-green depths. "I can't make any promises, Tobias. As a damper I can sense your energy has the potential to be huge, but it's impossible to detect when it'll surge or ebb away. Without a measuring instrument -"

"It's okay," he cut her off with a finger over her lips, grinned when she bit it. "I understand. What do you need from me in the meantime?"

"Peace, love and an endless supply of ice cream?"

"Done." Tobias stared up at the emerging stars above them, hope flaring hot and sharp in his gut. Determined to be patient, he twined a strand of her red-tinted hair around one finger and shifted the topic sideways. "We should talk about our fathers."

"They can't know about us. Not yet." Aislinn's palms smoothed along his collarbone, her soft energy gentling his. The darkness deepened around them as the blue sparks created by their frantic coupling winked out one by one. "I have no idea what Dad's plan is but I'm willing to bet the two of us working as a team isn't it."

"They did arrange for you to come home," Tobias pointed out. "Surely that's worth something?"

"They were forced into that, and you know it." Aislinn's face darkened. "If Dad finds out we're heartmates, there's no telling what he'd do."

"Wouldn't my father try to stop him? He's a second, after all."

"He might try; he'd likely fail. You have to understand that Rupert's a good General but a terrible second," she replied, kissing his sternum in an attempt to soften the words. "He won't stand up to Andre the way a second should."

"Because of love, or fear?"

"Love - but in this instance, I think it's fear born of love," Aislinn said quietly, pity softening her voice. "After the peace summit bombing, Dad changed. He became obsessed with catching the bearkin, to the point where he walked such a fragile mental tightrope everyone treated him with kid gloves."

"Everyone?" He couldn't resist teasing.

She snorted a laugh. "Okay, everyone except Flynn and I. I'm sure Rupert thought, in the beginning, that if he gave Andre space and support, he'd come around. Now, they're both in too deep to turn back. I often wonder what Rupert sees when he closes his eyes at night; what nightmares haunt him." Aislinn met his gaze, a knowing glint in her eye. "Zeke would never let you turn into that. Nor would I, for that matter."

Tobias remembered the towering, vicious rage that had gripped him when Aislinn had first returned, the way Zeke had cajoled, threatened and glared him out of doing anything truly stupid. With a slow blink, he cleared those nebulous fears from his mind and looked up at the woman so warm and deadly above him. "I meant what I said in the watering hole, you know. I'm yours."

"Dad will challenge you on that."

"Let him." Tobias shrugged, tracing her cheekbone with his thumb. "If you think we should bide our time, then we will - but we can't hide the truth forever."

"I don't want to hide it forever; just until we understand Dad's motives." She crinkled her nose. "The mood he's in, he'd charge you with treason for looking at me wrong."

He gave Aislinn a wicked grin. "I've been looking at you wrong for years and nobody's noticed it yet."

"Given that I was the last of our group to work out how you felt, I'd say that's the biggest lie you've ever told yourself."

*Where are you?* Flynn's voice crashed into Tobias' thoughts with a ferocity that made his eyes roll in his head. *Kaira's down.*

Aislinn shimmered against his skin and quite suddenly Tobias held an auburn-furred wolf in his arms. *Gentle, dammit!*

*Sorry - it's the fucking singing that does it.* Flynn's voice quieted at once, no longer a bludgeon across their senses. *Better?*

*Yes. Where's Kaira?*

*Lena says...* Flynn paused, and Tobias took advantage of the silence to shift into his own wolf form, his sandy brown fur mingling with Aislinn's where she still sprawled atop him. *About a third of the way round the patrol route, at the base of a cliff. Something about a hollowed out tree trunk.*

*We know where it is.* Aislinn nuzzled briefly at Tobias' jaw, then rolled to her feet. *Where are you?*

*In the fruit orchard,* the tigerkin answered.

*We're closer.* Tobias flipped upright and gave himself a shake, settling his fur into place. *Keep an eye on the rest of the pack, in case this is a diversion.*

*Will do - call if you need backup.*

It only took a few minutes to reach the location Flynn had described. The cliffs that formed a protective border around one edge of pack land rose steep and stark beside them, a dark outline against the clear southern skies. Tobias paused beside the hollowed out trunk of a tree that had once been so large it'd take two of him to get his arms around it, raised his nose to the cooling air and sniffed.

Night-time, eucalyptus, earth... Kaira's honey and orange blossom scent, mingled with an odd chemical smell. Tranqs, he realised, lips peeling back from his teeth. Aislinn, her pose mirroring his, let out a sub vocal grunt. When he looked her way, she waved a paw at the surrounding area, nipped his shoulder and made her way deeper into the shadows of the cliff. A moment later Tobias heard the soft huskiness of her voice, answered by the sturdier rumble of Lena.

Leaving the two women to tend their fallen friend, Tobias did as she'd asked and began a methodical back and forth of the immediate area. He found the place where Kaira had been tranqed, evidenced by the heavier layer of her scent and the sharp tint of pain in the air surrounding it. Lena's lavender and sandalwood also lingered but try though he might, Tobias could find no evidence of an intruder.

Aislinn stepped out of the shadows in human form and Tobias shifted as he went to meet her. "How is she?"

"No actual injuries, just sedatives." Aislinn wrinkled her nose as she surveyed the area, a used tranq dart dangling from her fingers. "I only smell the four of us."

"Agreed. They had to be either up on the cliffs or in one of the trees." Tobias held his breath a moment, hesitant to voice his next thought. "Lena -"

"I already asked," she said, tapping her nose. "She had nothing to do with it."

Relieved, Tobias nodded. "Bearkin, then?"

"Seems most likely." Aislinn paused, chewing on her lower lip. "Kaira's an Iberian lynx. Similar size to my wolf form, with big enough ears and a bushy enough tail that in the dark and from a distance, a mistake is more than possible."

Understanding struck. "Olaf said he wanted you alive. He could've planned the psychic attack earlier to weaken you, then sent his men in for abduction."

"Yes." Aislinn looked toward the top of the cliff. "Stay here."

Without giving him a chance to protest, she dematerialised and streamed off into the night, a shadow among shadows. Tobias propped one hand on his hip and blew out between clenched teeth. "Dammit, Ash."

"Annoying, isn't it?" Lena's low voice preceded her out of the darkness, her ebony skin kissed by the moonlight until it shone. "I've only known Aislinn a few months but in that time, I've witnessed her flout regulations on countless occasions, jeopardising not only her own safety but that of others."

"And?"

Sensing the thinly veiled temper in his tone, Lena's teeth flashed white in the dark. "Every one of those times has resulted in a successful mission which would likely otherwise have become disaster."

"Sounds about right." Tobias' lips crooked in the corner. "She's always been like that, right from the day she was born."

Lena's eyes flashed with humour. "I'm not surprised. I thought at first she was reckless, but I've since come to realise that her mind is sharp enough to process information and reach conclusions very quickly."

A huff of laughter tickled Tobias' ears and a moment later, Aislinn rematerialised beside him, her body flowing together like so much midnight smoke. It was different to what he'd learnt to notice before, a more detailed glimpse behind the curtain of her powers. Something inside him stretched, reaching… and then recoiled as if slapped.

"Tobias?" Aislinn's cool fingers on his face, her eyes narrowed in the dark. "What is it? Do you need-"

"I'm fine," he cut her off gently, capturing the slender fingers on his jaw and pressing a soft kiss to her knuckles. "Just a headache. Did you find anything?"

"No." Irritation turned her voice to gravel and Aislinn stomped over to Kaira's inert body. "No scent trail, no evidence of a stake out, nothing. It makes no sense."

"The wind, perhaps?" Lena tipped her head back to stare at the top of the cliff. "It's strong enough to carry a scent away."

Aislinn shook her head. "There's enough vegetation up there that a scent should've lingered. I checked the nearby trees, too. Nothing."

"Strange," Tobias mused, moving to join her. "Bears - in either form - would be far too big to conceal their scents completely."

Aislinn exhaled through gritted teeth. "Whoever it was, they're long gone."

Tobias stared down at the lynx on the ground. Pale tawny fur broken by black spots covered a sleek body that, whilst distinctly smaller than many predatorial cats, was just as deadly. Kaira's tufted ears were overly large and pointed, her face framed by an elegant, black-furred ruff which tapered down to a point either side of her jaw. "I've never seen a lynx like this before."

"Iberian lynxes are endangered in the wild and Kin versions of them are also rare," Aislinn answered. "Kaira inherited this form from her Spanish mother, who works in animal conservation. She's a warrior too, in her own way."

At that moment Kaira stirred, lashes flicking up to reveal night-glow eyes of a gold-tinted green. She tried to move, muscles tensing, and ended up barely twitching her whiskers. A growl echoed in her throat but it was angry rather than afraid, the glare she turned up to Aislinn indignant.

"Tranq darts," Aislinn answered, holding up one of the projectiles. "I've found two so far. Any more?"

A grunt that had Aislinn performing another, more thorough search of the soft-furred body at her feet. When she removed a third tranquilliser, her face dark with fury, Tobias said; "They didn't know how many they needed."

She nodded. "Seems less and less like bearkin to me - Olaf is nothing if not intelligent."

"If not them, then who?" Lena asked.

"I don't know." Aislinn clenched the dart in her fist for a long moment, lips pursed. "For now, we pretend it's the bears. Whoever's really behind this might make a mistake born in arrogance."

"You have suspicions?" Tobias asked, recognising the glint in her eye.

"Nothing more than my imagination at this point." Aislinn feathered her fingers through Kaira's fur. "We need to get you up. Want me to carry you?"

Before the lynxkin had an opportunity to answer, two wolves loped out of the bush; one a sleekly muscled creature with a coat of ash blond and the other smaller, more vicious looking, with a shaggy coat of silver-streaked brown.

The newcomers stopped ten paces away as Aislinn's growl - no less effective coming from her human throat - echoed in the night. The rangier wolf peeled his lips back and growled in return, but the subtle air of command surrounding him was as nothing compared to the towering wall of energy that Tobias and Aislinn shared.

Andre melted into human form. "We're here to take over the watch. Report."

"One soldier down but recovering," Tobias returned, gesturing towards Kaira. "The rest of the pack are safe back at the settlement."

Andre gave a crisp nod, brown eyes trained on Tobias' face. After a few moments of unbroken staring, the older alpha grunted to the wolf by his side. Rupert shimmered into his human form and snapped off a crisp salute. "Area's clear."

"I'd expect nothing less," Andre replied coolly, "From my junior Alpha."

Tobias didn't as much as blink at the backhanded compliment. Instead, he looked over his shoulder to where Aislinn and Lena stood guard over a recovering Kaira. "I'll see our wounded safely to Jemima's and arrange for double patrol rotations. One pack member, one squad member at all times."

"Agreed." Andre stepped back on that single word and returned to his wolf form, melting into the dark as though he'd never been.

"Any news on the meeting yet?" Rupert's voice, holding a surprisingly tentative note. Tobias turned to find his father standing at military rest position, his hands clenched tightly to fists.

"No."

"Perhaps we should -"

"I'll pass on word when I have it."

A shadow passed over Rupert's face but it was impossible to decipher in the dark, so Tobias didn't bother. A moment later, his father nodded, returned to his own wolf form and loped off into the bush.

Aislinn appeared at his side a moment later, eyes trained on the place where their fathers had disappeared from sight. At the precise moment that they passed beyond range of his senses, she sighed. "Dad's pissed."

"How can you tell?"

"Because I know him. Rupert tried to warn you, too - you weren't submissive enough."

"I'm not submissive at all," Tobias growled. Quiet, yes. A pushover? No. Not even before he'd woken one day to find the hormones of an alpha surging through his veins. "I've helped Grandma Redding run this pack for over a decade."

"Something my father expects you to put aside the instant he walks into the room," she reminded him. "He'll be looking for any excuse to take you down a peg or two."

Tobias shrugged, less interested in internal politics than he was in Kaira's safety. "Is she ready to travel?"

"Yes. We'll head to Jemima's like you said, and then I need to pay my mother a visit." Aislinn grimaced. "I promised."

"I know." Tobias brushed a kiss across the tip of her nose. "I'll see you at home, then."

Her answering smile lit up his night. "Fair warning; I'll probably have Flynn in tow."

"Of course you will." Tobias sighed but there was no real frustration in it. "Damn tigerkin's the worst cockblocker I've ever met."

A short, wicked laugh. "I'm going to tell him you said that."

"I'm counting on it."

********

Marguerite was waiting with Jemima when they arrived at the Smythe's cottage. Leaving Kaira and Lena with Tobias and the pack's medic, Aislinn borrowed a wrap-around robe and motioned her mother outside. "Zeke said you wanted to talk."

"You're angry with me. I suppose I deserve it." She sighed, her shoulders hunched. "Would you believe I didn't know about your father's deception?"

"I can smell lies, Mum - I already know you weren't aware." Aislinn pressed her lips together, staring at a white rose with such intensity it was any wonder the bloom didn't wilt under the pressure. "I'm not angry at you directly so much as by association."

Marguerite tugged nervously at what remained of the elegant chignon she'd worn to the picnic. "I only wanted you to see the world, to get a taste for it."

"The problem is, you didn't think about what I wanted." Aislinn shook her head. "You forced me to go, and in doing so, you took me *away* from my world."

A sharp breath. "You cannot ever say that in front of your father. He will weaponise it."

"I know." Aislinn smiled and, since she knew her mother was too frightened to bridge the gap, tugged the older woman into a hug. "It's all right, Mum."

The night was softer for a few minutes, Marguerite's slender frame shaking with silent emotion. "I have a favour to ask. If you're not using your room, would you mind if I slept there?"

Aislinn noted the shadows beneath her mother's eyes and the way she hugged her arms to her chest as though to soothe an ache. Underneath it all, however, lay a thread of steel. She raised an eyebrow. "By yourself?"

"Stephanie's staying with me tonight - but yes, once she makes up with Rupert, I'll be by myself." Marguerite drew a deep, shuddering breath. "I cannot accept the man your father has become. I started to realise it the day he locked you in hospital and wouldn't let me visit - and I knew for sure the day I gave Flynn your phone and begged him to keep you safe."

Aislinn stiffened at the undertone in her mother's words. "Did Dad hurt you?"

"No, but I think the fact that we both assumed he would says enough," Marguerite murmured. "Your father hasn't crossed that line but he's crossed so many others that I don't know him anymore."

"You're thinking about breaking the mating, aren't you?"

"Yes, though not immediately." Marguerite frowned, elegant even in her distress. "I need some time to think before that happens, and look into the legal implications. The pack's suffered enough without me causing more chaos."

"Those aren't good reasons to stay in a toxic relationship and you know it," Aislinn snapped, narrowing her eyes.

Marguerite stared off into the night for a long moment. "I suppose I like to think that maybe, just maybe, he'll wake up and fight for me. Foolish, but until I'm ready to let the notion go, we'll stay mated."

"Take my room and anything else you need." Aislinn tightened her grip on her mother and pressed a kiss to her temple. "I love you, Mum."

"I love you too, sweetheart."

They lingered together as the stars burned above, standing silent in the roses with fingers interlinked. In the end, her heart a painful lump in her throat, Aislinn kissed her mother again and made her way back to Tobias' house. She arrived to find Jaxon and Zeke drinking shots while Dominic kept count, the party continuing on blissfully unaware of either Kaira's injuries or Aislinn's painful discussion with Marguerite.

"It's not even midnight," Zeke protested when he caught Aislinn's eye. "Where's my Alpha?"

"I dug a hole and buried him up to his neck."

Zeke howled with laughter and tackled her onto the couch, the scent of a fresh sea breeze touched with limestone wrapping Aislinn in a familiar blanket. When they rolled off the couch and thumped onto the floor, he straddled her, palms braced either side of her head. Golden curls so like Sienna's and yet somehow not in the least bit feminine tumbled around Zeke's face, his sapphire eyes impossibly blue. He looked her over, his breath tinted with tequila, and murmured, "Looks like someone had a hard day at the office."

"Something like that."

"Shots if you can get me off."

Aislinn raised an eyebrow. "Ezekiel Smythe, I never knew you felt that way."

As the second choked and blushed furiously, she gripped one of his wrists, palmed the opposite shoulder and flipped them both over in less than the time it took to blink. Trapped beneath her body with the hard length of her forearm against his throat, Zeke squawked in surprise, legs flailing for a moment before he tapped the floor in a sign of defeat.

When Aislinn stood, she rubbed her palms against her thighs and turned to find the rest of the room watching in shocked silence. Dominic swallowed, his smooth, olive skin pale in the artificial light. "How did you move that fast?"

"I didn't. He was slow."

"But -"

"Sorry guys, but I'm *really* not in the mood." Aislinn stalked to the bench, snatched up one of the tequila shots and tossed it back. "I need some space."

Conscious of the eyes on her back, she stormed up the stairs to Tobias' room and slammed the door behind her. Pictures rattled on the walls, a pointed reminder that she'd put too much force into the motion but rather than bring calm, the realisation only ratcheted her temper up another notch. Aislinn dragged the borrowed robe off her body and flung it on the floor, opened the window and leapt out. A two story fall was nothing to her Kin strength and she was running for the trees before her feet hit the ground, seeking the solace of exhaustion. Barely was she beyond the first few trunks when a warm, familiar weight cannoned into her from the side, slamming her mercilessly into the dirt.

Aislinn twisted beneath the naked man she knew inside and out, glaring up at Flynn and baring her teeth. "What do you want?"

"Same thing you do," the tigerkin growled. Silken black hair slithered across his forehead as he drew back a clenched fist. "Blood."

She shifted her head a fraction to the left and his fist slammed wrist-deep into the earth, sending a shower of dirt over their bodies. Flynn's elfin face twisted with a feral rage he'd show no-one else, lithe frame quivering as he wrenched his fist out of the ground. Aislinn caught the second blow in cupped hands, using Flynn's momentum to roll over and push up to her hands and knees. He grunted as the back of her head connected with his jaw but managed to wrap his free arm around her ribs, toppling them both backwards into a rolling, scratching, kicking mess. The fight that followed was dirty and vicious, neither allowing the other room to land a proper punch or kick, both Kin using the leverage of each other's bodies to lift and slam and roll into obstacles without mercy.

Sweat and blood slicked their bodies by the time Flynn found his feet, slamming Aislinn spine-first against the wall of the house. He drove his knee hard into her gut, ignoring the rain of paint chips and leaf litter that peppered the top of his head. Wheezing through the pain, Aislinn elbowed him hard across the face, snapping the tigerkin's head to the side as she tried to wriggle free. He lost his grip on her waist, but his other hand twisted in her hair and wrenched her head back, baring her jugular. Several more quick-fire blows traded places and by the time Flynn's teeth pressed into her skin, Aislinn's claws were digging into the vulnerable flesh of his throat.

A draw.

Time stood still, the night hushed in the wake of their fight. Flynn's gaze flicked to her lips and he leant forward, longing writ plain across his face - then those amber eyes squeezed shut and he sank curved incisors into his own lip, bumping his forehead against hers and dropping his hand from her hair. "Stalemate," he rasped. "Again."

Aislinn loosened her grip on his neck. "I'll get you one day."

Flynn rumbled something which may have been a laugh or a growl. "Hopefully not in front of an audience."

"An audience?" Aislinn blinked, then flushed as he stepped away to reveal the group of Kin clustered on the back deck, Tobias among them. "Well, shit."

"Don't worry." Flynn's teeth on her ear, his voice so low that even her friends' sensitive wolf hearing wouldn't be able to pick it up. "They don't know how these little bouts used to end and I won't tell."

"Flynn -"

"Don't." He pressed a quick, warm kiss to the hollow below her jaw and stepped away. Raising his voice, Flynn added, "You're almost back to normal speed."

Gritting her teeth, Aislinn twisted her face into what she hoped looked more like a smile than a grimace. "Good."

"The bleeding's going to be a pain in a stealth situation, but… I'd put you at ninety per cent recovered." Flynn flicked a glance up at their audience. "What? Cat got your tongues?"

Zeke leant over the deck's railing, his knuckles white against the wood. "Where the *fuck* did you learn to fight like that?"

"From Flynn," Aislinn answered, spitting blood onto the ground.

The men looked, as one, at Flynn. He shrugged. "Inside of a box."

Surprise flitted across their faces but any further questions were cut off as Tobias dropped lightly off the edge of the deck and prowled up to Aislinn. "You're bleeding everywhere."

"It'll heal."

A single, raised eyebrow. "Want to tell me what's going on?"

"What?" She frowned, considered how the fight may have looked from other angles, and came up blank. "Nothing's going on. We needed to wash off some tension, that's all."

"And it was lovely," Flynn purred, his accent thickening as his tone dropped into bedroom range. "Nobody does it quite like Ash."

A growl vibrated in the air and fur rippled up Tobias' arms. Aislinn slapped a hand to his chest before it could go further, shoving her energy against his until the transitional surge settled. She turned to Flynn and bared her teeth. "Stop it."

"No," the tigerkin purred, his voice a velvet rasp. "He's gotta sort this out, or we're dead."

"Transition isn't going to be cured overnight, Flynn."

"I'm not talking about transition. Use your nose, princess." Flynn dipped his head and pressed a hot, wet kiss to Aislinn's shoulder, watching Tobias from beneath lowered lashes the entire time. "He's jealous."

Aislinn's mind blanked. She was aware, on some level, of Tobias snapping and snarling and leaning into her restraining hand while Flynn continued to kiss and lick his way across her shoulder towards the curve of her neck, but it was as nothing compared to the roaring in her mind.

Jealous. Flynn was right - she could scent it in the air, see the proof in the set of Tobias' jaw and the temper flashing in his eyes. She could scent, too, the desire Flynn didn't bother to hide. The air was thick with an overpowering cocktail of sweat, blood and emotion, two massive masculine energies slamming against her own.

"Enough!" Whether by the grace of the death in her voice or perhaps the slight edge of hysteria, they both froze. "You're both being assholes. I already warned the others that I'm not in the mood, and now you both want to start a pissing contest?"

Tobias leant into her hand and Aislinn shoved him backwards with enough force to send a normal Kin flying. Except this was Tobias, with his interminable strength that only grew as the minutes passed. He wobbled in place and frowned. "I didn't start anything."

"*Really*?" She hissed. "I warned you Flynn would be here."

"I know."

"Then what the fuck is going on?"

Instead of answering, Tobias turned on his heel and headed back to the house. "I'll get you a towel."

"Why, so you can cover up what you don't want to see?" Temper sparking even hotter, Aislinn loosed a growl and flipped him off. "Don't bother."

She dematerialised before he could respond, streaming up to the roof and sliding into the ensuite through the ventilation shaft for the exhaust fan. Emotion made her body heavy and Aislinn trembled as she turned on the shower and stepped into the spray. Scalding water sluiced blood and grit from the myriad of scratches and bites across her skin - and she sank to her knees in the cubicle as the tempest inside her turned inward, quiet sobs shaking her frame.

Too much. They wanted too much of her, too many pieces. She'd barely begun to fit herself back together - how was she supposed to manage anything else? Fury and agony rent her insides in equal measures, coated in a loneliness that went soul deep and threatened to bind her chest until she couldn't breathe.

Buried so deeply in her own pain, Aislinn didn't know the door had opened until gentle hands lifted her and the scent of butterscotch and cream wrapped around her senses. Tobias settled her carefully in his lap, lips warm against her temple and arms locked tight around her body.

"Ash," he murmured in a voice thick with regret, "I'm sorry." She thumped a fist against the solid wall of his chest and he took it with a grunt, his next words carrying the hint of a wheeze. "Please, Ash. Please talk to me."

"I can't," she gritted out between sobs. "Everywhere I turn, someone's looking at me like I've grown a second head or deeply disappointed them or both. I can't do this. I'm not who you remember, not who you want me to be."

"Ah, shit." When she refused to turn her head at his prompting, Tobias rubbed his cheek against her hair. "Don't say that, beautiful, it's not true. I wasn't thinking straight back there. I'm sorry."

"You looked at me like -"

"I *know*." A sharp exhale. "Flynn already spoke to me about it."

Something in his tone made her lean back, lashes sweeping upward. A fist-shaped bruise was spreading across Tobias' cheek and Aislinn knew that in less than an hour he'd have a spectacular black eye. For some reason, it made her choke out a laugh. "He has an interesting way of talking, doesn't he?"

"I deserved it." Pressing his lips together in a thin line, Tobias brushed her hair back from her face. "Flynn was right; I was jealous. That fight was something else, something private. It rubbed my fur the wrong way - not because I don't trust you, but because I felt like it should have been me."

"You saw," she whispered, fighting the urge to flinch.

"The way he looked at you? Of course. It's the way I looked at you when you first arrived - not that I did it where you could see." Tobias' mouth quirked into a bitter grin. "I don't blame you or Flynn or *anyone* for that, Ash. He's got his own battles to fight and he's winning them, if tonight's any judge." Another swift exhale. "I swear my jealousy was nothing more than feeling like I wasn't there for you when you needed me to be. Seeing him support you that way…"

"Flynn and I are blood bonded to each other. He's important to me, too."

"I know. I *know*." Tobias ground his teeth in frustration. "I just don't know how to make it work."

"Neither do I." Aislinn forced herself to breathe, pressing her face closer to his chest. "But it's important to me that it does. I can't live without Flynn any more than I could live without you."

"I'm sorry."

Aislinn let her lashes drift close, the last of her tears mingling with the hot water from the shower. "I'm not strong enough for this."

"Then I'll hold you together until you are." Quiet, implacable strength, unshakeable certainty. "I'll learn to deal. Flynn will learn to deal. We'll find a way, if you just give it a chance. Please?"

"All right - but if either of you fuck with me, I'm going to tear off your cocks and shove them down the other's throat."

"Deal." His chest rumbled with a laugh. "You know, I've never had anyone threaten me quite the way you do."

"I'm serious, Tobias."

"I know." He was quiet for a long moment. "Can I wash you?"

Aislinn's heart stuttered in her chest at the tentative question, the last of her tension melting away. "Yes."

Tobias cleaned her body with gentle hands, checked the scrapes and split scars which had already begun to seal, rinsed her off and towelled her dry. When he swept her up in his arms and carried her to his room, Aislinn didn't protest. The raucous sound of merriment continued downstairs but instead of asking her to join it, he closed the door behind them and dressed her tenderly in soft pyjama shorts and, eyes twinkling with mischief, one of his own t-shirts. Tobias propped several pillows against the headboard and reclined against them, settling her weight between his legs and her head on his chest. He drew the quilts over them with equal care, rumbling deep in his chest as she stroked her fingers over one pectoral muscle and down his ribs.

She felt his body twitch and harden against her but instead of following through, Tobias shifted his hips until they were both comfortable, his erection a hard warmth against her spine. He settled one arm across her body, the other combing through her still damp hair, and said, "Go."

Haltingly at first and then with growing confidence, Aislinn began to speak, telling him of the conversation with her mother, her worries over Olaf, her uncertainty about the heartmate energy between them. She spoke about her time in Ireland, about the duties she'd done, about people she'd killed and people she'd saved. She told Tobias about the house she shared with Flynn and Kaira, about the unique friendship with the tigerkin that had often ended up being physical in spite of their best efforts to break it off. And last of all, she told him about the attack, about the awful time afterwards as scientists prodded and doctors harrumphed over her ruined body. As she spoke, pouring out her soul to the man who'd always caught her, who'd always glued her back together, Tobias stroked her hair and listened without a word. His presence was everything, his strength bottomless. Each word he absorbed healed a hole inside her and when Aislinn finally slipped into sleep, she did it with his arms locked tight around her waist and his chin resting on her head.

When she woke in the early hours of the morning, dawn a grey promise on the horizon outside Tobias' window, they were still in the same position. A curious weight had Aislinn opening her eyes to see Flynn's tiger body sprawled over their combined laps, his soft breathing tickling the inside of her wrist. One of Tobias' hands still curved across her ribs and the other was curled into Flynn's fur, extending his impossible strength to the other male, inviting him in. Though others would no doubt look upon the trio as something unusual, for the first time in years Aislinn felt only deep contentment, surrounded on all sides by the shocking vitality of two men who, despite being opposites, were determined to put their demons to rest and come together.

For her.

# Fifteen

Tobias woke with a start, heart hammering in the gentle morning light. Aislinn lay curled between his thighs, Flynn's heavy tiger weight oddly comforting over the top - and both his bed mates were stiff with tension.

*I assume we all heard that,* Flynn said, turning amber eyes in their direction. Tobias nodded, aware of Aislinn doing the same. He opened his mouth to speak when he heard it again; the faintest scritching of claws on... glass? Wood? *Someone's trying to open the window next to ours from the outside.*

They rolled out of bed as a unit, the chill of early morning puckering Tobias' naked flesh. The clock at his bedside blinked 5.40am and he suppressed a groan as he padded over to the window. Mornings were not, and had never been, his strong suit.

"I'll go next door," Aislinn whispered, her fingers trailing down his arm in the ghost of a caress. "See if we can trap them."

Grunting in understanding, Tobias tried to slide the window open without revealing himself. It wasn't an easy task, the wood grating against the frame before it was barely halfway. A shadow flickered at the edges of his vision and he abandoned all pretence at stealth, flinging the window up and hauling himself outside in time to see a silhouette disappear over the guttering and onto the roof. Though he wasted no time following, only empty, open rooftop waited when he landed on the dew-slick tiles. "Damn."

"Tobias?" Aislinn's voice, behind and to the left, from the room their shadowy intruder had been attempting to enter.

Tobias stalked across the roof, dropped to his knees and crawled headfirst over the edge. Aislinn jumped aside as he lowered himself into the spare bedroom. "Nothing - they ran for it."

*Why this room, specifically?* Flynn poked his nose under the bed, striped tail lashing back and forth in agitation. *Jaxon's not here; hasn't been all night.*

Aislinn propped both hands on her hips. "Isn't this your father's study?"

"It was once," Tobias agreed, motioning to the battered desk against one wall - a desk still covered in ancient papers. "I stuck a bed in here a few years back when the boys started dropping by more often."

"Hmm." Aislinn wandered over to the desk and started poking through the papers. "I wonder whether the intruder was looking for an easy way in… or something more."

Tobias frowned, saw Flynn tilt his head in similar confusion. "You've lost us."

"If this used to be your father's study," Aislinn elaborated, "And someone was looking for - let's say, I don't know, his laptop - but didn't know you'd turned the space into a bedroom, wouldn't this be the first place to check?"

"Well yeah, I guess, but Dad's staying at Grandma's," Tobias growled, running a hand through his hair.

*Only you and Aislinn knew that, though,* Flynn said, his feline eyes widening in sudden comprehension. *Most Kin, either in or outside of Pack land, would assume General Greenwood would return to his own home.*

Aislinn reached out to poke gently at Flynn's nose, got a half-hearted nip for her efforts. "Bingo."

"So what were they after?" Tobias racked his brain for anything of value Rupert may or may not have kept on his laptop. "I highly doubt it was Dad's collection of classical jazz music."

"There's no way to know - whoever it was is long gone now," Aislinn sighed, dissatisfaction in every stiff line of her body. "Did you see anything at all out there?"

Tobias shook his head. "Just a shadow. Could've been anyone."

"Dammit," she hissed, hands clenching to fists.

*No use bleating about it now.* Flynn arched his spine and yawned. *Like you said, they're long gone.*

"Mmmm." Aislinn nodded, chewing idly on a fingernail. "All right. Let's eat some breakfast and get ready for the meeting."

"You got a response?" Tobias raised an eyebrow.

She brandished her glittery pink phone and nodded. "Came in just before you woke. Nine o'clock sharp, horsekin meeting circle."

"That's at least an hour's drive," Tobias mused, looking at the clock on the wall. "You're right - we better make a move."

They padded back down the hall and into his room, Aislinn dressing swiftly while Tobias rummaged in his drawers and Flynn curled up on the bed with another yawn. *Wake me when you're finished primping.*

"Are you kidding me? That fur's sleeker than my hair," Tobias muttered, finally locating shorts and a t-shirt. "One of us loves their grooming, kitty cat, and it's not me."

Flynn whuffed a feline laugh and closed his eyes. As Tobias dragged his clothes on, his gaze wandered out of habit, crossing the common lawn, scaling the walls of Grandma Redding's house, past the man sitting in the tree and up to Aislinn's window. Wait... what? Moving slowly so as not to attract attention, Tobias stepped back out of sight. "Ash, there's someone sitting in the tree outside your old bedroom window."

"Huh?" She stopped midway through tying up her bikini top to twist and stare.

*He's right.* Flynn was already heading out the door and by unspoken agreement, both Tobias and Aislinn abandoned their clothing and shifted into wolf form to follow. *If we're quick, we might catch him.*

*Only one?* Aislinn queried as they raced down the stairs.

Flynn's whiskers twitched as he bared his teeth. *I hope not. I'm not in the mood to share my breakfast with you losers.*

Tobias swallowed a laugh as his paws hit the lounge room floor. Zeke was asleep on one of the couches in nothing but his jocks, golden hair tumbled haphazardly all over the place and long legs dangling from the cushions to drag on the rug. Jaxon was curled in his wolf form on a nearby armchair, snoring loud enough to wake the dead. Dominic was nowhere to be seen but a glance at the clock told Tobias he'd gone to take his place on patrol alongside Jacques after the duty roster had been rearranged the night before. *Should we wake them?*

*No,* Aislinn and Flynn in unison. Aislinn's jaw dropped in a silent laugh and she added, *It'll take time we don't have - and there's a better chance at surprise if there's less of us.*

Tobias cast a final look at his second and then eased out through the dog flap. *Zeke won't like it.*

*He'll live.* Aislinn nipped him on the shoulder and they set off across the common lawn, moving low and fast.

*I'll go left,* Flynn said, flowing alongside with such grace that Tobias felt a momentary stab of envy. *T-Fuzz, straight on. Ash, duck right in case he tries to escape that way.*

Considering he'd already intended to go point, Tobias didn't argue. Aislinn shot off towards the front right corner of the Redding household while Flynn went left, picking up speed with an ease that said he'd been holding himself back to match their pace. Tobias reached Grandma's front fence and leapt, hitting the tree trunk with tremendous force. He was rewarded with a shout of surprise and the tinkle of broken glass as the tree slammed against the house.

A shower of sparkling shards scattered the ground but the spy was nowhere to be seen, his momentum having carried him through the window and into the room beyond. Flowing from wolf to man in less than a second, Tobias leapt straight upward, caught at the very branch the peeper had been using, and flipped through the broken window.

Aislinn's childhood bedroom was peppered with shattered glass, shards of which bit painfully into Tobias' shoulder as he rolled over the impact area and came to his feet outside the blast radius. A back section of his brain registered the sleep-mussed forms of both Marguerite and Stephanie, eyes wide in surprise as he charged into the hall.

"Bathroom!" Grandma Redding appeared at the top of the stairs in time to point at the still swinging door across the way. Tobias burst into the white-tiled room with his teeth lengthening inside his mouth - and stopped.

It was empty.

Rage flooded him in a hot wave and he choked, gripping the edge of the hand basin as he fought for clarity. The window was open but a glance outside showed Flynn prowling beneath; it was impossible for anyone to have slipped out without the tigerkin noticing. Breathing through the crashing cymbals inside his head, Tobias scanned the bathroom, even going so far as to tug open cupboards... until he heard a scritching sound from above, caught the faintest whiff of engine grease.

"Fuck." He leapt for the exhaust fan above the shower, tugging loose the already wobbly cover, but it was too late. "*Roof!*"

Two seconds later the house shuddered under the weight of a heavy body. *Gone,* Flynn growled, his head framed in the hole where the exhaust fan should have been. *Too fucking slow.*

Tobias' vision clouded red as the tidal wave of his own rage swamped his senses. Seconds later it leeched away, the fierce fire smothered by soft, soothing shadows. When he blinked it was to find Aislinn's face in front of his, fingers gripping tight to his shoulders and blue-green eyes tinted with concern. She was talking, the sunlight glinting off her lips in a spectacular, sparkling display that Tobias itched to possess.

Aislinn squeaked as he hauled her close, thrusting his hands into her thick, wavy hair and curling his fingers around the back of her skull. Tobias slanted his lips across hers, swallowing her shock, his kiss hot, wet and demanding. He wanted her melted against him, soft and pliable - would accept nothing less. For a scintillating fraction of a second he got what he craved; then Tobias slammed backwards into something hard and cold, water sluicing across his face.

He came up gasping, Flynn's now human - or at least, as human as he could be - face only moments from his own, water cascading down around them. "No," the tigerkin murmured, low and deadly. "Get it together."

"Damn." Tobias swept a hand over his face and shook water off it, staring at his dripping fingers. Flynn straightened and the water cut off just as the bathroom door swung open to admit Rupert and Andre.

"What sort of incompetence," Andre snarled, lips curling back from his teeth in a very lupine expression, "Lands the three most powerful Kin in the world in my mother's bathroom *without* the intruder?"

"Shut up, Dad," Aislinn sighed, shaking her head. "At least we got here - you were in the same bloody house and didn't sense a thing."

Andre snarled and turned to Flynn. "Report."

"Target is male, short and in bad physical condition. Disguised his scent with engine grease but..." Flynn's eyes narrowed, nostrils twitching. "I swear I caught the hint of something botanical."

"Oh well, in that case, we'll just round up every short, unfit male in the area and ask you to search them for weed." Andre bared his teeth, his voice thick with venom. "Useless, the lot of you."

"Andre." Rupert put a warning hand on his alpha's shoulder as Flynn went deathly still.

"Don't Andre me, I know -" the older alpha broke off and blinked. "Tobias, what the fuck are you doing in the bath?"

"Er…" Tobias looked down at the porcelain tub in which he found himself sitting. "I slipped?"

"Really?" Andre raised a brow and turned to Aislinn, who was leaning nonchalantly against the sink. "He slipped?"

"Transitional surge," Aislinn supplied, her hands on her hips. Naked hips, Tobias realised. Naked woman. Naked. He closed his eyes, folding his arms over his lap as electrical energy flickered at the base of his spine. Don't look, Tobias. Do *not* look. Think of cold showers. Coldcoldcoldcoldcold-

"A transitional surge," Rupert echoed, an odd note in his voice, "That made you throw him in the bath?"

Aislinn shrugged and though her face was cool, her blue-green eyes glittered with mischief. "Flynn even ran the shower to help out."

"If we can get back to the *point*," Andre snapped, "I want to know why that asshole was looking through the window at my mate."

"Probably something to do with the reason someone tried to break into Dad's study a few minutes earlier," Tobias grunted, battling his rabid hormones with pure, unadulterated willpower. "It woke us up."

Andre frowned. "Explain."

"We heard a noise outside. I chased the intruder across the roof but they seemed to disappear into thin air." Tobias shook his head, staring pointedly at the bland white rim of the bathtub. He needed to concentrate on something other than a naked Aislinn Redding but his body was thrumming, determined to distract him with images of milky skin and gentle curves. "Now that I think about it, there was no scent there, either."

"Why would someone try and break into my study in one moment - especially given I haven't used it in over a decade - and then go to Aislinn's window the next?" Rupert screwed up his face in confusion. "Particularly given she wasn't there."

Flynn's voice thrummed with quiet fury. "Bearkin don't know that."

"No," Aislinn agreed. "Bearkin won't fit through the exhaust duct for a bathroom fan, either."

"No scent, no visual, no fucking clues." Flynn snarled and thumped his fist against the wall hard enough that the cabinets rattled. "I hate to say it, but we're better off shelving this until after the meeting."

Andre gave a sharp nod. "Agreed. Aislinn?"

"Nine am at the Horsekin meeting circle."

"Very well." The senior alpha tapped a finger against his chin. "Tobias will remain here to watch over the pack. You and Flynn shall accompany Rupert and I."

Tobias sat up very straight. "I beg your pardon?"

"He needs to attend," Aislinn said smoothly, before her father could so much as send a stormy look in his direction. "As his damper, I can't let him out of my sight."

"Transition aside, the message requested my presence," Tobias growled. "Grandma Redding can protect the pack without me, especially given the extra team you brought in."

Andre's brows beetled but it was Rupert who spoke up. "It does give us a little more flexibility. Leave Jacques and the others here with Joanne and the rest of us will go."

"A show of strength isn't a bad idea," Andre said, as though he'd never attempted to separate them in the first place. "Very well. Tend your wounds, put some clothes on and meet us at the garage in twenty minutes. Bring Ezekiel with you - even junior alphas should move with their seconds in tow."

"Yes, sir."

"Excellent. I'll brief my mother; she's standing guard over Maggie and Steph." Without waiting for a reply, Andre shifted on his heel and swept out, Rupert following silently along behind him.

Flynn watched them go, mild panic settling over his features. "Clothes?"

"Clothes," Aislinn replied firmly, patting his arm. "You can do it."

"I can also do *this*." The tigerkin dragged her close with an arm around her neck, using his other hand to muss her hair. She squawked and flailed at him, laughing, and Tobias was arrested by the smile that spread across Flynn's face in response. As inhumanly beautiful as the rest of him, it was like the first sunrise after a hundred-year storm - breathtakingly spectacular whilst more than a little wild. Tobias fought the urge to shake his head, wondering how he'd managed to best Flynn when it came to Aislinn's attentions. When the tiger wasn't busy hating everyone around him, he was extraordinary. The moment ended swiftly, with Flynn releasing his hold and dragging Aislinn upright. He pressed a chaste kiss to her forehead and then flicked Tobias a sharp look. "Get used to it."

"I didn't say anything," Tobias returned, realising even as the words tumbled through his lips that he'd been growling deep in his chest. Flynn's smile took on a devilish edge and, after a second, pointed brush of his lips over Aislinn's temple, he strode out. Tobias watched the doorway with narrowed eyes. "I hate him."

"Liar." Aislinn reached out a slender leg and toed the door shut. When it clicked into place, she sighed and shoved away from the basin - revealing two hand-sized sections of crushed porcelain. "Cute liar, but liar nonetheless."

Unable to look away from the damage he'd done without realising, Tobias thrust a hand through his hair. "So what's the plan for handling our fathers on this excursion? We hate each other?"

"More or less." Aislinn shrugged. "If anyone asks, we made temporary peace but had a fight at the pack picnic and are back to being antagonists."

"I'm not sure I can be an asshole on purpose."

"Sure you can." Her smile was all jagged edges. "You did it well enough before. Just channel angry Tobias."

He slid his hand out of his hair and down over his face. "I don't like angry Tobias. Before this all started, I was even tempered Tobias. Calm, gentle Tobias. Pat your dog and kiss your baby Tobias."

"That man still exists - he's just swimming in rough seas for a little while." Frowning down at the basin, Aislinn tapped her chin. "I better do something about this."

Tobias blinked as she twined her fingers together and brought the combined strength of both fists down on the edge of the sink, smashing it into tiny pieces. "How does that help?"

"You want to tell Grandma *you* broke it? Better she thinks it was our bad guy." Aislinn crossed to the bath and stuck her hand out. Tobias took it and allowed her to pull him upright, both of them flinching as a very real spark arced between them. "Whoa!"

"Sorry."

"Why?" Aislinn stepped into the tub, pressing her curves against his flesh. "I wasn't protesting."

"Ash." A frisson of energy wriggled down his spine. "I -"

"Shh," she whispered, tugging him down to check his bleeding shoulder. "No glass. Lucky." Aislinn fetched a washcloth from a nearby shelf, her skin sliding tortuously against his. "Now, hold still."

"Ash," Tobias tried again, his voice gravel as she damped the cloth and bathed the blood from his shoulder. "I'm losing it."

"No you're not." She dropped the cloth and slid her arms around his neck. "I've got you."

Before he could reply, Aislinn touched her lips to his and all conscious thought disappeared. Tobias wrapped his arms around her as tight as they would go, pressing their bodies together as though he could meld them with force alone. She wriggled deliciously in his grip, plunging her tongue into his mouth with such fiery heat that his body responded, the growing erection brushing against her leg.

Aislinn chuckled, nipping at his lower lip as she drew her head back. "Down, boy. Bad alpha."

"Can't help it," Tobias spoke through gritted teeth. He wanted to pull her closer; he wanted to let her go so he could touch her, he wanted to kiss her again and again. Sparks danced in front of his vision and he saw Aislinn's eyes widen. "What?"

"There's literally a storm inside you." Her voice was awed, hands reverent as she brushed them over the jagged lightning cracking and rolling underneath his skin. Aislinn traced one finger along his forearm and the lightning chased her touch. "I've never seen anything like this before."

"I think…" Tobias trailed off, alternately pleased that he could do something Fabulous Flynn couldn't, and embarrassed at how swiftly such an external display of his feelings could give them away. "I think it's because of you."

"Seems that way." She spread her fingers over his ribs and smiled as she pumped him full of cool, soothing energy. "Transitional energy takes pre-existing emotional reactions and exaggerates them exponentially. Anger is the most common but desire is pretty high on the list, too. It makes for some funny and often embarrassing moments if there's no damper around; particularly if you're in one of your other forms."

Tobias blinked rapidly, trying to process the implications. "Are you saying that if I lose my mind in my wolf or midform I might…"

"Yup," she nodded, then grinned. "Why so shocked? They're all variations of you - and transitioning into an alpha is about becoming more of a wolf, not less."

"I just..." he trailed off, cleared his throat. "I never considered doing *that* in one of my other forms."

Aislinn raised an eyebrow but didn't challenge the half-truth. "Some Kin prefer it that way."

"Have you ever -"

"No."

Tobias wasn't sure why he was relieved to hear that response; he simply was. He watched Aislinn's hips sway as she stepped out of the tub and swallowed the urge to chase her. "I suppose it would take an enormous amount of trust."

"I suppose so. I've never really thought about it."

"We trust each other," Tobias announced, unsure why he felt it necessary to say aloud. "Don't we?

Aislinn paused with her hand on the door, surprise flitting across her face. "Of course we do."

"So it wouldn't be bad... if that happened."

"What are you trying to tell me, Tobias? You want to shag me in wolf form?"

Yes. No. Maybe. "I can't control myself when the transitional energy shoves in. I don't want you in *any* position where you feel like I'm forcing myself on you, no matter my shape. I'm not Olaf."

Aislinn's face softened. "No, you're not. If it puts your mind at ease, I want you no matter what form you take; you're still Tobias to me. Relax."

She stepped out into the hall and Tobias stood alone in the bath, the lingering vanilla and honeysuckle of her scent tickling his nostrils. Relax? Tell him something like that and then ask him to *relax*?

"Lunaida above," he muttered, shaking his head to clear it and sending the last few droplets of water flying around the room. "Woman's trying to kill me."

*********

The pack's garage rose in Aislinn's vision as a dark silhouette against the rising sun. Flynn stalked quietly alongside her, clad in shorts that hung perilously low on his hips and clenching a balled up t-shirt tightly in one hand. On her other side, Tobias was deep in low-voiced conversation with Zeke, bringing the lanky blond up to date with the situation and receiving a patrol report in turn.

Their voices hummed across her senses, background music to the tumult of her thoughts. Aislinn glanced down at her hands and found them opening and closing, as though she sought to grip something of value but didn't know what it was. Only she did know; had realised it with shocking intensity in her grandmother's bathroom.

Her damper powers were fading.

Tobias' temper had been difficult to smother, his desire all-but impossible. Neither episode had been anything more than ripples in the vast lake of his rapidly growing power and should have been easily extinguished. The only explanation was, of course, Olaf and the damned Mark he'd laid upon her body. After all, if the bearkin could steal her strength, her very life force, and block her bond to Tobias - why not her other powers as well?

It was a clever, brutal plan that a dark part of her mind admired; taking away her damping ability turned both Tobias and, to a lesser extent, Flynn, into ticking time bombs. Bombs that, when they went off, would do a great deal of Olaf's work for him - either by forcing her to flee or leaving the pack in tatters, their strong members killed by rogue alphas nobody could control.

Grass turned to gravel underfoot and Aislinn looked up to see the yawning doors of the garage. Andre and Rupert waited with crossed arms and tapping feet, the former in suit pants and a shirt with the sleeves rolled up, the latter in camo shorts and a white t-shirt that pulled too taut across his chest. Apparently a preference for clothes that were too small ran in the family - though Tobias looked hotter than the sun with his tousled hair, glistening musculature and bronzed skin, whereas Rupert looked like he'd been pushed and prodded until, though he was technically confined, bits and pieces poked out everywhere.

Tobias' father stepped forward. "We'll need two cars."

"Rupert and I will take this one." Andre tapped the sleek silver hatchback he was leaning against, then gestured to a similar vehicle alongside. "You can take that one."

Flynn stopped dead. "No."

"Hey." Aislinn laid a hand against his arm, felt the muscles clenched so tight they quivered. His amber eyes were wild, lip curled back from his teeth to show the long fangs which marked him as anything but human. "Look at me."

He obeyed, leaning into the hands she stroked over his face, long lashes drifting closed. "I can't."

"I know." She raised her voice. "We'll take the ute."

Andre's snarl cut like a knife. "I thought his transition was settling."

"It is," Aislinn snapped. She didn't have the time, the patience - and most importantly, the right - to talk about the skeletons in Flynn's closet, particularly with a man who would immediately weaponise the knowledge. "We'll still take the ute."

"The red one has space for all of us." Zeke snatched a set of keys from the rack on the wall and stalked over to the vehicle in question. It was an American make, with a broad bench seat that fit three adults and a deep, long tub on the back.

"I'll drive," Tobias announced as Zeke unlocked the door and slid inside. "I know where we're going."

"Are you sure that's wise, given the incident in the bathroom?" Aislinn frowned. "Zeke can do it - or I can."

"You are absolutely *not* driving," Flynn growled, jerking back long enough to drag his t-shirt on over his head. "No fucking way."

Aislinn fisted a hand on her hip. "I'm not that bad."

"You're worse," Rupert announced, shuddering. To Tobias, he said; "Do not, under any circumstances, let her behind the wheel. Not unless your life depends on it."

"Maybe not even then," Flynn muttered. He turned and in three quick, fluid strides, crossed to the ute and leapt into the tub. "You hear me, T-Fuzz? Don't let those keys out of your sight."

Growling swear words under her breath, Aislinn slid into the cabin beside Zeke, who dropped a companionable arm around her shoulders. "You must be a pretty shitty driver if Rupe and Flynn are agreeing, little sister-mine."

Aislinn said nothing as Tobias slid into the driver's seat and dragged the door shut with the clanking of dented metal. She waited for the engine to start, filling the shed with a dull roar that would obfuscate even the sharpest of ears. "I'll have you know I'm an excellent driver."

"I'm sure you are." Tobias pulled out of the garage behind Andre's sleek hatchback. Rupert looked ridiculous inside of it, his head hunched and his beefcake arms wrapped around his ribs. "They really could've chosen a better car than that."

"Dad's thinking low profile," Aislinn returned, "And don't condescend to me, you giant alphajerk." She glared at Tobias' unrepentant grin, then swivelled to peek out the window to check on Flynn. He lay on his back in the tub, staring resolutely up at the sky, arms and legs akimbo like some sort of elfin starfish. The tigerkin never so much as glanced her way, but flipped her off with a long finger nonetheless.

"He okay?" Zeke asked, having followed her gaze. "I thought Flynn was the terminator."

"He is; I've seen him rip arms and legs off with his bare hands." As she'd intended, Zeke turned away from the tigerkin to demand more information. Aislinn gave it gladly, talking until she was sure they'd forgotten Flynn's odd behaviour and then requesting they share stories in turn. When conversation dwindled to companionable silence, Aislinn connected her phone to the ute's stereo system and prodded both men until they reluctantly joined her in singing along with her chosen music. Every so often she glanced over her shoulder to check on Flynn but the tigerkin never moved from his silent vigil of the cloudless sky - though Aislinn did catch him tapping his fingers in time to the beat.

When Andre's car pulled off the road and into a car park marked by wooden logs, Tobias followed and all six of them were soon standing beneath the shade of the tall gum trees bordering the area. After a cursory look over his shoulder, her father shoved the car keys into the pocket of his trousers and set off into the bush, seemingly unbothered by the idea of trekking through the underbrush in formal pants and patent leather shoes.

Flynn captured Aislinn's fingers in his as he used to do when they were in Ireland and dragged her along, leaving Tobias and Zeke to bring up the rear. Ten minutes later, they emerged into a large clearing. Joseph was already there, head thrown up in a way that was quintessentially equine in spite of his human shape. He held a chipped mug and wore jeans and a faded flannel shirt that spoke of comfort rather than formality. Aislinn tugged her fingers out of Flynn's and ran across the clearing to enfold the stallion in a hug, startling a laugh out of him while he juggled his coffee in one hand and returned her embrace with the other.

"You look better than when I last saw you," Joseph chuckled.

"I can only imagine." Aislinn flicked a lock of red hair off his face. "Where's Jen? You need a haircut."

"Protecting the herd," Joseph answered, swatting her hand away with mock irritation. "Seeing as I'm here with the lot of you instead."

"Really?" Aislinn made no effort to contain her disappointment. She'd known Joseph on and off throughout her time in Ireland and enjoyed the company of his wife and second, Jennifer. "Who did you bring with you, then?"

"Steve, and someone else I wanted you to meet. Hello, Andre." Joseph stepped sideways to shake Andre's hand, nodded at Rupert, Zeke and Flynn and raised an eyebrow at Tobias. "You look better than when I last saw you, too."

Aislinn glanced over her shoulder and blinked. Dappled by sunlight and shade, thumbs jammed casually into the waistband of his shorts, there was an unmistakable aura around Tobias. It wasn't just his spirit that shone bright from the golden starbursts in his blue eyes - his body, too, seemed different, as though he'd gained muscle, weight and presence overnight. A change he was clearly unaware of as he shrugged and said; "I don't know about that; I haven't had breakfast yet."

"I believe I can assist you there." Joseph smiled, gesturing behind him to the large tent on the opposite side of the clearing. "I've got tea, coffee, and muffins."

"Muffins!" Aislinn was already moving, rubbing her hands together in anticipation. As she ducked inside the tent, an impossibly thin, lanky man unfolded himself from a camp chair. Dressed in a t-shirt full of holes and battered cargo shorts, Steve's olive green eyes were alight with a smile as he gave Aislinn a tentative wave - which became a gasp as she tugged him into a hug.

"I'm not really a hugger," Steve muttered, but his arms came around her nonetheless, thin fingers patting awkwardly at her shoulders.

"You'll learn," said Aislinn cheerfully. "Joseph said there were muffins."

"There are." His relief at escape was obvious enough that Aislinn snorted a laugh. "I'll get you one."

The man who'd been kneeling in the corner stood as Steve passed by, stepping gracefully in front of Aislinn. He bore a natural olive complexion tanned darker by the sun, with glacier-pale eyes that tilted up slightly at the corners. Creamy coloured hair, so pale a blonde as to be almost white, tumbled in glorious waves around his face and down his back, brushing his waist. He was perhaps six foot two, just shorter than Tobias, with shoulders marginally narrower but muscles that were so well wrapped around his powerful frame they deserved a fanfare all of their own. He was dressed like a character straight out of an old martial arts movie, complete with baggy, pleated trousers and a set of crossover, wide-sleeved tops with a broad sash to hold everything in place. Dangling from graceful fingers was a headband that immediately made Aislinn's brain say 'ninja.'

"Hello," he said, his voice smooth and cool as his eyes. "My name is Baringa Kurugashi. You must be Aislinn Redding."

Aislinn stared. Finally she cleared her throat and managed; "I'm sorry, did you just say *Baringa*?"

He blinked, long and slow, lashes the colour of fallen snow caressing his cheeks in a gesture so beautiful her heart ached. "My mother is a devoted fan of Australian equine literature."

"Baringa," Aislinn murmured, then smiled. "It's lovely. As you guessed, I'm Ash."

He took her extended hand and brushed his lips to her knuckles, the scent of ginger and winter frost tickling her nose. "An honour."

"Charming and dangerous," Aislinn observed, accepting a paper plate from Steve. She stared down at the neatly sliced and lavishly buttered muffin, then batted her lashes at the crocodilekin. "I think I love you."

"Er…" Steve blinked rapidly, his cheeks turning an adorable shade of pink.

"Solaeden save us," Tobias announced from the doorway, his face full of horror as he stared at her muffin, "There are *two* of them."

Aislinn hummed in delight as she picked up the first piece and bit into it. "Unlike some other men in this tent, Steve knows the correct ratio of butter to muffin. I think I'll keep him."

Curious, Baringa leant over to look. He'd tied the headband across his forehead, using the back of the strip to secure his incredible hair in a ponytail. It flowed down his back like foam on a waterfall, shorter tendrils escaping the front to brush his cheeks and forehead. If Aislinn thought he looked like a ninja before, his appearance screamed it now - except for the delicate way his nose crinkled as he said; "That is enough butter for five muffins."

Aislinn swooned dramatically against an astonished Steve. "Defend our honour, brother in arms. These infidels should not besmirch the sacred butter!"

His cheeks flaming even more pink, Steve managed; "I like butter."

Baringa snorted and though his face did not change expression, Aislinn swore she saw a spark in his glacier eyes. "A warrior who bears her scars with grace and maintains a sense of humour. Joseph said I would like you, Aislinn Redding, and he was correct."

Now it was Aislinn's turn to blush as Tobias, lowering his voice so that nobody outside the tent would hear the way it had turned tender, said; "Told you so."

Aislinn gave him the finger and took another bite of her muffin. "I'm still marrying Steve." She levelled her gaze at Baringa, who'd floated to the buffet and was pouring himself a cup of tea. "So, who and what are you, exactly?"

"I am who I have said I am," Baringa replied, then smiled a short, quick smile that turned him from handsome to oh-shit-I've-melted. "I am also a horsekin stallion, a professional ballet dancer and a shinobi… a ninja." He looked briefly into his cup. "I like chai tea and cinnamon donuts. Will that suffice?"

"No." Aislinn frowned, crossing her arms. "Are we dunking the donuts in the tea or not? Are they hot or cold?"

The ninja, who had just sipped his tea, made an undignified choking sound which evolved into a surprised laugh. "Dunking. Hot."

Aislinn rubbed her hands together in glee. "Excellent. Tobias, we're keeping both Steve *and* Baringa."

"Lady have mercy." Tobias rolled his eyes and crossed the room, holding out his hand. "Sorry for the belated introduction - Tobias Greenwood."

"I gathered," Baringa's voice was dry. "Baringa Kurugashi."

"Kurugashi? As in, Kurugashi Enterprises?" Tobias drifted to the buffet table, grabbed a muffin and winked at Aislinn as he ate it whole, without even a smidge of butter, like a true infidel.

Baringa inclined his head. "My father and older sister, yes - I'm afraid the corporate life is not for me. I prefer a different kind of hunting."

There was a scratching at the tent and then Zeke poked his head in. "Foxes are here. Better come out before Flynn eats one." Irritation warred with amusement as he turned sapphire eyes on Aislinn. "According to Andre, you're the only one who can keep 'that creature' in line. Oh, hey, Steve-" Zeke caught sight of Baringa and raised an eyebrow. "- And scary but cool samurai guy. I'm Zeke. Please don't stab me unless you promise to leave a hot scar the ladies will adore."

Baringa stared at the tent flap as it drifted closed, then blinked at Aislinn. "Is he yours?"

"Mine," Tobias grunted, thrusting a hand into his hair and tangling it irreparably. "Come on, Ash - we better run interference."

"For Flynn or Zeke?"

He rolled his eyes again. "Both. Remember I hate you."

"I hate you, too." She blew him a kiss and Tobias ducked out of the tent with a low, not-at-all-hating growl.

Steve heaved a sigh. "I guess I'll bring tea and coffee outside. Baringa, give me a hand?"

The stallion muttered a response that Aislinn didn't hear as she strode to the tent flap and, after taking a moment to straighten her spine, twitched it aside to step into the early sunshine.

Joseph stood talking quietly with Andre and a tall, rugged looking woman whom Aislinn guessed was Carrie-Anne, the foxkin Vixen who'd single handedly reunited her enormous and famously skittish pack after a fallout between her father and two uncles had resulted in civil war. Carrie-Anne had thick orange-red hair cut in an asymmetrical bob, the left side sitting above her ear and the right side brushing the tip of one shoulder. She wore cargo shorts, work boots, a dark green shirt and a frown which, judging by the deep furrows on her brow, was her standard expression. Standing five paces back from his Vixen, arms crossed over his chest and eyes darting over the clearing, was a tall man with dark auburn hair and a neatly trimmed beard.

"Hart?" Aislinn grinned as he turned, brown eyes widening in recognition. "Holy shit, it *is* you!"

"Ash? Well I'll be damned." Hart blinked, then grinned a grin that took ten years off his face. The foxkin covered the distance between them in swift, long strides and tugged her into a back slapping hug. "Healing sleep did you wonders, by the look of it."

"I'd say the same of you." She gave him a contemplative look. "You know, I thought you were old and crusty but now you're not covered in bearkin blood, I think I was mistaken."

"Biting a bear on the balls has a way of ageing a man," Hart replied sagely, his arm around her shoulders in the easy way of a Kin used to a close-confines pack. He wore his strength easily, muscles rippling beneath heavily freckled skin that was still pale in spite of all the time he must spend in the sun. When he looked down at her, his eyes twinkled with mischief. "Does this mean I get a second chance to buy you that drink?"

"Drink?" Aislinn blinked and then snorted. "I didn't think you were serious about that."

Auburn eyebrows shot up. "Why not?"

"You were investigating a murder!"

"And you were hauling home some useless transitional asshole who almost killed you," Hart said with an easy shrug. "Besides, it looks like the bears killed Freddie and Macey - that's why I'm here. What about you? I hope you ripped your charge a new one."

Aislinn bit her lip to keep from laughing. "Oh, I gave him a piece of my mind, don't you worry about that."

A deep, rumbling growl caught her attention and Aislinn turned, recognising Tobias' voice. He stood on the opposite side of the clearing, his gold-shot eyes trained on Aislinn and Hart - or more specifically, the arm Hart still had lazily around her shoulders. The noise interrupted conversation clearing-wide but before anyone else realised what was going on, Flynn got in Tobias' face and started snarling right back.

"*Aislinn.*" Andre's voice cut through the crowd, swift and sharp.

"Excuse me." She smiled sweetly at Hart and slid out from under his arm. Crossing the clearing and well aware every single eye was focussed on her, Aislinn shoved between Flynn and Tobias, a hand splayed on each of their chests. "Stop it."

Tobias snarled and Flynn hissed, batting Aislinn's hand away. He caught her gaze with his amber one, a silent signal in a language they'd perfected over years of working under intense scrutiny. Reversing the trajectory of the hand he'd shoved aside, she spun him in place and landed a solid kick to the back of his knees which sent the tigerkin sprawling. Tobias grabbed her other wrist in a strong grip that was entirely more real than Flynn's; with a quick hunch of the shoulder and a swift pivot, Aislinn rolled him over her spine to land beside Flynn with a startled yelp. She crouched between them, one knee on Flynn's back and the other foot across Tobias' neck. "If you two don't put a lid on it, I'll geld you both. Got it?"

Flynn's shoulders shook with what may have been rage but Aislinn knew was really feline amusement. "Fuck off, Ash."

"Make me. Tobias?"

Blue and gold eyes narrowed to slits but her heartmate's gaze was steady. "Fine. Now get your foot off my neck."

Aislinn obliged and stood, surprised when a warm, male hand steadied her elbow. Hart leant down to speak into her ear, his smoke and sawdust scent filling her lungs. "Who are these idiots?"

"That's my Alpha," Zeke growled - but he was shaking his head in resigned amusement.

"Hart, meet Tobias Greenwood and Flynn Tigerkin, transitional asshole and rogue Kin agent respectively." Aislinn waved a negligent hand at the two males as they got to their feet.

Hart whistled between his teeth. "You gotta deal with both of 'em?"

"You have no idea." She snorted and looked over at Andre. "Happy now?"

"No," her father snapped. "Keep that tiger on a tighter leash."

Flynn flowed to Aislinn's other side and slid a proprietary arm around her waist. "Better?"

Andre turned away, his face white with an old, cold rage that only surfaced when Flynn lavished Aislinn with his attention. To her surprise, Hart didn't relinquish her elbow as Andre called the meeting to session; rather, he pressed his lips closer to her ear. "You involved with the tigerkin?"

"Only as his damper."

Hart looked surprised, then glanced at where Tobias now stood glowering with Zeke and Rupert. "I thought you were *his* damper."

"Like you said - I've got them both." Before the foxkin could ask any more questions, she dragged Flynn across the clearing and offered a hand to Carrie-Anne. "Aislinn Redding. Sorry about Macey - Freddie was a friend of mine."

"Carrie-Anne Cartwright. Thanks." She flicked a glance at Hart. "I heard you kept my cousin safe in Gerup. I owe you."

Aislinn smiled. "He held his own well enough. You've got good people around you."

"I appreciate that." The older woman's frown lifted into what might not be described as a smile but, given the dour expression she'd been wearing earlier, was definitely an improvement. "Steve said you wanted to talk bearkin."

"I do." Aislinn took a deep breath and lifted her chin. "Olaf Gruybere is in the area. He's the one who brought the bearkin in, following me - though I didn't know it when I arrived. They killed Freddie and Macey in an attempt to discover my location." She held Carrie-Anne's gaze. "I'm sorry. If I'd thought there was danger, I'd never have let Freddie go off on his own."

She nodded sharply. "I understand."

"Olaf wants my head," Aislinn continued. "I don't intend to give it to him. I asked Steve to organise this meeting so we might talk about joining forces to catch the bears and keep our people safe."

Baringa, hovering by Joseph's left shoulder, crossed his arms. "Why wouldn't we just hand you over? It would be more expedient."

"Bait, you mean?" Aislinn cocked her head, considered. "I'm not against the idea but Olaf's clever. It would need to be carefully planned and right now, we don't have the numbers to set up something like that and defend our vulnerable at the same time. Zeke?"

Zeke obligingly passed over a smaller copy of the map he'd been making in the den, complete with marks showing the bear incursions. Aislinn hunkered down on the ground and spread it out, using stones to hold the paper flat. Joseph was the first to crouch beside her, spreading weathered fingers over the print-out. "They're trying to drive you north-east."

"Through my earth?" Carrie-Anne dropped to one knee on the stallion's other side. "Hart, does this data match yours?"

Aislinn heard the hesitation in his voice as the foxkin said; "Ellie's got that data."

Carrie-Anne's eyes narrowed a fraction and then she put two fingers in her mouth and whistled. A moment later the bush rustled and a petite woman with luxuriant curves and rich, curly brown hair jogged out. She was dressed in a loose black tank with a pink unicorn on the front and a pair of frayed denim shorts. Green eyes glittered out of an angular but pretty face dusted lightly with freckles. Joseph raised an eyebrow as Ellie dug her phone out of her pocket and handed it to her Vixen without a word. "Hiding your people in the trees, Carrie-Anne?"

"No more or less than you, Joseph," Carrie-Anne returned, accepting the phone and swiping at the screen. "Seems the wolves are the only ones honest enough to bring all their people to the actual party."

Aislinn shrugged, deliberately not looking at her father. "We have nothing to hide, and enough chutzpah to flatten the lot of you. Why bother?"

Flynn growled in emphasis and whilst Joseph looked faintly taken aback, Carrie-Anne gave her a grim smile. "I like you. According to Ellie's data, this map is basically correct. Except," she held out a hand and Ellie fished into her pocket again, withdrawing a black marker. "We've had reported sightings in the last few days of both bears and slain wildlife here, here and here."

Aislinn frowned at the marks but it was Tobias who said; "Close together and out of the original radius."

"But still on my land," Carrie-Anne grunted. "It's pretty rough country out there - ideal place for them to hide. Only thing is, it could be a trap."

"I don't think it is," Aislinn murmured, brushing a fingertip across the still-damp ink and then staring at the stain it left on her skin. "Olaf's injured. I'm willing to bet my left nipple he's holed up somewhere around there to recover."

"Huh." Carrie-Anne stood and gestured to Hart, who followed her a couple of paces away. While they whispered to each other at a sub-vocal level, Aislinn noticed Ellie sidling closer to Tobias until she could at last lay delicate fingers on his forearm. His smile reached his eyes as she stood on tiptoe to whisper in his ear.

*I searched for you in the pubs and clubs...* Tobias' voice, wracked with grief and frustration, swam out of her memory. Aislinn's stomach knotted at the realisation that Tobias and Ellie had shared more than coffee in the past - and judging by the way she wet her lips as she waited for him to respond, the foxkin was hoping for a repeat performance.

Not that Aislinn could blame her, with Tobias' new alpha energy taking him from shit-hot to outshine-the-sun. However, she discovered with bone-jarring intensity, the thought of Tobias even smiling at Ellie made Aislinn want to murder people. Specifically, curvy women with curly brown hair and nice boobs. Definitely them.

"Aislinn?" Joseph's face appeared in her line of sight, blocking Tobias and Ellie from view.

"Sorry?" She blinked and offered the older stallion a half smile. "Lost in thought."

"I *said,* Steve told me he's willing to back you no matter what. Considering he's only with me voluntarily, I have no way to prevent that." The prime stallion bit his lip a moment and then shrugged. "That said, I have no love for the bearkin and what they've been doing. I invited Baringa here because not only is he deadly and loyal, his job takes him worldwide. He'd be a valuable ally for us both."

"When he's not considering turning me over to the enemy," Aislinn returned dryly.

"Shinobi can be like that," Joseph acknowledged with a smile. "For the sake of your damper's interest, Baringa has a fully functional midform and successfully navigated his transition alone."

"Alone?" Aislinn repeated, aghast.

"The story is his to tell, but I will say to you - do not make the mistake of underestimating him because he's what other Kin might call a prey animal." Joseph's eyes crinkled at the corners. "I've never met anybody who is less prey in my life."

"Demon in horse's clothing, eh?" Aislinn smiled and nodded, accepting the subtle offer hidden in Joseph's words. "Thank you, your majesty."

Joseph rolled his eyes at the title. "Don't push it, princess."

"Do you think the foxes will side with us?" She murmured, cutting a glance at the near silent but definitely heated exchange going on between Hart and Carrie-Anne.

"Hard to say. They want revenge for Macey and Freddie but Olaf is nobody to be trifled with." Joseph sighed. "That and Carrie-Anne doesn't get along particularly well with your father. It would've been better if Andre had stayed behind."

"Tell me about it," Aislinn grunted. Andre and Rupert had watched the meeting so far in stony silence, though Tobias' burly father kept glancing towards his son with an uncertain look on his face. They'd positioned themselves a few paces back, close enough to hear the main discussion but not so close that Aislinn's tainted scent would carry to Andre's nose on the faint breeze. The sight of it only deepened Aislinn's anger, but looking away brought her back to Tobias and the lovely Ellie, who was pressing ever closer to his side while she continued murmuring in his ear.

Flynn's sudden snarl was very much predator, vicious and low and, oddly enough, a welcome relief. Aislinn surged to her feet as he grabbed her by the shoulder, fingers digging into her skin with the faintest hint of claw. "Engine grease," he growled, dragging his t-shirt off over his head with the other hand. "On the wind."

Aislinn didn't argue; Flynn's nose was one of the best. Fur was already rippling across his back and shoulders as he bent to strip his shorts off, earning an appreciative gasp from Carrie-Anne that might have been due to what he had under his shorts, or the way Flynn's body stretched into the midform which never failed to impress.

"Go," Aislinn said in response to his questioning look - and Flynn, tail lashing and chest rumbling, shot off into the trees. "Tobias! Zeke! Engine grease on the wind!"

"Engine grease?" Joseph repeated, brow furrowed in confusion as Tobias and Zeke shimmered into wolf form and disappeared into the bush.

"Aislinn!" Andre stomped over, eyes glittering with malice. "What is the meaning of this? They're not yours to -"

"Whoever tried to infiltrate the Den Mother's house this morning obscured their scent with engine grease, if you recall," Aislinn snapped. She looked across the clearing at Steve. "I could use your help."

The croc was already half out of his clothes, revealing a sunken chest and stark ribs that made him look starved. "I'll go via the river, try to cut them off. Baringa?"

"Yes." The other male slid out of his clothing in one rolling movement and Aislinn had a split second to appreciate a muscled body that would have made sculptors cry before he shimmered and began to change.

"Holy shit," she managed. "He's a centaur."

Baringa's very male, very human torso remained, with a horse's body replacing his lower half. His coat was a creamy-white, his luxuriant tail a silver-tinted waterfall that matched the long hair still secured by his ninja headband. He bent and scooped what looked like a long, thick knife out of his clothing and gave it a shake. With a silken sound, it spread into an enormous, four pointed star with a hole in the centre. Baringa spun the star in his fingers once, as though to ensure it had settled properly, then dug out a second, repeated the motion, and galloped into the trees without a backwards glance.

"There are not many horsekin who hold a midform and not a one I've ever seen who looks like that," Joseph said as she turned wide eyes on him. "Will you be joining the search?"

"Yes," she said, even as Andre barked a quick; "No!"

"If you go out there you're a sitting duck," Rupert added, "And you leave us with one less guard for the head alphas."

Aislinn raised a brow. "Are you telling me that you, Hart and Ellie aren't enough? It's not like Carrie-Anne and Joseph are slumps, General. Don't try and shackle me with duty talk."

*Hurry up - I think there's more than one.* Flynn's peevish voice, intense enough that Aislinn knew he spoke to her alone. *I've got a scent from the way we came and another cutting off south-west, around behind the tent. I'm giving you ten seconds to respond before I turn around.*

Aislinn yanked her top off over her head and dropped it on the ground. She heard Hart's sharp intake of breath as more of her scarring was revealed, saw her father's face tighten. He grabbed her wrist in a crushing grip. "Have sense, Aislinn. Bad enough to display what scars you have, but really-"

"Save the shame for yourself," Aislinn snapped. As she'd anticipated, her father stepped closer, looming over her in a vain attempt to intimidate with size alone. She smiled. "Thanks for that."

Comprehension dawned too late. Aislinn dissolved into Andre's shadow and streamed away while Carrie-Anne swore low and hard. The sun forced her to re-materialise a scant few paces further along, but the confusion gave her enough time to shift into wolf form, shake off her remaining clothes and streak into the trees. *I'm almost at the tent. Stay on target.*

*About fucking time.*

*I love you too, asshole.* Aislinn circled around the back of the tent, nose to the ground as she hunted for the scent trail Flynn had mentioned.

*Ash?* Tobias' voice. *Zeke and I found a pot of grease.*

*Odd for the bearkin to be that clumsy,* she replied. Then, because she couldn't help herself, *Tell Ellie the next time she touches you I'll break her godsdamned wrist.*

*She wasn't -* he began, only to be cut off by Flynn's laughter.

*She fucking was,* the tigerkin chuckled. *I could scent her pheromones from where I was standing. She's in heat and you've got a bulls-eye between your legs, T-Fuzz.*

Tobias swore but Aislinn's attention was captured by a fresh wave of grease-heavy scent, laced with undertones of ozone. *I have something.*

*Be careful.*

*Yeah, yeah.* She followed the trail into a narrow gully whose vegetation was so thick, Aislinn's wolf body could barely squeeze through. A snagged mess of tree roots had her scrabbling for grip and then, in a bout of frustration, dissolving into the shadows to stream through to the other side. *I don't get it; it's physically not possible for a bear to come this way.* She solidified in a small, clear space beside a water soak, deep in the gully and far, far from prying eyes. *In fact - oh, shit.*

Tranq darts thumped into her chest and flank in quick succession. She stumbled, tried to turn and fell as another dart pierced her hindquarters. Someone was shouting; she dimly recognised Flynn's mental voice and clung to it with all her strength.

*Flynn,* she managed, the effort required to form words monumental. *Tobias. It's -* and then the chemicals flooded her system and Aislinn collapsed to the ground, unconsciousness sweeping over her in a tingling wave.

# Sixteen

Flynn's telepathic instructions to the search team echoed over and over inside Tobias' head as he dove through the bush, frantically hunting for any sign of the woman who was his entire world.

Zeke met him in the gully where she'd been taken and together they did a thorough check of the surrounds - but it was as though Aislinn had simply winked out of existence, her scent diffusing into nothingness.

*Anything?* Flynn asked.

*No,* Tobias poked his nose into the hollow beneath a fallen tree, found it empty. *You?*

*Nothing.* A pause. *Some of the others found lingering hints of engine grease, but they're spread seemingly at random though the bush.*

*A distraction.*

*Yes.* Another pause, Flynn's voice thick with growling frustration. *I'm going to call everyone in - meet back at the horsekin circle.*

Though the yearning chasm in his chest begged him to disagree, Tobias knew they'd stand a better chance of finding Aislinn if they worked together, so he turned back the way he'd come. He met a fox who smelt of smoke and sawdust halfway there and though Hart did little more than yip in acknowledgement, Tobias slowed his pace to match the other male's. They reached the meeting circle and shimmered back to human form, Tobias immediately pushing both hands into his hair. "Anything?"

"No," Hart shook his head. "The bastards were clever about it."

"Or we were stupid." Tobias yanked at his hair, the sharp pain in his scalp bringing clarity - and a sidelong look from Hart. "Something on my face?"

"No. It's just occurred to me that I've got an Alpha to protect and we're suddenly one damper down." The fox's brown eyes hardened. "How much of a danger are you right now?"

It took every ounce of willpower Tobias had not to strangle Hart then and there. His heartmate - his *heartmate* - had been kidnapped and all the foxkin could think about was Tobias' hormones? Hart's life was saved by the sudden appearance of Zeke, who shimmered into human form and immediately began shouting for a phone. Tobias stomped over to his second, swiping Joseph's flannel shirt off the ground along the way and shaking it until a phone clunked onto the grass.

"Here." Tobias thrust the device into Zeke's outstretched hands.

"Thanks." Zeke clapped him on the shoulder and turned away, punching numbers into the keypad and lifting the phone to his ear. "Dom? Yeah, it's me."

Unable to keep still, Tobias paced the circumference of the clearing on the off chance a new scent trail presented itself. Halfway through his second lap, Baringa stepped out of the trees. He still wore his midform, enormous ninja stars held down by his sides as he gave Tobias a swift once-over. "You smell as though you are in great distress."

"Of course I'm -" Tobias broke off, mind working sluggishly. There had been no reprimand in Baringa's voice, only cool warning. "You're observant, Kurugashi."

Baringa inclined his head. "So I'm told. I suggest either finding or faking calm, because the wolfkin Councillor is on his way." The horsekin hesitated, then offered a small, humourless smile. "When you reveal the truth, make sure it's to your advantage and no-one else's."

"I'm not even going to ask how you know."

The stallion raised a pale brow. "I've got eyes?"

"Right. I have a feeling it won't be long before the secret's out, but I appreciate the advice." Tobias jigged up and down in a vain attempt to settle his restless energy. "Where's Steve?"

"Searching the nearby waterways."

"Flynn?"

Baringa pointed a graceful finger straight up. Tobias followed the gesture and spotted a flash of orange in the branches of a thick tree. "What the fuck is he doing?"

"My guesses are either running a perimeter patrol or trying to contain his emotions before they spill into bloodshed." Baringa's tone was conversational, as though he were discussing a local sports match. "You have an interesting pack."

"Flynn's not my pack."

"He acts like he is; tigers are notoriously antisocial."

"I'm going to take that as a compliment when I'm in a better mood," Tobias growled.

Not in the least daunted by the carnivore dominating his voice, Baringa nodded. "It was meant as such. Now breathe - here they come."

Andre stalked out of the trees with a face like a thunderstorm, Rupert hopping awkwardly along behind him with one leg in a pair of shorts. "Well?"

"Nothing," Tobias ground out, crossing his arms over his chest to hide the way his hands shook. "Steve's checking the waterways but for now, it seems like we've lost her."

"I want holds on all public transport in the immediate area and double security on flights, boats - anything that can get a Kin out of the country in the next twenty-four hours," Andre instructed.

"Consider it done." Rupert tugged out his phone and stepped aside to make the call.

Andre shoved both hands in the pockets of his suit pants, his voice carrying the edge of a growl. "I want to know how the bears got so close in the first place. First pack land, now this meeting - we should've been secure."

"It seems an impossible task without inside assistance, doesn't it?" Joseph's voice preceded him out of the trees, his bare chest dripping with moisture and his jeans muddied.

Andre snarled. "You accusing my pack of having a mole?"

"I think the situation speaks for itself." Joseph held out a fist, unfurling calloused fingers to reveal a few strands of dark brown fur that shimmered red in the dappled sunlight. "I found this by the creek where Steve went in."

"So they either took her down the creek to a bigger boat, or they crossed the water to confuse the scent trail." Zeke handed Joseph his phone. "Thanks for the lend."

The prime stallion blinked but pocketed the device without otherwise betraying his surprise. "In that case, I suggest we widen the search area with the waterways in mind."

"No, that won't be necessary." Andre's face was thoughtful. "The bearkin want information; they'll take Aislinn to their base and try to make her talk. If we play this situation correctly, we have the perfect means to catch Olaf."

"You're not serious." Hart's face blanched with horror. "Do you know what they're likely to do to her?"

"Forget that," Zeke snapped, "Do you know what they've already *done* to her?"

"Better than you." Andre shrugged. "Aislinn is a warrior. This is her job."

"What part of rape and torture is anyone's *job*?" Zeke shouted.

Hart choked. "Those scars…"

"Yeah." Zeke's sapphire eyes were chips of fury. "Those scars."

Hart made to step forward and was stopped by a warning hand from Joseph. "Andre, think for a moment. She's your daughter, for Solaeden's sake."

"I'm not for a minute suggesting we abandon her." Andre removed one hand from his pocket, examined the curve of his nails. "Allowing Aislinn to become bait is a solid tactical move - one that your own man suggested, I might add."

Tobias found it impossible to speak, his voice stolen by the red fog of rage creeping inch by slow inch through his body. A cool hand gripped his shoulder a fraction too hard, Baringa's voice soft in his ear. "He wants you to lose control; it gives him the authority to pull you off the search."

Aware the other male was correct, Tobias fought furiously with his own instincts, jaw clenched and hands fisted so tight he drew blood from his palms. Someone had to stop Andre, had to wipe that smug look from his face, but he knew if he moved so much as an eyelash he'd erupt - and Aislinn needed him sane.

Carrie-Anne stepped out of the bush at that moment, her frown so deep it created shadowed grooves in her face. "Just when I don't think you can disgust me any further, Andre, you manage it. Giving up your own daughter? What will your mate think, I wonder? Rest assured, she'll find out." She flicked a glance at Hart. "We owe Aislinn for her work in Gerup. Find Ellie and begin co-opting volunteers for a wider search."

Looking immensely relieved, Hart inclined his head. "Yes, Vixen."

"The horsekin are at your disposal," Joseph added. "Steve will co-ordinate my herd."

At long last, Tobias' jaw unlocked. "Count us in, too."

"No." Andre held up a hand, his face smooth as polished marble. "As a Councillor, I rescind those orders. All troops will stand down until further notice. Anyone defying the Council will be tried for treason."

Joseph shook his head. "Andre, old friend, this is madness."

"It is war," Andre corrected, "And Aislinn is my soldier."

"You're wrong," Tobias snapped, tension singing through his bloodstream. "Aislinn is my heartmate and I'll tear the world apart until I find her."

A collective gasp went up through the crowd and Andre's face turned white, then tinged green, then began to purple with rage. "You lie."

"You're all alphas - you can scent the truth." Tobias growled low in his throat, fur rippling across his arms and chest before he forced it down. "Zeke?"

"Do it."

Tobias drew a deep breath, an unnatural calm stealing through his bones. Aislinn had warned him this moment would come - he wouldn't fail. Straightening his spine, he looked Andre dead in the eye. "I hereby renounce my oath to the Redding pack and take up the mantle of Alpha wolf. My birth pack is no longer my home, my heart wanders where it wills. Though the song of my family echoes always in my heart, I hereby claim my right to form a pack of my own, which I swear to lead to the best of my ability and guard with my dying breath, from this moment forward until my bones are bleached by the sun and the mantle is passed on to another."

"*What?*" Andre blanched, his shoulders stiff with shock. Behind him, Rupert gasped, clutching at his chest as the bond tying his son to the pack severed. Tobias felt it snap, too - but instead of pain, there was only a soaring freedom.

Carrie-Anne stepped forward and lifted her chin. "As Vixen of the Cartwright foxkin, I hereby acknowledge Tobias Greenwood as Alpha of the Greenwood pack."

Though it only needed one other alpha to witness his ascension, Joseph too stepped forward, his eyes glittering with something that

Tobias thought might be respect. "As Prime Stallion of the Victorian Horsekin, I hereby acknowledge Tobias Greenwood as Alpha of the Greenwood pack." He reached out to clap Zeke on the shoulder. "Take care of your Alpha, son."

Zeke swallowed and nodded. "Always. Tobias?"

"Round up the others. We go for Ash."

"*No!*" Andre launched himself at Tobias, shifting to wolf mid leap. Fur rippled over Tobias' body, limbs cracking and stretching as he donned his own wolf form. He caught Andre's salt and pepper-furred body with his teeth, spinning on his haunches to launch the older Alpha over one shoulder. Andre landed awkwardly, claws scrabbling for purchase in the grass as he turned to come rocketing back. The rangier wolf had years more experience but it was as though he moved in slow motion, his every intention laid bare. Tobias swatted Andre aside like a naughty pup, his claws drawing lines of blood where they collided with the other male's face. He put more than half his strength behind the blow and when Andre hit the ground he stayed there, body limp and eyes closed.

Silence blanketed the clearing. Ten seconds passed. Twenty. Still Andre failed to rise. As nausea twisted in Tobias' gut, Rupert rushed forward and pressed two fingers to his Alpha's throat. "He's alive."

"If Andre cannot continue, the challenge goes to Tobias." Carrie-Anne made to step closer and stopped as Hart grabbed her elbow. "What?"

The male foxkin narrowed his eyes at Tobias. "Are you still in there?"

Tobias nodded and returned to his human body. "I don't need the help of transition to beat lowlife scum."

Hart blew out a sigh of relief and released Carrie-Anne's arm. "Good; I don't fancy suicide by crazy Alpha."

Tobias couldn't help the laugh which escaped him - one that cut suddenly short when he met his father's stark expression. "You two really fucked this up."

"What else could I do?" Rupert shook his head as he gathered Andre's body into his burly arms. "He's my Alpha."

"A good second knows when to obey, when to support and most of all, when to disagree," Zeke said, his sapphire eyes flinty. "*You* taught me that. Andre may have failed the pack but you failed him. Worse than that, you failed your own son."

Rupert was silent for a long moment, his eyes lined with silver. At last he sighed. "I'll have Jemima sedate Andre to check for deeper injuries. It'll buy you until nightfall; after that, I can't make any promises."

"Understood." Tobias stooped to retrieve his clothing, jerking his chin at Zeke to follow suit. He paused before Joseph and Carrie-Anne, who wore equally grave expressions. "Let me take the fall for this; if something goes wrong, we need good people here to lend support against the bearkin. I'd also appreciate it if you both speak to Grandma Redding about helping to defend Redding pack land - I've just taken the only trained warriors they had."

Joseph offered his hand, eyes creasing in the corners. "You're an excellent Alpha, Tobias. Rest assured, my herds will watch over your former pack - and your new one, should that ever prove necessary."

"Thanks." Tobias accepted the shake with a strained smile. "Now, if you'll excuse me, my heartmate's waited long enough." He let his hand drop, raised his voice. "Flynn! Get your flea-bitten hide over here!"

*No need to shout.* Flynn melted out of the trees a bare six paces away, his amber eyes cold when they landed on Andre's unconscious form. *It's about time.*

"Don't start now," Tobias growled - but he was unable to stop the feral smile tugging at his lips. "Any more leads?"

Flynn nodded. *Steve found a metal dinghy covered in engine grease and tracked them to a road. Looks like they put her in a car.*

Joseph fisted a hand on his hip. "So the trail is lost?"

*On the contrary.* Flynn's lips curled back from deadly teeth. *We've got a direction and the freedom to search without impediment… unless you assholes want to get in our way.*

"Way I see it," Carrie-Anne said, "You disappeared into the bush so fast not even Solaeden could catch you."

*Good.* Flynn's tail flicked and he turned away, slipping back into the bush. *Come on, T-Fuzz. Let's go tear out some throats.*

"I thought you'd never ask."

*******

Aislinn woke with sand in her eyes, bile in her throat and the smell of wet jumper thick in the air. It took her a moment to realise the scent belonged to her - and the moment she did, memory came back in a painful rush.

"I wouldn't move, if I were you - the wire around your legs will cut you into tiny pieces at the slightest provocation." Her captor sounded so incredibly bored that Aislinn's curiosity overwhelmed her need for caution and she opened her eyes.

They stuck like glue.

He chuckled, then a moment later a warm cloth sponged at her face. "Now try."

This time her lids fluttered up on command, revealing the gritty interior of a low-roofed burrow, with tree roots poking from the walls and dangling from sections of the ceiling. Apart from the hard table to which she was bound, the room was devoid of furniture or decoration, limiting the number of potential hiding places or objects which could be used as a weapon.

Smart.

Aislinn rubbed her head on her forelegs, using the opportunity to inspect the wire that bound her forepaws together. As Captain Boredom had warned, it was a high tensile wire often used in garrottes and was, if she struggled, well and truly capable of amputating her limbs. Not that it mattered, since she could blend into the shadows and -

Except she couldn't.

Panic struck and Aislinn tried a second time to dematerialise, with equal lack of success. There were plenty of shadows; the room was lit only by the flickering flame of an old hurricane lamp set in an alcove on the opposite wall. Still, no matter what she tried, her powers refused to co-operate.

"I assume you've tried your little trick by now," drawled her captor, crouching down in front of her. He seemed familiar somehow; reedy and the sort of rumpled that came from true dedication to not bothering with one's appearance. Dirty blond hair fell in matted clumps around a pinched face whose thick black glasses reflected the meagre lighting and made it impossible to see his eyes. "I'm afraid the tranq is still in your system. We might've overdone it a little."

Aislinn growled.

"Don't worry - when the tranq wears off you'll be back to normal." He scooped up a tranq gun from the floor, checked the settings, then slouched back against the far wall. "It's nothing as accurate as that serum the bearkin have; your system will be building up an immunity even now."

Nothing as accurate as the bearkin? That answered one question - he wasn't a bear. Aislinn rubbed her chin on her front legs, testing the wire a second time while she racked her brains. *Where* had she seen him before?

"I'm a little disappointed you're not making more of a fuss." He yawned, slouching even further. One knee was bent, the arm holding the pistol resting on top. His fingers bore not only the calluses of a warrior, but nicks and burns she might associate with a doctor, or - Aislinn's head jerked up in astonishment and his thin lips curled. "Looks like your brain's finally catching up to the rest of you."

Yes. Now if she could just remember his *name* -

"Gerard, who are you talking to?" A voice like claws on a blackboard preceded the unmistakable form of Professor Percival Postlethwaite into the room. His greying hair had been carefully combed but the roof was low enough that the hanging tree roots had already began to ruffle it. Upon spying Aislinn, he drew a shining pocket-watch from his waistcoat and frowned at it. "Awake already?"

"I told you the tranq would wear off fast." Gerard shrugged. "Drugs never last long on Kin like her."

Percy squinted at Aislinn as though personally offended by her metabolism. "Shoot her again. She's notoriously troublesome."

Gerard waved a lazy hand. "If we pump her full of too much gunk, we might kill her. Then all of this will be for nothing."

"If she kills us, this will also have been for nothing." Percy's lips pursed in thought. "As soon as you think it's safe, put her back out."

"Sure." A long, lazy blink. "How was your conference call?"

The Professor made an annoyed sound in the back of his throat and slid his pocket-watch away. "It took more work than expected, but everything is arranged."

"Thank the gods; we've been here for hours."

Hours. It was impossible to tell without windows but Aislinn guessed from the comment - and the lack of hunger in her stomach - that it was still the same day, likely even before noon.

"I share the same frustration." Percy filled his cheeks with air, then shrugged. "We'll be back on track soon enough."

Aislinn's brow furrowed.

"Look at her face," Gerard chuckled. "She really *is* clueless."

"Instinctive cunning and intelligence are not the same thing, my dear assistant." Percy regarded Aislinn with an avian tilt of his head. "These wolves possess one and not the other."

Aislinn blinked. *Did he just call me stupid?*

"They're still predators - they'll be looking for her." Gerard waved the tranq gun wearily. "Especially the tiger."

"Hence the precautions we took with that odious grease - those fools will be looking for bearkin, not us," Percy replied, his nose wrinkling. "It's too bad the stink isn't so easily removed."

Professor and assistant stared at Aislinn for long, silent moments before Gerard made a face. "Hard to tell if it's the engine grease, the river water or the stench of bear that's the most overbearing."

"Quite. I look forward to having her thoroughly disinfected at the earliest opportunity."

Aislinn bared her teeth and growled.

"It's in your best interest to behave, Miss Redding." Percy adjusted the sleeves on his tweed jacket, his tone officious. "The Council have agreed with my professional opinion that you are, by extension of your connection to the bearkin, dangerous and have ordered you officially placed under my care."

*What?* Aislinn tried to sit, but the wire around her legs cut painfully into her flesh and she dropped back to her belly.

"Indeed," Percy looked vaguely amused. "I think your father would be equally surprised to discover that was part of the reason for my visit; the rest of the Council lost faith in him after the hospital incident, I'm afraid."

That came as no surprise to Aislinn - though the irony that her escape had now led to a similar version of the same captivity wasn't lost on her.

"I must admit," Percy continued, "I was stymied by the electromagnetic pulse that destroyed all of my electronics - but that was solved with the arrival of the backup team. I'd wager that eaglekin hasn't even noticed his tablet device is missing."

Aislinn growled again, her hackles stiff with drying mud as they stood straight on end. Brayden might look easygoing, but he'd be no less forgiving than any other predator when he discovered his things had been tampered with.

"Don't be mad," Gerard drawled. "After all, unless you tell the eagle, he'll never know. For shit hot agents, you guys *really* suck."

What? Aislinn's growl died and she tilted her head in obvious confusion. Percy clicked his tongue between his teeth. "Really, Gerard, no need to wax chatty just because you have a captive audience."

"Why not? We did all that hard work with the tranqs and the attempts to retrieve the alpha's laptop - seems a shame not to let her in on the secret." Gerard's eyes sparked with malicious humour. "Two wolves and a tiger, outdone by a barn owl and a sewer rat? Pathetic."

Wait. The Kin who'd shot Kaira, who'd attempted to break into Tobias' and then Grandma's house… were *Percy* and *Gerard*? Aislinn huffed a laugh and shook her head. She'd been so consumed with the bearkin, even the obvious hints hadn't presented as they should.

Percy shot Gerard a quelling look. "It's a scientific fact that we smaller Kin are often overlooked by the larger, more egotistical ones. So few stop to consider that whilst my owl form is small, I am nevertheless strong enough to support the weight of a rat."

"And a tiny, modified dart gun," Gerard added with a self-satisfied smirk.

Shifting in a vain attempt to ease the ache of her bindings, Aislinn considered her situation from a new light. If Percy had attained the cautious backing of at least one other Councillor before he'd petitioned to join the trip, her father's reputation was more damaged than she'd guessed. Once they returned to Ireland, it would be all-but impossible to escape - but she had no intention of allowing that to happen. With every passing moment, her strength returned and as soon as she was able, a simple dematerialisation would set her free.

As though hearing her thoughts, Gerard hefted the tranq gun and flicked a look at his wristwatch. "How long until transport?"

"Likely nightfall, at this stage." Percy sighed, fisting both hands on his hips. "I was hoping to make a start on my research sooner rather than later, but I suppose it can't be helped."

"Don't you have your portable kit?" Gerard asked. He jerked his chin in Aislinn's direction. "I'm going to have to shoot her again anyway. May as well make the most of it."

Percy looked down his nose, his face waxing contemplative. "Hmmm. I do have a number of experiments which could be conducted here - nothing too delicate, of course, but it'll give us a starting point once we return to my laboratory."

*No!* Aislinn scrabbled at the rug with her bound paws, trying to move her body to a better position.

"Hey!" Gerard rolled his wrist, levelled the tranq gun and unloaded three darts with an ease that made Aislinn re-evaluate his skillset as a 'lab assistant'. She managed to evade the first but the other two hit home, sinking deep into her hindquarters and deadening them immediately.

*Damn.* Unconsciousness crept up Aislinn's body one inch at a time. For every cell that went numb, her resolve hardened - she wouldn't go calmly into whatever torture they had planned. If these two males wanted a pound of her flesh, they'd have to pay for it in full.

# Seventeen

Sienna stared up into the bright summer sky, watching Brayden's eagle form slowly dwindle from sight. She remembered the breathtaking beauty of his brown feathered wings and head, his stomach and legs shocking white with black speckles. A martial eagle, he'd explained; one of the largest predatory eagles in the world. Stroking her fingers down those feathers had been an exquisite sensory exercise that even now had her skin tingling in delightful recollection.

He'd been sweet and gentle after the concert, walking for hours with her through the orchard before she'd shyly confessed that Aislinn had vouched for his ability to worship. Brayden had laughed and kissed her, his scent citrus and sunshine and incredibly decadent. Then he'd worshipped her as promised; right there in the middle of the orchard.

They'd lain chatting under the stars about her dreams to take her fashion designs global; he'd immediately begged to see her work. Enchanted, Sienna had driven them both - still stark naked - to Ysera's Boutique, where Brayden paid the same detailed attention to her dresses as he had to her body; and then he'd worshipped her there on the floor, and later on the shop counter, and later again, on the sofa in the upstairs office. A thorough, intense worshipping that Sienna knew would become the benchmark for all her future encounters.

The sun rose on them both thoroughly exhausted but Brayden hadn't allowed time for Sienna to be shy; he'd demanded she model one of her creations while they went in search of breakfast. After returning to the store with bellies full of wild blackberries, he'd worshipped her all over again.

He didn't care that she was Ezekiel Smythe's younger sister. He didn't care that she was waif-petite. He didn't care that her breasts were too small and her eyes too big, that her fingers were too spindly or her joints too knobbly. In fact, when she'd shyly admitted to hating the almost constant nudity that went hand in hand with being Kin, Brayden's jaw had all-but hit his chest.

"What?" Sienna's tiny finger tapped his jaw, her brows furrowing. "Why are you making that face?"

"Didn't I just tell you how beautiful you are?" He demanded, shaking his head as if to clear it. "Sienna… No, you won't believe me, will you? No wonder Aislinn got involved." Bright hazel eyes twinkled mischievously. "I'd hate to disappoint either of you ladies, so it looks like I'll just have to keep on worshipping until you realise you're a goddess in your own right."

And he had.

When Zeke called to say Aislinn had been kidnapped and Tobias had left the pack, Sienna's heart froze solid in her chest but Brayden kept his cool, taking the phone from her nerveless fingers and exchanging swift, professional words with her brother.

"I have to go." Phone on the counter, hands strong and warm on her shoulders, lips inflammatory against her own. "I need to join the search."

"What do I do?"

Brayden's face had softened, his dark blond hair tumbled from their exertions and bronze body sheened with sweat. "You swore to Aislinn; now's the time to prove it."

That was how she'd ended up with a hastily scrawled list in Brayden's surprisingly neat handwriting, detailing what supplies she'd best gather and stash in the car while he took wing in the azure skies above.

"Well," Sienna whispered, staring into the now-emptied sky; "Better get started."

She slipped back into the boutique and locked the door, heading upstairs to her office. Gerup was still a ghost town after the bearkin attack a few days earlier, but someone might report back to Andre if questions were asked - or worse, any stranger could be a bearkin waiting for an opportunity to strike. Biting her lip, Sienna began ratting through boxes of half-finished clothing, putting together a hodgepodge outfit of gaudy prints and flowing, bohemian layers that she topped with a light headscarf to disguise her golden curls. It wouldn't fool the locals if someone looked closely, but it might be enough to do what needed to be done.

Brayden's list in hand, she exited the shop and tottered down the street, skirting shards of broken glass to step through the window of the abandoned general store. It was testament to the trust inherent among Kin that nobody had looted it before now and Sienna felt a twinge of guilt as she began to search the wreckage. Maintaining her concentration was difficult when every shadow made her jump and every sigh of the summer breeze made her flinch.

"Come on, Sienna," she whispered, curling her fingers around the wire shopping basket half-filled with canned food and sundries. "Stop being such a baby."

Though she forced herself to keep going, the words bought little comfort. She wasn't a warrior like Aislinn or a level-headed medic like her mother; she was a fashion designer with a knack for colour, a penchant for pretty shoes and a minor in business management. By the time Sienna had ticked off as many items as possible from her list, her hands were shaking and her lungs fluttered unsteadily in her chest. She made her way to the counter and, devoid of money or anything of value to leave in return for the goods, penned a careful note to the store owner and tucked it into the cash drawer of the dormant register. It wasn't much but it would have to do.

The searing heat of the afternoon beat down as Sienna stepped into the silent street. Shrinking deeper into the dubious protection of her gauzy headscarf, she trekked back to Ysera's Boutique, letting herself in the side entrance as she'd done when Brayden had been egging her on with his broad smile and twinkling eyes.

Brayden. Whilst Sienna had no illusions about the fact that their arrangement was a temporary one, it would nevertheless have been comforting to have the eaglekin back by her side. He wouldn't ruffle her hair like a child as Zeke often did; nor would he berate her for her fears like her mother. Locking the door behind her - though it would do precious little if a bear really wanted to get inside - Sienna packed her 'purchases' into a pair of heavy rucksacks she'd found in the spare wheel well of the car. It was pack procedure to have a stash of basics in all vehicles and some of the things she'd been unable to find at the general store were already inside.

Putting the packs behind the counter in case she needed to make a quick exit, Sienna checked her phone and then, feeling somewhat odd about it, Brayden's. No messages on either device although, in reality, it was likely Flynn was co-ordinating the search with his incredible telepathic ability.

Mere thought of the tigerkin sent a shiver down Sienna's spine and she rubbed at her arms. Oh, he was Bad Boy sexy all right but he was also dangerous and terrifying with equal emphasis. She knew he'd been close to Aislinn - Sienna blushed at the thought of how close - but she couldn't for the life of her imagine how anyone could put up with a presence that intense. There was something about Flynn, like he was a hurricane in a skin suit that might go off at any minute and raze the entire town. Not like Tobias, who wore strength and comfort the same way other people wore shorts and a shirt; no, Flynn was a thing of nightmares. Kinky, dirty, sweaty nightmares, but nightmares nonetheless.

A scritching sound at the Boutique's front door snatched Sienna's attention and made her heart thump unevenly in her chest. With a terrified lump in her throat, she tiptoed to the front of the shop and peeped around the edge of the curtain. A rotund, middle-aged woman stood under the awning, eyes darting nervously from side to side and a sunhat clenched tightly in her fists. Recognising Martha Crawford from the bakery three doors over, Sienna immediately drew the curtain aside and unlatched the door.

"Martha? Is everything okay?" She asked as the mousekin shuffled inside.

"I was going to ask you the same," Martha answered. "I was helping Cliff with the bread and I saw you skittering up and down the street like your own shadow might get you."

Sienna pasted what she hoped was a reassuring smile onto her face. "I suppose we're all feeling like that since the attack."

"Too right." Martha shuddered, closing her grey eyes briefly. "Bearkin, all the way out here! It's no wonder so many've decided to visit relatives out of state."

"Why didn't you go?"

The older woman shrugged. "Cliff wanted to make sure the community had what it needed when things settled down. Our home's here, you know?"

"Of course," Sienna agreed. Lunaida above, Cliff and Martha were *mice* and they had more courage than she did! Cheeks pinking with shame, she dared to reach out and pat Martha's soft shoulder. "I happen to know that the Cartwright foxes, the Victorian allied herds and the Redding pack are working together to provide security from here on out." She placed a finger alongside her nose. "Trade secret."

Martha looked relieved. "Good to see the toothy types haven't forgotten those of us who're less able to defend ourselves. No offence, my dear."

"None taken." Sienna smiled brightly; a smile she'd learnt long ago put others at ease. Her head began to ache, as it often did when her newly acknowledged empathic ability was operating at full speed. "Is there something else, Martha?"

"Oh, well, it's nothing… just, have you heard from the Beauforts at all? Agitha's sick, you know, and with everything being closed down I don't know if she's able to get her meds." Martha bit her lip with tiny, white teeth. "I wanted to drive out to the burrow and check but it's a long way in uncertain times."

"And it's between here and pack land," Sienna added, nodding when Martha exhaled in a gust. "She never really recovered from the miscarriage, did she? Emotionally, I mean."

Martha's face was sad as she shook her head. "No, poor girl. Human and Kin genealogy just don't mix."

The differences between humans and Kin were a long-debated mystery nobody had been able to solve. Though their human bodies looked near enough to be considered identical, the two races were biologically incompatible and pregnancies either miscarried, resulted in stillborn babies, or worse - babies who lived only a few hours before they gained an angel's wings.

Sienna pressed her lips together in a thin line. "I can't begin to imagine the toll it takes mentally. If only there was a way."

"Scientists, magicians, holy men and doctors've been trying for centuries to fix that." Martha shook her head. "Can't help who you fall in love with, I guess."

"No." Sienna thought of her confused, misspent emotions where a certain Tobias Greenwood was concerned, and winced. "Would you like me to drop by the Beaufort's burrow on my way home later?"

"Oh, yes, please. They've likely gone to Agitha's family in Perth but I'd feel so much better if someone checked." Martha's smile was filled with gratitude. "Would you wait another half hour? I'd like to bring by a loaf of bread."

"I'll wait." Sienna smiled again and after a brief, awkward embrace, she let Martha back out and locked the door behind her.

True to her word, less than thirty minutes later the mousekin was back with two fresh loaves of bread and a meat pie, because Sienna looked far too thin and should put something good in her stomach. Having not eaten since breakfast, she wasn't about to argue and wolfed down the pie in a matter of minutes. It was only afterwards, as she sank down in the chair inside her office, that Sienna thought guiltily that she should have saved some for Brayden but it was far too late for that now. Warm and comfortable, she dropped her head back against the headrest and closed her eyes.

The next thing she knew, a pair of warm, male lips were tracing their way up the column of her throat and along her jaw. Citrus and sunshine surrounded Sienna as she woke, opening her mouth on instinct. Brayden's kisses were long, slow and drugging, one big hand cradling her head and the other sliding behind her shoulders to tug her against his chest.

"Good evening," he chuckled when her eyes fluttered open.

Sienna blinked in a valiant effort to clear her foggy brain. "What time is it?"

"Sun's setting, so… about eight?" Brayden raised an eyebrow. "Bit hard to wear a watch, I'm afraid. Ruffles the feathers."

"Ha. Ha." Framing his face with her much smaller hands, Sienna nipped the tip of his nose in a way she'd discovered drove Brayden Maxwell a little bit wild, and was rewarded with a tightening of his embrace and a laughing shower of kisses as he tumbled her out of the chair and onto the floor.

"Too many clothes," he complained - and set about rectifying the problem immediately.

"Wait! Aren't you hot and tired and hungry?" Sienna protested. Her words ended on a breathy gasp as he bared a strip of abdomen and began kissing his way across it. "Brayden!"

"Hot, tired and hungry," he agreed, raising his head to show all three of those things glittering in his bright hazel eyes. "No?"

"Yes," Sienna managed, completely disarmed by the intensity in his expression. "But I do have actual food - fresh bread."

"Later," he declared, and went back to peeling layer after layer of clothing off her body. Everything he removed garnered a murmur of sensual appreciation; every bit of skin he bared got kissed with the same dedication that Brayden applied to everything else she'd seen him do.

"You don't have to take it all off," she gasped, writhing helplessly as his tongue flicked over her hip.

"Yes I do." His words were a seduction all their own, his breath hot and damp across her skin. "I need to see all of you." Brayden's fingers hooked in a layer of gauze, drew it carefully away. "You're too beautiful to be covered."

Undone. She was completely and utterly undone and there were no more protests to be made as Brayden used his lips and hands over her body, winding her tighter and tighter until one single, luscious lick across her core had her shattering into a million pieces. Then he was inside her, the welcome intrusion shoving her further into ecstasy. When the last shiver faded, Brayden angled his pelvis so that he was buried deeper than before, grinning as her eyes went wide, and paused.

"What?" She managed.

His grin turned decidedly wicked. "Are you ready?"

Sure the sane answer was 'no,' she nevertheless nodded. "Yes."

"Good." Bracing himself on one elbow, he trailed the other hand down her body, leaving goose bumps in the wake of his touch. Brayden palmed her hip, fingers firm without being too hard, and captured her mouth with a kiss so tender Sienna's eyes pricked with tears. "Hold on now, gorgeous."

A simple enough suggestion but as he began to move, employing what surely had to be some sort of witchcraft, Sienna wondered if she was even going to remember her name after it was over. Gentle and sweet and devoted, Brayden magicked her body to heights she would have heretofore declared impossible, sweeping her away on a tide of sensation until Sienna was sobbing his name between kisses, her body consumed by fireworks that seemed never-ending.

Brayden collapsed on top of her as his own release scoured them both. He was deliciously heavy, their lungs working in tandem to garner air without inconveniencing the other, hearts racing at such a speed that she knew he'd enjoyed himself just as much as she had.

"You've killed me," she muttered, limbs quivering like jelly.

"Not sorry," he chuckled, pressing a kiss to her shoulder. "I didn't hurt you, though? I might have lost my mind a little at the end." Sienna took so long to answer that he raised his head, one eyebrow quirked. Seeing the astonishment on her face, Brayden's brow furrowed. "What? If I hurt you, I-"

"No," she shook her head. "I was just thinking you were perfectly gentle the entire time and I've never felt so good in my life - and you're worried you *hurt* me?"

"Well, that's a relief." His expression smoothed into one of very male satisfaction. "I'm not the pistoning kind."

"*Pistoning*?" Sienna blinked in horror. "Is that even a thing?"

"Of course." Brayden yawned and snuggled into her neck. "There are plenty of men out there who think it's all about ramming and jamming."

Sienna choked, then dissolved into a round of helpless giggles as he began lipping the sensitive skin where neck joined shoulder. "Stop that."

"Make me." A teasing challenge - but a second later, he lifted his head and yawned again. "I didn't find Ash."

"Oh."

"I know I should've told you straight away but I couldn't resist your sleepy face," Brayden admitted, cheeks colouring. "Besides, I'm no good in the dark; Jacques has taken over until Andre wakes."

"Andre," Sienna growled. "I'll never understand his motivations."

Brayden shrugged. "Broken people do strange things sometimes. How did you go with the list?"

Happily trapped under his body and feeling equally guilty about that happiness, Sienna related the entirety of her afternoon. Brayden listened quietly, nodding now and then as he agreed with something that had been said or a supposition she injected into the narrative. Barely had she finished talking when both of their phones, now on Sienna's desk where he must have dumped them before waking her, beeped insistently.

"No rest for the wicked," she muttered.

"Guess not." Brayden sighed, carefully disentangling his body from hers. "Hot damn but I hate it when duty calls."

Flushing with embarrassment, Sienna caught the phone he lobbed her way and checked the message. "Zeke, asking me to meet up with him and the others. You?"

"Jacques." Brayden grunted, his face creased in displeasure. "We've been recalled - he's warning me to be ready to hunt the lot of you."

Unable to stand the furrow between his brows, Sienna smoothed it away with her fingertips. "You already caught me. Several times."

"Well." Dropping his phone, Brayden grinned. "Someone did promise you a worshipping on my behalf, didn't they?"

"Yeah." She hesitated, suddenly self-conscious. "If that's the only reason you-"

"Don't," he cut her off gently, tipping up her chin until their eyes met. "Sienna, I thought you were delightful from the moment I met you. Ash just gave me permission to act on it and not get my balls ripped off. In fact, in other circumstances I might be tempted to break my non-dating rule." Now it was his turn to look hesitant. "This was-"

"It was perfect," Sienna murmured, stopping him with a finger over his lips. "And don't worry, I know it wasn't forever. You showed me I'm more than I ever thought I could be, inside and out - but I'm not expecting you to mate with me because of it."

"I'm not sure if I'm disappointed or relieved to hear that." Brayden sighed, then clambered to his feet and offered a hand. "It's been a pleasure to get to know you and I don't mean that in a kinky way."

"Likewise." Sienna smiled and allowed him to tug her to her upright. He bent his head as she stood and they kissed gently, a sweet, chaste kiss from two people connected on a deeper level by the intimacy they'd shared. "I guess I'll see you around?"

Brayden's look was anything but innocent. "I hope so."

And then, before it could get awkward, he kissed her again and headed down the stairs. By the time Sienna gathered the packs, stashed them in the car and locked up the shop, Brayden had winged off into the oncoming night. She didn't watch him leave this time, aware that their interlude had come to an end and determined to treasure the experience with a smile - even if her lips trembled a little.

Sienna slid into the car and started the engine, heading towards the place Zeke had instructed her to meet; a place she'd carefully avoided mentioning to Brayden and he'd carefully avoided asking about. She considered the route as she drove, tapping her nails against the steering wheel. The Beaufort burrow was on the way and even though Brayden had flown overhead several times during the day and seen nothing out of the ordinary, Sienna decided to stop by anyway. After all, she'd promised Martha - and who knew what would happen once she met up with Zeke and the rest of the boys?

Decision made, she pulled off the side of the road a respectful distance from the burrow, as was polite when visiting those who lived underground. Concealing the car behind a stand of gum trees, Sienna adjusted her clothing - the bohemian wrappings she'd worn earlier - and stepped into the bush.

As she approached the path leading to the burrow Sienna paused, nostrils curling. What was that smell? Lingering behind a tall paperbark, she inhaled again. It smelled like… cars. Like a mechanic's garage or something equally greasy. Making a face, she crouched down to get a clearer whiff of the scent and caught faint undertones of… bergamot?

Who in the world smelt like earl grey tea? Someone who clearly didn't like it, Sienna reflected, if they were trying to cover it with some sort of oil or grease. Uneasiness settled in the pit of her gut. Agitha and Tomas weren't farmers and kept their car garaged in town to avoid littering the bush where they made their home. Why would the smell of engines be so very strong here?

Biting her lip, Sienna cast a glance over her shoulder. She should go back to the car and get her phone; call Zeke. But then a strange, keening howl, muffled as though underground, split the night - and was cut suddenly short. Recognition straightened Sienna's spine and widened her eyes.

Aislinn.

Without stopping to think, Sienna called her wolf form and raced into the darkness.

********

Aislinn woke screaming, the noise tearing from her lupine throat as a distorted howl which Gerard cut off via the simple expedient of jamming a wadded up tea towel into her open mouth. She tried to struggle but her limbs, still bound in pairs by razorwire, were tied to the kitchen table.

Percy, who'd been cutting into her hindquarters with a scalpel, stepped back in irritation. "Really, Gerard, are you paying attention at all? I almost slipped."

"I didn't think she'd regain consciousness so quickly." Gerard yawned, sounding just as bored as he had earlier. "Darts wore off too quick."

Percy took another step back and rested a wrist on his hip, carefully curling the bloodied scalpel away from himself. "This really will *not* do. Get the tranq gun."

"Can't shoot her again so soon," Gerard reminded him. He flicked a look at the clock, a faux gingerbread house affixed to the kitchen wall. "Got another hour before our ride is here; best save it until then."

"Hmm." Percy pressed his lips together in a thin line. "Very well. Fetch me something else to tie her down with, then; I'll be mightily displeased if Miss Redding ruins the hard work I've done so far."

Gerard expelled his breath in an exasperated gust, rolling out of the rustic wooden chair in which he'd been sitting as he sterilised a range of cruel-looking tools that were more like a torture kit than a scientist's belongings. "Fine. Back in a minute."

As soon as Gerard was out of the room, Aislinn chanced a glance at her hindquarters. They'd shaved her right hind leg, exposing the skin - and Olaf's thick, black Marking - underneath. Percy had begun to make an incision around the Mark and it was that pain, Aislinn knew, which had broken the thrall of the tranquillisers. Not before he'd managed to get almost half way around though, the neat cuts leaking blood into her remaining fur. The tea towel might have prevented her from biting, but it did nothing to stop the threatening growl which rumbled in her chest as she turned her eyes back to the Professor.

"Really, Miss Redding," Percy huffed. "I am not trying to kill you, merely assess if the Mark is only skin deep, or whether it extends further into muscle and bone. I also intend to find out whether an excised Mark holds form, if it grows back or if it duplicates. You should be honoured; this is a ground-breaking opportunity."

*A ground-breaking opportunity?* Aislinn stared death into Percy's eyes until at last his gaze skittered away. How long would it take Gerard to find whatever he was looking for? How long until her body recuperated enough for her shadow powers to return? It seemed a fool's hope to believe one would come before the other, but it was all she had.

A scrabbling noise echoed from the other end of the burrow and Percy frowned. "Gerard? You foolish rat, what are you doing up there? How long does it take to fetch another length of razor wire?"

Hatred rose in Aislinn's heart, thick and fast, along with a curious sense of desperation. Maybe it'd be better to shift, to amputate her own limbs - she'd die of the blood loss in minutes but at least she'd take Percy and Gerard with her. Even as the dark thing inside her urged her on, Aislinn paused. If she did this, here and now, she would never see her heartmate again; would leave him forever bereft. Not only that, but Olaf would be free to continue his murderous rampages - and who was going to stop him? Who would step in to avenge the women who were already lost? Who would protect the women he might target in the future? Aislinn's vision blurred and she laid her head on her forepaws. No, she wouldn't break. There was nothing the Professor could do to her that hadn't already been done - and there was everything, *everything* to gain from surviving. So she'd count every sin and measure every drop of blood the Professor extracted - and when the time was right, he'd die.

The same scratching, scrabbling sound came from the other end of the burrow and this time, it had a distinctly wet edge to it. Percy cleared his throat. "Gerard?"

Nothing; only an ominous quiet. Percy's fist tightened around the scalpel and he took a half step towards the archway when a golden bullet shot through it, hitting him square in the chest. Both Kin tumbled, Percy shrieking as lupine jaws snapped near his throat.

*Zeke!* There was no mistaking the golden sheen of that fur coat as the wolf, already covered in blood, made a second lunge for Percy's face. The Professor bought his hands up in an instinctive move to defend himself and the scalpel embedded deeply into the wolf's shoulder. It yelped and faltered, allowing Percy to get a leg up and kick his attacker away. The wolf rolled unceremoniously under the table and Aislinn strained at her ropes to peer over the edge.

The wolf was female, fine boned and lovely even covered in blood. Aislinn met a pair of terrified sapphire eyes and felt her breath catch. She hadn't mistaken that golden fur but she *had* mistaken the wolf who wore it. This wasn't Zeke; this was Sienna, and judging from the way she was slowly backing up, lips pulled back from her teeth in a growl that lacked any real conviction, she had no idea what she was doing.

Aislinn rumbled deep in her chest, a sound she hoped was encouraging, and jerked her head in an effort to communicate while Percy struggled upright. Sienna returned her look with one of confusion and then it was too late; Percy launched himself across the room in a very un-professorly movement. He snatched up the tranq gun Aislinn had been trying to indicate and fired three shots in quick succession.

Sienna yelped and dove aside, saved by a combination of dumb luck and Percy's wild aim. The golden wolf slipped in her own blood and crashed into a side table, knocking the case of tools Gerard had been sterilising down on top of herself. Percy's second round of darts was better aimed but Sienna was protected by the thick steel of the case which had fallen across her and the tranqs bounced harmlessly away. She got her feet beneath her and leapt - and while the lunge was anything but elegant, her teeth fastened around Percy's wrist and dragged him to the floor.

The Professor shrieked and shifted forms, leaving Sienna with a mouthful of feathers as a fist-sized owl flapped towards the front of the burrow. Sienna dove after him, the next few minutes filled with snarling, screeching and crashing before the sharp sound of shattering glass heralded a new silence. Moments later, Sienna staggered back into the room in her human form.

"Ash," she sobbed, her face and chest covered in blood. Sienna seized the scalpel still embedded in her shoulder and pulled it out with shaking hands, dropping to her knees beside the table to cut at the razor wire. "I killed him, Ash. Solaeden save me, I tore out his throat."

Gerard or Percy? Not that it mattered at this point; either dead left the other at a disadvantage. Aislinn rumbled encouragingly in her chest as Sienna fumbled with the wire, finally throwing down the scalpel with a scream. When the younger woman's breath began coming in gasps, Aislinn nosed at her bloodied cheeks. Sienna blinked, sapphire eyes focussing at last.

"Ash... by the Lady." Swallowing heavily, Sienna carefully extracted the tea towel from her mouth and Aislinn whimpered in relief as the ache in her jaw eased. "I don't know what to do!"

Heedless of the blood and muck, Aislinn rubbed her cheek against Sienna's chest and stayed patiently still while the other's trembling arms held her close, squeezing almost painfully tight. Second by agonising second, Sienna's shaking faded and her breathing calmed.

When she finally leant back, Aislinn nudged at her shoulder, whined, and pointed her muzzle at the fallen case of tools.

"Oh. Oh!" Sienna hurried to the case and began digging through it, eventually turning out a pair of wire cutters. Her fingers were slippery with blood but she managed to get the cutters under the edge of the razor wire and bear down, separating the strands with a click that was music to Aislinn's ears.

Feeling returned to her forepaws in a tingling rush and she groaned deep in her throat, curling her front legs reflexively under her chin whilst Sienna moved on to the back ones. The moment the second lot of wire fell away, Aislinn called her human body and wrapped Sienna in a tight embrace. They were both sobbing now - relief, grief, gratitude and pain swirling together in a tight knot of emotion.

Aislinn made a monumental effort to swallow her tears, smoothing Sienna's golden curls as she did so. "Are you okay?"

"I killed him," Sienna repeated, her body once more a mass of trembles.

"I know," Aislinn returned, kissing her gently on the forehead. Now that her mind was clearer she could tell it was Gerard's blood coating Sienna and felt a dark twinge of satisfaction that the bored ratkin had met his end in such an ignominious way. "I'm sorry you had to do that. But, Sienna, where are the others? Why are you here alone?"

"Oh!" Sienna drew back to dash at her tears and Aislinn felt a surge of pride in her friend. "Everyone thinks the bears stole you; they've spent all day searching. I was on my way to join them but I promised Martha I'd drop in to check on Agitha and Tomas and then when I got closer I could smell this odd, engine kind of smell and then I heard you scream and..."

"Okay," Aislinn soothed, "It's okay. Why don't you explain it once we're out of here? Over a cup of tea." She flicked a glance at the gingerbread house clock and hoped that whoever Agitha and Tomas were, they'd gone somewhere safe long before Percy and Gerard had arrived. "We've got to get going - the Council are sending lackeys to fetch me."

"Damn! Percy got away, too." Sienna straightened at once. "We have to meet Tobias and the others at Cracked Forks' Bridge."

"Cracked Forks' Bridge?" Aislinn swung her legs off the table and winced at the pain in her hip. She saw Sienna eyeing the incision that curved over her buttock and ribs and tried to smile. "It's just a surface wound - it'll heal."

Her ankles protested the weight she set on them but held and after a moment's unsteadiness, Aislinn swept the burrow with practised efficiency. She recovered two dead phones, a dead laptop and Brayden's stolen tablet, but nothing else of use. Shoving the electronics into a canvas shopping bag and mouthing a silent apology to Agitha, she shoved the bag into Sienna's shaking hands, blew out the hurricane lamp and led the way to the front of the burrow.

True dark had fallen, but Aislinn's night vision was that of a wolf and she had no trouble spying Gerard's body slouched against one wall. His throat was messily torn and she winced at the evidence that Sienna had struggled with him, the kill far more intimate - and traumatising - than a quick, clean strike. Admiring her friend's courage anew, Aislinn checked Gerard's body, discarding several grisly looking knives and a half eaten apple before she was satisfied he had nothing hidden on his person that could be used to track them.

"He really was a cock," she murmured, running a now-bloodied hand through her hair, "But he also wasn't just a lab tech. Where did you come from, Gerard, and how did you end up with Percy, of all people?"

"I jumped him from behind," Sienna whispered, surprising Aislinn by moving to stand beside her and prod Gerard's leg with her toe. "I winded him, I think, but he was strong."

"Did he know how to fight?" Aislinn glanced up and down the length of Sienna's body, noting several rapidly forming bruises. "Yes, he did. Interesting. You did well to get one up on him, Sens."

"I didn't want to."

"That," Aislinn told her quietly, "Is a good thing. Come on."

It was almost anticlimactic to slip out the front door, locking it behind them on instinct. Aislinn followed Sienna through the night-dark bush to one of the pack cars, stashed a respectful distance away beneath the shelter of some trees, her eyes and ears peeled for any sign of Percy's tiny owl form or, worse, whatever backup he'd requested.

"Wait here," Sienna murmured, disappearing off in another direction. When she returned, she was dressed in a pair of flowing pants and a crop top, her fists clenched tightly around the car keys and what turned out to be several pieces of gauzy fabric. "I'll drive."

"Are you sure?"

"You're injured worse than me," Sienna returned evenly, then shoved the fabric into Aislinn's hands and pointed imperiously at the vehicle. "I also need to do something other than think."

Aislinn slid into the passenger seat without further protest. Sienna started the engine and pulled out onto the road and the first few minutes passed in silence whilst Aislinn busied herself turning a fringed shawl into a makeshift bandage which also functioned as a skirt. The remaining fabric was too short to be good for much, but Sienna began murmuring quiet instructions on how to knot the pieces together and by the time they hit the main road and began picking up speed, Aislinn had a passable substitute for a bikini top. Her breasts spilled up and out like she was the damsel in someone's corny fantasy but her nipples were in and she decided that, for now, would have to do.

"Okay," she ventured at last, "Why Cracked Forks' Bridge?"

Sienna drew a deep, slow breath and shot Aislinn a sidelong look. "There was a fight with Andre. I don't know the specifics but Tobias swore out of the pack and took on his mantle as Alpha. Pack land is closed to us and as of sunset, Andre initiated a search to have us arrested and imprisoned for treason." Sienna shivered and tightened her grip on the wheel. "From here on in, we're on our own."

# Eighteen

Cracked Forks' Bridge was a dark shadow jutting into a sky littered with cut crystal stars. On any other occasion Tobias would have thought it a beautiful patchwork of shadow and light; tonight every star was a leering, lecherous bearkin face and he a shrinking violet with no hope of rescue.

His only saviour was Flynn, who punched him astonishingly hard every time he started to panic beyond the ability to think. The resulting brawls left them both bloodied and bruised but feeling temporarily better for having spent their impotent energies.

"What I don't understand," Tobias said for the tenth time as Zeke appeared at his side, "Is how they disappeared off the face of the fucking earth so damned fast."

"We're missing something," Zeke agreed, rolling to the balls of his bare feet and back down again. "I still say they've taken shelter. Jacques assured me that Brayden's top notch when it comes to needles in haystacks so if he didn't see anything, then there wasn't anything to see."

Tobias thrust a hand into his hair, carefully avoiding the eye that was almost swollen shut from his most recent spat with a certain tigerkin. "Now Brayden will be hunting us, first thing tomorrow morning. How hard do you think he and the rest will try to catch us?"

Zeke sighed, golden curls tumbling around his face as he looked further down the narrow gorge. "Flynn thinks they'll go as easy as they can - but if they slack off too much, the Council will replace them. We'll have time, just not bucketfuls of it." His head jerked upright. "Do you hear that?"

"A car." Tobias spun towards the precarious pathway up the side of the cliff. "Alert the others; primary defence positioning."

Zeke melted into the darkness, leaving Tobias to climb at a pace that would have alarmed him a week ago but was now normal. He paused just shy of the clifftop as the car rolled to a halt. The air was thick with the iron-rich scent of blood, the fumes of the exhaust and… with a hoarse shout, Tobias levered himself over the edge of the bluff.

Aislinn and Sienna barrelled into him at full speed and they all went down hard, but the pain was secondary to the women in his arms. Tobias hugged them hard enough that they laughed protests, Sienna clinging like a limpet whilst Aislinn peppered his face with kisses, her hands tangled in his hair.

Zeke appeared less than a minute later and Sienna disappeared into her brother's arms with a strangled cry. Tobias heard Flynn's voice, and Jaxon's, but he didn't care about a single thing except wrapping both his arms around Aislinn and kissing the life back into them both. She melted instantly, her body soft and lusciously curved against his, a sinful addiction he'd never get enough of.

"Get a room," Flynn growled.

Aislinn raised her head a fraction, her breath tickling across Tobias' lips. "Stop watching."

"I can't," Flynn replied. "It's like a car crash; impossible to look away."

"You're a car crash," Tobias grunted. Aislinn laughed and kissed him again but it was softer, sweeter, something so tender it tugged at his soul. "Let's get down to the camp and out of sight."

Flynn promptly snatched Aislinn out of Tobias' grip and crushed her against him, his embrace so tight the tendons stood out on his arms. The tigerkin buried his face in her hair and his chest heaved like a bellows as he absorbed her scent - and for the first time, Tobias smiled to see them reunited.

"Hey," Aislinn chuckled, patting at Flynn's face with shaking hands. "Come on now, it hasn't even been twenty-four hours."

"Too long," Flynn growled, his voice muffled by thick waves of hair. "I already lost you once."

Making a sound of affectionate exasperation, Aislinn flicked a look over her shoulder at Zeke. "What do you want to do about the car?"

"Andre will be looking for it," was the immediate response. "So will any bearkin who saw it." Zeke flicked a look down at Sienna, who he'd tucked under one arm. "How did you manage to get Ash away from them, little sister mine?"

"It's a long story, but no bears are going to recognise the car," Aislinn said quietly. She looked up at Jaxon. "Keys are in the ignition. Dump it somewhere inventive."

"Done." The stocky wolfkin nodded, jogged to the car and slid inside.

"Wait!" Sienna ran to the boot, opened it and dragged out two bulging rucksacks. "Okay, *now* dump it."

Tobias caught the bag Sienna threw in his direction and unzipped it a fraction to peek at the contents. "When did you get time to manage this?"

"Earlier today," Sienna answered, shoving the second bag at her brother as Jaxon drove off into the night. "Now, if nobody minds, I *really* need a drink."

"I've got scotch," Flynn offered.

Sienna nodded. "Please."

"Come on." Aislinn extracted herself from the circle of Flynn's arms, took Sienna by the hand and led her to the cliff. "The boys can meet us down there."

Zeke blinked. "Did they just jump?"

*Looks like it.* Flynn prowled to the edge of the cliff in tiger form, whiskers twitching as he peered over the edge. *They're halfway down already.*

Tobias moved to Flynn's side and leant over to look for himself. The two women slithered to the bottom at that very moment and, still holding hands, moved unerringly in the direction of the camp. "Looks like we need to do a better job of covering our scent trail."

Trusting the example his heartmate had set, Tobias stepped off the edge. The hairs on the back of his neck stood on end and his stomach flip flopped uncomfortably but the cliff was underfoot moments later. He slid down to a narrow ledge, teetered and dropped again, one tiny shelf at a time, until he'd made it to the bottom in less than a minute.

Zeke swore as he followed, Flynn laughing as he bounded alongside in complete defiance of the laws of physics. They landed in time to flank Tobias as he jogged along the base of the cliff to where a steep overhang hid the pack's campsite from view. There was no fire, simply a stack of blankets spread out towards the back of the overhang and a haphazard collection of supplies they'd managed to gather from their final, hectic visit with Grandma Redding. Tobias added his rucksack to the pile and moments later Zeke did the same. There was a general shuffling and murmuring, then Flynn, back in human form, produced a flask of something from somewhere and handed it to Sienna with a sarcastic flourish.

"Thank you." Sienna unscrewed it and swigged with enough fervour that Tobias' eyebrows shot up.

"Solaeden's balls, Sens, are you okay?"

"No," Sienna answered shortly, offering the flask to Aislinn.

"I better not," the other woman murmured. "Tranqs are still in my system. I've had enough unconsciousness for one day."

Flynn caught Sienna's enquiring glance and grinned. "Finish it."

She did, then tossed him the empty container. "A few days ago you offered to teach me about those pressure points. Is that offer still open?"

"I thought you said I was too scary?"

Sienna's face turned hard. "I've discovered there are worse things than a tiger with a bad attitude."

Flynn howled with laughter, doubling over with his hands on his knees. When he straightened, he wiped away tears and said; "We'll start tomorrow."

"Tonight," Sienna corrected, then looked at Aislinn. "Put us on watch together."

Aislinn nodded, looking not in the least surprised. "Whatever you need."

Zeke folded his arms across his chest, brow furrowed. "Someone want to fill us in on what we're missing here?"

Jaxon arrived at that moment and Sienna began to talk, haltingly at first and then with increasing confidence, about how she had spent the day with Brayden - Tobias noticed Zeke trying not to look traumatised - and ended up discovering Aislinn by accident.

"Percy and *Gerard*?" Dominic exclaimed, eyes wide. "You're shitting me."

Aislinn snorted. "I didn't believe it until I saw it, either. Percy got away - he'll be making trouble as soon as he can."

"They have to find us first." Zeke frowned. "What about Gerard?"

"He won't be a problem." Sienna looked down at the ground and Tobias realised with a start that the stain on her chest was not mud but dried blood. "I tore his throat out with my teeth."

Zeke choked on that but his younger sister kept talking, her voice a monotone of relentless detail as she described struggling with Gerard, attacking Percy and freeing Aislinn.

"Percy stole Brayden's tablet to contact the Kin High Council and plead his case," Aislinn broke in, rubbing at her head as if to ease an ache. "He convinced them I'm mentally unsound and they voted to have me returned to Ireland - by force, if necessary. Once there, I'm to be submitted for Percy's study." She blew out a long, slow breath. "By law, that gives him every right to abduct me without reprise."

"That little asshole," Zeke spat.

Aislinn nodded. "It means Sienna acted out of turn rescuing me, too. I'm freed but we're in a worse mess than we were before."

"I'd rather us all in a mess than the alternative," Flynn growled. "If T-Fuzz hadn't flattened your father I fucking well would have."

"Using me as bait is a sound tactical decision, but part of me is still disappointed." Aislinn made a face. "I guess it's true what they say about leopards and spots."

"You are *not* a tactical decision." Tobias stormed across the camp and caught her shoulders in a tight grip, lowering his face until they were nose to nose. "You are a *person*."

"You won't win, T-Fuzz." Flynn yawned and stretched. "They've been beating it into her far too long. Come on, Sienna, let's take first watch. I know a place you can bathe that bastard's blood off and I promise I won't peek - not even a little."

Sienna gave the tigerkin a wan smile. "Sounds good; I'll never be clean, but it'll be nice not to be sticky."

Flynn's elfin face twisted, his expression almost impossible to read in the dark. He swept Sienna into his arms like a child, ignoring her startled squeak to nuzzle the side of her face. Her arms were stiff as they went around his neck in reflex but slowly relaxed as Flynn murmured in her ear. The hint of a blush tinted Sienna's cheeks but she nodded and the two of them disappeared into the night.

"Tobias…" Zeke trailed off, looking equally enraged and helpless as Flynn carried his sister away. "She ripped Gerard's throat out with her *teeth*. How do I help her with that?"

Tobias filled his cheeks with air and blew out slowly. "Fucked if I know."

"Ash?"

"First off you need to accept what she's done - really accept it, as one warrior to another. If she sees you the way you are now, it'll break something inside her that's already fragile." Aislinn sighed and for a moment Tobias could have sworn he felt her heart aching inside his own chest. "I wish I could say it gets easier from here but it doesn't; the reality is that good guys have to do bad things sometimes."

"I guess." Zeke looked utterly dejected, the t-shirt and shorts he'd borrowed from Dominic hanging loosely off his wiry frame and his sapphire eyes pools of midnight in the darkness. "It's just... she's my sister."

Tobias stirred, but Aislinn stilled him with a gesture. Stepping into Zeke's space, she tipped up his chin with a single finger. "Your sister just took down a trained soldier and saved my life - you should be so proud of her it hurts. I know I am."

Zeke blinked, then snorted a humourless laugh. "You always know what I need to hear, don't you?"

"It's my job," Aislinn replied, and Tobias felt his heart expand at the compassion in her tone. "Sienna is my pack now. I'll guard her to the death, even from soppy losers like you."

"Oi!" Zeke barked a laugh, batting her hand away. "I'm pretty sure I can take you in this condition, little sister-mine. Watch yourself."

Aislinn rolled her eyes. "Puh-lease, you couldn't take me if I was unconscious and had both my legs amputated. As for my injury, it's not so bad."

"Let me see," Tobias said, his body trembling with the need to touch her, to reassure himself she was okay. His heartmate shrugged and tugged down the scarf she'd been using for a skirt. Brutalised flesh bordered the black lines of Olaf's Marking, the whole area smeared with dried blood. Choking down his rage at the reminder of her torture, Tobias focussed on the wound. "It's sealed, at least. What the fuck was Percy trying to do?"

"Excise the Mark in the name of science," Aislinn said dryly. "He tried to tell me it was an honour."

Tobias traced the new skin with a gentle finger. "I'm going to kill him."

"Get in line." She caught his hand, twined her fingers through his. "We should get some rest. If I don't sleep soon, I'll be useless."

"What about a watch roster?" Zeke asked, stretching and yawning.

"You and Jax go next," Tobias said. "Followed by Rory and Dom, then Ash and I last. Two hour shifts."

Aislinn looked up into the sky. "I think we should move sooner than that - the longer we linger here, the higher our chances of being found."

"You and Sienna need the rest," Tobias countered, tugging her towards the back of the overhang. "It's worth the risk."

She followed reluctantly, chewing her lower lip as he arranged a pair of blankets into one larger surface. "I really think -"

"No." The word trembled in his throat. Gripping her shoulders, he willed her to understand. "I almost lost you, Ash. All over again."

"Stop. I'm not going anywhere, not now I've found you." Aislinn tugged at his t-shirt and he drew it off, relaxed into the hands she smoothed over his chest. "I'm safe."

"Hold me until I believe it." Tobias kissed her, trying to rein in the screaming emotions inside of him, then shucked his shorts and shimmered into wolf form. Aislinn's fingers combed through his fur as he circled twice on the blanket before dropping to his belly.

Fabric rustled and a moment later Aislinn's wolf body curled tightly against his. It was warm and comforting and intimate enough to shut out the rest of the world, to calm his heart even as it threatened to overflow. He wanted to stare at the perfection that was Aislinn Redding all night long but before he knew it, Tobias slipped softly into the realms of sleep.

*******

Dominic woke them with a gentle shake. If not for the stiffness in Aislinn's bones, it would've been easy to assume no time had passed at all; the stars still glittered overhead and the complete lack of Lunaida's moon gave the night a surreal feeling. Then Tobias nipped at her ear and padded off to the area they'd designated as a bathroom, and everything was laughably normal again.

Aislinn shimmered back to human form, shook her limbs out, took one look at Dominic and hugged him tightly. "Why so sad?"

287

"Sad?" His voice was a surprised whisper of sound in her ear, his eucalyptus and rain scent more potent than usual. Dom's arms came around Aislinn by reflex but he stiffened rather than relax and when she looked up, it was impossible to miss the burn of a blush tinting his cheeks. "Um…"

"Oh - I'm still in heat." She stepped back from his embrace, well aware her scent, heavy with both bearkin and pheromones, had to be overwhelming. "Sorry. Now tell me why you look about thirty years older than you are."

Dominic ran a hand through his silky hair, tumbling it adorably. "I swore to Tobias and I don't regret it, but it means I've left Deanna alone."

"She'll understand." Aislinn braved the distance between them to lay a comforting hand on his arm - but only for the barest moment. "Didn't you say she was dating one of the foxes? Surely he'll step up in your absence."

"Noah Acheson," Dominic supplied, nodding. "I hope he does; he seems genuine and she glows when he's around. I just… she's been my responsibility for so long. I know I wanted to roam but now it's happening, I feel guilty leaving her."

Aislinn offered him her best lopsided smile. "Uh oh, someone's having a testosterone moment." When Dominic looked affronted, she chuckled. "You can't be everywhere and do everything, Dom. Give poor Noah a chance."

Dominic's offended expression melted into one of rueful acceptance. "Yeah, you're right. Thanks, Ash."

"Any time. Try and get some sleep, okay?" She pointed at an empty blanket. "No telling when we'll have to move."

He shot her a wink, already backing away. "You can't tell me what to do, you know. You're not my Den Mother."

"I'll show you Den Mother in a minute," she growled, raising a fist - then they both snorted a laugh, and Dominic shifted to wolf to curl up on one of the blankets she'd indicated.

Tobias returned at that moment, twining his fingers through Aislinn's as they made their way out of the campsite to take their turn on watch. The lookout point wasn't far; a small heap of rocks which supplied a good view of the gorge in either direction, as well as a vantage point of the clifftop and Cracked Forks' Bridge above. The shape of the rocks meant that whoever was on duty could lounge in the lee of the pile without being noticed, particularly on a night as dark as this one. Except, of course, for the fact that tiny blue lights had begun to glow beneath Tobias' skin, so that he seemed entirely made of stars.

"You're shaking," she murmured, spreading both hands across his chest.

"You're in heat." Tobias cleared his throat, his voice a rasp. "Every single part of me is feeling very primal right now."

"I guess whatever surcease you bought us the other day has worn off." Aislinn frowned. "How bad is my scent?"

"On a scale of one to 'watch Tobias rip everyone's heads off,' we're at a comfortable mass murder."

"Damn."

"It wasn't that strong before you went to sleep," he grumbled. "I think the tranqs must've diluted it."

Aislinn nodded, using her shadows to smooth the flickering lights from his skin one by one. It felt like trying to carry honey in a sieve, but she managed it. "Want to tell me why Flynn punched you in the head?"

"To derail my anxiety-fuelled transitional surges," Tobias rumbled. "How did you know it was him?"

"I'd know the imprint of that right roundhouse anywhere." She reached up to brush gentle fingers over what remained of the bruising. "He likes you."

"He *likes* me?" Tobias caught her hand and pressed a laughing kiss to her palm. "Ash, we've spent the entire day beating the shit out of each other."

Gripping his jaw so that he had no alternative but to meet her gaze, Aislinn spoke in a low monotone. "If Flynn didn't like you, he'd have let transition take you over and then used it as perfectly good justification to kill you. Instead, he chose to put his body on the line to save your life."

Tobias was silent for a long time, his steely blue eyes and their golden starburst centres almost luminous to her night vision. She let him work through the knowledge, saw the moment his face darkened in potent realisation. "He's accepted me."

"Yes." Quiet words, but her fingers tightened on the strong line of his jaw. "Flynn doesn't let *anyone* in, Tobias. Nobody."

"Except you."

"And now you." Because of her - but the motivation didn't matter, only the acceptance. Aislinn tugged Tobias down until they shared breath. "Flynn will fight for you and he will die for you. He's not my tigerkin anymore, he's ours. Do you understand?"

"Shit." Tobias screwed up his face. "That's a lot of responsibility, Ash."

"Do me a favour and don't screw it up, then."

Surprise flitted across his face, then he laughed. "I'll try."

"Good." Aislinn laid her head on his chest, watching the far end of the gorge and listening to the steady beat of his heart beneath her cheek. "I'm glad you had each other."

"So am I." Tobias' hands lifted to clench in her hair. "You know, I thought the boys were mad when they talked about the scent of a female in heat making it impossible to think, but right now I can barely string two words together."

"Wait." She leant back far enough to stare into his face. "I know we have longer cycles than humans but this happens every six to eight months. Surely you've smelt an unmated female in heat before."

"Never." His thumbs traced her cheekbones. "Only you."

Aislinn froze. Memory prodded her:

*"But when did you... how long have you..."*

*"Solaeden's balls, I don't know." He reached up to brush her hair back from her face and pressed a kiss to the corner of each eye. "As long as I can remember. Longer."*

"I... always?" She managed.

"Always." Tobias' eyes softened, lips curling into a wicked bedroom smile that displayed all four of his pointed canines. "I was born loving you."

The words hit her like blows. Even as a child, he'd known; had lurked in the wings while she'd been blissfully oblivious. The connection between them must have formed before she left, before she'd ever been old enough to go into heat - while he waited, lost and hurt, half a world away. The knowledge burned deep inside Aislinn's soul and left her feeling edgy, desperately reaching for something she couldn't quite access. "I want to mate with you."

Tobias choked, eyes wet with tears, blue sparks blossoming beneath his skin until he was a beacon in the dark. He wrenched back her head and kissed her - a hot, wet kiss that carried his entire heart.

"Now," he demanded, his voice hoarse. Words bubbled out between kisses as he traced the edges of her lips, her cheeks, her eyes. "I can't wait, I can't. I can feel you right there and I can't reach you and I'm dying inside."

"We can't do it here; everyone will see and hear. Besides, I don't have the machine to measure your transitional strength."

"I don't care," Tobias mumbled, his face buried in her hair, his teeth scraping her shoulder. "I've waited my entire life to hear you say those words."

Logic said no but it had nothing on her body, which shouted *yes* with every single, aching cell. Slave to the tide of emotion and sensation, she whispered, "Do it."

The words had barely left her lips when Tobias slanted his mouth across hers. Aislinn sank into the embrace, revelling in the liquor-sharp scent of his arousal as she shifted her body so that the heavy length of his erection rubbed against her. Tobias groaned, sliding his hands beneath her thighs and lifting her up against the rocks. It put her far higher than she wanted to be, her legs wrapping his waist and the erection she very much wanted inside her now pressed against the cold stone. Aislinn murmured a wordless complaint against his lips, tugging at his tangled hair with her hands.

"Slowly," Tobias growled, nipping at her jaw. "I don't want to rush this."

"I do." Aislinn gasped as he licked a path down her scars towards her breasts. "I'm going to explode if you don't-"

A high pitched screech rent the night air, echoing through the canyon and causing the hair on Aislinn's arms to stand on end. She and Tobias froze as it rang out a second time, ululating wildly as the owner of that voice pushed his boundaries in an effort to send it as far as possible.

"What was that?" Tobias whispered into the silence that followed.

"A warning." Aislinn spread her hands across the broad expanse of his chest and poured her shadows into his skin. Her bones ached, her breath coming in gasps as she dredged at a power which was now only whispers, but the sparkling blue lights flickered and died. She toppled and Tobias caught her with a curse. "I'm fine."

"Liar," he hissed. "What's wrong?"

"My powers aren't working properly," she snapped, giving him just enough truth to get by - the rest would have to wait. "We need to find the others."

"I'm not going anywhere until your head's on straight."

"For the love of -" Grinding her teeth, Aislinn forced herself to take a deep breath, drawing strength from the implacability of her heartmate's tone. With a supreme effort, she sat up and met his eye. "My head is working just fine. We have to get back to camp."

Tobias frowned but when she shoved at his chest, he helped her to the ground without protest. When it became clear her balance was solid, he released her elbow and met her gaze. "Who was that?"

"Jacques."

"Jacques?" Tobias repeated, falling into step as she raced back towards the camp. "He doesn't sound stupid enough to announce it if he's found us."

"He's not." Aislinn skidded to a stop at the edge of the blankets, eyeing the shadowy forms of her no-longer-sleeping packmates and friends. "Where's Flynn?"

*Here.* He padded up from the opposite direction, shimmering into human form as he went. "At least the fucker's paying his debts."

"Ash?" Sienna's voice wobbled, her eyes wide with fear. "Have they found us?"

"No," Aislinn shook her head. "It was a warning. Someone's on our trail - someone who's not Jacques."

Sienna gasped. "Percy."

"More likely the team sent to extract me, but yes, that's my guess." Waving Flynn over, she added, "It also means they've got a way to find us."

Flynn knelt by Aislinn's side, spreading his hands over the wound on her hip. "Owlkin's smarter than he looks - I can feel it."

"Get it out."

The tigerkin's hands were already clawed. "Keep her still, T-Fuzz."

Strong arms banded Aislinn's waist as Flynn's claws dug into her flesh, opening Percy's incision with terrifying ease. She didn't need the support, knew it had only been a way to distract Tobias, but Aislinn leant into his strength anyway.

Flynn worked quickly, his touch delicate as he made a three inch long cut and, punctuated by growls and gasps from their audience, thrust two of his delicate fingers into the soft flesh bordering Aislinn's hip bone. She grunted but bore the pain, gripping Tobias' wrists with white-knuckled fingers. Moments later Flynn withdrew, a shining silver disc the size of a grain of rice held firm in his bloodied grip. "Got it."

"GPS tracker," Aislinn muttered, accepting the device. Resting his palms against her ribs, Flynn leant in and began licking the blood from her wound. Ignoring behaviour which was no doubt horrifying the others, she rubbed blood off the tracker and looked at it more closely. "Standard Council issue; nothing fancy. Location lock, no heat signature or vitals records."

"Mistake," Flynn declared, finishing his self-imposed task and getting to his feet. "But good for us."

"What do we do?" Sienna asked, hands over her mouth.

"What we always do." Flynn shrugged. "I'll take the tracker and go one direction, you lot go the other, and we'll meet up at dawn."

"Split up?" Sienna shivered. "That sounds dangerous."

"Less dangerous than staying put or leaving the tracker here," Aislinn murmured, patting at Tobias' iron grip until he let her go. "Don't worry; we've done this before."

"I'll keep an eye on you through the bond," Flynn said, licking his fingers clean of blood, "And track you down after I ditch the GPS somewhere suitable." Amber eyes held Aislinn's. "Run, and run hard. If you feel anything, don't come back for me."

"Flynn -"

"Promise," he snarled, top lip curling.

"No."

"Fuck you."

"I love you too."

They glared at each other for long, valuable seconds, then Flynn spat a curse in Gaelic and threw both hands in the air. "Fine. We both live, or we both fucking die."

"Exactly." It was a pact they'd made years ago, and no power on earth would make Aislinn desert this broken, beautiful man who held a part of her heart. "Don't die, and we won't have to argue about this in the afterlife."

Flynn snorted, his temper easing somewhat at her teasing words. "I'm going to whip your ass into next week when I get back."

"Good." Aislinn opened her fingers, revealing the GPS tracker.

"Wait." Tobias shoved between them before Flynn could reach for it. "I have something to ask you first, tigerkin."

Flynn raised an eyebrow. "If it's for a kinky threesome, the answer is only on Thursdays."

Rather than answer, Tobias scooped up a hunting knife from a nearby rucksack. He set the tip of the blade to his inner elbow and cut a long, thin line all the way to his wrist, then flipped the blade in his hand and offered it to Flynn.

The tigerkin stared at the knife, then at the welling blood, then at Tobias. "Why?"

"You know why."

Flynn's amber eyes wandered to Aislinn; went back to Tobias. "You need to be certain."

"Do I look unsure?"

Silence fell and only Aislinn saw the faint tremor in Flynn's frame as he accepted the knife and sliced a matching gash in his own arm. The two men turned their bleeding hands side on and clasped, fingers wrapping around elbows and forearms pressing together down the length of the open wounds.

Two sets of eyes met; one amber, one gold-touched blue. Neither spoke, neither moved. Aislinn held her breath, heart hammering in her chest, as they remained that way for the requisite thirty seconds - enough of a blood exchange to cement the bond between them. She saw them both jerk as one of the oldest contracts of all time locked into place; the only way for two Alphas to swear fealty to one another. They were family now, indelibly bound for the rest of their lives.

Moving in tandem, both arms dropped away to reveal the cuts were already beginning to heal, mingled blood a smear across skin both pale and tanned. Flynn stared down at the wound with a raw look in his eyes, while Tobias turned to Aislinn with the ghost of a smile that meant everything.

"*Now* he's ours."

# Nineteen

Zeke wasted no time yanking a map out of his pocket and spreading it on the ground. "How do we want to do this?"

"I'm no expert, but I'd assume completely opposite directions would be too obvious." Tobias scooped up a blanket and used it to wipe his arm, the cut already sealed over. He offered the fabric to Flynn who accepted without a word, amber eyes unreadable as he mirrored Tobias' movements and scrubbed his own skin. "Ash? Is that about right?"

"Pretty much." She crouched before the map, muttering under her breath as she walked her fingers over a variety of landmarks. "If we can buy ourselves a couple of days..."

"Brax is too far," Flynn growled, inching closer. "And they'll be watching the fuck out of him."

"I know that."

"Brax?" Tobias couldn't quite keep the edge out of his voice.

"An old friend who owes me a couple of favours. Lives north of Sydney - I'll introduce you sometime." Aislinn bit her lip. "Flynn, head south west as if we're trying to circle back to Melbourne. We'll go this way." She tapped the north west part of the map, where a swathe of black crosses marked out the most recent bearkin sightings. "If we can deliver Olaf - or at least his head - we might gain some bargaining power with the High Council."

"That's a few days' run," Tobias pointed out, fists on his hips. "Even if we manage to avoid our fathers and the Council, we'll arrive exhausted."

Aislinn grinned. "That's why we're going to drive."

Jaxon growled low in his throat. "I dumped the car, Ash. You *told* me to dump the car."

"I did. But look here." She jabbed a red circle about a third of the way between their location and the area they assumed Olaf was hiding. "This was a possum community. The bearkin wiped them out pretty early on but I happen to know they were a modestly sized settlement - I'm willing to bet there's a few cars there whose owners won't mind if we borrow them."

*And if we're in cars,* Flynn purred, his tail lashing, *It'll be harder for brown-nose and golden boy to spot us from above.*

"Yes. Think you can catch us by dawn?"

*Not even a challenge.* Flynn's tiger head craned over the map. *Is there room to hide bodies?*

"Yeah, the country's pretty rough." Aislinn stroked one hand through his fur, lips pursed. "Try and avoid it, though. We're in enough trouble as it is."

Tobias sat back, wondering if his face mirrored the shocked expressions the rest of his companions wore. It was abundantly clear, in that moment, the different path that his life had taken from Aislinn's. Something tingled in his chest, and he blinked up into Flynn's amber eyes. *Regretting your choices, squeaky clean?*

"No." Tobias rubbed his heart, soothing the strange sensation. When the tiger purred, he realised it was their blood bond, and dropped his hand into his lap. "Just angry at what you've been forced into."

Flynn's eyes glittered in approval, but it was Aislinn who answered. "There's no point in anger; we're here, and we have to deal with it."

*We will.* The tigerkin rubbed his face against Aislinn's. *The sooner I start, the sooner I'm back.*

"Go." She kissed his nose. "Stay safe."

Flynn nudged her a final time, then disappeared into the darkness.

Zeke sighed, folded up the map, and stood. "All right guys and gals, let's get the hell outta here."

Spell broken, everyone set about stuffing clothes and blankets into rucksacks while Rory used some old branches to sweep the camp of their presence. Tobias helped strap rucksacks to Jaxon and Dominic, their wolf bodies the largest apart from his own. Aislinn hefted the final pack, smiled when he growled, and shrugged. "Fine, fine. You carry it."

He stood still while she strapped it in place on his chest, assuming her own wolf form immediately after. With his nose at her shoulder, they ran, leading the others up a tumble of boulders and onto flatter ground.

After a quick sniff to ensure they were all in one piece, Aislinn cut across country. Time passed in landmarks, the bones of the earth peeking out between tall candlebarks. Thick forest blurred the horizon; not the scrubby type of bush Tobias was used to but the sort of dense, moisture-laden greenery often layered with rotten logs, ferns and the gods knew what else.

Aislinn ushered them into the trees as the first of the sun's rays gilt the land behind them in shades of bronze and gold but there was no time for relief; Tobias knew if they didn't keep moving, Brayden would spot them the minute he neared the area. Chest heaving like a bellows, he paused only long enough to ensure the rest of his companions were under cover, then followed them deeper into the undergrowth.

After half an hour's worth of slipping between trunks, slithering over mossy logs and dodging fallen branches, the pack arrived without warning on the rocky bank of a creek. Aislinn slowed to a walk, nose to the ground as she inspected the bared ground before shimmering into her human form.

"Rest here." She crouched to unclip Tobias' rucksack, then moved to do the same for Dominic and Jaxon. "We'll move on when Flynn arrives."

Tobias flopped to the ground between Zeke and Sienna, relinquishing his wolf form to better feel the cool press of the earth against his skin. "It's been a long time since I ran that far flat out."

"Tell me about it." Zeke turned towards Tobias and groaned. "I hope you're not going to call down another thunderstorm, because I cannot move right now."

"Huh?" Tobias looked down to discover the blue sparks under his skin had multiplied, flowing up and down his arms like twinkling Christmas lights. "Damn. Ash? Am I dangerous?"

"No." Aislinn knelt beside him and smoothed a palm along one bicep. "Running makes kinetic energy, which is what's got you all sparkly. Once you learn control, this sort of static build-up won't happen."

"One more thing to add to the list."

Aislinn shrugged, unconcerned by his growling displeasure. "It is what it is. We'll work it out."

"I hope so." Cool energy washed over his body, leaving behind a wave of goose bumps. Most of the blue sparks faded - but not all, and Tobias was reminded of her admission back in the canyon. "You okay?"

"Tired." Aislinn worried her lower lip with pointed incisors and then shrugged. "That'll do for now."

Tobias watched her return to his rucksack, where she dragged out empty canteens and water purifying tablets. He opened his mouth, shut it, opened it again, then took the canteens she offered, rolled to his feet and went to the creek.

*She wasn't lying, but something's not right.* Flynn's voice was solid inside his mind, private. Tobias looked up to see the tiger on the other side of the creek, his face turned away as he looked downstream. *I don't like it.*

Neither did he but there was no way to answer without revealing their conversation to Aislinn, so he said, "I assume everything went as planned?"

*Of course. They never even spotted me.* Flynn jumped the creek and padded towards the pack, the word 'amateurs' hanging unspoken in the damp air.

Tobias couldn't help but grin as he filled the final canteen. There was something about the tigerkin's irrepressible nature that was reassuring - not that Tobias had been worried about his safety. Of course not. Still, what did it say for Aislinn's malfunctioning powers if Flynn had made a point of mentioning them? Frowning, he handed the now full canteens to Rory, grabbed Aislinn's hand and tugged her against his chest. "You sure you're okay?"

"I told you, I'm tired," she murmured, her voice so low he had to strain to hear it. "Torture does that to a girl."

Tobias' nose crinkled. Still no lie, but Flynn was right - something was off. Lowering his head to sip at her lips, he whispered, "I know you're screwing with me, Aislinn Redding."

She didn't miss the steel in his tone, the warning of a conversation to come later. With a noise half affectionate and half frustrated, Aislinn leant up to nip his jaw. "You haven't changed a bit, you know that?"

"I'm taking that as a compliment."

"My eyes are burning," Dominic announced, zipping up Aislinn's pack and holding it out. "Seriously, the vomit factor is more than even I can bear."

Tobias snorted. "Liar; you're as smooth as they come."

"And yet, I'm single." Dominic yawned, stretching a muscular body that Tobias had witnessed earn him lovers without the other wolf having to say a single word.

"We're heartmates." Aislinn shrugged. "He didn't need to try very hard."

Tobias spluttered indignantly at that, but Dominic nodded. "It's true, he was always hopelessly devoted to you. I've comforted many a sobbing woman over the devastatingly oblivious Tobias Greenwood."

Tobias snatched the pack out of Dominic's hand with a growl. "I am *not* oblivious."

"No? What about Jocelyn Underfield?" Zeke piped up, dusting his hands on his thighs. "Or Rebecca Fletcher?"

"Jocelyn needed someone to finish her decking, and Rebecca couldn't manage her groceries after she broke her wrist." Tobias frowned. "They weren't interested in me."

Rory chuckled softly. "Not at all. Neither was Lauren Saurice."

"Or Heather Valtroix," Jaxon added, his green eyes sparkling. "She came by once a week for months."

"To pick up Grandma's preserves for the farmer's market!"

"Let me guess," Aislinn's voice was thick with ill-concealed laughter. "Heather had a terrible habit of turning up when you were in the garage? With no shirt on? Or maybe helping Grandma mow the lawn? Also with no shirt on? Or when Grandma was out somewhere and you doing some sort of handyman type chore… with no shirt on?"

Tobias' cheeks flamed. "No, it wasn't like that! I mean -"

"Tobias is right," Zeke agreed, hiding his snigger behind one hand. "He had a shirt on some of the time."

"Oh, that's not a problem, his clothes don't fit him anyway. A shirt on Tobias is as good as a shirt off Tobias - better, sometimes." Aislinn cut a wicked glance at Sienna. "Am I right?"

The younger woman sighed dreamily. "Why do you think I never ordered bigger shirts for any of them? I wouldn't have anything to drool over, otherwise."

All five men stared in astonishment. Zeke, sounding scandalised, said, "Really?"

"Well, I clearly wasn't ogling *you,* seeing as we're related, but I'm sure someone was. Not that any of you ever noticed, of course." Sienna reached out to run a hand down Dominic's sculpted abs in a gesture so sensual the other male yelped in surprise. "Tobias isn't the only one blind to the nose on his face. Your losses."

*Are you wolves coming or what? I'm going to fucking freeze at this rate,* Flynn grumped. Trying - unsuccessfully - to shake off his astonishment, Tobias turned to see the tiger ankle deep in the creek.

"What do you say, Sens?" Aislinn chuckled. "Time to push on?"

Sienna's answer was a final flick of Dominic's ribs before she shimmered back into her wolf form and padded over to stand beside Flynn in the water. Aislinn shifted to join them, followed quickly by the rest of the pack.

Tobias shrugged into the rucksack at his feet and shook it into place against his chest. *Pretty sure you could boil the water with your temper alone, kitty cat.*

Flynn growled, but his voice in Tobias' head was anything but irritated. *We need to get her to talk.*

*You think I can make her?* Tobias snorted. *You've got rocks in your head. She's independent to a fault.*

*Too bad.* Amber eyes narrowed as Tobias followed his packmates into the freezing creek water. *She gets until the next rest. Then either you get her to fess up, or I will.*

*******

The creek meandered a little but Aislinn knew it would eventually take them to the possum settlement, with the added bonus of erasing their scents in the process. The trees above were thick enough to provide cover from prying avian eyes and though they travelled in knee-deep water, the going was much easier than traversing the forest floor would have been. It was approaching sunset when Aislinn finally climbed out, her paws frozen in spite of the constant movement.

The trees above swayed in a northerly breeze and though their party was deep enough in the undergrowth to warrant only the faintest trickle of air, the sickly sweet stench of death increased the further they travelled through the thinning bush. Aislinn curled her lip back from her teeth, wishing she had something to dim her acute sense of smell - and promptly froze when a chittering noise cut through the otherwise silent air.

*Everyone stop.* Flynn melted out of the thick forestry, rubbing briefly against Aislinn as he moved into a clear space and sat. Within a minute, two little possums scurried out of the undergrowth to hide behind the tiger's front legs. *Nobody move - you'll scare them off if you're not careful.*

The possums chattered and chirruped at Flynn until, with a long-suffering sigh, he lowered himself onto his belly and allowed them to climb onto his head. With his two new charges firmly in place, the tigerkin got to his feet and disappeared into the forest without another word.

Aislinn resumed her human body and stretched. "Take five, everyone. We need to wait here for Flynn."

The scent of butterscotch and cream tickled her nose and Aislinn was unsurprised when Tobias' strong arms came around her from behind, his face nuzzling into her hair. "I know you said before that he can talk to wild animals, but seeing it in action is something else entirely."

"That's nothing," she snorted. "Wait until he's being trailed by a family of ducklings, or being kissed by giant koi in the botanical gardens' oriental section."

"Hmmm." Tobias' voice was distracted, arms tightening around her waist. "Your scent is driving me insane."

Aislinn patted his hands in a soothing motion, confirming with a swift glance that the other males, likely without even noticing, had followed Tobias' lead and drawn closer. She frowned, equal parts frustrated and embarrassed by the way her scent was affecting everyone - except Sienna, whose face said she knew full well the boys' primal brains were in the drivers' seats. "You need to reel it in."

"I don't know if I can." Stark words, a rueful laugh.

"Of course you can. You're an adult, Tobias - act like one." Shoving out of his arms, Aislinn dematerialised and streamed into the forest, ignoring Tobias' surprised exclamation. Keeping to the thicker shadows, she flowed over branches and under ferny boughs until she located Flynn, already heading back the direction he'd come. The two little possums still crouched on his head, beady eyes bright and little fists curled deep in his striped fur.

*Safe,* he said to her on their private channel. *Signs of death but no bodies.*

Of course he'd sense her near. Smiling inwardly, Aislinn curled around his shoulders, no more than a whisper of darkness. *I'll start scoping out weapons and possible shelter. I... need a few minutes to myself.*

*Roger that.*

Aislinn streamed towards the settlement, concentrating on her surrounds. Gorgeous cottages clung to the sides of larger trees, high enough off the ground to be mostly hidden from below. Bigger residences draped gracefully between close-growing trunks, each dwelling built with a cattywampus charm that made little to no impact on the natural environment. Branches supported buildings as much as they were part of them, growing around and through walls, windows and even floors.

As Flynn had promised, there were no bodies, though Aislinn swept beneath every door and curled through every room to make certain. Broken furniture littered the floors, fractured walls and shattered glass testament to the furious battle which had taken place.

Aislinn shimmered into her human body inside a busted living room, her heart as torn as the bloodied carpet. These people, like so many before them, had died with no hope of a saviour. With the entire community gone, who would seek justice on their behalf? Who would lay their souls to rest, grieve their passing, honour their memories?

Aislinn palmed a kitchen knife from the bench and flicked her wrist, burying it hilt-deep in the opposite wall. She couldn't prepare a meal with such a blade but she knew how to throw it, how to fight and kill with it. For so many years she'd tried to duck her father's legacy, fulfilling her duties without any emotional attachment and dreaming of freedom. But these possumkin - and the countless other lives Olaf had destroyed - would never be free unless someone actually *did something.* Most Kin didn't have those skills, much like Aislinn lacked the skills required for civilian life. However, much as she sucked at a regular nine to five, she *did* have the ability to dispense justice - a bloody, vicious kind of justice, but justice nonetheless.

Claiming such a future would require her to set aside the shattered woman Olaf had made, to embrace the wilder side which even an assassin's deadly training had never squashed. Not a simple task, but the more she stood in that broken room, surrounded by the echo of slaughtered dreams, the more certain Aislinn became that this was her path - to fight dirty, to fight hard, to never stop.

But… would Tobias still want her, if she chose to walk that road? Aislinn ran trembling hands over the vivid network of scars on her chest, smoothed palms over the ridges on her ribs and abdomen, then raised a hand to the torc around her throat. Tobias had fought for her - she wouldn't dishonour either of them by pretending to be anything other than herself. It was time to heal the last of her fractures and let him see her in truth.

With those thoughts foremost in her mind, Aislinn stalked to the front door of the tree house and tugged it open. There'd been no weapons anywhere obvious, but these people *had* fought for their lives. Somewhere, this remote little community had to have something that could be turned to their advantage. She dematerialised, continuing her search with more purpose. It didn't take long to find an attic full of gym mats, exercise equipment and, up the back in a corner, a locked chest.

Aislinn yanked the padlock straight off, the wood no match for her Kin strength. Inside, carefully wrapped in black cotton, she discovered an ancient nine-ring broadsword and a collection of combat knives in various shapes and sizes.

"Well, hello," she murmured, lips stretching into a grin. The combat knives had rubber grips designed specifically for Kin use and though some had begun to decay, just as many were in good condition. Aislinn wrapped the best ones in a spare cloth, then turned back for the nine-ring broadsword. Curling both hands around the hilt, she backed onto the mats and indulged in the first half of a kata designed specifically for blade work. The sword was exquisite, a well-loved antique whose edge was as sharp as the day it was forged. Whoever had owned that sword had loved it dearly and though it deserved better than to be left to rot, it was no use to a wolf needing speed and stealth. With a regretful sigh, Aislinn set it back in the chest and closed the lid.

Tucking the bundle of knives under her arm, she lowered herself back into the main building. It was impossible to dematerialise and still carry the weaponry, so she jogged through the dining area on foot and carefully nudged the remains of the front door aside. It was quite a drop to the forest floor but nothing impossible; with a rush of adrenaline, Aislinn stepped off the landing and landed in a crouch between Rory and Dominic.

"Shit!" Dominic's eyes were wide as he leapt away, while Rory slid into a fighting stance before he recognised her and relaxed.

"You should be more alert," Aislinn said calmly, straightening to her full height as the rest of the pack whipped their heads around in astonishment. "Never forget to look up."

Flynn's laughter broke the tension, ringing inside their heads like a symphony of silver bells. Even the possums, still on his head, chittered in amusement.

"Solaeden's balls, Ash," Dominic spluttered, one hand spread over his heart. "There's nobody here."

"*I'm* here." She tossed him the wrapped bundle. "Take care of these, will you?"

He unrolled the cotton and whistled. "These are proper looking knives."

"Too bad they didn't save the possums," Aislinn returned.

Dominic nodded. "If I add these to the couple we've already got, that's one knife apiece."

"That's pretty good." Aislinn smiled. "Try and make sure the sizes fit both hands and mouths."

"Yeah, I know the way of it." Nodding a second time, Dominic turned to the rucksacks and began dragging out the other knives.

*Any sign of the garage?* Flynn asked, his tail lashing back and forth.

"No." Aislinn shook her head. "Only residences and common areas. I was hoping we might be able to shelter in one for the night, but there's a lot of blood and broken things."

*I don't think we should stop that long anyway. If I know brown-nose at all, our twenty-four hours' grace is about up.*

Aislinn's lips quirked at the edges. "Poor Jacques. Doing his duty and you're all grouchy at him."

*I should have shoved that fucking apple so far down his throat he choked,* Flynn growled.

"Where's Tobias?"

*Out with Zeke, looking for hidden ground buildings that might house a car.* No doubt catching the guilty look on Aislinn's face, the tiger chuckled. *I'll go check on them; you mind the kids.*

"All right." Hoping she didn't sound too relieved, Aislinn watched him jog away and then turned to a muttering Rory. "What?"

"Kids," the wolfkin repeated, his face scandalised. "*Kids.*"

"Flynn's seen the harder side of life - He's older than his years." Aislinn wrapped an arm around Sienna's shoulders. "How was he as a trainer?"

"Hard, but not unkind." Golden curls tumbled across pale shoulders as Sienna tilted her head. "I'm not so scared of him now."

"Good." Waving Dominic over, Aislinn bade him hold out one arm. "Show me."

Before the handsome wolfkin had time to blink, Sienna struck the inside of his wrist with a single finger. Dominic squeaked, his hand immediately going limp. "What the fuck, Sienna?"

"It'll wear off." Sienna turned a bright smile on Aislinn. "Tell Flynn I got it right first try?"

"Definitely. Technique was good and you're fast. Did he show you this way, too?" Aislinn forced her fingers together until they were shaped like the head of a spear.

"Yeah," Sienna nodded. "But he said that as long as I'm accurate, it's not the shape of the blow that counts. I can…" she crinkled her nose in thought. "It's hard to explain. I can kind of sense them, so I don't need to learn where they are - not once he showed me what to look for. I just have to practice."

"What did you do?" Rory asked, watching as Dominic tried unsuccessfully to make his fingers work.

"I struck a chi point."

"A what?"

"Like a pressure point, but different." Aislinn tapped the inside of her wrist. "It's a hard skill to master - but potent, if you can. I never had the patience."

Rory raised an eyebrow. "It's like Dom's paralysed from the elbow down."

"He is," Aislinn answered. At Dominic's startled look, she bared her teeth in a vicious smile. "Like Sienna said - it's only temporary."

Dominic regarded his floppy fingers with new interest. "That's incredible, Sens. I never even saw it coming."

"Flynn said speed is my best ally against a larger opponent, and pretty much anyone who's over the age of ten is going to be a larger opponent." Sienna turned her hands back and forth in such a way that Aislinn wondered what she saw. "I need to be faster."

"You couldn't have stopped Gerard," Aislinn murmured. "He chose his own path."

"Correct, but I might have been able to avoid tearing his throat out with my teeth and bathing in his gory remains," Sienna replied. "I have a lot of things on my bucket list, but 'blood waterfall' wasn't one of them."

"That's a good thing."

"Is it?" Sienna's face crumpled, her skin pale. "Seems to me like we need more warriors."

"Self defence is important, but what we need more than anything is a healer with a huge heart." Taking both the other woman's hands in her own, Aislinn stooped until they were eye level. "Leave the bloodshed to me."

# Twenty

Tobias was sweaty, frustrated and ready for a fight by the time he and Zeke located the possumkin's cleverly hidden garage. Partially submerged in the forest floor and covered by several decades' worth of leaf litter, the tumbledown shed was so well integrated into the environment that the two wolves passed it twice before Tobias noticed the faint glint of a window.

He shifted into human form to clear the piled up branches and interlaced ferns, Zeke toiling by his side until they revealed a pair of rickety wooden doors held shut by a rusty chain.

"Bloody hell," Zeke muttered, snapping the chain like it was made of paper. "This building looks ancient."

"It probably is." Tobias curled his fingers around a weathered plank and prised one of the doors open. "No reason to fix something that's not broken."

Zeke gave a snort, squinting into the gloom. "You say that, but I'm pretty sure the place is held together by luck and forest fairies."

"Forest fairies?" Tobias ducked into the shed, coughing through a thick layer of dust. "By the Lady, it doesn't look like they got out much."

Two cars; one a bright, mandarin orange, the other a more sedate silver-blue. A quick search revealed a pair of rusty nails with keys hanging from one wall, several jerry cans of fuel and a pile of hessian sacks that smelt like hay. Tobias opened the blue car, revealing a faded velour interior which, though it smelt musty, was clean and spacious. He tossed the other key to Zeke, then slid into the driver's seat and tried the ignition. The car coughed, spluttered and turned over, the soft hum of a well-loved engine filling the shed's darkened interior. He looked across at Zeke with a grin of triumph, only to find his second shaking his head.

"Flat battery," Zeke mouthed.

Tobias gave the steering wheel a light pat and, leaving the old girl to warm up, hopped out and went to the orange car's open window. "Pop the bonnet, let me see."

Zeke raised an eyebrow, feeling around under the dash. "Because you're so mechanically minded."

"I can start the lawn mower," Tobias retorted. "Just let me look, okay? What's the worst that could happen?"

His second gave a loud guffaw and yanked; the bonnet popped. Tobias heaved it open, setting the metal rod in place to keep the lid up while he inspected the engine inside. It was grimy but nothing seemed particularly wrong - not, as Zeke had already pointed out, that he was particularly mechanically minded. He'd never needed to be, with Frank Smythe being both enthusiastic and knowledgeable in his role as the Redding Pack mechanic.

Tobias stared unseeing at the engine, blinking furiously to hold back a sudden wash of tears. From the day he'd become an Alpha, he'd imagined working, living and growing old as part of the Redding pack and now he was cut off from it, with a fledging pack of his own and no idea what the future held. The shock had been bearable with Aislinn by his side but she'd stormed off - and the worst part was, he couldn't even blame her. He owed her not only an apology but the commitment to be better; a task that seemed, at this very moment, all but impossible.

*Start the car, Tobias,* he thought, forcing air into his lungs. *One step at a time. Start the fucking car.*

Zeke had said the battery was flat. If the blue car was running, maybe they could jump start this one. Wiping his eyes on his bicep, Tobias leant forward and located the battery. Resting one hand on the side of engine bay, he began to brush away the layer of grit coating the terminals so they could connect some jumper leads.

"Need a hand?" Zeke got out of the car, the sudden weight transference causing it to lurch unsteadily. Tobias stumbled, inadvertently gripping the top of the battery for balance. Raw energy roared through his veins, crackling down his arm and flooding out through his hand. There was a thunderous *boom* which rocked the world, and Tobias flew backwards out of the shed to thump spine-first into the dirt. He skidded on his shoulders, gravel shredding his bare skin and legs over his head, before coming to rest in a tangled heap at the base of a nearby fern. He coughed, a weak, wet sound, then groaned and managed to topple sideways so that all of him was approximately face down on the cool, solid ground.

Warm hands gripped his shoulders and turned him over; Tobias blinked. "Why is there two of you?"

"There isn't," Zeke muttered, running both hands over his shoulders, chest, ribs, hips. "Nothing seems broken."

"Fucking lucky," said the other Zeke - who was actually Flynn, Tobias realised. "Ash would've been mad if I'd laughed and he was actually dead. That was the most amazing thing I've ever seen, T-Fuzz."

"Fuck you," Tobias growled, blinking again. His eyes couldn't quite focus but given that Flynn's hair was black and Zeke's blonde, he knew in which approximate direction to aim his rude gesture. "Fuck you *twice*."

"I'm not that into you," Flynn answered cheerfully, leaning close enough that Tobias could see all four of his sharp, curved canines. "Smells like someone cooked your bacon. What happened to him, goldenrod?"

"I don't know." Zeke hauled Tobias into a sitting position and held him still when a wave of dizziness threatened to steal his senses. "I was half out of the car and there was an explosion and he was just *gone*."

Flynn's brow furrowed, a delicate move that only made him more exquisitely attractive than normal. "I rolled up in time to see T-Fuzz hit the dirt, but nothing else. How you didn't break a bone, I'll never know."

"I just…" Tobias coughed and spat bits of fern out of his mouth. "I lost my balance and touched the battery and then… pow."

"Hmm." Flynn raked an amber eye over Tobias' naked, bleeding body. "Goldenrod, do us a favour and start the car."

"Battery's flat," Zeke explained. "That's what started all of this."

"Start. The. Fucking. Car," Flynn repeated, lips peeling back from his teeth.

Tobias made to rub both hands over his face and paused, noting the skin on his palms was it's usual, customary bronze - no longer a single blue spark or flicker of light underneath. "Zeke, he's right. Try it."

Muttering under his breath, Zeke stomped back into the shed. A moment later, the orange car coughed, groaned - and roared to life. Not quiet and subtle like the purring blue, no, this engine was pure muscle, a lion bolted into a metal shell. Even though he'd half expected the result, Tobias' jaw still hit his chest as Zeke came racing back to them. "What the hell?!"

"Transition," Flynn replied, lips stretched in a very feline grin. He reached out to pat Tobias on the thigh. "You, brother, are a fucking lightning rod."

"Solaeden's balls," Tobias groaned, flopping backwards into the dirt. "Are you telling me I charged the battery just by touching it?"

"Something like that." Flynn's voice was getting more smug by the second. "You attract electricity and store it for the EMP, but it looks like if you come across a handy container, a transfer of energy is initiated. I can't wait to get you to touch more shit and see what blows up."

"I hate you," Tobias said weakly. "More than I hate Brussels sprouts - no, more than I hate taking a shit and finding out too late that there's no paper. That's how much I hate you, kitty cat."

The tigerkin's laugh was rich and musical as he dropped to the ground beside Tobias and began nuzzling his shoulder and neck. "Feeling's mutual."

Tobias cleared his throat as the taller man lined their bodies up, throwing a possessive leg over Tobias' thighs. "I thought you weren't that into me."

"I'm not." Flynn's breathing turned ragged but even Tobias, dazed as he was, could hear it wasn't desire. "I need touch and I can't touch Aislinn right now without wanting to fuck her six ways from Tuesday. You're my blood brother - I need *you*."

Feeling more and more at sea, Tobias slid his arm beneath Flynn's shoulders and tugged him closer, using all his strength to anchor the other male against his chest. Flynn's striped arms locked around Tobias' waist and squeezed back, a bone-wrenching demand for reassurance which had Tobias using his free hand to stroke Flynn's hair. "Touch Ash and I will fucking murder you."

"She'd kill me herself - why do you think I'm here instead?" Flynn growled. "You need to do something about her, and I don't mean her pheromones."

Tobias blinked, sighed, looked up at Zeke. His second, to his credit, had raised both eyebrows but otherwise seemed unaffected by the sight of two Alphas canoodling on the ground. "Check both cars over. I want a full report on their condition."

"You got it." Zeke flipped a lazy salute and sauntered off.

Tobias watched the other male disappear into the shed and then turned his head fractionally. "Explain."

"Olaf's scent is getting stronger," Flynn rumbled, his lips against Tobias' pulse in an intimacy he'd only ever before allowed Aislinn. "And hers is getting weaker. I think even you can do that sort of math, T-Fuzz."

"Shit." His fingers tightened in Flynn's silky hair and the tigerkin nipped his throat in reprimand. Smoothing his grip out, Tobias continued petting, his mind now clear enough to race ahead. "Olaf's draining her. That's why she couldn't damp me earlier."

"A blessing in disguise, seeing as you just started the car," Flynn agreed, "But I don't know how long it'll take before she's useless, meaning either we'll kill each other *and* Ash, or the bears will."

"Why wouldn't she tell us?"

"Are you kidding me, boy wonder? You said it yourself - she's independent to a fault. She's not hiding it because she doesn't trust us, she's hiding it to try and protect us." The tigerkin was silent for a moment, his breath warm on Tobias' skin. "That, and if I know Ash at all, she won't like admitting she's got no viable solution to the problem."

"Yeah, she's always been like that," Tobias grumbled, flinching when Flynn's hand smoothed over his ribs. "Careful, asshole, I'm ticklish."

"Not sorry," Flynn answered, wriggling impossibly closer. "It's this or an insane rampage. You choose."

"Mother Moon, what the fuck happened to you?"

The tigerkin stilled. "Ash didn't tell you?"

"She said it was your story." Tobias sighed, adjusting the angle of his head to give Flynn better access to the soft flesh under his ear. "I'm not normally the pushy type, but I'd feel a little less violated if you gave me something."

"I'm not in a good space, but... do you understand the concept of sensory deprivation?"

"Yeah." Tobias went cold. "How long?"

"Seven years. In a box."

Seven *years*? "How old were you?"

"I don't know. My earliest memories are of that box." A pause. "I don't know how old I am now, either, so don't fucking ask. The best we can do is 'under thirty,' because transition ceases once you hit the big three oh."

Tobias went quiet, turning that over in his mind. The first seven years - at least - of Flynn's life, locked in a box. "In human form?"

"Tiger. I didn't know I was Kin, or human, or anything other than a thing in a box." His voice was a growl, his body shaking. "I'm a fucking basket case and I know it, but touch helps. Gives me an anchor."

"Otherwise?"

A hesitation, a sharp breath. Turning their bodies inward on instinct, Tobias pressed Flynn against his chest, used his leg to hook the other male closer until the shuddering lessened. "Otherwise people die," Flynn mumbled, his lips against the hollow of Tobias' throat. "And I don't remember it."

Anything, Tobias realised, to feel *something* - to get out of the box which was likely behind the tigerkin's eyelids every time he closed them. "Enough," he said quietly, stroking Flynn's ridged spine with one hand. "I know enough."

They lay like that for several long minutes, until Flynn once again relaxed and began to rumble with a purr. Tobias waited until the tigerkin shifted against him before loosening his grip, the two of them sitting up in unison. Flynn looked breathless and pale but his gaze was steady as he met Tobias' and said; "I don't hate you so much now."

"Thanks." Tobias smiled in spite of himself. "I suppose I can live with having a weirdly affectionate blood brother."

Amber eyes dropped to a softly striped forearm. The wound which had joined them was gone now but Flynn traced the place it had been, face unusually still. "I've never had a brother before."

"Me either."

"Am I supposed to not kill you?"

Tobias chuckled. "I think so."

"How about a little maiming?" A perfect black brow arched. "Or you think Ash would rip our heads off?"

"I don't think she'll care if we brawl," Tobias mused, watching Flynn's delicate finger trace the invisible gash over and over again - as though to remind himself it was real. "So long as we both come back to her afterwards, with our limbs more or less attached."

"I hate saying this, but you need to complete the mating." Flynn's expression settled into something so otherworldly Tobias wondered if he'd simply disappear. "I don't care what it takes, just seduce the fuck out of her and Mark her. We need to get rid of Olaf before he gets rid of Ash."

"She agreed to it back in the gorge, but…" Tobias thrust a hand into his hair and tousled it. "I don't know if it's even possible, let alone trying to manage the ceremony amidst all this chaos."

"What if you were alone?" Flynn picked up a leaf, examining the fine tracery of veins inside it. "This place is a write off. No food, no real shelter - but according to Zeke's map, there's a human town a few hours north. If you take one of the cars, and Ash, you could go for supplies and catch us up later."

"She won't want to leave the others without an Alpha." The moment the words were out of his mouth, Tobias blinked. "Mother moon; you're an Alpha. Sabre, I mean."

Flynn's grin was all teeth. "Too fucking right I am. Unhinged maybe, but every ounce in charge nonetheless."

"She won't like it."

"Which is why we're not going to tell her." Amber eyes narrowed. "I know I said we need to beat the truth out of her, but that's like asking the sun to rise in the west. New plan; let her bend the truth, thinking she's getting away with it, while we play the same screwed-up game."

"I don't like lying, not even by omission."

"Front her, then." A one-shouldered shrug. "Fucked if I care; just save her life."

"All right. Do you think you can manage without the two of us, though? Touch-wise," Tobias added, holding up both hands for peace when the tigerkin's face darkened.

"The answer is both yes and no. I won't like it, but I'll handle it because the alternative is much fucking worse." Flynn flicked a leaf into the air and watched it spiral to the ground. "Time's short - in more way than one. Take her and go and *do not* come back until she's safe."

Tobias nodded, raised his head and whistled. Zeke strolled out of the shed, wiping his hands on a greasy rag. "Both cars look good. Full tanks, extra fuel, everything in place. Tyres are a little low, but nothing dangerous."

"Good." Tobias pushed upright, held out a hand to Flynn and was surprised when the tigerkin actually took it. "We're splitting up. Ash and I are going to get some supplies, the rest of you keep going. We'll catch you later on."

Golden lashes lowered, rose again. "Okay."

Flynn laughed. "He's a good second, T-Fuzz. There was more meaning behind that one word than you can manage in an entire speech."

"Shut up," Tobias growled. "Get back to the others and bring them here, won't you?"

"I'll do you one better." Shimmering into tiger form, Flynn raised his head to the breeze. For a moment Tobias worried he was going to roar out loud, but the sound, when it came, echoed inside his mind. *T-Fuzz is down. Bring the others.*

Tobias gaped. "How is that one better?"

*Because I didn't have to go anywhere.*

Shaking his head, Tobias crossed to Zeke's side and gripped the other male's shoulder. "You okay?"

"It's been an interesting few days, but I'm handling." Zeke tilted his head, the setting sun burnishing his golden curls. "Should I be protecting your virtue from a tiger, though?"

"He just needed to borrow a little strength."

A pale eyebrow shot up. "Is that what the young kids are calling it these days?"

"Very funny," Tobias growled. "Are you up for this, or not?"

"Sure." Zeke filled his cheeks with air, blew it out slowly. "We'll look for a secure place to camp not too far from here, then travel slowly tomorrow. Will a night and a day be enough?"

"Should be." Tobias shrugged. "If you don't hear from us after that…"

Sapphire eyes connected with his and Zeke nodded. "We'll come looking."

********

Aislinn drummed her fingers on her opposite elbow, wondering if the steam coming out of her ears was actually visible. The blue car they'd borrowed from the possumkin purred quietly along, not missing so much as a beat for all it'd been locked away for what smelt like years. The countryside was a gently rolling combination of hills and valleys, the elevation such that in the winter, these slopes would be blanketed in snow. Tobias drove in careful silence and though she was staring pointedly out the front windscreen, Aislinn knew every cell of his body was trained on her.

"You planning to be mad at me the entire way?" He asked, half turning in her direction for the fortieth time in as many minutes.

"At this point, yeah."

Tobias tightened his grip on the wheel and turned back to the road, washed yellow by the car's headlights. "This isn't as bad as you seem to think. We're going north, the others are going north-east. There won't be much time lost and you know we need to eat, at the very least."

She spoke through gritted teeth. "Splitting up makes us more vulnerable and we could've hunted."

"Flynn will keep them safe, if that's what you're worried about."

"For Solaeden's sake, Tobias, they're not children." Aislinn dropped her head into her hands with a snarl. "Just forget it. I can't deal with you right now."

"Are you… trying to *avoid* a fight?" He sounded surprised. "You love fighting."

"Stop trying to charm me, Tobias Deklyn Greenwood."

"Why? Is it working?"

She gave him the finger and he subsided with a gritty chuckle. They drove in silence for another twenty minutes, the road lined with gnarled trees whose leaves were curled by the day's dry heat.

"Is your Mark hurting?" Tobias asked suddenly.

"Huh?" Aislinn looked down at the skin she'd been furiously kneading. "Yeah, actually, now that you mention it."

"You didn't think to say something earlier?" The first cracklings of actual temper showed in his voice and Aislinn looked up to meet blazing blue and gold eyes.

"It's been aching since I woke up on Percy's table. I didn't think about it then, but now that I'm paying attention, the feeling's worse."

Tobias took a deep breath and when he spoke again, his voice trembled. "Olaf's killing you, isn't he?"

Damn. "He's trying."

"Why not just tell me?" Tobias asked, hurt evident in every word. "Why shut me out, leave me guessing?"

"I didn't -"

"No, listen. Flynn was the one who guessed what was going on, and yeah, I can see you probably have some convoluted reason for keeping it from everyone else, but… from me?" Tobias glanced her way, his face vulnerable in a way only Aislinn ever got to see. "You said you wanted to mate. Do you, really?"

"Of course I do," she managed, wrapping both arms around herself. "Why would you question that?"

"Because you keep looking for excuses to put it off." Tobias gripped the wheel so tightly it creaked. "I get that you wanted to use the measuring device to map my power levels, but, Ash, we both know it's a pointless exercise. I can feel my energy pushing at my skin, desperate to get out. I can feel *your* energy railing against those damned walls you keep rebuilding, trying to reach me. My soul is in knots, battered and bruised from the constant smack down, and I'm willing to bet yours is the same." The steering wheel groaned a protest and he took a deep breath, his knuckles relaxing ever so slightly. "You know you own me - everybody fucking knows you own me. Why say you love me, agree to mate, then put your life on the line to turn me down?"

Ice formed in Aislinn's gut. "I'm not turning you down."

Tobias barked a short, wet laugh that hit her right in the solar plexus. "How would you describe it, then?"

"I meant what I said back at the gorge," Aislinn said at last, rubbing her hands over her biceps. "But you know just as well as I that this cure -"

"Dammit, Ash, I don't want to cure you, I want to *be with you*." He thumped his chest in emphasis, then frowned. "You look like death warmed up. Are you sure you're okay?"

"I don't know. I'm cold and aching. Almost as if Olaf – oh gods, Tobias!"

A pair of headlights shone in the side window, attached to an enormous four wheel drive that smashed into the back of the car and sent it into a terrifying spin. Aislinn braced herself against the dash whilst Tobias fought for control but it was no use; there was a sickening crunch as the sedan thumped into a tree on the opposite side of the road. The seat belt dug in painfully tight and Aislinn jerked backwards while Tobias flung forwards, his head hitting the driver's window hard enough to crack it.

"Tobias?" She unclipped her seatbelt, grabbed his shoulder and shook.

"I guess this car's too old for air bags," he slurred, wiping his face and staring down at the resulting smear of blood. "Well, shit."

The car shunted sideways with a metallic scream, the driver's side door suddenly gone. A bear stood in the opening, teeth bared, swinging the mangled metal like a sword. Tobias ducked and the car shuddered beneath the blow. As the bearkin drew back for another swing, Aislinn shifted to her midform and dove across Tobias with a roar, tackling the bearkin to the ground and shredding his throat with her teeth.

Tobias stumbled out of the wreckage behind her, blood trickling down his face from a cut at one temple. He opened his mouth to speak but the sharp retort of a gun stole his words, the bullet's impact wrenching his body backwards.

Fear choked Aislinn but Tobias was already moving, fur sweeping across his skin as he shifted to his midform between one breath and the next, his clothes shredding like a scene from a bad movie. He launched himself at the four wheel drive which had rammed them, slamming feet first onto the roof of the vehicle and smashing the windscreen with a clawed fist. Reaching into the cabin, Tobias played a brief tug of war with the occupants before his transitional strength won out, the driver's truncated screams motivating the remaining bearkin to abandon the car - and their deceased comrade - and sprint for cover.

*Shit.* Aislinn stepped into the shadows and dematerialised as the men came her way, ducking the dismembered body parts Tobias flung in their direction.

"Solaeden save us," one whimpered, his English heavily accented as he ducked a severed foot. "He's lost it!"

"You shouldn't have shot him," another answered in Russian, his voice gravelly. "Boss warned us there was a wild card."

Flowing over the ground like so much water, Aislinn snapped the necks of both bearkin before either had a chance to say any more. The third ducked away from her reaching fingers and called his bear form, his black fur melting into the darkness so that he seemed little more than glittering eyes and brilliant white teeth. Aislinn blocked a feint, ducked the real swipe and stepped under his guard, feeling a sting in her ribs as she flipped the bearkin onto his back. She stumbled, legs suddenly rubbery and veins filled with a terrible burning - only to realise the claws she put to the bearkin's throat were not claws at all, but human fingers.

"Shit." Aislinn threw herself to the side, snarling as she pulled a syringe out of her ribcage. "You need some new tricks, General."

"Why would I bother, little wolf, when this trick works so very well?" Olaf stepped into the open, motioning his ally to stand down. "I'd advise you to call your friend to order, or I'll be forced to shoot him some more."

"Fresh out of serum?" Aislinn drawled, hefting the syringe like a knife and tossing it into the shadows where her black-furred opponent had last been. "Tobias, stop tearing that bear's limbs off and come here so we can surrender like good little victims." Her answer was a throaty roar, and a shower of meaty chunks on the ground at her feet. "Sorry, General, looks like you're on your own."

"Ah, the joys of transition." Olaf's face creased in open delight. "Will he turn on you next, I wonder?"

"Brave words for a man who's watching his inbred cousin be torn into bite-sized pieces," Aislinn returned, surreptitiously trying to shake the agonising burn of the shifting serum out of her limbs. How big was the dosage in that syringe? How long would she be down and out? "Don't you care for your mangy little family?"

"My men knew the risks before they chose to accompany me on this mission. Speaking of..." Gimlet eyes narrowed. "I know Regina gave you the formula and I *will* have it, one way or another."

"This again?" A whisper of sound behind and to the left; Aislinn stepped backwards as a stun-rod passed through the space where she'd been standing. She swept the rod out of her attacker's grip and rammed it through the back of his head, kicking the body aside. "How many times do I have to tell you: I don't have the bloody formula!"

The bearkin general opened his mouth to respond and paused as the wind changed, carrying the scent of fresh blood. They turned as one to watch Tobias step from the trees, his fur slick and his eyes bright with battle fever. He stopped a few meters short of Aislinn and spat the severed head of a man onto the ground at her feet.

"Um." Aislinn frowned down at the head and back up. Her heartmate rumbled deep in his chest, nudging the grisly trophy closer with a clawed foot. "I… thanks?"

Olaf choked. "Did he just give you that head as a *present*?"

"Seems that way." Aislinn strained her senses, but couldn't pick up anything beyond the blood drenching Tobias' fur. When she tried to move away from his offering he whimpered, top lip curling back from razor sharp teeth. Sighing, she stopped and held out a hand. "It's okay; I love it. Best gift you ever gave me."

Tobias bent his head and nuzzled her fingers, streaking blood over her palm. Aislinn scratched his chin, making soothing noises even as she scanned the area. Olaf had taken several discreet steps backwards, putting him out of Tobias' immediate line of sight - but hadn't been foolish enough to make himself a target by fleeing. In fact, he had a decidedly smug look on his face.

A whistling sound broke the silence and Tobias shoved Aislinn aside as a rope cut through the air. He caught hold of the length but it wrapped around his body, tipped by a three pronged hook that slammed deep into Tobias' shoulder.

Olaf's power barrelled into Aislinn a second later, taking her knees out from underneath her. Tobias jerked sideways to break her fall, his midform large enough to both cushion and shield her as they fell to the ground together. Staring into the golden starbursts of his eyes, Aislinn realised that even in the grip of transitional psychosis, without a single coherent thought in his mind, he loved her - and if she didn't do something soon, he'd die for her.

Pressing a kiss to his bloodied snout, Aislinn got her legs beneath her and ran. Olaf's power pummelled her again but she went with the fall, landing half in and half out of the blue car they'd purloined from the possumkin.

"Oh, little wolf of mine." Olaf's voice was throaty, his patent leather shoes crunching the asphalt as he approached. "I think *that* might have been the last of your energy."

"It was," Aislinn rasped. His psychic fist closed around her chest and she slumped, her left hand scrabbling under the passenger seat and her right trapped beneath her body. By the time Olaf flipped her onto her back, her heart was little more than a twitching bird inside her chest. She met his gloating smile with one of her own. "Lucky you've got plenty."

Turning inward, Aislinn wrapped herself in Olaf's frigid mental touch and yanked. He choked, stumbled - and she sat up, one hand fisting in the collar of his formal shirt while the other buried a combat knife deep in his gut.

The bearkin General leapt back with a roar, clutching at the rubber-coated hilt protruding from his stomach. Aislinn sucked in air and rolled to her feet, racing into the bushland on the side of the road. Olaf's power struck again but she was expecting it this time and wrenched the psychic reins from his grasp, sending the icy energy back where it came from.

"Find her! *Kill her!*" Olaf shouted, agony and apoplexy warring in his voice. "I want her head!"

Palming the second, smaller knife she'd dragged from the car, Aislinn cut through the trees and wriggled underneath the four wheel drive the bearkin had used to ram them off the road. Feet loomed; she slashed with the knife and her opponent screamed, dropping to the ground to clutch at his legs. A second slash and he fell silent, eyes wide and glassy.

Aislinn slipped back under the car as two more bearkin moved into view; one in human form, holding the end of Tobias' rope and the other in bear form - neither of them the black bear. Eyes narrowing, she did some quick calculations, scented the air, and felt a swift surge of hope.

Olaf was gone.

Holding that shining thought close like armour, Aislinn rolled out into the open, throwing the knife as she gained her feet. It thunked into the eye of the male in bear form and he slumped quietly to the ground while his partner swore and danced out of the way.

With nothing left now but pure bravado, Aislinn stalked forwards, forcing her expression into something resembling a smile. "Looks like your pals have deserted you, friend."

The man holding Tobias' rope watched her with wide-eyed apprehension. "There's no shame in dying for a just cause."

"I hope you truly believe that." Aislinn snapped her teeth and the man jerked backwards - then toppled as Tobias tore his head from his shoulders with an awful, sucking sound.

The night went silent.

Aislinn had a split second to scent the air before Tobias stepped over the dead bearkin, tipped her chin up with clawed fingers and growled softly. She looked into his wild eyes and saw no rage, only devotion. "They're gone. We're safe."

He wasn't really in there - there was no way he'd be draping an intestine around her shoulders like a scarf if he was - but he rumbled affectionately, his soul responding to her not as a warrior, but as a heartmate. She swallowed a thick knot of emotion and spread one hand over his thumping heart. When he didn't protest, she gripped the shaft of the hook embedded deep in his flesh. "I need to take this out, Tobias. You need to let me take this out."

Another rumble. It was as good as she was going to get. Aislinn set her teeth, braced against the wall of his chest and tore the hook free with brute strength alone. Tobias howled, scrabbling at her shoulders, her sides - and then he dropped to the ground, shimmering back into human form as unconsciousness claimed him.

# Twenty-One

Sienna wiped her mouth with the back of one wrist and frowned at the night-darkened smear of blood. "Damn."

"Again." Flynn curled his hands into fists. "Faster."

She wanted to rage at him, wanted to cry, wanted to tell the ridiculous man it was impossible to go faster. Instead, Sienna took a deep breath, adjusted the loose t-shirt she'd borrowed from Zeke and nodded. "Again. Faster."

His grin was a deliberate taunt and Sienna felt something dark and wild rear its head in response. Ever since she'd sunk her teeth into the pulsating skin at Gerard's throat and torn, his heart's blood cascading into her mouth and across her chest in a sticky deluge, her skin didn't fit right. The woman who had laughed and loved with Brayden Maxwell was gone, her healer's soul shredded by the life she'd ended with such brutal finality. That it had been necessary didn't help; she'd had another option at her disposal and hadn't known how to harness it - a flaw Sienna intended to rectify even if it meant training with a certain irritating tigerkin every day for the rest of her life.

"Go." Flynn cut through the night like a knife, slipping beneath her fledgling guard and sweeping Sienna's feet in a movement so quick she didn't even bother trying to follow it. Instead, she bunched her fist in his t-shirt and dragged him down with her, landing a glancing blow to the chi point inside his wrist. Bringing up both feet, Sienna planted them in Flynn's abdomen and heaved; he went over her head and disappeared out of sight. She rolled to her knees - and was promptly flattened in the dirt. "Better, pretty puppy, but I still win."

"I got you," she panted, lying quiescent as he ran all four of his sharpened teeth back and forth across the side of her neck. "You know I did."

Flynn dangled a limp hand in front of her face. "Too bad you got your throat torn out in the process."

Still, it was progress and Sienna could tell by the tone of his voice that Flynn was pleased. Footsteps echoed at that moment and her tall, gangly brother stepped out of the bushes, his face moving from resigned to alarmed in less than a second. "Oh, come on! That's my sister, man."

Flynn laughed deep in his throat and backed off, hauling Sienna upright by the collar of her borrowed t-shirt. "Don't worry, Goldenrod; she's not my type."

Under any other circumstances the comment would've made Sienna bristle but it was plain as the nose on her face that the tigerkin was in love with Aislinn, so she stood silent while the two males spoke. Instead of focussing on their words, she watched the energy currents flowing through their bodies and practised turning her second sight on and off - a process she hoped would become less cumbersome as time went on.

Flynn had taught her how to feel the chi energy; a human psychic website had taught her how to open her 'inner eye' and see those chi points as very real things. While Flynn was focussed solely on teaching her to disable or even kill an opponent with a quick tap in the right spot, Sienna knew beyond doubt that the nature of her skills was a peaceable one, something that would allow her to encourage the body to heal, de-stress the mind or, by striking a point and temporarily deactivating it, remove pain entirely.

Realising that the men had fallen silent and were both staring, Sienna frowned. "Pardon?"

"I asked if you had anything to add." Zeke's sharp eyes filled with concern. "You good, little sister mine?"

"Sorry, I was distracted." Sienna attempted a smile. "Run it by me again?"

"It doesn't matter," he muttered, face turning hard as he spotted her split lip. "Dammit, Flynn, I told you to be gentle."

The tigerkin shrugged. "Best way to learn is the hard way."

Zeke growled deep in his throat and Sienna promptly stepped between them, swatting her brother on the arm. "Stop it. He's baiting you on purpose." She shot a glance over her shoulder. "You're supposed to be playing Alpha, remember? Try and act like it for two minutes."

Flynn let out a long-suffering sigh. "Just because I'm blood bound by both T-Fuzz and Ash to protect your sorry carcasses -"

"Which you volunteered for," Zeke interjected.

"- doesn't mean I have to strut around with a stick up my ass ticking boxes on a fucking checklist."

"Maybe you should've thought about that before you started licking Tobias' neck like an ice cream," Zeke snapped.

"What on earth - you know what, don't tell me." Sienna held up both hands in surrender. "I don't want to know."

"Liar." Flynn's grin was razors and tangled bedsheets. "You can't wait to - shit!"

Zeke rushed to catch the collapsing tigerkin while Flynn growled and tried to bat him away. Sienna watched in horror as the chi point over Flynn's heart turned from pale yellow to a deep, dark red. "The blood bond!"

"I'm fine, I'm fine," Flynn rumbled. Yanking out of Zeke's grip, he dropped to all fours and shifted into his tiger form. He was still dressed in the denim shorts and t-shirt he'd dragged on earlier, the garments taut around his feline frame. *Someone's injured. Maybe both of them.* He turned to Zeke and his tone was pure command. *Round everyone up. We need to move.*

The tension which had been all but setting fire to the air between Zeke and Flynn disappeared in a blink as her brother straightened. "I'll need five minutes. Sens, will you warm up the car?"

"Sure." She caught the keys he flung her way. "Meet you there."

Zeke tossed a wave over his shoulder, already running for the bush. Sienna made her way towards the car, Flynn trailing silently in her wake. "You okay?"

*Fucking fantastic,* came the acerbic response. *Why wouldn't I be?*

"Oh, I don't know, maybe because your heart is about to explode?" Sienna whirled and struck him behind the shoulders with a single finger. "Better?"

*I...* Flynn stumbled to a halt as the chi point which had been so angrily red slipped back to soft yellow. *Thank you.*

"Welcome." Sienna coaxed him back into a walk, watching the flow of his energy to ensure it was back to normal. "Maybe you should travel inside the car this time."

*No.*

"I'm not sure it's a good idea to ride on the roof - what if that happens again?" She stopped beside the ridiculously orange vehicle and unlocked the doors. "You'd fall off."

*Still better than being inside.*

"You're insane."

*Possibly.* Flynn screwed up his nose in thought, whiskers twitching. *I've often wondered, but I guess a lunatic can't really diagnose themselves.*

"Right." Not under any illusions that her brother would actually let her drive when she knew full well it was one of his guilty pleasures in life, Sienna shoved the key in the ignition, leant over to take the car out of gear and then turned it on. Flynn was still watching silently when she stepped back, letting the door swing closed. "You look ridiculous in those clothes."

*Now you know why I spend most of my time naked.*

"I guess I can't argue with that." Fighting a smile, Sienna bent to grasp the hem of his t-shirt. "Arms up. Or legs. Whatever."

*What are you doing?*

"Undressing you, idiot. You can't ride on top of the car with clothes on - it'll impede your movement."

After a long moment, Flynn settled onto his haunches and raised both long, dangerous forelegs over his head. Sienna carefully peeled the t-shirt off, smoothing ruffled fur after it was gone. Without prompting, he lowered his front half and stood as she undid his shorts, tapping first one hind leg and then the other in a silent signal to step out.

The silence between them was so peaceful, Sienna found words slipping free. "Aislinn asked me to help set up a place for people who are injured... you know, when this is over." Sienna rubbed a fist over her chest. "Physical injuries are one thing but rape, trauma, loss... there are so many other maladies out there which are swept under the rug. At first I just wanted to help Ash, you know? Be a part of her life. Now I want to give those people someone to talk to, something to do, something to hope for."

*Why do you sound sad, then?*

"I…" Sienna paused, swallowed around a sudden lump in her throat. "I don't know if I'm fit for it now, carrying my own fractures."

*At the risk of sounding like a soppy fucker, it's your fractures that make you perfect.* Flynn huffed a hot breath against one of the hands twined in his fur. *You can't be what those people need unless you've seen darkness and truly understood it. Gerard has done that for you.*

"I guess."

*Whoever knew a lazy ratkin could have such practical uses?*

Sienna startled, then began to laugh. Rumbling deep in his chest, Flynn shoved his head against her shoulder and she threw both arms around his neck, burying her face in his fur. They were still like that five minutes later, when Zeke and the rest of the pack came jogging into the small clearing where the car was parked.

Her brother's hand was gentle on her shoulder. "Sens?"

"I'm fine." Sienna pressed a soft kiss to Flynn's nose and stood, flashing Zeke a smile that was both diamonds and dust. "Just needed a hug."

"Okay." Sapphire eyes so like her own, wide and guileless and full of love. "I'm not sure where Ash and Tobias are, but we know where they were going."

"That's a good start." Sienna slid into the back of the car, allowing Dominic and Rory to settle her between them. "Ten bucks says Flynn falls off in the first half hour."

Dominic listened as the tigerkin arranged himself on the roof. "Make it twenty, and I say the first ten minutes."

Rory's chuckle was soft, his voice a gentle whisper as he added, "Thirty - and he stays on the entire way."

"Deal." Sienna held out a hand, palm up.

The two men fitted their hands over hers. "Deal."

"You do all realise," Zeke drawled, sliding into the driver's seat while Jaxon slammed into the passenger one, "That we're very possibly driving to someone's death?"

"Sure." Sienna's grin was a vicious baring of teeth. "Bet you fifty bucks it won't be any of us."

Her brother blinked, long and slow. "Deal."

*******

A quick search of the surrounding area revealed a second, less damaged four wheel drive hidden in the trees. After making sure they were truly alone, Aislinn carried Tobias to the car and settled him in the back seat before retrieving their rucksack from the ruined blue sedan.

Shoving the pack on the floor in front of Tobias, Aislinn climbed into the driver's seat and dragged the door shut behind her. The keys were still in the ignition and, sending up a prayer to Lunaida for luck, she turned them. The car rumbled to life first try, though there was an ominous rattle in the engine bay. The instruments also showed a low petrol gauge; they'd make it to their destination but no further than that. Having fixed the route in her mind before they'd split from Flynn and the others, Aislinn put her foot to the floor and peeled out onto the road.

There was probably a speed limit, but she had no idea what it was and lacked the facility to care; Tobias' wounds needed to be tended as soon as possible. Worry over a second ambush had her driving for a good fifteen minutes before she pulled into an empty truck stop, turning the engine off and climbing into the back seat. The spacious area was consumed by Tobias' bulk, blood and sweat turning his skin into a grisly slip and slide. Despite the nightmarish appearance, his pulse was steady and his breathing clear. Reassured, Aislinn began a thorough search of Tobias' body, finding the hole where the bullet had gone into his shoulder and come out the back, leaving a gaping wound the size of a tennis ball. There was also a lump on his head, several rope burns, copious amounts of gravel rash and most importantly, two nasty gashes in his upper chest from the hook she'd torn out with such reckless abandon. Despite the outwardly severe appearance, the injuries were all punctured flesh and shredded muscle; provided she could stop the bleeding, Tobias' body would heal itself.

Hoping the bears had stolen their vehicle from someone prepared, Aislinn thrust an arm under the passenger seat and was rewarded with a blanket and a first aid kit. Flipping the lid on the tin, she dug out a bottle of disinfectant, some cotton wool and a veritable treasure trove of bandages.

"Sorry," she whispered, unscrewing the bottle and pouring it over Tobias' chest.

His eyes flew open, arms flailing as he gasped for air. "Ash?"

"Shhhh." Aislinn put a hand on his chest and Tobias subsided at once. "We're safe for now."

He lay silent as she tended his wounds, his clenched fists the only outward sign of discomfort. When she'd finished with the disinfectant, he lifted himself onto one arm so that she could get the bandages around his torso. "What happened to Olaf?"

"He's gone. Run away," Aislinn clarified, seeing his eyebrows lift.

"Damn. You didn't chase him?"

"I was a little busy trying to keep us alive," she snapped, blinking away sudden tears. "Someone decided to get himself shot, among other things."

"Hey." Tobias captured her trembling hands in his own. "We're okay, Ash. We're okay."

"Shut up." Aislinn yanked her hands free and leant down to tie the bandage in place, ignoring his grunt of pain. "Don't you dare frighten me like that ever again."

"I didn't exactly plan it," he replied, amusement lifting the veil of discomfort. "In fact, I don't remember a thing. Did I...?"

*Tear a man's head off his shoulders? Gift me an intestine scarf? Have a giant, completely inappropriate hard-on in your midform in the middle of a life and death battle?* Aislinn gave him what she hoped was a reassuring smile as she tucked the blanket over his lower half. "Nothing I couldn't handle."

"Really?" He narrowed his eyes. "You look awful."

"Yeah, well, they got me with the serum and my powers, among other things, are down for the count. But we're alive, and most of them are not, so it counts as a win in my book."

"They got you with the serum?" Tobias looked aghast. "How long will it last?"

"Well, I couldn't shift for a month last time but I think that was mostly due to trauma. Besides, this needle was a *lot* smaller than the original syringe they jabbed me with." She leant in, brushing her lips against his cheek. "Let's hope for a day, maybe two?"

"Shit." He dropped his head back against the seat. "What now?"

"We find somewhere safe so that you can rest and heal. Olaf is injured too, so we can afford a day in a motel - but no longer than that." Aislinn frowned. "I'd like to go back to the others but we're going to need more medical supplies and the human town is closer."

Something elemental shifted behind Tobias' eyes but he only said; "Problem one, money. Problem two, if we go to the humans naked and covered in blood, it'll look suspicious."

"Problem one I can solve, providing these are packed according to standard emergency protocol." Rummaging through the rucksack, Aislinn located the discreet compartment at the bottom and nodded. "There's a wad of cash here - it should be enough."

Tobias raised a shaking hand to rub at his head. "I should know that."

"Relax," she soothed. "You took a pretty big blow to the head; you might be foggy for a while. As for problem two, there's spare underwear and a little towel in here, so I can clean up and deal with anyone we come across."

"All right… What about me?"

"Try and get some sleep while we're driving. With any luck we'll arrive before dawn, so you'll get a couple of hours."

Tobias reached up to tuck a lock of hair behind her ear. "I meant, I'm still naked."

"No you're not." Aislinn kissed his fingers and laid them against his chest. "You've got a blanket and a bandage on."

He growled and reached for her but she was too quick, laughing as she hopped back in the front of the car. She shimmied into the sports bra and underpants, discovering with glee a small pair of black jogging shorts and tugging those on as well. Tobias remained silent and when she glanced back, it was to see he'd fallen asleep.

"Rest," she whispered. "I've got you."

Feeling unaccountably raw, Aislinn started the car and pulled out of the truck stop. After ascertaining they weren't being followed, she adjusted the rear-view mirror to show Tobias' face instead of the road behind her. Even in sleep he exuded a masculine energy that made her want to snuggle under the blanket alongside him.

*"You know you own me - everybody fucking knows you own me. Why say you love me, agree to mate, then put your life on the line to turn me down?"*

Aislinn's heart contracted at the deep, visceral need in his remembered words. Mother moon, she'd made a mess of things - and she couldn't blame anyone but herself.  She slammed her hands against the steering wheel and immediately felt guilty but Tobias slept on, oblivious to her inner turmoil. Probably just as well; admitting she'd been so focussed on her own pain she'd not noticed his would've cut twice as deep if he'd been awake.

A crossroads came up out of nowhere and Aislinn swung to the right, pushing the car as fast as it would go. Better to concentrate on the road than think - at least until they were somewhere a little safer.

It was just after five thirty in the morning when she pulled into the driveway of the Outback Motor Inn. After a quick check in the mirror to confirm her reflection wasn't as terrifying as she thought it was, Aislinn slid out of the car, dragging the rucksack with her.

"Hello?" The door cracked open before she had the chance to knock, revealing an elderly gentleman wrapped in a plaid dressing gown.

"Hi. Sorry to disturb you so early, but I was wondering if you had a room available?" Aislinn offered what she hoped was a sweet smile.

"Hmmm. Well, we don't have any guests right now but I'll be honest, we don't usually check anyone in this early." He squinted, trying to make out her face. "Are you all right? You've got blood on you."

"My husband fell while we were hiking. He's all right, but I need somewhere to let him recover. I can pay," she added, digging a wad of notes out of the rucksack.

"Good heavens! How long are you planning to stay?" The man exclaimed.

"Two days at most, plus meals and a little extra for helping us out."

"Well I don't normally offer much more than breakfast but I can make an exception this once, seeing as you're in a pickle." A pause. "I'm Bruce."

"Ash." She pushed the wad of bills into his wrinkled hands. "Pleased to meet you."

Bruce grunted. "Stay here, I'll get you a key."

Aislinn jigged on the spot, watching the street as she waited. All was quiet and Bruce returned in less than a minute, dropping a silver key into her palm.

"Rooms are around the back, yours is number four. I'll have to go to the store for supplies so breakfast will be about nine. I'll knock on your door." He frowned. "If you're hungry in the meantime, there's some staples in the room."

"That's fine. Thank you," Aislinn called, jumping backwards as he closed the door in her face. Rather than be offended, she hurried back to the car and leapt in, following Bruce's instructions around behind the office.

To her delight, the 'rooms' were in fact little cabins. Nine in total, they were arranged in a semicircle around a small, well-tended garden and had concealed parking spaces behind each one. Aislinn parked the four wheel drive close to the building so it wouldn't be seen from the road, then opened the door and moved their few possessions inside.

The accommodation was simple but neat, with one bedroom and one bathroom. The open plan living area held a round table and two chairs, a small couch and a bench with a kettle and bar fridge. Best of all, the cabin had front *and* back doors, giving her plenty of escape options. Clearing a path from the back door to the bedroom, Aislinn returned to the car, double checked nobody was watching, then rolled Tobias' sleeping form into her arms. A Kin wouldn't so much as blink at the sight of her carrying a man at least twice her size and weight, but a human would - and flapping jaws led to confrontations.

Positioning Tobias carefully on the bed, Aislinn checked his wounds and pulled up the covers, knowing he preferred a sheet at the very least. Guilt cut deep and she bit her lip as she stared at the filthy, bloodied man on the bed. He really was her everything, and she - she was such a *bitch*.

Hunger and misery gnawed at her belly and with little else to do, Aislinn trudged out to the fridge. Discovering bread, cheese and milk, she made two cheese sandwiches, poured a tall glass of milk, and downed the lot without really seeing any of it. That done, she retired to the shower to scrub herself twice over. Most of the blood belonged to others but the accident and ensuing fight had caused several of her scars to split open, the worst of which still oozed when she ran the loofah over it. Sighing at further proof that her body was failing, Aislinn dried herself carefully then rinsed her clothes in the sink and hung them on the towel rail.

Tobias hadn't moved when she returned to the bedroom and Aislinn crawled into bed beside him, tucking her body around his warmth and burrowing her head into his shoulder. Even covered in blood and grime, his presence was a comfort - and a torture. She owed him better than this. Better than a half life, a half bond, a half lover. Aislinn pressed a soft kiss to his skin, heard him murmur in response even in the depths of his exhaustion. When he woke, she vowed, she would fix this. Once and for all. Keeping that thought foremost in her mind, Aislinn curled her arm around Tobias' waist and fell asleep.

# Twenty-Two

Tobias woke to an insistent banging on the door, a pounding rhythm that matched the one in his head. He groaned, rolling over in the soft bed and rubbing at his face. Bed? Door? His eyes flew open and he was on his feet in an instant, gasping at the pain in his chest and shoulder. Aislinn lay sleeping in the space he'd just vacated, her hair spread across the pillow in a glorious display of dark brown and red wine. They must have made it, then. But who on earth was knocking?

Tobias made his way out into the living area of their accommodation, grabbing a cushion off the couch to cover his groin as he went. After fumbling for a moment with the unfamiliar lock, he yanked the door open.

An elderly gentleman bustled in, carrying a tray covered with hot food. "Morning, young man."

"Um. Good morning."

"I'm Bruce. Forgive the expression, son, but you look like shit," Bruce said, depositing the breakfast tray onto the table. "Must've been one hell of a hiking accident."

"Yes. I'm very clumsy," Tobias replied, his eyes riveted on the tray.

"Hmmm. I took a tumble in my youth, too. Buggered my knee and now the blasted thing aches when it rains. You need to be more careful, youngster, or you'll end up like me." He blinked at Tobias out of steely grey eyes. "I got your wife's name - Ash - but I can't say as I remember yours."

"I... sorry, I'm Toby." Tobias offered his spare hand.

Bruce eyed the bloodied skin and shook his head. "No offence but I'll shake after you shower. Look, your missus paid for all meals but she gave me far too much. Is there anything else you need?"

"Well, my clothes got torn up in the fall. I'd be grateful for something to wear."

"Easily done, son. I've got some old clothes you can have. Like I said, your missus gave me far too much cash and I don't like to feel as though I'm ripping you off," Bruce said, unpacking the laden tray onto the table.

Tobias' stomach grumbled as the aroma of bacon crossed the room. "Keep any extra, we just appreciate having someone to help us out."

"If you say so. I'll admit we haven't had many people through lately so it's nice to see some fresh faces. I'll drop the clothes back in a few minutes but otherwise lunch will be at midday. Enjoy." Bruce stumped out, slamming the door behind him.

"Bye," Tobias muttered, tossing the pillow back onto the couch.

"What? Where?" Aislinn appeared in the doorway, a sheet clutched to her chest and her eyes glazed from sleep.

Tobias gestured at the table. "Breakfast."

"Oh. Right. Great," she added, rubbing at her face. Then; "How are you feeling?"

"Like I got hit by a truck," he admitted, holding fast while Aislinn prowled around him in a circle, her eyes narrowed as she assessed his body. "But better than yesterday. Hungry."

Aislinn raised an eyebrow. "You don't want to shower first?"

He looked like a nightmare, he knew - but he was also literally starving to death. "I'll wash my hands."

"Boys." Aislinn snorted, then disappeared into the bathroom.

Tobias washed his hands as promised and sat down at the table, overjoyed to see two enormous servings of sausages, bacon, eggs, hash browns and grilled tomatoes. He was half way through his meal when Aislinn returned, wearing a black sports bra and some tiny jogging shorts. Tobias choked on a mouthful of bacon, glad that a loud knock covered the sound. When did gym clothes become so sexy? He watched Aislinn open the door, admiring the curve of her butt in the morning sunlight and listening to the hum of her voice as she spoke with Bruce.

Aislinn closed the door and turned to Tobias with a smile. "Clothes?"

"Breakfast," he grunted, shovelling a hash brown into his mouth.

Aislinn laughed, dropped the shopping bag Bruce had given her onto the couch and sat down next to him. "This smells fantastic."

Tobias watched her chew, watched her throat work as she swallowed, felt his blood begin to heat. Wondering if his voice sounded as strangled as he felt, he said; "So. Plan?"

"Not sure… Give your shoulder a little more time to heal, I guess. We can stay here tonight but tomorrow we'll have to keep moving." Aislinn frowned, toying with half a fried egg. "I also need to get rid of the car and find a new one."

"What about the others?" Tobias pushed his empty plate away and fetched the jug of orange juice off the tray. "Seeing as Olaf's not where we thought he was, we should probably could call and pass on an update."

Aislinn shook her head. "No need. I woke up to a billion messages - Flynn felt you go down through the blood bond and they're already on their way here."

*Dammit.* Tobias clenched his fist around his fork and tried to think. When the silence grew suspicious and he felt, more than saw, Aislinn's brow rise, he poured her a glass of juice and offered it. "Is it wise for them to join us?"

"I don't want to endanger the humans here either, but I don't think we have much choice. Olaf's…" Aislinn fidgeted, brows furrowing. "Angry. The moment he's capable, he'll come looking for us. We need the numbers."

A growl echoed in Tobias' throat before he could swallow it. He finished his juice and stood, stomping across the room to snatch up the bag of clothes. "Gods forbid we could have one fucking moment's worth of actual fucking *privacy*."

"Tobias?"

He turned to see her frowning, head tilted to one side. Tobias wanted to scream at her, to shake her, to tear his heart out until it stopped hurting. He'd dared to believe, wounded and groggy in the back of the car, that they had a chance - but with only a night left, perhaps less, before the rest of the pack caught up? More likely the skies would open and bury him in snow in the middle of a scorching summer's day.

Particularly when all he could do was shout; "Forget it!" In a voice that didn't sound like his at all, it was so ragged and hopeless. Still, it was satisfying to watch her flinch when he snapped his teeth and stormed off towards the shower - even if it made him feel like a royal asshole while he did it.

*******

*Coward.* Aislinn listened to the shower turn on and dropped her fork, no longer hungry. Instead, she got up and went out the back door to look at the car. Behind the place where it was parked, there was a slight incline into bushland. Maybe they could just take the hand brake off and push? She sauntered down the hill, attempting to look like she was simply out for a morning stroll, and slipped into the scrub. Her skin burned when she attempted to call her wolf body, a sure sign the serum was still in effect, so Aislinn was forced to slide through the inhospitable undergrowth in her bare human feet.

*Coward.* The incline ended abruptly in a sharp overhang, at the bottom of which more thick, gnarled scrub awaited. If she could nudge the car in this direction, the little cleft might provide enough cover to hide the damned thing until they left the area. Aislinn raised her eyes to the sky, a clear cerulean marked only by the blazing sun. Probably not a good idea to try and dump the four wheel drive in the middle of the day. She'd come back when it was dark.

*Coward.* Her skin was covered in a thin sheen of sweat by the time she made it back to the motel. Aislinn yanked open the back door of the four wheel drive and crawled inside, rummaging in the cargo area until she discovered a length of rope, a crowbar and a hunting knife in a leather sheath. They smelt of human rather than bear and she spared a thought for their owner before dumping her newfound supplies on the back seat.

*Coward!* Ugh. Aislinn slumped to her knees, dropping her head into both hands. She *was* a coward. She'd said she was going to fix this and instead, she'd deliberately ignored the elephant in the room. What in Lunaida's name was wrong with her? *Get a grip, Ash. Get a gods-damned grip.*

A subtle difference in the background noise alerted her that the shower had turned off. Aislinn took a deep breath, gathering the things she'd found in the car and sliding out onto the ground. If the rest of the pack arrived and found them ready to tear each other's throats out, her heat escalated to fever pitch - well, she might as well slit her own throat now and save the bears the trouble. The Mark on Aislinn's hip twinged, as though Olaf had caught the train of her thoughts, and she hissed. *No.* There was no way in hell that foul creature was going to take any more of her life - it was time to suit action to her words.

Starting with the man in the shower.

Firming her resolve, Aislinn went back inside, closed the door and flicked the latch. She took a moment to stuff her new treasures into the rucksack then went out and sat on the couch to wait. Time seemed to draw on interminably and Aislinn fidgeted, crossing and uncrossing her arms and legs, drumming her fingers on her scarred knees. In the end, she pushed herself to her feet, moved the little table to the other side of the room and started running through a kata, closing her eyes and letting the familiar movements calm her down.

A soft sound disturbed her and she opened her eyes to see Tobias standing by the bench, wearing a pair of grey tracksuit pants and drying tumbled brown hair with a wet towel. His skin glistened in the sunlight, golden starburst eyes dragging at her soul. The five o'clock shadow which had darkened his face earlier was now gone and Aislinn realised that was why he'd taken so long in the bathroom.

"Hey," she said, standing up straight.

"Hey," he answered, setting the towel on the bench and running one hand through his damp hair to settle it. The movement drew attention to his chest and shoulder, now missing the bandage Aislinn had wrapped around it last night.

"How is it?" She asked, daring to step closer. The wound was still angry and red but the flesh had closed over, his Kin body healing it far more efficiently than human medicine ever could - though he'd need extra food and rest to complete the job. When Tobias didn't answer her question, Aislinn reached up a hand to touch, gliding her fingertips over the new flesh as gently as she could. He hissed and she froze, looking up at his face. What she saw was not pain but a terrible intensity that was almost worse.

"Don't stop," he rumbled.

She bit her lip, dropped her hand and took a deep breath. "I owe you an apology."

"Oh?" The golden stars in his gaze sharpened and Tobias stepped closer, fingers curling under her chin and tipping her face towards his. "What for?"

"Everything," Aislinn murmured. "I'm sorry, Tobias. I never meant to hurt you."

"I know." The corner of his mouth twitched. "The fault is just as much mine."

"How do you figure that?"

"I appear," he murmured, brushing his thumb over her lower lip, "To be a glutton for your very specific brand of punishment."

Whatever indignant response she'd been about to formulate disappeared as Tobias lowered his head, brushing his lips against hers. He began to draw away but the chaste kiss wasn't nearly enough to quench the sudden fire in Aislinn's veins. She grabbed at him, slinging one arm around his neck and fisting the fingers of the other hand in his damp hair. Tobias had barely opened his mouth to return the kiss when Aislinn thrust her tongue inside. Recognising an invitation when it came, Tobias wrapped his arms around her body, fingertips skimming her ribs. Everywhere he touched was on fire and Aislinn hummed in wicked delight, smoothing her palms across the uninjured section of his chest and down to his hips. Hooking her fingers into the dangerously low waist of his pants, she tugged Tobias' pelvis against her, the bulge of his erection pressing firmly into her ribs. Breath ragged and voice husky, she spoke against his lips. "Mate with me."

He froze.

"Ash," Tobias pulled back, panting, his hands cupping her face. "Don't start something you can't finish. Don't do that to us. I love you but I'm not a saint."

"I love you too," she said, surprised at the fierce defiance in her words. "I was afraid before, but not of the bond. I was afraid of what would happen if we reached for each other and it didn't work. I thought if we had the measuring device, it would... it doesn't matter. I want this. I want you."

"Are you sure?"

"Yes!" Aislinn shouted, satisfied when he startled away from her. "I want our life back, Tobias. *Our* life, the way it should be. For Solaeden's sake, stop talking and let's *do* this!"

"Gods above, yes." He scooped her up in his arms in spite of his injury and carried her into the bedroom, placing her on the bed as though she were made of glass.

Aislinn wrapped her legs around his waist, terrified that if she let him go, Tobias would dissipate like mist on a sunny morning. He groaned as his erection rubbed against her core, recognising the super sensitive flesh even through layers of clothing. She gasped, managed; "My powers are fried. I can't sense your transitional energy. If you're in a lull you might not be strong enough -"

"I'm strong enough." Tobias bent his head and kissed her again, a long and lingering kiss that left her breathless. Aislinn could do nothing but fist her hands in his hair as he trailed kisses along her jaw, running his hands up her ribcage. In one smooth movement, he hooked his fingers in her sports bra and drew it off over her head. "Gods save us both but you're beautiful, Ash."

Tears pricked her eyes as Tobias lowered his head, kissing his way along the brutal lacework of her scars, sliding down her body to tug one nipple into his mouth. He suckled slowly, laving his tongue over the hardened peak until she moaned and writhed beneath him. He held her in place with his larger body, pausing to look up at her with those beautiful blue eyes, their golden starburst centres dark with desire. With their gazes firmly locked, Tobias' tongue slid slowly out of his mouth, lapping gently at the other breast, his expression tender as he lowered his head to pay exquisite attention to the nipple he'd neglected before.

"Tobias," she managed, not quite sure what she was trying to say but needing to say it anyway. This wasn't like any of the other times they'd been together - energy crackled in the air, stole her ability to think. "What -"

"You're in heat," Tobias chuckled, sliding one hand down her ribs and into the waistband of her shorts. "And I'm your heartmate. Our souls might not be joined, but our bodies recognise each other. They know we left this too long."

Just like that he was gone – and so were her pants and underwear. Tobias stood at the end of the bed, one hand caressing her leg, his eyes burning over her body. Aislinn wiggled self-consciously but a soft, reassuring squeeze on her thigh made her stop, her entire body trembling. Something tugged at her gut, a deep, low pull that stole her breath as it reached for Tobias and was slapped away. "I can't reach you."

"I'm right here, Ash. I'll always be right here."

Tears welled in her eyes and Aislinn blinked to clear them as Tobias stripped off his pants. Even through the haze of her emotions it was impossible to miss his jutting erection, moisture already beading on the tip.

Tobias crawled onto the bed beside her, his body hot and hard as he pressed against her side. "Last chance to change your mind."

Pain echoed in his voice, an uncertainty she'd put there herself - an uncertainty that made her angry at fate, at the years which had separated them, at her own cowardice. "Mother Moon, Tobias! Just do it already."

"Just *do* it?" he barked a short laugh. "I've waited half my life for this moment. There will be no 'just doing' of anything."

Tobias trailed one finger down the side of her face, tilting her jaw up for a fiery kiss that left her panting. As his hand dipped ever lower, crossing her belly and sliding over her hips, Aislinn shut her eyes, squeezing them tight. Her body ached to have him crawl inside and make her whole, her lungs labouring for air. By the time his fingers dipped to caress her most sensitive spot, her blood had turned to honey in her veins. She moaned as he teased her, a gentle touch that was both incredible and incredibly frustrating. He made a hoarse sound in the base of his throat and quite suddenly the weight of him was gone off the bed, leaving Aislinn cold and bereft, her body crying out for his return. "Tobias?"

"Trust me," he said and a moment later she screamed, her eyes flying open. Sparks zinged up her body, followed by a very satisfied male laugh as he licked her again. "Surprise."

"You..."

"Should I stop?"

"No!"

He laughed again and lowered his head, nipping his way up her inner thigh. "Good."

Nobody had ever touched her the way Tobias did then, his fingers gentle whilst his tongue lapped and laved, invading her body in the most intimate of ways. It was an exquisite torture and she could only writhe on the bed, one hand fisted in the sheets and the other in his hair. Her body demanded more and she bucked her hips against him, eliciting another laugh. Tobias complied with her silent command, his fingers sliding in and out, his tongue flicking over her, the gentle grazing of his elongated canines driving her ever higher. With no warning, he sealed his lips over her clit and sucked. Aislinn cried out as her inner muscles clenched, wave after wave of pleasure turning her inside out. Tobias was relentless, refusing to stop until she was limp and moaning – and then he crawled up her body, the tip of his erection rubbing against her slickened entrance.

"Yes?"

"Yes." Aislinn wrapped her legs around his hips and her arms around his neck, drawing Tobias down against her. His kiss was aggressive, as though he would consume her, his passion a desperate, living thing. In contrast to the wild demands of his mouth, Tobias' hips moved slowly as he invaded her with infinite care. Aislinn groaned at the glorious sensation, her inner muscles flexing and stretching around his shaft until, buried to the hilt, Tobias stopped.

He nipped at her lips and pulled back, eyes bright. Aislinn offered her right hand and Tobias clasped it firmly, supporting himself on one arm, his eyes never leaving hers. When he opened his mouth the ritual words trembled with emotion. "For you I offer my one true heart, to be writ across your soul for all eternity and worn with love upon your flesh until our bodies return to the earth and our souls soar in the heavens."

"I offer in exchange my one true heart, to be writ across your soul for all eternity and worn with love upon your flesh until our bodies return to the earth and our souls soar in the heavens," Aislinn answered, her heart thundering in her chest. Tobias bent his head, burying his face in the tangle of her hair until he found the soft flesh of her neck where it joined her shoulder.

"Mine," he grunted and bit her, hard enough to draw blood.

Aislinn dug her fingers into his biceps and returned the gesture with a sharp bite of her own. "Always."

Energy welled between them, a furious heat that set them both panting. A primal urging swept up Aislinn's body and she dug her heels into Tobias' legs. He groaned and began to move, slow, deep thrusts that sizzled in and out of her. Aislinn's hips took on a life of their own as she milked him, her muscles clenching in rhythm with his movements, her only wish to take him deeper, higher.

Tobias released his grip on her neck to capture her mouth instead, his body picking up speed, each thrust more glorious than the last. Aislinn clutched at his broad shoulders, her body no longer her own as he took her, his thrusts so hard and deep she knew that he, too, had lost all semblance of control.

"Tobias! Oh gods, Tobias, please," she begged, tossing her head as the pleasure mounted, bordering on pain. Her body shattered, eliciting a shout which Tobias echoed moments later. The feeling of him pumping into her intensified the orgasm a hundredfold and Aislinn clung to his body, the only real thing in a sea of sparkling stars.

At last they were spent and Tobias fell forward, his weight a warm comfort against her chest. He made to move but she locked her ankles, growling in warning until he relaxed.

"Did it work?" he mumbled, raising his head.

"I don't know."

Aislinn had no sooner spoken when iron bands of cold clamped across her body, pressing down and squeezing the breath right out of her. She gasped, the sudden iciness causing her teeth to chatter and her body to shake. Tobias called her name and with the sound of his voice came a strange tingling, followed by a tide of heat that pushed the iciness away. The chill retreated until it was localised on her right hip – and then it disappeared.

"Ash?" Tobias repeated, his eyes filled with concern. "Are you okay?"

"I -" she broke off on a gasp as power slammed into her, pure and primal in its fury. Shadows wrapped around her as the dam gate binding her damper powers lifted and the raw, tingling electricity of Tobias' energy crackled through her veins, shattering already fragile shields so that her own wild energy surged forth. And then, snapping into place like a wire going taut, she felt the heat and light and strength of the heartmate bond. Her hearing sharpened, her sense of smell went crazy. She blinked at cracks in the ceiling which hadn't been there before, gasped at the super-sensitivity of her skin. Love - true, pure, unadulterated love - poured into her, filling her from toes to crown, bubbling in the back of her throat and shocking her heart into a desperate, erratic rhythm. When it at last settled, her senses returning to an approximation of what they had been before, she stared at Tobias' terrified expression and croaked; "I think it worked."

"It did?" he leant backwards, pulling out of her body with infinite care. "Lady Lunaida!"

"What?" Aislinn looked down at herself. Her right hip, which had previously carried Olaf's enormous Marking, showed only pale, creamy flesh. Unable to quite believe what she was seeing, Aislinn's hands followed her eyes up her body to the new Mark, slightly smaller but infinitely more welcome, spanning across the left side of her ribcage just below her breast. In contrast to the violent looking lines Olaf had left, Tobias' Mark was smooth and symmetrical, full of loops and dips and curls. It was beautiful. "It *did* work."

"Shit!" Tobias yelped and Aislinn looked up to see his hands clamped over the junction between his right shoulder and his neck. He flopped down on the bed beside her, eyes rolling back in his head and jaw clenched as he experienced his own version of the sensations which had just rearranged Aislinn, body and soul, into something new. When his breathing finally relaxed and he stared at her in astonishment, Aislinn pried at his hands until he revealed a Marking identical to her own in size and design, the swirling centre exactly over the spot she'd bitten during the mating ceremony.

"Mine," she whispered, tears welling in her eyes as she reached up to touch the elegant black lines. "We did it."

Tobias was still staring at her body, his face pale. "Oh Ash, I'm sorry."

"What? Why are you sorry?" Aislinn smiled at him, confused by the sadness in his soul where it twined around hers. "That was amazing and it worked. Fuck you, Olaf."

"Look," he murmured, his fingers trailing gently across her collarbone.

Aislinn looked. The thick scarring which had crisscrossed her body for months was still there, the bone deep ache of her injuries still lurking beneath the satisfied humming of her inner female. "Oh."

"The transition must have made a difference after all."

"Don't you dare! It worked, Tobias. I'm free and we're together. This is nothing," Aislinn snapped, waving a negligent hand in spite of the tears rolling down her cheeks. "I've learnt to live with it and I'll keep learning. The scars don't matter."

But they did, and from the way Tobias collected her tears with a gentle thumb, he knew it. "I wanted to make you better."

"You do make me better. You make me better every moment of every day." He was inside her now, a crackling, living presence that was already making her body soften and her blood sing. "Forget about the scars - you fill me up until there's nothing left but love. Now, I suggest you do it again before I become very cross with you."

Tobias' head snapped up as she lunged forward, tackling him backwards onto the bed and rubbing her body against his. "Ash!"

"What?" She hummed, nipping at his neck and rocking her sensitive core against his rapidly hardening shaft. "I'm serious."

Tobias tried to speak but she wasn't interested, leaning forward to capture his mouth with hers, hot and demanding as she used her body to whip his into a frenzy. Aislinn's core was already slick from their earlier lovemaking but a fresh wave of desire washed over her and the scent of her arousal had Tobias' eyes widening beneath her kiss.

"Touch me," she demanded, breaking away long enough to grasp his hands and drag them up to her breasts. "Love me."

"What are you doing?"

"Making up for lost time," she answered, slowly impaling herself upon his thick length. "Or are you telling me you're spent?"

Tobias growled in response, his hands sliding down to grip her hips. He set a pace that was both too much and not enough, each second a sparkling lifetime - and when their bodies erupted they both cried out, consumed by a mutual fire that left them panting and sweaty and shuddering in each other's arms.

Aislinn leant forward for a long, lingering kiss, the aftershocks of such an intense orgasm reluctant to let her go. Tobias rumbled deep in his chest, kissing a trail along her jaw and tugging her body flush against his. The smooth lines and swirls of the mating Mark drew her and Aislinn kissed the centre of the design, smiling as he jerked beneath her touch.

"Sensitive," Tobias grumbled - but it was a good natured grumble, so she did it again, then laid her head against his uninjured shoulder, drawing his butterscotch and cream scent deep into her lungs.

"I love you," Aislinn whispered.

"And I love you." Tobias pulled the cotton blanket over them both. "Now rest."

"Hmmm." Conscious that Tobias was still healing from their altercation with the bearkin, Aislinn curled her fingers against his chest and closed her eyes. "I better get thirds when we wake up."

His laugh was throaty, sexy and absolutely delighted. "Promise."

"Good." Aislinn sighed and relaxed, the steady rhythm of their synchronised heartbeats serenading her to sleep.

# Twenty-Three

Someone was knocking on the door.

Again.

Tobias grunted in disapproval, surfacing to discover Aislinn lying half on top of him, her hair spread across his chest. He slid out of bed with utmost care, settling her into the space he'd vacated before grabbing his tracksuit pants off the floor and yanking them on. The knocking became more insistent and he hurried to flick the latch and open the door.

"About time," Bruce muttered, bustling in with the lunch tray. "Sorry it's late but I -"

"What is it?" Tobias asked, frowning in concern. "What's wrong?"

Still staring, Bruce pointed at the join between Tobias' neck and shoulder. "Was that always there?"

"Oh, that." Tobias reached up a hand to touch his Mark, cursing himself for not thinking to cover it. "Yeah, I got that done when I was just a kid. You know how it is."

"Huh. Must be going senile in my old age." Bruce shook his head, grey brows drawing into a frown. "Anyway, sandwiches. Dinner will be about seven. Enjoy."

"Thanks." Tobias held up a hand to wave but the older man had already stomped out, slamming the door behind him. "Charmer."

"Deja vu." Aislinn's voice preceded her out of the bedroom, thick with amusement.

"Tell me about it." He turned to greet her with a lopsided smile, heart expanding as he took in mussed hair and a lush body wrapped in their bed sheet. "You look - holy shit!"

"Tobias?" Aislinn froze as he rushed across the room towards her, ripping the sheet off her body. "What's wrong?"

"Solaeden save us," he whispered, running his fingers over her skin. The scars which had so plagued his heartmate were gone, leaving only the flawless, creamy flesh he remembered in his dreams. "Ash, *look*."

"Oh!" Her smaller hands joined his and together they explored her body, poking and prodding and tugging at pristine skin. When she looked up, her blue-green eyes were brimming with emotion. "We did it. I feel... I feel better!"

Laughter bubbled up from nowhere and Tobias dragged her into his arms, taking her mouth in a long, deep kiss which had his whole body twitching for more. Aislinn wrapped her legs around his waist and when she leant back, Tobias was presented with an astonishingly good view of her breasts - which he promptly buried his face in and motorboated like crazy. Aislinn squealed and slapped at his shoulders, a reaction which ceased as soon as he began to nip and lick at her skin, pulling a nipple into his mouth so he could suck hard. She was panting when he leant back, flicking her an apologetic look from beneath his lashes. "Sorry."

"For what?"

"For making you wait for your lunch," he answered, then lowered his head to her other nipple. Aislinn groaned and he felt her core turn molten against his abdomen. Overcome with joy, giddy with desire, Tobias turned and pressed her against the wall, one hand supporting her backside so that he could rain down kisses on her pristine collarbone, her shoulders, her neck.

"Tobias," she gasped, writhing against him. When he didn't answer, she reached between them and shoved at the waistband of his pants. He spared a hand to help and Aislinn grabbed his erection as soon as it was free, sliding her hands over the hot, hard flesh in a caress as exquisite as it was wild. Guiding him towards her, Aislinn used the tip of his shaft to tease her clit, groaning at the sensation. Tobias growled against her breast as she did it again, knowing there was only a short amount of time he could put up with such perfect torture before he embarrassed himself everywhere. The only solution was to make her equally as desperate, so he returned to her nipple with single minded determination, circling the hard peak with his tongue and grazing gently with his teeth. Aislinn immediately retracted her hand and used all her considerable strength to bear down on him. "Now."

Surrendering willingly, Tobias drove home with a quick, hard thrust that drew cries from both of them. Aislinn braced her shoulders against the plaster as he began to move; long, powerful strokes that had her nails digging into his shoulders. He claimed her mouth as she shattered around him, his own orgasm barrelling up his spine until Tobias was unable to tell where he ended and Aislinn began. It took everything he had to keep his feet, to breathe past the thick knot of emotion in his throat. "You are my world, Aislinn Jaide Redding."

Flushed and sweaty, Aislinn grinned. "Say that again."

"My world," Tobias repeated, shifting his hips and drawing a gasp from her in emphasis. "Warrior, woman, Den Mother, friend - there's not a single piece of you that I don't adore."

She bit her lip, pointed incisors stark against pale skin. "I wish I could put my feelings into words like that."

"You don't need to," Tobias answered honestly. "I can feel you through the bond."

"You can?" Aislinn blinked, laid a hand over her heart. "I guess I'm still getting used to it. You know, considering you're not trying to kill me."

Tobias chuckled. "I may yet have a go at that, depending on how irritating you intend to be."

"Oh, I plan to be incredibly irritating," she answered, her smile as wide and goofy as his own. Her free hand feathered across his chest. "Look, Tobias. You too."

Tobias followed her gaze to see that the vicious gash left by the hook had completely disappeared, his bullet wound also sealed. "Getting better is fun."

"I'd say it was the sleep more than the exercise that did the trick," Aislinn laughed.

Tobias pouted. "Way to puncture my ego, Princess."

"All in a day's work, lover."

Tobias grinned, carefully disengaging their bodies so he could lower her to the floor. "Lunch?"

"Definitely." Aislinn rescued the discarded sheet and wrapped it around her torso. "Thanks to your insatiable libido, I'm hungry."

"That makes two of us." Tobias gave her his best bedroom leer, tugged his pants back up and dropped into the chair beside hers.

"Oh look," Aislinn snickered as she lifted the lid on the tray. "Your favourite."

The sandwiches were fresh and soft, brimming with creamy egg and lettuce. Tobias' stomach rumbled and he devoured three in a matter of minutes, reaching for a fourth before he put his mind to work. "So, seeing as we've been successful in banishing Olaf from your body, what now?"

She toyed with her half eaten sandwich. "Whilst our own personal worlds have been thoroughly rocked, nothing's changed externally. We're still being hunted by the Council and with the exception of Olaf, nobody else will know we've mated."

"Do you think the mating will make things better or worse?"

"Worse," she muttered. "Neither Percy nor my father wanted us to mate and now that we have, they're going to be pissy about it. Gaining leverage is more important than ever - and with Regina's formula out of reach, Olaf is our next best bet."

"He's desperate and wounded, which is going to make him more dangerous than before." Tobias ran a hand through his hair, contemplating a fifth sandwich. "I guess it also makes him more vulnerable, though."

"Yes." She nodded, her blue-green eyes hard. "On top of that, Olaf learnt a lot about his powers while he and I were unwittingly bound. I wouldn't put it past him to capture another woman for the express purpose of killing her remotely while the Council looks on. I can't stand by and let that happen."

"Fuck," Tobias growled. "All right. As soon as night falls, we hunt. Unless you think we can sneak off during the day?"

"Probably not. I don't like the idea of sitting around, but if we wait until dark I can -"

The sound of smashing glass filled the room and Tobias ducked on instinct, dragging his heartmate to the floor and rolling them under the table.

"Go right," she whispered, pressing a butter knife into his hand. "I'll go left."

Tobias gained his feet and turned towards the broken window in time to see a fist swinging towards his face. He dodged, stepping in to deliver a cracking blow to his attacker's head with one elbow. Tobias followed his opponent to the floor, straddling the other's chest and -

"Stop!" Aislinn cried. Tobias looked up to see she'd tangled her opponent in the bedsheet and held a vicious hunting knife to their throat. "Back off or I'll kill Lena."

The man underneath Tobias growled. "You wouldn't."

"Don't test me, Jacques. Promise to behave or it's lights out."

Tobias brandished his butter knife in emphasis and Jacques sighed, yanking off his ski mask. "Very well. I submit."

"About time - you already knew this was horse shit." The new voice preceded two more people from the direction of the back door. Shoving dirty blonde hair back off his face, Brayden looked Aislinn up and down and grinned. "Look at you!"

Releasing her captive, Aislinn spread her arms wide and twirled. "Yup! All fixed."

Brayden's clear hazel eyes sought Tobias'. "You sly dog, you."

"Nothing sly about it." Tobias shrugged and grinned. "We did it in broad daylight."

"If you all don't *mind*," Jacques growled from the floor, "I'm still being sat on."

"Serves you right," Kaira growled, shaking an admonishing finger. "Tobias should sit on you all damn day as far as I'm concerned."

"I'd rather not." Tobias gave the owlkin beneath him a stern look. "You gonna behave?"

"*Oui.*"

"Good choice." Aislinn crossed to help Tobias up, sliding an arm around his waist. "You okay?"

"Yeah." He set his butter knife back on the table. "Your owlkin is slow."

"Hah!" Her grin was brief but bright, then Aislinn turned to pin Kaira with a sharp look. "Report."

The other woman tugged on a lock of cobalt hair and sighed. "Way I understand it, Andre had an interesting discussion with the Council when he woke. He wanted you apprehended, but apparently Percy owns your ass now."

"So, he's still alive," Aislinn mused. "How disappointing."

Jacques sat up and rubbed a hand over the bruise forming on his jaw. "Professor Postlethwaite requested an emergency extraction after you tried to kill him."

Tobias growled, but Aislinn laid a gentle hand on his chest and stroked the sound away. "Torture has a habit of making me unreasonable."

"*Excusez-moi?*" Jacques' hand fell to his lap, jaw slack. "Torture?"

"What were you expecting?" Tobias snapped, baring his teeth at the other male. "Percy wasn't in it for the tea and biscuits."

"There are procedures," Jacques began, then threw his hands in the air. "*Merde!* Why bother? None of you follow the procedures anyway."

"Sometimes it's more important to think for yourself," Aislinn returned, shrugging. When Jacques' answer was a vicious string of French curses, she chuckled. "Have you been this pissy the entire time I've been gone?"

"And then some," Kaira muttered, dragging her black jumper off over her head and dumping it on the floor. Underneath, she wore a series of tight crop tops in varying shades of grey which displayed the muscular expanse of her stomach and well rounded hips, upon which rode dangerously low black shorts. Knives were strapped to waist, thigh and calf, and Tobias had no doubt she also had one stuffed into her combat boots. "I'm so glad you're back in charge now."

"What about the mission?" Jacques demanded. "We can't just ignore it."

Tobias wrapped one arm around Ash's shoulders and tilted his head to the side, deliberately drawing attention to the Mark on the lower curve of his neck. "You were sent because Percy wanted to play science god but there's no longer anything to experiment on, so the mission is null and void. Congratulations."

Jacques sputtered indignantly but Lena, brows drawn into a frown that made her look even more fearsome, stepped forward. "Let it go - we all know the Professor's report was questionable at best. Do you really believe Aislinn to be mentally unsound?"

Silence reigned for a full minute, then Jacques sighed and shook his head. "*Non.*"

Tobias felt the tension drain from Aislinn's body and he dropped a kiss on her hair, glaring at Jacques all the while. "What did that useless excuse for a Kin tell you?"

"That Ash was not of a sound mind and refused medical treatment, attacking him, killing Gerard and escaping with some young upstart as protection." Jacques narrowed his eyes. "I'd never have called you a young upstart, though - you're more than Alpha enough."

"That's because it wasn't me," Tobias growled. "It was Sienna."

Brayden's mouth fell open, his face white as a sheet. "*Sienna*? Is she okay?"

"I'm not sure," Aislinn murmured. "She's not injured, but she was the one who killed Gerard."

"Mother moon," Brayden whispered, looking nauseous. "That would have shredded her. What were those two idiots thinking?"

"I don't know, but there was more to Gerard than the lazy lab tech he let us see." Aislinn chewed on her lip in thought. "He was the one who tranqed Kaira and he knew how to truss me up with razorwire - among other things. Sienna saved my life, but she's no longer the woman you knew."

"I saw her *two days ago*," Brayden exclaimed. Then, noticing the stares of everyone else around him, added, "What?"

"There are times," Kaira said slowly, "when you're incredibly embarrassing, you know that?" Then, before the eaglekin could answer, she thumped him hard on the arm. "You *pervert!*"

"Hey! Ow!" Brayden leapt back, hands held up to ward off further blows. "She asked me to!"

"You chauvinistic, good for nothing -"

"Kaira, I'm serious!"

"- useless, hopeless excuse for a walking cock!"

"*She asked me to!*"

"*That still makes you a man whore!*" Kaira roared, prodding him in the chest with a finger.

"Stop it." Aislinn caught Brayden as he stumbled, shoving him onto the couch. "Sienna really did ask - and I gave him the hint in advance. She needed a little adoration."

Kaira narrowed her eyes. "Promise?"

"Promise," Aislinn answered. "Now, can we focus? Because the human who's been feeding us is nice, in a grumpy kind of way, and I don't want to ruin his place."

"Fine, fine," Kaira waved a hand, then frowned. "Where's the rest of your pack?"

"On their way."

Tobias felt an extraordinary warmth unfolding in his chest as he realised that, at long last, their pack was truly one. He looked down at Aislinn and wasn't surprised to find her eyes already on him, the hubbub of the room fading as their gazes locked and held, his Mark warming from the centre outwards. He saw Aislinn's hand drift towards her ribs and knew she'd felt it too, saw the secret smile that was his alone. Cutting through the chatter, Tobias said, "I couldn't give two shits about the Council right now. Our foremost concern is catching Olaf."

Kaira crossed her arms under her chest. "Big call, wolfkin."

"Think about it - if Olaf hitches a plane, he could go anywhere." Tobias dropped a kiss to his heartmate's forehead, then raised his eyes to the room. "Ash believes he'll bind someone else if given the chance, and I agree. Any of you fancy your female relatives being turned into psychic time bombs?"

Lena shuddered. "You're right. He delights in tormenting our people."

"I will do everything in my power to stop Olaf Gruybere adding to his list of conquests," Aislinn murmured. "Everything."

Brayden shared a look with Jacques and the Frenchman rolled his eyes. "*Bien*. What about the Council?"

"On my head," Aislinn replied.

"Ours," Tobias corrected, tightening the arm he had around her shoulders.

His heartmate gave an inelegant snort. "Fine. *Our* heads."

Jacques narrowed his eyes. "The Professor?"

"Can go fuck himself."

Yellow owlkin eyes continued narrowing until they were no more than slits. "And the operation itself?"

"As soon as *our* pack arrives -" Aislinn cut a glance at Tobias, "- and night falls, we dump the car and move out. Olaf's injured and I'm not willing to waste even a moment tracking his furry ass down."

Jacques sighed, got to his feet, then held out his hand to Aislinn. She clasped it and the owlkin bowed his head. "We are yours again. Don't make me regret it."

"Looks like your wish has come true, Ash." Brayden grinned from ear to ear. "We're going on a bear hunt."

********

The afternoon passed all too slowly. No matter how many times Aislinn stared out the window, the blazing sun had barely moved, the cabin's little air conditioner labouring to keep the room cool.

"You look better than you have in months," Kaira said quietly, joining Aislinn by the window. Brayden and Jacques were both gone; one on aerial surveillance and the other, knowing him, sulking somewhere. Lena had shifted into cat form and gone bounding off in search of food, with the paltry remains of Bruce's sandwiches having been ruined by the shattered window.

"I feel better than I have in months," Aislinn admitted, her eyes on the road where Tobias, unseasonably draped in a hoodie and those pale grey tracksuit pants that were driving her wild, had so recently disappeared. "Actually, I lie. I feel better than I have in *years*."

Kaira brushed calloused fingers over the Mark on Aislinn's ribcage, visible now that she'd eschewed the sheet in favour of her sports bra and jogging shorts. "I'm not surprised. Not just a mate but a heartmate - I'm jealous."

"Sorry." Aislinn gave her friend a sheepish smile. "If it helps, there's a lonely, mass murdering bearkin out there who got dumped yesterday."

"Oh!" Kaira's face brightened. "When you put it that way, how could I possibly resist?"

Aislinn laughed. "I'm glad you're here."

"So am I." Kaira chuckled. "Do you remember the day we met?"

"Of course; I rocked up at the Council's training academy prepared to hate everyone. Flynn *did* hate everyone. You were the pretty little rich girl who'd been granted entrance because her father owned the whole godsbedamned island and you had a literal band of worshippers watching your every move." Aislinn grinned wide enough to bare her teeth. "Who better to tackle into the castle moat?"

Kaira's face misted with recollection. "I was so jealous of the way you were so *you.*"

"It's a flaw, I'll admit. Why bring it up now?"

"I don't know, I just..." She made a face, ran a hand through brilliant hair Aislinn knew she only dyed to annoy the socialites who fawned at her father's feet. "Did you ever think, after that brawl in the moat, that we'd end up here?"

"No," Aislinn answered honestly. "I thought we'd end up eaten by giant moat eels." She tilted her head to one side, considering. "Or dying of some kind of fungal infection."

"Oh please," Kaira scoffed. "You used to live with orphans in an ancient sewer system."

"Storm drain. It was an ancient storm drain."

"Whatever." Kaira waved a dismissive hand, their argument as soft and comfortable as an old quilt. "Just admit it, you're a scummy peasant."

"And you're a stuck-up noblewoman, Lady Balcourte. I don't know how I put up with you."

Kaira twisted her hands together and squeezed both elbows inwards, plumping up her cleavage until it was nothing short of barbaric. "Because of my charming personality?"

"Uh huh." Aislinn snorted a laugh and turned to look back out the window. "So says every vapid excuse for a male who gets lost in that crevasse."

Kaira made some sort of appropriate response but Aislinn didn't hear, pressing both hands against the window pane. The bush had changed. At first, she wasn't sure exactly what it was, only a feeling deep inside insisting something was different. Then she saw it; a set of antlers so tall and wide Aislinn would never have believed a creature could wear such a crown if she hadn't seen the silhouetted head and shoulders of the deer to which they were attached. And… they were covered in leaves and dotted with burgundy bottlebrush blooms.

"Ash? *Ash*!"

Aislinn blinked but the deer was gone, dissolving like a mirage in the desert. "Did you… see that?"

"See what? Bearkin?" Kaira immediately began reaching for the wickedly curved knife shoved into the waistband of her shorts.

"No," Aislinn shook her head and pointed. "A deer."

"A *deer*?" Kaira squinted out the window. "I can't see anything, but I'm happy to go check."

"I'll do it," Aislinn murmured, already heading for the door. She crossed the small car park, slipped behind the four wheel drive and into the bush, calling her wolf form as she went. The shifting serum must have worn off because she was on all fours a moment later, padding through the bush to the very place she swore she'd seen the strange creature.

Nothing.

Nothing but the thick undergrowth - so thick she had to shove through it like a rookie - and the faintest, lingering trace of burnt sugar. A scent which faded so quickly Aislinn was sure she was imagining it, because what sort of deer had flowers on their antlers and smelt like a sweet shop?

Shimmering back to her human form, Aislinn returned to the cabin, stopping along the way to snatch up her clothes and wiggle back into them. Kaira was waiting by the door, hands on her hips and lips pursed. "Anything?"

"Nope." She rubbed at her eyes and sighed. "I guess I'm just tired."

"Maybe." Kaira looked dubious. "You know if there are any deerkin herds close to here?"

"Not off the top of my head but Tobias might." As though he'd heard her, Tobias appeared out of the heat haze, loping down the drive and letting himself in through the cabin's front door.

"Spoke to a few locals, found a glazier who can take care of the smashed window," he said as he closed the door behind him. "I charged it to the Redding Pack account because I didn't know what else to do. We'll have to owe them - what?"

Aislinn watched his brow draw into a frown and sighed. "Do you know of any deerkin herds in the area?"

"No." Tobias dragged his hoodie off and shook his hair until it flopped messily over his face. "The closest herd I know of is near Adelaide, and they're pretty reclusive. Why?"

"Ash is hallucinating," Kaira announced.

"Just tired." Aislinn held up both hands as Tobias' brow creased further. "Promise! I thought I saw something but when I looked twice it was gone. Nothing to worry about."

Looking completely unconvinced, Tobias grunted. "If you say so."

"I do." Aislinn crossed her arms over her chest. "Forget the whole thing, both of you. We have more important things to do."

"Like?"

"Like…" Aislinn trailed off and then grinned as a bright orange car pulled into the drive, the engine roaring so loud the remaining windows rattled. "Like letting the rest of the pack in."

Tobias intercepted her as she made for the door, brows lowered. "Ash."

"I'm *fine*." She went up on her toes, brushed a kiss across his lips - then another, and another, until he growled and kissed her back. With a final nip of his jaw, Aislinn was out the door, throwing herself into Zeke's open arms.

"Well I'll be damned!" He crowed, catching her as though she weighed nothing. "My little sister wolf, back to normal." Zeke planted a kiss on her nose and stepped back, running a critical eye over her body. "Marriage suits you."

"Mating!" Sienna slapped her brother's shoulder and then flowed into Aislinn's embrace. "By the twin gods but I'm glad to see you."

Aislinn held her packmate close, her eyes roving the tree line as Dominic, Rory and Jaxon got out of the car. "Flynn?"

"I ate him," Jax muttered, bumping at her with his shoulder.

"Oh come on now, he wasn't that bad, was he?" Aislinn peeled one arm from around Sienna and widened her embrace - into which all three of the remaining men attempted to pour themselves. Laughing at the onslaught of affection, their recognition and acknowledgement of a pack now completely joined, Aislinn did her best to hug and kiss the lot of them while Zeke watched with a shit-eating grin on his face.

Then Tobias was there and instead of helping, he shoved Zeke on top of the pile and proceeded to bear hug the lot of them, until there was a fair amount of squealing from Sienna and grumbling protests from the other males. Fingers brushed Aislinn's wrist and she knew without looking they were Tobias', her heartmate's touch registering on a level nobody else's ever would. She twined her fingers with his and, when the pack loosened and stepped backward, allowed him to tug her against his side and press a kiss to the top of her head.

Dominic grinned as he inspected his Alpha pair. "I guess you two will do."

*They better,* Flynn's voice echoed from the treeline. *Because I sure as all fuck am done with the lot of you.*

Laughing, Aislinn pulled away from Tobias and pelted across the car park, leaping into the bush just as Flynn's human form unfolded from the thick undergrowth. Strong, wiry arms came around her and they tumbled unceremoniously into the scrub, the tigerkin nuzzling at her throat and squeezing until she thumped his chest in a silent reminder for air. "Why were you running, you idiot?"

"I wasn't - not all the way. I had to get off the roof when we got closer to the human town. Didn't want to send the wrong vibes." Flynn's elfin face crinkled. "You smell like T-Fuzz."

"And he smells like me." Aislinn shoved the tigerkin but he held on, sniffing her until she relented. "Is it really that bad?"

Flynn snorted a laugh that held a brittle edge. "The mating or the stink?"

"Either. Both?"

"The mating is good for you. We all knew it was coming and I can no longer smell your heat-scent, which is great, because I was half an hour away from fucking you blind," Flynn said glibly. Then, while Aislinn punched him in the kidney, he added; "As for the stink, I can say with certainty I prefer T-Fuzz over that misbegotten asshole of a bear. *Your* scent is strong again, like you - and once you shower, I'm sure my blood-brother's influence will be minimal."

"You're a monumental fuckwad, you know that?"

He grinned, showing all his long, curvy teeth. "That I am."

"If I'm mated to Tobias," Aislinn murmured, her heart curiously heavy, "What does that make us?"

"Ah, fuck, Ash, don't do this to me." Flynn's humour faded, his forehead bumping against hers. Long, dark lashes drifted closed. "Are you familiar with the term *Anam Cara?*"

Aislinn frowned. "My Gaelic isn't very good, and you know it."

"It means soulmate, but not necessarily in a romantic way." He flashed a smile that was sharp and beautiful as a blade. "The literal translation is 'soul friend.' Two souls, who need each other always, tied together for eternity."

"*Anam Cara,*" she repeated, running a hand through his soft hair. "I like it."

"Good, because you're fucking stuck with me," Flynn growled, lashes sweeping up as he kissed her forehead.

"Hey," Tobias growled, wrenching them both upright. "Stop kissing my heartmate."

"I blood bonded her first," Flynn argued, kissing her temple.

"I *saw* her first."

Amber eyes glittered. "I fucked her first."

"Flynn!" Aislinn gasped, her jaw dropping.

To her surprise, Tobias laughed and leant in close. "I'll be fucking her forever, tigerkin, so stick that in your pipe and smoke it."

There was a low, feline growl, matched a second later by a lupine one and then, while Aislinn debated which of them to murder first, both Alpha and Sabre started to laugh and caught each other in a backslapping hug.

"Thank you," Flynn murmured.

"And you, brother," Tobias returned.

Aislinn struck out with both elbows, earning joint grunts. "I'm right here, you idiots! And I'm not the ham in your stupid man sandwich!"

Employing not just her elbows but also her shoulders, she wrenched free and turned to find both males watching her with equally wicked grins. It was Flynn who said, "Welcome to the torment that is the rest of your life, *Anam Cara*."

"Oh, piss *off*," Aislinn snarled, and turned to stomp back to the cabin.

The mingled laughter of her heartmate and her soulmate followed - and because neither male could see her face, Aislinn smiled and basked in their love.

# Twenty-Four

Tobias knew absolutely nothing about running a hunt and kill operation, and was infinitely glad when Aislinn took firm control of the situation. She issued commands with precision and grace, her team's trust evident in their immediate responses, no matter how unusual the request. Tobias ran odd jobs when asked but spent the majority of his afternoon leaning against whatever flat surface would have him, doing his best to learn by observing.

Sienna sidled up and tapped his elbow during a particularly interesting conversation about how far Flynn could run flat-out in tiger form under heavy load. Catching Aislinn's eye and getting a nod in return, he allowed Sienna to tug him outside and around the back of the cabin. "What is it?"

She held out her arm and a moment later, an enormous eagle landed on her wrist. Tobias eyed the creature with his cheeks full of air; it had to be Brayden but he'd never expected the other male's eagle form to be quite so impressive. As though sensing Tobias' surprise the eagle spread his wings, revealing a wingspan that had to be well over eight feet, the setting sun burnishing his dark chocolate feathers in copper and bronze. If not for Sienna's Kin strength, Tobias doubted she'd have been able to hold a bird which was easily forty inches from beak to tail, covered all over in those same dark feathers - bar the chest and stomach, which were bright white with dark brown splotches.

"I need to ask you something," Sienna said, drawing his attention away from Brayden and back to her sweet, innocent face. "Are you having unprotected sex with Aislinn?"

Tobias' jaw dropped open. "Am I *what*?"

"Thought so." She nodded, held out her other hand for the previously unnoticed paper bag that Brayden dropped into it. "Do you want to be a father, Tobias?"

"Well, yeah, but -"

"Right now? In the middle of a war which is only going to get bloodier before it's done?" Sienna rolled her arm and Brayden dropped to the ground at her side, folding those incredible wings close to his body. Staring up at Tobias from beneath golden lashes, Sienna added; "I'm waiting."

A hot, dark flush crept up Tobias' neck and over his cheeks. "No."

"Right." Sienna began unrolling the top of the bag, holding his gaze as she spoke. "We all know unprotected sex is no problem most of the time, given that Kin don't suffer from sexually transmitted diseases and can only conceive when they're mated and in heat. However, you and Aislinn are now mated - and she's in heat."

Oh. *Oh.*

"I didn't -"

"I know," Sienna cut him off, and seeing his panicked expression, smiled softly. "It's all right, she's not pregnant. Yet." While he continued to stare, she stuck her arm in the bag and dug around. "Do you know what causes pregnancy, Tobias?"

"Uh -"

"Irresponsible ejaculation."

Brayden's ill-disguised avian laugh was enough to give Tobias back some modicum of sense. "You're right. I need to look into it."

"Don't bother." Before he could as much as blink, Sienna snatched his wrist and plunged a pressure injector into the underside of his forearm. "Consider this a mating present from my mother."

"Shit!" Tobias leapt back, shaking his arm whilst whatever she'd injected burnt its way through his veins. "Holy hell, Sens, what was that?"

"A contraceptive injection," she said calmly, slipping the used injector back into the paper bag and rolling it closed. "It lasts a few weeks. Long enough for us to get over this little hump -" a snigger, "- and for you and Ash to have a proper conversation, like mature adults."

Tobias stared at the injector mark on his arm, then at Sienna, and then finally at Brayden. "What the fuck just happened?"

The eagle said nothing, even going so far as to hide his avian head beneath one wing. Sienna spread a hand on Tobias' sternum, her face solemn. "I'm the pack healer now, whether I like it or not - and it's my job to make sure neither you nor Ash go blundering around like idiots. Which, apparently, you were both doing."

"Sorry, Sens," Tobias managed, staring down at her tiny hand. "You're right."

"I know. You're just lucky I care enough to break the inherent rules of being a wanted fugitive to send my mother a text message. Given that Brayden's *not* a fugitive and can cover that sort of distance quickly, he was kind enough to pick up what we needed - and yes, before you ask, you owe him one." Sienna scowled until Tobias nodded. "Once Ash is out of heat in a couple weeks, you can irresponsibly ejaculate wherever and however you like for the next six to eight months. But when you smell her going back into heat again," Sienna tapped the side of her nose in warning, "You come to me straight away, Tobias Greenwood - and you better be either asking for another injection or advice on cute baby clothes. Got it?"

"Got it," he echoed. Sapphire eyes glittered with an anger he usually only saw on Zeke but behind it, Tobias knew Sienna had been worried. "I'm sorry, Sens. Really. And you," he flicked a glance at the eagle peeping out from behind her, "She's right. I do owe you one."

Brayden made a squawking sound that was suspiciously close to derisive laughter and Sienna turned to prod him in the chest with a finger. "Don't start with me, Brayden Maxwell." The eagle ducked his head a little lower and made another, more genuine sound. Sienna's prodding finger turned to a soft caress. "That's better."

Still not sure whether to be grateful, terrified or somewhere in between, Tobias rubbed at the injector mark on his arm and dared to take a step backwards. Sienna watched him retreat and in that moment, he thought she looked suddenly lonely. "Are you okay, Sens? Really?"

"Me?" She blinked, and the expression was immediately replaced by the bright, glittering smile he'd known all his life. "Of course. Why?"

"You just looked -" he trailed off, saw Brayden shake his eagle head. "Tired."

"I am." She sighed and nodded. "Don't worry, I'll be fine."

"Okay." Tobias stared hard at Brayden and he stared back, his raptor eyes giving away nothing. "After this is all over, we've got some plans to make. As a pack."

"I'm not sure how much control we'll have over our choices." Sienna tipped her head towards the late afternoon sun, closing her eyes. "We both know the Council are going to want us back in Ireland, one way or another."

"Yeah." Tobias sighed. "Is Ireland what you want, though?"

"What *I* want?" Sienna's delicate brow furrowed. "I want to be around the people I care about, to have a clothing store of my own featuring my designs, and to help those who can't help themselves - where I am doesn't matter, as long as I'm doing those things. Also," she cracked an eyelid, "I *chose* Ash to be my Den Mother. If I had the choice again, knowing full well it would lead me back to that bunnykin burrow and the awful rat inside, I'd still swear to her."

Tobias couldn't help it; he grinned. "That emotional intuition sure is something."

She shrugged but he could tell she was pleased. "You'd be amazed what several hours in the back of a car with only the internet for company can teach you. Particularly when Rory and Dominic are playing the most irritating game of I Spy ever."

"Solaeden save me from *that*." Tobias rolled his eyes. "You'd think they were five years old."

"Tell me about it! They kept trying to slap each other over my head." Sienna made fake ducking motions, bumping Brayden hard enough that he spread those glorious wings to keep his balance. "Oh. Sorry, Bray."

He chittered gently and Sienna's face softened. Feeling suddenly like he was intruding, Tobias ducked back around the corner of the cabin. Two steps later he slammed into Aislinn; she clutched at his chest for balance and they stared at each other for a moment before breaking out into laughter.

"What are you doing?" Tobias asked, kissing her nose.

"Looking for you." Aislinn's blue-green eyes danced. "We've got a task. Why are you rubbing your arm?"

He hesitated, then showed her the injector mark and gave a brief, low-voiced run down of his conversation with Sienna. By the time he'd finished, Aislinn's jaw was on her chest and her cheeks were flaming red. "Are you okay?"

"I think so," she said finally, shaking her head. "I just never thought about… that."

"Me either," he agreed. "Luckily Sens is on top of it. You don't mind?"

Her lips quirked in a lopsided smile. "Little late to be asking, isn't it? You're already shooting blanks." Tobias took a half step back in surprise and Aislinn chuckled. "Don't worry. I want children one day - but not today."

"Good," he answered, more relieved than he dared admit. "Now, you said we had a task?"

Aislinn slid her hand into his. "Yup. You're going to help me steal a car."

"I am?" When she raised an eyebrow in the face of his astonishment, Tobias managed; "But -"

"Do I need to spout bullshit about returning it afterwards to massage your conscience?"

"No." He frowned. "It's just not dark yet."

Aislinn grinned. "Oh, my sweet, hunky partner in crime - don't you worry about that. Just come along and let me teach you how to be properly bad."

Alternately enchanted and mystified, Tobias drew on the hoodie she handed him whilst Aislinn shrugged into the black knit sweater Kaira had been wearing earlier. It was at least a size too small and stretched gloriously over her breasts, hugging every delicious curve. Unable to help himself, Tobias gathered her thick, wavy hair in his hands and bent to kiss the column of her throat. "You look amazing."

"I'm wearing jogging shorts and a knit that's cutting off my circulation," she snorted - but her body had already softened against his. "Stop that."

"Why?"

"One, because we have criminal activities to indulge in, and two, because Zeke is leering at us through the window."

Tobias jerked back and gave Zeke full view of his middle finger. His second laughed, made little kissy faces in the window, and then disappeared as Dominic tackled him out of the way. "Gods above but they're idiots."

"Our idiots, though," Aislinn chuckled, tugging him out to the street as if they were going for a stroll. In the late afternoon heat. In long sleeves. Yeah, subtle.

"I really don't understand how you expect this to work," Tobias muttered. "We look exactly like the out of towners we are."

"Trust me," she said lightly - and oh, if he had a dollar for every time Aislinn Redding had said *that* to him before he'd been dragged off on some half-baked adventure.

*Wait.*

"Ash?"

"What?"

Tobias chewed the inside of his lip, waiting until they were out of sight of the motor inn before he stopped in the shade of a nearby tree. "Now that we're mated... there's probably a more romantic way to say this, but what name are we using?"

In Kin society, when a pair mated, one half usually changed their name to reflect the joining. Whilst it was open for discussion which name was used, for an Alpha pairing couples traditionally took the surname of the more powerful member. Tobias knew, deep in his bones, that he and Aislinn stood on completely equal footing - and as long as they were together he didn't care what name they used, but he *did* want them to be a unit. He watched with trepidation as she leant in, her lips brushing his, and whispered; "I think Aislinn Greenwood has a rather nice ring to it, don't you?"

He kissed her. Hard. What else was a man to do when his heart was in a puddle at her feet? When they finally pulled apart, flushed and panting, he found tears in the corners of his eyes. "Are you sure? I thought you'd want to stay a Redding."

"Not really." Aislinn linked her fingers through his and continued along the footpath as though she hadn't just completely rearranged his reality. "Aislinn Redding died in a study with green paint and too much wood panelling, surrounded by bearkin. If I go back to Ireland as Aislinn Redding, I'll be expected to slot back into Aislinn Redding's life and do the things she did and say the things she would have said." A tiny headshake, the steadily setting sun picking out her red wine highlights and setting them ablaze. "Aislinn Greenwood is new. A blank slate, with a fresh pack and a different attitude to boot. It will be easier for me - and thereby, us - to find our own path this way."

Tobias' heart ached as he nodded, squeezing her hand a little tighter. "That makes sense."

"It also takes us out from under Grandma Redding's shadow, puts distance between her and the people we want to protect - from both the bearkin and the Council." Aislinn flicked a glance at him from under her lashes. "I'd also be lying if I didn't say I hate my father enough right now not to want to be associated with him, even by the accident of my name."

"My father didn't do us much better."

"His crimes are lesser," Aislinn murmured. "I can see how he got pulled into it; a second who saw his Alpha failing and decided to support a scheme he likely thought temporary, just to keep the peace. Only, by the time Rupe realised it wasn't ever going to be better, it was too late to right the wrongs. Say what you will about your father but he's been loyal, even if that loyalty was misguided."

"I hate that he failed, but you're right," he said at last, his voice hollow in his ears. "They're pretty good reasons."

"Oh, baby, don't look like that. I'm not finished." Her lips curved slightly at the edges and Aislinn paused on a street corner, looking up and down with the air of a human checking for traffic when Tobias knew the reality was very different. "Would you believe me if I said I always wanted to be Aislinn Greenwood?"

"What?"

Her smile widened and she crossed the street before she answered. "When I was younger - before I left for Ireland - I'd practise writing my name in the back of my notebooks. You know, make up a fancy signature and all that."

Tobias nodded. He'd never understood it himself but Sienna had done the same thing, obsessing over her name until she found the perfect flourish for every letter. "And?"

"I never once practised Aislinn Redding," she admitted, her cheeks darkening. "I practised Aislinn Greenwood. Over and over and over. I told myself it was because our friendship made us close enough to be like family, but I burnt every one of those notebooks so nobody would see. It was too precious to share."

"You knew," Tobias murmured, rubbing a clenched fist against his heart. "Somehow, somewhere, you knew."

Aislinn stopped, leaning on someone's white picket fence. "I never placed much faith in fate - but now, looking back? I have to wonder if some part of me knew I was never really me until I was part of you. Until you were mine. Until we were… whatever we are, together."

"That might be the single most romantic thing anyone's ever said to me." Tobias waited until she gave him a dangerous look and then grinned. "I'm serious!"

"You're a jerk, is what you are," she muttered - but she was laughing, her eyes sparkling.

"You love me," he teased, leaning down to nuzzle her hair.

"I do," she murmured, leaning into his caress. "You've always been my voice of reason, Tobias - and I have a feeling that no matter what happens today, this situation is going to get worse before it gets better. The bearkin want war and if the Council get their way, I'll be front and centre."

"We."

She inclined her head in acknowledgement. "All of us. Thanks to Percy, our bargaining chips are minimal; Olaf, if we can get him, and Regina's formula, which we don't actually have. I'm probably going to end up doing things that are insane, cold blooded and downright awful in the name of not only the greater good but of protecting our pack. The High Council won't hesitate to sacrifice us and I, for one, don't like that idea very much."

"If we go to war, we do it together." Tobias turned her to face him, cupped her face in his hands. "Tell me what you need."

She blinked, her expression suddenly vulnerable. "I need you to reel me in when I go too far. I need you to hold my hand the way you hold my heart. I need you to push me to be better and I need you to love not only the person I was, or the person I am, but the person I'm going to become. Because if I lose you-"

"Stop," he murmured, feathering a thumb across her trembling lips. "There's nothing you could ever do - *ever* - to turn my love cold. Whatever you need, now and always, I'll freely give."

Tears pricked the corners of her eyes; he kissed them away and earnt a husky laugh for his trouble. "I don't deserve you."

"Yes you do," he returned, unable to stop the smile which threatened to split his face much the same way his heart kept threatening to split his chest. "I have my own flaws, need the same things from you in return."

She quirked a brow. "You want me to hold you back from your insufferable mischief? Because that's *so* you, Tobias."

"No, fat head." He rolled his eyes. "I mean that maybe I'm a little too serious; I'm probably going to need some egging on, and a whole lot of 'take a chill pill, Tobias' - which, by the way, is one of Zeke's favourite sentences."

"It's a good sentence."

"Somehow I thought you'd say that." Tobias snorted and shook his head, knowing that he was going to have a hell of a time with both Zeke and Aislinn getting on his last nerve every damn day - and what did it say about him that he was looking forward to every second of it? "My point is, you can ask everything from me because I'll be asking everything of you. That's what being a heartmate is."

"I thought it was about sticking your cock in my -"

"*Ash.*"

She grinned. "I know, I know. Just testing your resolve."

"Consider it tested," he growled. "Now are we stealing a car or not, Mrs. Greenwood?"

"Why yes, Mr. Greenwood, we most certainly are." Her answering smile lit up his entire world. "That one, to be exact."

Tobias looked over his shoulder and promptly choked at the vehicle he saw parked in a nearby driveway. "Is that... a panel van?"

"An ancient one," she agreed, her tone deadly serious. "Older cars are easier to pinch and according to Jacques, the people who live here are away on an interstate trip and won't be back for months."

"*Jacques* found that out?"

"It's amazing what people will tell a confused French tourist with terrible English and a weakness for iconic Australian cars."

Tobias absorbed that for a minute. "But... *Jacques*?"

"He has his uses." Aislinn chuckled, pressing a kiss to the inside of his wrist. "When he's not sulking, of course - but don't tell him I said that."

Slipping out of his arms, she unlatched the gate on the white picket fence and sauntered to the front door. There was, obviously, nobody home, but Aislinn made a show of knocking and shrugging before slipping a folded note out of her pocket and poking it under the screen door. Dusting her hands on her thighs, she wandered over to the panel van and stopped by the driver's door.

"What are you doing?" Tobias asked, following after her.

"Stand here," she said by way of answer, angling his body so that he blocked out the sun. "Thanks."

A second later Aislinn dissolved into a soft, barely-there shadow that streamed around the edge of the door, rematerialising in the driver's seat. She wound down the window and grinned at him, brandishing a five cent piece she'd found in the console. "Ready to fall in love with me all over again?"

"What are you -" Tobias broke off as she jammed the edge of the coin into the ignition as though it were a key and twisted. A second later the panel van coughed, then roared to life in a frenzy of old pistons and exhaust. "Holy shit."

"Sexy, right?"

"The sexiest." He leant in the window to nip at her jaw. "How did you - no, don't tell me. Flynn."

She winked, then reached over to pull up the lock on the passenger door. "You guessed it, lover. Now, if you wouldn't mind getting into the car? I've done what I can, but eventually someone's going to ask questions."

Trying not to look either guilty or hurried, Tobias made his way around to the passenger side and slipped in. "What did the note say?"

"Hey cuz, thanks for letting me borrow the car while you're away. Found the spare key where you said, call me when you get back. Love, me." Aislinn adjusted the seating position, tested the clutch, and smiled wide enough to show her pointed incisors. "You'd be amazed how well that works."

"Huh. And did you actually leave a number?"

"Maybe." She winked, then put the car in gear and reached for the handbrake.

"Wait," Tobias said suddenly. "Didn't Flynn say never to let you drive?"

Aislinn's grin widened. "Want to find out why?"

"No." He shook his head but she'd already yanked off the handbrake and Tobias scrabbled for his seatbelt while the woman he loved launched the van onto the road as though it were a rocket. "Shit! Ash!"

"Oh come on, Tobias," she chuckled while he desperately strapped himself in. "You know me better than anyone. How bad can it really be?"

The van peeled out onto the main street, turning so hard Tobias swore the road came up to meet his window. "I love you," he gritted out, "But when we get back, I'm going to kill you."

Aislinn's laughter rang out in the cabin and even in his moment of unbridled terror, Tobias had to admit it was the best thing he'd ever heard.

*******

Aislinn stared out the window as the countryside rushed by, the deep purples and muted ebony of an Australian summer night doing nothing to soothe the tension singing through her bones. "It's almost midnight. Where are they?"

Kaira held up her phone. "GPS has Jacques ahead of us now, ETA less than five minutes."

"In that case, I'll look for a place to stop," Lena murmured from the driver's seat. The panel van's previous owner had retrofitted the back with two long benches running perpendicular to the driver and passenger, allowing for a great deal of seating inside. Aislinn and Tobias reclined on one of those benches, with Kaira in the front beside Lena. The rest of the pack had crammed into the orange car with Zeke, leaving the remainder of the panel van vacant for Jacques and Brayden to return to. Flynn, being Flynn, rode on the van's roof, his whiskers flapping the breeze and his eyes closed.

When Lena pulled off the road at a section that looked just like any other, Aislinn flung open the back doors of the panel van. A snowy owl and a martial eagle immediately swept inside, one alighting gently on the back of the driver's seat and the other tumbling across the floor in a confusion of white and brown feathers. With Tobias' strong hands securing her in place, Aislinn leant out and yanked the doors closed again.

"Gods above us," Brayden snarled, shifting back to human. "I will never enjoy flying at night."

The snowy owl stretched and changed until Jacques perched on the back of the chair instead, long legs stretched out in front. "If you practised more, you'd find it easier."

Brayden snarled at his companion and then turned to Aislinn. "It's done; the four wheeler is ditched and your little human friend Bruce is none the wiser."

"Good." Aislinn nodded as the eaglekin dragged himself onto the bench opposite her. "Thanks, Bray."

"As for Olaf, I saw nothing of note." Jacques carded both hands through his hair and tugged it back off his shoulders. "We'll have to rely on Zeke's map work and your gut instinct."

"Right - so he's injured," Aislinn ticked it off on her finger, "Angry, and missing half his people. He's also free. I say he's going to try and get out of the country to regroup."

"On that note, I have a text." Kaira's head appeared from behind Jacques' naked backside. "Sienna says that Zeke says we should try the farm with the crop dusting strip."

"I did a flyover earlier today," Brayden said. "It's the only airstrip in the area, but there was no sign of life. If the bearkin are there, they're keepin' low."

Jacques crossed his arms over his chest. "Hell of a risk, Ash. If we're wrong -"

Kaira's phone rang. After a quick glance at the caller ID, she cleared her throat and answered. "Daddy! It's so good to - of course not, Daddy, why would you think that?" Her face abruptly clouded. "*Really*." Jacques froze and then began to edge his way down the seat towards the floor. Just when he would have leant forward to crawl away, one of Kaira's hands shot out, burying itself in his black hair and wrenching viciously enough that he winced. "Yes, Daddy. I understand. Thank you, Daddy. I'll tell her. Love you too." After blowing a wet, sloppy kiss at the phone, Kaira hung up, hauled Jacques up by his hair and shouted; "You called my *father*?"

"Not exactly," Jacques hedged. When Kaira growled and bared her teeth, he added, "I mean it! He rang me because…"

"Because he knew you'd blab everything the moment he asked!"

"He's one of our superiors!" Jacques cried, clutching desperately at her wrist. "Ow! *Merde*, Kaira, you're going to pull my hair clean out!"

"You good for nothing, dishonest -"

"I had to!"

"- disease-ridden, brainless -"

"Kairaaaaa!"

"- *faithless bag of feathers!*" Kaira thumped Jacques' head against the side of the van until his eyes began to roll in his head.

"Enough," Aislinn snapped. Kaira dropped Jacques' naked body with a sneer of disgust. He made to sit up but Aislinn grabbed him by one ankle and, with a yank, had the owlkin at her feet. "What did you tell Lord Balcourte?"

"Nothing that would jeopardise the mission or your safety." Flushed and dazed, blood trickling from his hairline, the Frenchman swallowed heavily. "Just that we'd caught up with you and decided Olaf was the more imminent threat."

"And how did you convince him of that?"

"I didn't have to." Jacques raised a hand to his face and winced when it came away bloody. "Word got out that Professor Postlethwaite petitioned for your custody on grounds of mental instability. Rumours are flying; you're dying, you're a bear, you're half-wolf-half-bear, you're a spy, you're a goddess, you're weaker, you're stronger. Freddie and Macy's murders were also leaked and Bhaile Roinnte is in chaos. The bearkin are no longer the bogeymen on the other side of the world - they're here and they're real."

Aislinn drummed her fingers on one of his incredibly pale thighs. "Did you say anything about the mating?"

"*Non!*" Jacques' eyes went wide. "That's none of my business. Besides... Lord Balcourte might not've been as eager to sanction our assistance if he'd known."

"Jacques Elegante," Aislinn murmured, her lips quirking into a smile. "Are you telling me you lied to a superior?"

"It wasn't a lie," the owlkin hedged. "He just never asked and I never mentioned it."

Aislinn burst out laughing. "Well now, Kaira, did you hear that? Our baby's growing up."

"Don't make me puke." The lynxkin snorted, blue and purple hair flipping as she shook her head. "All right, so I'm not going to roast him up for Sunday lunch. But that doesn't mean this is over," she added, waving a finger at the man on the floor.

"What else did your father say?" Tobias asked, crossing his arms over his chest. "Because I gather there's more."

"There is." Kaira's smile was tight. "Daddy said the media has been reporting savage animal attacks in the same area as that little farm we were just talking about; wildlife and a few humans taken."

Aislinn nodded. "It's the last piece of evidence we need. Head for the airstrip." Then, to Jacques, "Good job."

The owlkin's face relaxed and he dropped his head back against the floor of the van as it roared out onto the road. "I thought you'd think… you know."

"That you're a traitorous son of a bitch?" Tobias growled.

Jacques' face twisted. "I've always been loyal to my people, to the Council. That's the reason I joined the service and I don't regret putting it above all else - but the decision to hand Ash over to Professor Postlethwaite like some sort of lab experiment was *tordu,* wrong. It was wrong the first time and it was wrong the second time. She's given too much to her people to warrant being tossed aside like a tool no longer functioning properly. And, much as I don't often admit it, I… consider her a friend."

Aislinn smiled, reaching down to tug Jacques into a sitting position. "I always knew you were a softie deep down."

"Don't tell anyone," he grunted, running both hands through his long black hair and tying it in a knot at the base of his neck. "Satisfied, Alpha?"

"Very." Tobias looped an arm around Aislinn's shoulders and pressed a kiss to the top of her head. "I'd have hated to kill you for endangering my pack and my heartmate."

Jacques snorted, rolling to his knees. "That doesn't sound like something you would do, Greenwood, and I've only known you a short time."

"No," Tobias agreed, his fingers trailing over Aislinn's collarbone, "But I might've said something in front of Flynn and then sat back and watched while he de-boned you like a fish."

Aislinn burst out laughing, turning her head to kiss the Marking on his neck, clearly visible despite the thick hoodie Tobias wore. "That's my heartmate."

*"Foutu enfer,* you two are made for each other." Jacques' eyes glittered, his smile small but real as he settled onto the other bench seat.

"I'm glad I'm on your side - neither the bears nor the Council have any idea what's coming for them."

# Twenty-Five

Half an hour later, Kaira pointed to the left. "Turn here!"

Lena stomped on the brakes and yanked the wheel, jerking Aislinn out of Tobias' arms and throwing them both on the floor. The panel van juddered and Aislinn dragged herself up to see a badly corrugated dirt road with the bush close enough that stray branches scraped the van's sides.

"If we get much closer they'll hear us," Tobias rumbled, settling back onto the bench seat.

Kaira squinted at the map on her phone. "There should be a driveway up ahead; we can pull in near the farmhouse and go the rest of the way on foot."

The turn loomed out of nowhere but Lena had already slowed to a crawl and manoeuvred into the narrow driveway without issue. The farmhouse on the other end looked quiet, but the gate had been torn clean off its hinges and lay bent halfway across the front lawn. Uneasy silence filled the van as Lena parked under a stand of trees and turned the engine off. A few seconds later Zeke pulled the orange car in beside them and, with the growling engine now silent, they held their collective breaths and waited.

Nothing.

A large shadow slithered down the windscreen, landing silently on the panel van's bonnet. *I'll take the perimeter. You go inside.*

Aislinn met Flynn's amber gaze and nodded. "Everyone wait here; we'll be back in a few minutes."

Without waiting for an answer, she yanked the back door open and dissolved into the darkness, heading straight for the farmhouse. The curtains were drawn, no light peeping around the edges to suggest so much as a candle was lit inside. Her assassin's heart already knew what she'd find, but Aislinn still streamed underneath the front door and checked every room.

She returned to find her companions all crowded inside the panel van, their faces expectant. Tobias looked up as she rematerialised in the doorway, Flynn hard on her heels. "Well?"

Aislinn grimaced. "No survivors."

*Nobody made it outside, either.* Flynn nudged her leg with his soft pink nose and she dropped her hand to scratch between his ears. *There's some damage to the property from the back and a gutted supply shed.*

"How recent?" Zeke asked, his sapphire eyes dark as he looked out at the farmhouse.

Flynn's lip curled. *A week at least.*

Remembering the bloated bodies she'd seen, Aislinn nodded. "At least. I'd say they landed at the airstrip, then came this way for the farmhouse before anyone could send up an alarm. The earliest reported attacks were barely a day's run from here - it'd be easy to set up a rotating roster to sweep through the area whilst still having fresh people on hand in case of emergency."

"Damn, little sister-wolf," Zeke murmured. "Remind me never to piss you off - I don't want to stand between you and the rest of the world."

Aislinn levelled a finger at Tobias. "That's what he's for."

"You mean he's not egging you on?"

"No." She pointed at Flynn. "That's what *he's* for."

Flynn's jaw dropped open in silent laughter. *I'm good at it, too. T-Fuzz has his work cut out for him.*

"I'll manage." Tobias crossed his arms over his chest. "Now, do we have a plan? Olaf's injured, but I'm willing to bet actual money that he's not snoozing and drinking white russians."

Aislinn tapped her index finger on her chin. "If we want to win any sort of brownie points with the Council, we have to do this straight."

*We haven't gone straight down the barrel in years,* Flynn argued, one ear flickering. *It's a risk.*

"Yeah, but I no longer have swing with the Council to justify our weirdness," Aislinn reminded him. "Everything about this has to be clean."

The tigerkin growled, but after a long moment his head dipped in agreement. *All right. Lay it out, then.*

"Jacques, I want you in the air. Kaira, go with Dom and Brayden and cut east. Lena, take Zeke and Rory and go west. Keep to the perimeter, take out any patrols you find, meet at the back of the property and wait for the signal. Sienna, stay with me and Tobias, let us cover you where we can. Flynn, you're our tank, as always." Aislinn grinned wide enough to show fangs. "Take Jax and show him what you do best - something tells me he's going to have a knack for it."

*With a wolf form the size of a small horse? He'll be fucking perfect.* Flynn whuffed a feline laugh and stalked off into the night. *Come on, Jaxzilla. We've got work to do.*

After a nod in her direction, Jaxon jumped to the ground and followed after Flynn. The van rocked and when Aislinn turned back, everyone but Tobias had shifted into their animal forms. She held out her arm first for Jacques and then Brayden, heaving them skyward while the landbound Kin split off into their groups and melted away. Within moments only Sienna remained, her wolf form pale in the moonlight. Aislinn motioned her to wait and yanked Tobias closer, rubbing her hands up and down his biceps as if he was cold.

"What are you doing?" He whispered, kicking his discarded clothes into a corner.

"Creating static," Aislinn replied, delighted to see blue sparks gathering under his skin. "I want every advantage we can get."

"But I don't know how to use it," he answered, looking down at his chest in alarm.

"Just remember what Flynn said and embrace the transitional energy rather than fight it." When it looked like a small family of fireflies had taken up residence in his torso, Aislinn stepped back. "Okay, now shift." He did, his thick, golden-brown fur hiding the sparks completely. "Awesome. Let's do this before Flynn gets cranky."

As if on cue, the tigerkin's voice echoed inside her mind. *Where the fuck are you? I'm bored.*

"Busted," she mouthed at Tobias and leapt out of the van, calling her wolf form as she went. Her packmates fell in on either side and within seconds they'd cleared the property's neat lawns and were pelting through the bush. *We're coming. Try not to kill anyone before we get there.*

The countryside edging the little airfield was rough, littered with loose stones and sandy soil. Gnarled trees grew in copses and sun bleached rocks jutted up from the ground as though they were the bones of the earth itself. Twice Aislinn leapt over dried creek beds, their once polished pebbles now covered in dust.

*Ash.* Flynn's presence, warm and soft inside her mind. *Brown-nose says there's a slope ahead and if you don't pull up, you'll be in the open.*

*Shit!* Aislinn slowed just as the trees began to thin, pulled up in the shelter of the last few trunks. *Pass on my thanks to Jacques.*

*Before or after I eat him?*

*Before,* she answered, looking down the hill. Directly below was a hangar with an attached office and beyond that, a crudely asphalted runway. Aislinn drew the scent of old death and bearkin into her nostrils, lip curling. *This is definitely the place.*

*Gotta wonder how they live with that acidic edge to their scent.* Flynn's voice began to echo as he included everyone else in the conversation. *I've got visuals through the office window. Is everyone in position?*

*Yeah,* Kaira responded. *Not a border patrol in sight; I'd say they're all in the hangar, prepping to leave.*

*More fool them,* Flynn snorted. *Counting back from ten.*

While the tigerkin began reciting numbers in his smooth Irish accent, Aislinn kept her body low and led her companions down the hill. *This is it, guys. Kill the bears, stay alive, drinks are on me afterwards.*

*Three.*

*That's it?* Rory, his voice strained.

Aislinn chuckled. *'Fraid so.*

*Two.*

*See you on the other side.* Brayden, his cheerful rejoinder comforting in its familiarity.

*One.*

Kaira whooped loudly, the half-human sound igniting the adrenaline in Aislinn's veins.

*Zero.*

Dirt turned to pavement underfoot and Aislinn moved like a wraith across the tarmac as a window shattered to her left, followed by the snarl of a tiger and the deep growl of a wolf. Someone swore in

Russian, then several roars cut the night as the bearkin shifted to meet their attackers.

*Midform,* Aislinn hissed at Tobias.

*I can't control it,* he shot back. *I'm just as likely to attack the rest of us as I am the bears.*

*I won't let that happen.* The front door to the office burst open and a bear lumbered out, blood trailing from a slash down his face. *Trust me, Tobias. We need your strength.*

Following her own orders, Aislinn reached for her midform. Shifting from human to wolf was one thing - not painless, not painful, not nice and not unpleasant - but assuming her midform was the sharpest edge of agony and pleasure, a firestorm of raw nerve endings and rearranged body parts.

Aislinn and the bearkin slammed chest-first into each other, her claws driving deep into his ribs. He twisted his head to bury enormous teeth in her throat, but she dematerialised and her opponent's jaw snapped shut on thin air. Off balance, the bear staggered forward - and slumped to the ground as Tobias slashed his throat with a clawed hand.

A roar of pure, primal fury rolled across the tarmac as Aislinn rematerialised by the office door. She risked a look over her shoulder as Tobias, in his midform as she'd asked, planted one lupine foot on the bear's chest, wrapped clawed hands around that giant, brown-furred head, and twisted it clean off.

*I'm going to assume that means he's succumbed to the transitional rage and is no longer with us,* Jacques said calmly.

Aislinn ducked as the severed head - trailing several vertebrae - sailed through the doorway and thunked Flynn's midform in the face. *Yeah, I'd say so.*

*Motherfucker!* Flynn wiped spinal fluid off his cheek and kicked the severed head across the room. *Solaeden's balls, Ash - he comes near me and I'll rip his dick off and feed it to him!*

Aislinn sighed and ducked into the office, yanking on Flynn's studded collar with one hand whilst cuffing him across the back of the head with the other. *You'll do nothing of the sort. Now make yourself useful and open this door.*

*Mother Moon. You better keep a handle on him.* Flynn motioned to Jaxon and together, they slammed their combined weights against the door to the hangar. It buckled but stayed put.

Aislinn watched Tobias tear one of the dead bear's legs off and begin clobbering another bear over the head with it. *Everyone, keep an eye on Tobias. Lead him to the bears if you have to, but don't let him touch you. If he corners you, let me know.*

A chorus of acknowledgements echoed inside her mind, and Aislinn breathed a silent apology to her heartmate for putting him in such a position. That he'd succumbed to the rage at her request spoke of a deep trust she still wasn't sure she warranted, but would ensure she upheld.

*Hangar doors are opening,* Kaira reported - and over the cacophony of howls and snarls, Aislinn heard the grinding sound of metal on metal. *I count fifteen bears, plus Olaf in his midform. And -*

Whatever she'd been about to say cut off as another one of those primal roars shook the hangar and the air was filled with the sound of rending steel. The resistance on the other side of the door suddenly disappeared and Jaxon bowled right through it, Aislinn and Flynn hard on his heels.

*Well, shit,* Aislinn managed. Tobias had torn a hole through the wall with his bare claws and as she watched, he yanked two long, twisted pieces of steel free from the wreckage. Twirling them with the skill of a man who was an expert with a staff, Tobias buried one in each of the two bears who'd run to meet him.

Silence descended as everyone, friend and foe alike, paused to stare at the raging Alpha. Blood dripped down Tobias' fur as he tightened his grip on those two pieces of twisted metal, lifting the pair of dead bears clean off the ground. His eyes sought Olaf, standing behind a semicircle of bearkin in his midform. Muscles bunched as Tobias raised his arms over his head, bared his teeth at the bearkin General - and heaved both bodies at Flynn.

*Motherfucker!* Flynn roared as he went down, the sound breaking the spell and sending the bearkin into a frenzy of movement.

*Now.* Kaira led their companions into the fray, leaping for the bearkin closest to Olaf. Their numbers were even but the bears had a massive size advantage, making each altercation twice as deadly.

Aislinn ducked a swiping claw, disembowelling her opponent even as her mind churned over possibilities. Tobias couldn't control his midform or his powers but there was a chance, inside of a transitional rage, that his instincts would take over. Putting every ounce of authority she could muster in her voice, she shouted, *Tobias, get the lights!*

At first she didn't think he understood, then lightning crackled across his fur and the lights exploded, plunging the hangar into darkness. Olaf roared, his voice carrying the tone of an order which was abruptly cut off as Tobias tackled him to the ground. It was impossible to tell the two apart as they rolled across the concrete floor, snarling and slashing for all they were worth. Injured, Olaf should have been the weaker, but Aislinn knew Tobias wasn't thinking straight, his transitional rage stealing brain cells even as it gifted incredible strength - a strength Olaf, in his midform, also laid claim to.

Heart in her throat, Aislinn made straight for them. A burly grey bear got in her way and she blocked his frenzied blows, deliberately leaving herself open. When he lunged in, she pivoted and drove two fingers through his eye socket, shoving the body aside with a well placed knee even as she sought her heartmate. *Tobias! Behind you!*

The black bear who'd eluded Aislinn during their last altercation leapt on Tobias' back, pinning both arms by his sides. Before Olaf could take advantage of the situation, a black blur shot through the air and Lena, in her housecat form, landed on the bearkin's snout and began clawing at his eyes.

*Lena!* Brayden's eagle screech filled the hangar. The black bear released Tobias and staggered backwards, one of his eyes a bleeding ruin. Brayden swept in, talons outstretched to pluck Lena's body off the black bear's face. *I've got you.*

*I knew you would.* Lena's tiny black paws waved in mid-air as the eaglekin flapped hard for altitude.

*What are you doing fighting in cat form?* Brayden snapped. *We've talked about this.*

*It was the fastest way to* - Lena's words turned into a scream as the black bear leapt straight upward, his jaws closing around the catkin's hindquarters. With a vicious twist of his head, he ripped her in half.

*No!* Brayden tried to turn but was swatted heavily aside. He tumbled through the hole Tobias had torn in the wall, disappearing into the night with the top half of Lena's body.

Grief shivered through Aislinn, turning her soul to ice. Wrapping herself in a calm born of purest rage, she dematerialised, flowing between combatants to solidify on the black bear's back. He spat

Lena's hindquarters out and reared up, twisting both arms to reach Aislinn and throw her off - leaving him wide open for Flynn, who drove clawed fists into the bear's abdomen even as he sank enormous tigerkin teeth in the bastard's throat and ripped it clean out. The bearkin fell and Aislinn rode his shoulders to the floor, her calm fracturing as she spotted the grisly remains of a woman whose safety had been her responsibility.

*Pull it together.* Flynn grasped her around the waist and dragged her upright, amber eyes glittering with unspent emotion. *Make it count. Kill them all.*

*For Lena.*

*For Lena.* Flynn released her and leapt away, roaring as he tackled a bearkin who'd been backing Zeke and Dominic into a corner.

Spotting Tobias still locked in combat with Olaf, Aislinn dissolved into the shadows and went to assist. She was halfway there when Olaf gave a mighty roar and sent Tobias flying, his body limp as it crashed into the far side of the hangar amidst a collection of tool carts and fuel cans. He slumped against the wall, his bubbling breath somehow sharper in her ears than the rest of the fighting. *Flynn!*

*Fuck.* The tigerkin finished his opponent and changed direction, clearing a path for her to get to Tobias' side. *Use the heartmate connection; I'll keep them off you.*

Aislinn dropped to her knees beside her heartmate as he coughed and choked. Bright blue eyes met hers, the golden starbursts in their centres focussing with laserlike intensity. *How* did she connect to him? Olaf had always initiated contact and all she'd done was follow the icy energy back to his body - of course. Forcing herself to take a deep, steadying breath, Aislinn turned her attention inwards. This was Tobias; the boy she'd grown up with, the teenager she'd missed and the man she'd come to love above all else. He was in every breath, every pump of her heart. When she looked, *really* looked, their heartmate connection sparkled bright in the back of her consciousness. It took less than a thought to follow it.

All at once Aislinn could sense Tobias' heart as though it were inside her own chest. She knew without seeing that he'd broken several ribs and punctured a lung, felt his blood pounding through his veins in transitional fury. She could even feel her own fingers spread across his furred skin, providing comfort and warmth. Aislinn knew instinctively that with a thought alone, she could send him her strength and force his body to heal. Was *this* how Olaf had tried to kill her? How could he - how could anyone - wish pain and death upon someone they were connected to so intimately? Fury rose within her and Aislinn drew strength from it, pouring energy down the link until Tobias gasped and arched beneath her.

*Heal,* she told him, seeing herself through his eyes even as she saw him with her own. *Live. I need you.*

Deep inside her, beneath the layers of rage and pain and transitional chaos, she felt him stir. *Ash.*

An engine roared to life outside the hangar, the sound so deafening that Aislinn jumped. She looked up to see her friends and packmates still locked in vicious combat with the bearkin and though they were winning, they couldn't break through the line.

Olaf was going to get away.

Clawed fingers gripped her muzzle and Aislinn looked back at Tobias. His lung had already sealed, the onslaught of her energy shoving his ribs back where they belonged. Pain still marched in his eyes but his tongue was gentle as it licked softly across the tip of her nose. *Go.*

*Tobias -*

*GO.*

Aislinn rubbed her head against his jaw and dematerialised, streaming out the hangar doors. A cargo plane was rolling slowly across the tarmac, the great engines sounding more like a monster than a machine. Keeping low to the ground, Aislinn flowed across the asphalt and up through one of the air vents, rematerialising inside the empty holding area.

"I knew you'd come, little wolf. We have unfinished business." Olaf's voice preceded him out of the dark interior. He'd assumed human form to fly the plane and whilst he stood with shoulders squared, Aislinn could smell desperation. And blood. The angry scar from where she'd stabbed him two days ago cut a red line across Olaf's abdomen and fresh blood trickled out of four deep slash marks on his chest. For all the pain he had to be in, the Ursar's face was impassive. "You realise I cannot let you leave."

Aislinn bared her teeth and dematerialised, reappearing behind the bearkin General to swing scimitar claws at the back of his neck. He ducked at the last moment, throwing himself to one side and using a roll of cargo netting to drag his body upright.

"You know, I think I'll keep you alive for a while after I get the formula out of you." Olaf's lips twitched into a cold smile as he repositioned himself against the plane's hull. "Rather clever of Regina; who'd have thought she'd entrust her life's work to a *wolf*?" He tilted his head to one side, eyes narrowing. "She's dead, you know. Or were you too busy fucking that Alpha to notice?"

He was trying to goad her and damn if it wasn't working. Aislinn bared her teeth in a snarl, throwing her colossal midform at the side he'd left exposed. Olaf drew his hand free of the cargo net and she saw he held a sleek, black pistol, no doubt concealed behind the roll of netting for just such a purpose. A trap - one of the oldest in the book - and she'd fallen right for it.

The gun went off, a loud retort within the confines of the plane. Pain tore into Aislinn's knee but momentum carried her onwards and she crashed into Olaf with a roar, knocking them both to the floor. The bearkin called his midform as he fell, gathering both legs beneath him and kicking upwards. Aislinn slammed into the side of the aircraft, pain savaging her knee.

*Damn.* She jerked sideways as Olaf fired the gun again, his oversized claws struggling to manage a weapon meant for human hands. The plane swerved viciously before he could get off another shot, rolling Aislinn against the opposite wall and throwing the bearkin off his feet. The gun skittered into the darkness, a deadly promise amongst the shadows. Rather than try to race her for the weapon, Olaf snarled and launched himself towards the cockpit.

No. This had to end now. Aislinn tried to fade out and couldn't, the pain in her knee too blinding to think through. Fine; there was more than one way to skin a bear. Gathering her hands beneath her, she began dragging herself across the floor on her forearms and the one good knee. As she drew level with the wide door in the side of the plane, it opened and Tobias' head poked through.

Their gazes locked and she realised he was really there, staring out at her through clear, rational eyes. *Ash - we need to go.*

She bared her teeth and motioned towards the cockpit. *Olaf's still breathing. Use your EMP to bring down the plane.*

*I already tried,* he admitted, long lashes cresting furred, lupine cheeks. *I'm either out of juice, or it's not responding. I have no idea how it works.*

*What if you -*

*Dammit, you crazy bitch, get out already! I can't hold this much longer.* Flynn's voice faded in and out as the engines began to whine, straining to lift the aircraft off the ground. *If he takes off, we lose you.*

Glancing over Tobias' shoulder, Aislinn realised that in spite of whatever Flynn was doing to ensure otherwise, the plane was picking up speed. *Leave me here. We might not get another chance at this.*

*Your life isn't worth his!* A roar sounded from outside the plane, part agony and part effort. *T-Fuzz! Get her!*

The plane swung again, a last, vicious tug that sent Aislinn sliding helplessly across the floor and into Tobias. He caught her, tumbling them both outside as the engines reached fever pitch. *Got her.*

They hit the tarmac at an awkward angle, the asphalt stealing her breath and filling her head with stars. She shoved free of Tobias, calling her shadow form and this time, prepared for the agony of her knee, managed to dissolve. Before she was more than a few feet, Aislinn felt a curious yank deep in her gut and was suddenly solid again, face down on the runway. Spitting gravel, she got her hands underneath her only for Tobias to slam her sideways, rolling them over until he straddled her waist. *Stop!*

*No!* Aislinn brandished her claws but her heartmate held firm, his heavier midform pinning her flat. A howl tore from her throat as Olaf's aircraft lumbered into the air - and out of her reach.

* * * * * * * *

Tobias shimmered back to human form as soon as Aislinn slumped against the tarmac. Her blue-green eyes were wet, her lupine tongue lolling out of her mouth as her body laboured for breath.

"Let it go, Ash," he wheezed, risking his hand to caress her furred cheek. "Come back to me."

At first he thought she wouldn't answer, then abruptly Aislinn was back in human form. "Why did you do that?" she shouted, twisting one hand into his hair and dragging his face closer. "*Why did you do that?*"

"You weren't thinking straight," he answered honestly. "Olaf would've killed you as surely as you'd have killed him, and that's not acceptable to me."

Aislinn shrieked, a blood-curdling sound of grief and pain. Tobias wasn't surprised when she slapped him hard enough to rattle his brain inside his skull. "I almost had him!"

He coughed, tasted blood that had nothing to do with her slap and everything to do with yanking her out of a moving cargo plane, and bared his teeth. "I love you. I *need* you. I won't give you up - not now, not ever!"

Tears streamed down her face and after a moment in which he dared not even breathe, Aislinn spread a hand over his sternum. Warmth flooded his body, the same tingling heat which had partially healed his wounds before. "I let every single one of those women down today."

"No, you didn't. You fought for them and you'll keep fighting for them. Now stop that," he growled, swatting her hand away. "You've been hurt too."

"Shut up before I knock your head on the concrete."

"*Aislinn Jaide Greenwood -*"

"*Don't start, you lecturing asshole -*"

"For fuck's sake, both of you shut up," Flynn growled, limping out of the darkness. "Ash, do you know how *heavy* that monster of a machine is? I almost popped a shoulder trying to haul it across the runway. That bearkin is fucking nuts and you're just as bad."

Aislinn snarled, reaching again for Tobias' chest. He swatted her hand away. She tried again; he swatted again. Just as they were gearing up for a proper slap fight, Flynn's heavy, sweaty body tumbled them both sideways. Tobias grunted as he hit the ground, instinctively shielding Aislinn even as Flynn tucked his longer body around them both. They ended up in a curious tangle of limbs - and after a few moments of snapping, snarling and swearing, Aislinn began to laugh. Flynn's deeper voice joined in a moment later and Tobias pushed himself up on his elbows, spitting blood while the other two curled into each other, tears streaming down their faces as they howled in mirth.

"Solaeden save us," Aislinn hiccupped, "You wrestled a fucking plane!"

"And I was winning," Flynn laughed so hard he snorted. "I was winning!"

"Until he turned up the juice." Aislinn tried to school her expression, failed, and dissolved into another fit of giggles. "You should have seen Olaf's face!"

Tobias' brows climbed skyward. "Are you two always like this?"

"Yeah." Aislinn's laughter abruptly faded and she closed her eyes, tears once again trailing down her face. "I'm sorry I didn't get him. I tried."

Tobias and Flynn shared a look and as one, leant in on either side of her and licked up a trail of tears. Aislinn's eyes flew open and she squealed, thumping each of them in the chest. Tobias wore the blow with a grunt whilst Flynn snapped his sharp teeth at her knuckles. "Stop feeling sorry for yourself, princess."

"Why? I really, *really* wanted to kill him," she muttered - but the corners of her lips were tilting upward and Tobias knew they'd won her over.

"Next time." He reached out to stroke her hair, fisting one hand in the tangled locks.

"Will there be one?"

"We'll make sure there is," Tobias promised. "But for now, we need to let him go."

"Bit hard to do anything else when he flew off into the bloody sky," Aislinn grunted, closing her eyes and breathing deep. "What happened to the other bearkin? I notice Olaf deserted them without as much as a backwards glance."

"They were almost all dead when we left to come after you." Tobias narrowed his eyes. "Don't suggest going back in there; you're injured."

Flynn sniffed loudly. "I smell gunpowder. You let him shoot you?"

"Yeah, and it hurts like a bitch," Aislinn growled. "Got a point?"

The tigerkin gave her the finger and sniffed again, amber eyes focussing on her left knee. "A joint? Gods dammit, Ash, what if you've wrecked it?"

Long, elfin fingers immediately went for the leg in question and Aislinn growled. "Do it, and I'll snap you in half."

"You will not," Flynn muttered, beginning to probe the wound. "Ow! T-Fuzz, hold her the fuck down before I lose an eye."

Tobias caught Aislinn's flailing hands and pinned them over her head. When she opened her mouth for what was no doubt another vicious tirade, he leant in and kissed her. It was meant to be a simple, sweet kiss - partly to shut her up and partly to remind himself that she was most definitely alive - but she was soft and warm beneath him and before Tobias knew it Aislinn was groaning into his mouth and his erection was pushing rather painfully into the asphalt underneath them.

Aislinn jerked against him, hissing, and Flynn announced, "Got the bullet."

"Fuck you," she panted, turning her head away from Tobias long enough to bare her teeth.

Flynn merely laughed. "Don't throw out an invite unless you're prepared for the consequences, princess."

"You little -" Aislinn dissolved in the shadow of Tobias' body and a second later Flynn grunted as her fist connected with the side of his head. "I will shave off your eyebrows while you sleep!"

Tobias wrapped an arm around her waist and, wincing at the gravel rash on his undercarriage, sat up and dragged her into his lap. "Stop it."

"I thought it would be good if you two learnt to work together, but I am officially retracting that statement!" She slapped at his forearms but Tobias only tightened his grip.

"You did tell me," he reminded, leaning in to nip at her ear, "That it was my job to rein you in."

"I didn't say it would be a team effort!"

Tobias' lips twisted into a grin and he met Flynn's eyes over her head. "I guess that just goes to show what a phenomenally bad idea you had if the pretty kitty and I agreed on something."

"Don't worry, T-Fuzz, it's only a temporary insanity." Flynn peeled his lips back off his teeth. "I blame it on the adrenaline." He paused and blinked. "You're sounding a lot better."

"I -" Tobias frowned, realising he *felt* a lot better. "*Ash.*"

"What?" Her tone was sugar coated innocence. "As if I was going to ignore that lung you re-punctured in your foolishness. Your mother would have my hide."

Flynn flopped flat onto his back, howling with laughter. Tobias snarled and slapped his hand over her wounded knee, snapping his teeth when she tried to jerk away. "Don't. Push it."

"You don't even know what you're doing," she growled.

"No?" Tobias reached down the connection between them, immensely relieved that it was no longer a dead end, and tried to imagine her leg getting better. Moments later Aislinn gasped, gripping tight to his forearm.

"Not too much. You'll need your energy before this is done."

"Fair's fair, Ash." Tobias drew his hand away, staring down at what remained of the injury. "Did that help?"

Aislinn sighed and twisted in his arms, brushing her lips against his nose. "Bones are knitted and I'll be able to walk. Thank you."

"Well, this is lovely and all, but I'm going to help round up what's left of Lena," Flynn announced. He rolled to his hands and knees, sadness washing over his features before they hardened into the mocking arrogance with which the rest of the world was familiar.

"Wait." Tobias blinked, the words hitting home. "Lena's dead?"

"Yeah. Saved your ass and then got bit in half." Flynn shook his head, amber eyes tracking in the direction Olaf had flown. "Another reason to kill that asshole."

"She was a good warrior and a better person," Aislinn murmured, her face drawn. "She didn't deserve to die like that."

"Nobody does," Flynn replied, "But she knew what she was doing."

Aislinn screwed up her face. "Still."

"Yeah. Well, like I said, I'm gonna go give the others a hand." Flynn pursed his lips. "Glad you ain't dead, loser."

Aislinn curled one hand into the studded collar around his neck and yanked until they were nose to nose. "Thanks for the unwanted rescue, street rat."

Amber eyes narrowed and Tobias wondered if he'd be breaking up another fight - then Flynn's expression cleared like fog on a sunny morning, leaving behind a face so beautiful it almost hurt to look at. Ducking his head as if embarrassed, the tigerkin rubbed his hair against Aislinn's cheek, kissed her forehead and pulled away, loping off into the darkness.

They sat in silence after he'd gone, Aislinn relaxed against Tobias' chest while he wound a lock of bloody, sweaty hair around one finger. "So," he said finally. "What next?"

Her sigh was monumental. "Don't feel guilty, Tobias. It wasn't your fault."

"Lena died because of me."

"Lena died because she jumped on an angry bear's face while in her cat form," Aislinn snapped. "Yeah, she saved your backside but it was stupid and reckless and she paid for it."

"It was also brave," Tobias protested, then frowned when she cut him a glance. "You set me up for that."

"Sure did - don't dishonour Lena's memory by wallowing in guilt. She deserves better."

"All right." Humbled by her strength, Tobias pressed a soft kiss to Aislinn's temple. "So what now, really?"

She dropped her head against his shoulder, eyes drifting closed. "After the cleanup, we'll have to argue over who to report Olaf's escape to. Then we'll need to stop Jacques arresting us or something weird like that."

"Sounds tiring." Tobias buried his face in her hair, luxuriating in the feel of it against his skin. "Lucky you've got me around to give you a hand."

"Forever," she agreed - and only his Aislinn could make that sound like a threat.

Laughing, Tobias burrowed deeper and nipped at the column of her throat. "I think that sounds like just long enough."

"Good." Aislinn twisted in his lap, wrapping both arms around his shoulders. "Now kiss me, Tobias. Like you mean it."

"With a request like that, how could I possibly refuse?" Still laughing, Tobias drew her in for a fierce, possessive kiss that set their world on fire.

# Twenty-Six

Lena's tiny body was cremated on site, with the aid of some aircraft fuel and a hastily erected pyre. Aislinn stared into the flames until they were embers, tears streaming silently down her cheeks, surrounded by her pack and her friends. Once it was done, she scooped the ashes into an empty plastic container that Rory had found and cleaned specifically for that purpose. The ritual prayers she'd been taught as a child came out automatically, a warrior's last rites witnessed by those present at the time of her death. Brayden sealed the container with gentle fingers then shifted to his eagle form and carried it back to the van, where Lena would rest until they returned to Ireland and surrendered the ashes to her family.

"You sound like you've done that before," Tobias murmured, his lips against her ear.

"I have. Too many times." And it wouldn't be the last, either. Tobias likely guessed the same but didn't say anything, simply wrapped both arms around her waist and rested his chin on her head. Aislinn sighed, weary to her bones. "It's never easy."

"It shouldn't be," he replied. "The minute it is, you know it's time to find a new career."

"True." Aislinn turned in his arms and rested her head against Tobias' chest, allowing her lashes to drift closed while she borrowed her heartmate's strength.

How long they stood like that, she couldn't say - but then someone cleared their throat and she looked up to see Jacques, phone in hand, standing at the edge of the tarmac. "It's for you."

"Thanks." She put the phone to her ear. "This is Aislinn."

"Well, well. Someone's had quite the adventure." The male voice on the other end was calm and cultured, with a faint French accent. "Or so I'm told."

"Lord Balcourte." Aislinn straightened instinctively, giving Kaira a wide-eyed look.

"Aislinn, my dear, you've called me Arthur for years. I think it's a little late to fall back on formalities now, isn't it?"

"I wasn't a fugitive before, my Lord."

"*Arthur,*" Kaira's father snapped, his tone brooking no argument.

"All right, all right - Arthur," Aislinn relented. "Now, what can I do for you? I'll be honest, I was expecting this particular call to come from Andre."

"Luckily for you, I took a mild interest in the situation and deigned to go over your father's head," Arthur replied, laughter lacing his tone.

"You did?" Aislinn's jaw dropped. Lord Arthur Balcourte held a special position within Kin society in that he owned Bhaile Roinnte, the island on which the Kin High Council was based. He wasn't on the Council itself, but had the authority to step into Council matters at will and was often called upon to settle disputes as an impartial overseer. It was a power which could easily be abused but Lord Balcourte's reputation was iron clad, his gentle personality loved by all and his word universally accepted. Swallowing her shock, Aislinn managed, "I wouldn't have thought this a matter that required your particular touch."

Arthur laughed. "Oh my sweet, gentle Aislinn. If only you knew the furore the bearkin have created over here! There have been terrorist attacks in multiple locations - not just Australia, and not simply Kin. The human government is not impressed and the media is clamouring for blood."

"The delicate nature of politics once again going over my head," Aislinn said, trying to stop the man from going off on a tangent. "You're still on the phone with a fugitive."

"Scandalous," he whispered, causing Aislinn to roll her eyes. "And what if I told you, my dear, that that status is now revoked?"

"Eh?"

"You heard me," Arthur chuckled. "You're the best, Aislinn. The best. And once someone kindly pointed that out to the Council -" another chuckle, and Aislinn had no doubt who that 'someone' had been, "- and they realised that selling you off to Professor Postlethwaite like a prize cow was one of their sillier decisions."

Aislinn snorted. Only Lord Arthur Balcourte would dare speak of the Kin's ruling government like a band of unruly children. "Fine. So I'm off the hook for running out on Percy. Great. I'm still willing to bet actual pirate's gold they're not letting me off for the rest, though."

"Do you have actual pirate's gold?" Arthur queried, his voice quick with interest.

"No, Arthur. It was a figure of speech."

"Shame," he sighed morosely. "I should have liked to compare it to my collection." Before Aislinn could comment on that, because *of course* he had a collection, Arthur continued; "You're correct, however. The Council still wish to take you to task for your other perceived sins, if for nothing else than to have leverage over you."

"Heh."

"No need to sound so smug, dear girl. This could get quite nasty," Arthur warned, his tone verging on serious. "I managed to negotiate the alleviation of your immediate criminality on the condition that you return to Bhaile Roinnte post haste. The team which were called in to collect Professor Postlethwaite have delivered him safely to Melbourne airport and are now en-route to your current location. They will perform the cleanup Jacques has requested whilst you and your pack prepare for international travel."

"Wait just a minute," Aislinn growled, her fingers tightening around the phone. "If you think I'm going to trust a couple of teams who were on a search and destroy mission two days ago you've got another thing coming."

"I know that," Arthur said cheerfully. "But you needn't worry yourself, my sweet. I'm sending a secret weapon along to make sure there's no funny business."

"What secret weapon?"

"Oh no, no - that would quite spoil the surprise. Now, I'd prepare myself if I were you. According to my informants," another chuckle, "The helicopters should be there in the next few minutes."

"Arthur -"

"Give my love to Kaira, won't you? And do let's have tea and biscuits upon your return."

"Arthur!" Aislinn snapped - but Lord Balcourte simply made wet, kissing noises into the phone and hung up. "Arrrrgh!"

Tobias cleared his throat. "*That* was the famous Lord Arthur Balcourte?"

"Yeah. Try being his daughter," Kaira muttered, accepting the phone from Aislinn.

Tobias snorted. "Want my father instead?"

"Or mine?" Aislinn offered.

"No way," Kaira held both hands up in a gesture of peace. "Mine might be weird, but at least he cares. Sorry, Ash."

"Truth hurts," Aislinn shrugged. "Now, someone go and meet Brayden at the cars and move them down here. Once those choppers arrive we're going to have very little time and space to ourselves."

"We don't really need the cars," Jacques cut in. "The cleanup team will return them."

*And what about your rucksack, smart ass?* Flynn loped out of the blood drenched hangar, lips pulled back from his teeth in a silent snarl. *Unless you'd prefer the other teams to get their hands on your expensive lace underwear.*

"They're mesh, not lace," Jacques snapped, "and they're very supportive." When several sets of astonished eyes turned to him, the owlkin sighed and threw up his hands. "Fine! I'll go."

Silence prevailed until Jacques assumed his snowy owl form and flapped away into the grey dawn sky. Then Sienna snorted and quite suddenly everyone was laughing, the sound of their mirth a ragged chorus with which several wild kookaburras decided to join in.

********

The steady thump of chopper blades had Tobias looking up from the macabre task of counting dead bearkin, Sienna tottering along behind him with a clipboard she'd rummaged out of the office and a blood spattered pen.

"They're here," she murmured, her eyes narrowed at the twin silhouettes steadily winging their way in. "Why two?"

"Standard procedure," Brayden answered from where he crouched by a pile of body parts. "One assault escort, one transport."

Tobias dumped the bits of dead bearkin he'd been carrying, watching the other two Kin out of the corner of his eye. Whilst there didn't seem to be an actual relationship blooming, there was no denying Brayden's protective behaviour. Nothing had been said aloud but he always managed to find something to do within arm's reach, or at least earshot, of Sienna. If she noticed, she gave no sign - though she was quick to snarl whenever Brayden attempted to do anything that strained the injuries he'd sustained during the fight, the worst being a long but shallow gash running from shoulder to buttock that had occurred when he and what remained of Lena had gone tumbling end over end through the hole in the side of the hangar. Tobias winced, trying not to feel guilty over the fact that he'd been the one to create that hole, and turned away from the rapidly enlarging helicopters to find his heartmate beside him.

"We may as well stop," Aislinn said by way of greeting, handing him a grease-stained towel. "The cleanup crew will take over."

"Sure." Tobias looked down at the remains on the floor in front of him. "I was struggling to work out where all the bits on this guy went, anyway. Whoever tore him apart did too good a job." There was a short, telling silence, and he sighed. "It was me, wasn't it?"

Aislinn's hand was warm as she squeezed his shoulder. "Transition is as transition does." She flicked a look at Sienna and offered a bright smile. "Want to round up the others for me, Sens? If the choppers arrive and they can't see us all, there might be trouble."

Sienna nodded, put her clipboard down on a nearby fuel drum, and scurried off. Tobias watched Brayden trail after her, thumbs jammed casually in the waistband of his black jogging shorts. "I don't understand those two."

"I'm not bothering to try. Whatever's going on between them is their business." Aislinn shrugged, then squeezed his shoulder again. "You okay, spunk monkey?"

"Wow. There's a pet name I haven't heard in twelve years - and, for the record, haven't missed," Tobias grunted. When she poked him warningly in the ribs, he sighed and shook his head. "I don't know, Ash. Look at these bodies. *I* did that."

"You did it defending your friends and your pack and your heartmate." She slipped closer, spreading one hand over his heart. "It's hard to see the results of our more animal natures sometimes, but you need to accept that this is part of you, too, no matter how unpleasant. If it helps, I'm almost certain you'll be able to control your midform now. You were pretty rational whilst yanking me out of the cargo plane."

Tobias considered that, wiping his hands on the towel at long last and dropping it on the ground by the clipboard. "I assumed that was because you reached out to me through our bond and slapped a little sense in."

"I didn't do any slapping, per se." Aislinn nudged him with her hip and they wandered out into the open, where the rest of her pack and team were already gathering. "All I did was heal. The rest was up to you and now that you know how it feels, I think you'll be able to control your midform. For the most part."

"For the most part?"

"Surges of transitional rage will still happen, they just won't be automatically connected to your midform." She tilted her head in thought, eyes distant. "At least, that's how it went for Flynn."

"Oh, well, in that case," he muttered, "As long as I'm on the same path as *Flynn*, I should turn out perfectly fine."

Aislinn rolled her eyes but whatever she'd intended to say was drowned out by the approaching choppers. Rotor-made wind whipped Tobias' hair around his face and forced him to squint, raising a hand in front of his eyes as dust and gods knew what else pelted his half-dressed body. The aircraft touched down on the pitted tarmac, the whine of the engines immediately beginning to lessen. Several figures leapt out of the cargo transport and jogged over - and it wasn't until strong arms wrapped around Tobias' waist and squeezed that he recognised Stephanie Greenwood.

"Mum?" He stared down at her in surprise, returning the embrace and turning automatically to shield her from the wind with his body. "What are you doing here?"

Stephanie's grin was wide and she pointed at her ears, then in the direction of the hangar. Tobias looked over to see Aislinn similarly wrapped up in her own mother, with Grandma Redding watching from a few steps back. Beside her stood a short, weathered looking man in frayed black work shorts, a thin, faded burgundy tank and, of all things, an eyepatch. He looked Tobias over with his single grey-blue eye, barely visible through a mess of brown and white streaked curls that tumbled past his shoulders in greasy disarray. His skin was tanned a dark brown and appeared so weathered it might've been mistaken for real leather had Tobias not seen the man moving; a limping, awkward gait caused by the fact that his left leg was prosthetic. And not just any prosthetic - a sleek, black metal contraption that looked more like a prop from a steampunk movie than anything ever intended to be walked on. As the older man met Tobias' gaze, he drew his top lip back in a sneer and promptly turned to make several hand signals in the direction of the cooling down choppers.

Wondering what he'd possibly done to alienate a man he'd never even met, Tobias allowed Stephanie to drag him determinedly off in the direction of the hangar. She put the brakes on fairly quickly, however, when the distinctive smell of blood and death rolled out to meet her.

"This way," Aislinn said. With one arm linked through her mother's and one through her grandmother's, she swept off to the panel van and threw open the back doors with the air of someone showing off their castle. "Welcome to my temporary headquarters."

Rather than climb in, Marguerite Redding perched her tiny behind on the tailgate, smoothing her skirt suit into place. She was joined a moment later by Stephanie, who settled beside Ash's mother with an audible clank. Muttering under her breath, the petite woman began emptying the pockets of her cargo shorts into the back of the van, creating a pile of tools and paraphernalia that had Tobias' eyebrows winging upward. Clearly used to her friend's behaviour, Marguerite used her thumb and index finger to hold Stephanie's grease stained tank out of the way until the ritual was complete and both women were comfortable.

"So, what are you all doing here?" Aislinn asked, hands fisted on her hips.

"Well -" Marguerite was cut off mid reply by Stephanie's sudden squeal. She pointed at Tobias' bare shoulders, one hand over her mouth.

"What?" Tobias turned, but there was nobody behind him. "Ma? What is it?"

Stephanie tugged his arm until he bent over, tears streaming down her cheeks as she prodded at the join between Tobias' neck and shoulder. Grandma Redding loosed a loud snort. "You only just noticed? It's huge and he's got no shirt on, for Solaeden's sake."

"I'm short," Stephanie defended, smoothing her hands over Tobias' Mark again and again. "Oh, Tobias… oh, my baby boy."

"Are you okay?" Tobias asked, not sure whether to be worried or embarrassed.

"Of course I am," she barked, dashing at her tears. "I'm just so *proud* of you." Turning to Aislinn, Stephanie added; "And I finally have the daughter I always wanted."

A blush darkened Aislinn's cheeks and she slapped her hands over them. "Awwww, Steph, don't."

"I mean it!" Stephanie declared, yanking Aislinn into a three-way embrace with her son and squeezing them with all her Kin strength. "All mine, at last."

"You're not…" Aislinn trailed off, cleared her throat. "Disappointed?"

Stephanie stepped back in shock, her jaw slack. "Why would you think that?"

"Our fathers, collective," Tobias rumbled, putting his arm around Aislinn's shoulders and drawing her close to his side. "When I told Andre that Ash was my heartmate, he attacked me."

"What?" Marguerite gasped. "Where was Rupert?"

"Right there beside him." Tobias bared his teeth. "He stood back and watched while I pummelled Andre into the dirt and swore out of the pack."

"They offered me up to the bears - and then Percy - like a sacrifice," Aislinn continued, her voice quieter but no less intense. "After spending years trying to make us hate each other. For this." She waved a hand toward the hangar where the cleanup crew were, with the assistance of Sienna's clipboard, completing their assessment of the bearkin corpses. "They sundered families, separated heartmates and tore a pack apart for those bodies, that blood. And after all of it, Olaf got away."

"I swear to you we didn't know," Stephanie began. "I never thought -"

"It doesn't matter," Tobias cut her off quietly. "Neither Ash nor I have an interest in creating bad blood, but we need to think of our pack now. So again; why are you all here?"

Grandma Redding stepped forward and offered her hand. "Joanne Redding, on behalf of the Redding Pack and Lord Arthur Balcourte."

Sharing a glance with Aislinn, to which she nodded, Tobias gripped Grandma's hand and shook. "Tobias and Aislinn Greenwood, for the Greenwood pack."

"Well met." Grandma smiled, her face lighting up and her eyes twinkling. "These here are friends of mine, working in law and logistics respectively. With them on board as witnesses, I'd like to offer you and your pack sanctuary on my lands."

"What?" Aislinn gasped.

"You heard me, Den Mother," Grandma repeated firmly. "Your fugitive status has been revoked and the High Council has demanded your return to Ireland at the earliest convenience. Until then - and for every sunset afterwards - I'd like to offer you the unconditional sanctuary of the Redding Pack." Lowering her voice and stepping in so that Tobias and Aislinn instinctively leant closer, she added, "Come home; just for a while. Please."

Tobias, his heart thumping arrhythmically in his chest, shared another look with his heartmate. Aislinn smiled broadly and clasped hands with her grandmother. "It would be our honour to accept, Den Mother. May Lunaida's moon watch over you and yours."

"And to you," Grandma nodded, then clapped her hands. "All right. Steph, get to working out the transport arrangements. Marguerite, I need that official summons." When neither of the women moved, Grandma let out a sharp growl. "*Now!*"

Tobias watched as the females leapt to their feet and hurried away, neither daring so much as a backwards glance. When they were out of earshot, Aislinn sighed. "That was harder than I thought."

"Don't come down on them too heavily," Grandma said softly. "We've all three of us made mistakes and played our own part in this, but your mothers and I have sworn to both gods that we're going to fix what those fool men broke."

"The packs can't be re-joined," Aislinn murmured. "You know that."

"I do - but we can still be a family," Grandma said firmly. "Now, Aislinn, there's a cranky pirate over there who's been itching to talk to you. Would you kindly do me a favour and put him out of his misery so we can all go home?"

********

"Brax!" Aislinn threw herself into the older Kin's arms, laughing when he staggered backwards. "It's so good to see you."

"Watch the leg, you heathen," Brax grumped, his gravelly voice as gruff as ever. "Can't you see I'm a cripple?"

"The day you're a cripple is the day I grow wings," Aislinn retorted. "What are you doing here, you old dragon?"

"Council's calling me out of retirement, same as you," Brax growled. He set her on her feet and gave Tobias a scathing once over. "This your new toy?"

"Brax Montgomery, meet Tobias Greenwood, Alpha of the Greenwood pack and my heartmate." Aislinn gave both men a nudge and after matching grunts, they shook hands with the sort of white knuckled grip that meant bones were being tested. "Cut it out, both of you."

"Just checkin'," Brax replied without a hint of remorse. "Can't be giving you away to just anyone now, can I?"

*He's not just anybody,* Flynn mocked, loping over to join them in his tiger form. *T-Fuzz is the one. THE one.*

Brax looked Tobias over again. "Huh."

"Stop it," Aislinn hissed, blushing furiously. "Or I pull out your whiskers one by one."

Tobias, however, raised a questioning brow. "The one?"

Flynn's mouth fell open in a feline laugh, his tongue lolling out. *When Ash and I joined the Council's death squads, Brax was one of our trainers. Let's just say every training dummy she ever brained had your imaginary face painted right on it.*

"You're enjoying this a little too much, kitty pie," Brax cut in. "I recall you had your own faces to visualise."

Flynn hissed and, while Aislinn laughed, stalked off towards the transport chopper with his hackles stiff. "Oh, I've missed that. Nobody pisses him off quite like you do."

"It's a skill," Brax shrugged. "Now it looks like you're out of here, whereas I gotta stay and handle the clean up. Just wanted to say, seeing as we'll probably be seeing each other a little more often, that if you get anyone you wanna sling my way, don't be afraid to call."

Aislinn thought on that for a moment, then nodded. "I think I might, once we're settled."

"Just keep it to yaself," the older man grouched.

"Keep what to myself?"

"Good girl." And with a firm pat on the shoulder, Brax stumped away.

Tobias stepped to Aislinn's side, lowered his head, and whispered; "He scares me."

"He scares everyone, but don't worry. He's soft at heart."

"I heard that!"

"Keep hobbling, old man!"

"I will beat you to death with this leg one day, little girl!"

"I'd like to see you try!"

Brax raised both middle fingers, jabbing them in Aislinn's direction without bothering to turn around. Tobias shook his head. "Yeah. Soft at heart. Sure."

"Come on," she chuckled, bumping him with her shoulder. "Jax is loading our rucksacks onto the chopper. Let's go home."

His face immediately softened and in no time at all, the pack was piled into the transport chopper whilst Kaira, Brayden and Jacques slid into the assault chopper to man the guns. Flynn, who'd never liked flying, had a short but intense argument with the pilot about riding on the outside of the aircraft - an argument he lost when Sienna poked him in the back of the neck, causing the tiger to collapse into boneless unconsciousness.

After exchanging incredulous looks, Tobias and Jaxon took one end each of the enormous cat and tossed him none too gently into the helicopter, where Sienna took up a position beside his head in case he woke. Aislinn watched the show from her perch on Zeke's knee, a position the wiry second had dragged her into when it was clear the only other vacant seating was going to be between her mother and Stephanie. When Marguerite dared to hopefully pat the vacant spot beside her, Jaxon obligingly dropped into it whilst Zeke, not normally territorial in the slightest, secured Aislinn so tightly against his chest that she ended up with a mouthful of his golden curls.

"Why, big brother," Aislinn breathed against his ear, "I had no idea you felt this way."

Zeke rumbled a laugh but didn't loosen his grip. "Just making a point, gorgeous, and you well know it."

"They offered us sanctuary."

"I appreciate that, but they also gotta learn we're our own entity. If we want any hope of this pack, small as it is, getting anywhere in the shitstorm I'm damned sure is coming, we need to make a stand from the start." He nuzzled her hair and Aislinn allowed herself to relax in his strong arms, breathing in the sea breeze and limestone scent that was uniquely Zeke's. "Besides," he added, "Now that you and Tobias finally got your acts together, I can canoodle you as much as I want."

Aislinn laughed. "Big bad second needs his Den Mother's strength?"

"Always." A shiver ran down Zeke's spine and for a moment, he sagged against the side of the chopper. "I'm glad you're both okay, little sister wolf. Very glad."

"Oh, Zeke." Aislinn slipped an arm around his neck and squeezed. "I'm sorry we dragged you into this."

"I had to grow up sometime," he replied. At that moment Tobias appeared, dropping onto the floor in front of them. He slid his legs beneath the seat, shuffled forward until he was between Zeke's knees, and dropped his elbows on Aislinn's lap. Zeke's laughter shook all three of them as he said; "Personal space, dude."

"You got my heartmate, you deal with it," Tobias replied, propping his chin on his palms and staring up at Aislinn out of those steely blue eyes with the golden starbursts she adored so much. "I'm head Alpha now, you have to do what I say."

"If you think I'm gonna spend my life sniffing your badly washed ringhole, you got another thing coming," Zeke snorted. "I've got a backbone and I'm not afraid to use it."

Tobias' answering grin was brilliant. "I'm counting on it."

*******

It was afternoon by the time the choppers touched down on the Redding Pack's common lawn, the only clear space large enough to accommodate them. Tobias gripped Aislinn's hand tightly in his as they disembarked, the rest of the pack close behind. Grandma Redding stalked ahead with Marguerite and Stephanie as they moved to meet Andre and Rupert by the front steps of Grandma's house.

Tobias tried not to look too long at the friends and former pack-mates peering out of windows and around corners. The place he'd been born and raised felt somehow alien, his soul recognising on some deep level that he was no longer affiliated with the pack who called this land home.

"You're back," Andre said by way of greeting, brown eyes sharp as they assessed the bloody, dirty group of Kin amassed on the lawn.

"No need to sound so disappointed," Grandma snapped. "You and your precious Council wanted them, Andre. Here they are."

Andre ran his eye over the group again, finally settling on Aislinn. "We leave for Melbourne at dawn. Be ready."

"No."

Even the insects seemed to quiet as Andre stiffened. "No?"

"My pack and my team have been on the road for several days without rest. I won't move them at dawn." Aislinn's tone was cool and collected, her face set. "Not only that, there are lives which need to be tied up, arrangements made and families farewelled."

"I've no time for mucking about." Andre flicked the fingers of one hand in immediate rejection. "I'm sure you read your summons. The Council demands the attendance of you and your pack at your earliest possible convenience."

"I read it. And my earliest possible convenience is midday." Aislinn turned to face the rest of her pack. "Or do you need more time?"

Silence followed that comment until Sienna said, "I can do midday."

"Yeah." Dominic nodded agreement, his eyes already on the small house he shared with his sister. "Deanna's home, so midday should be fine."

Slowly, further agreements came tumbling out, and Aislinn finally turned to Tobias. He shrugged. "Where you go, I go. When you go, I go."

It was impossible to miss the sneer on Andre's face, even from the corner of his eye. But it was Rupert, standing beside and a little behind his Alpha, whose expression tugged at Tobias' heart. Pride. Pure, bright, unadulterated pride. And when Tobias met his father's eyes, the burlier man mouthed: *I'm sorry.*

It wasn't nearly enough but it was a start. Tobias inclined his head imperceptibly in response and saw tears shimmer briefly in Rupert's gaze. Aislinn squeezed his fingers and he looked down to find her smiling at him. "Together?"

"Always."

She turned back to face her father. "Midday."

"Dawn."

"Dusk, tomorrow."

"*Dawn.*"

"Oh, wait, I forgot." Aislinn wound a lock of hair around her free hand and sighed. "Sienna and I had appointments to get our hair done. Two days from now."

"Dawn, or -"

"I also promised Kaira we'd get matching tattoos next week," Aislinn continued, pursing her lips. "And maybe a quick mani." She splayed fingers that Tobias was willing to bet had never had a coat of nail polish in their life, and sighed again. "Killing indiscriminately really does wreck your cuticles, you know."

Trembling with outrage, Andre said; "I *order* you to be ready at dawn."

"Ooops," Aislinn giggled, waving the official summons she'd had stuffed in the waistband of her shorts. "You can't. According to this letter, due to my heartmating with Tobias my contract with the Council is void. Considering that Lord Balcourte is the one requesting - and sponsoring - my return to Ireland, that puts us under no authority but his. So," and she handed the summons to Zeke with a flourish, "My earliest convenience will, in fact, be *my* earliest convenience. Now have you got an intelligent response to make, or would you like to explain to Arthur why my pack and I are returning to Ireland via a month long vacation in Hawaii?"

Grandma Redding coughed into her hand, bending her head so that her greying red hair hid the laughter she was trying desperately to stifle. Marguerite's head whipped back and forth between her mate and her daughter so fast Tobias feared it might pop off, and Stephanie Greenwood was openly smirking. Unable to help himself, Tobias bent until he was nose to nose with Aislinn and said; "I always wanted to go to Hawaii."

"To celebrate our mating, I thought," she answered, her grin wicked. "Seeing as there's no rush and all."

Tobias released her hand so that he could cup both cheeks, tilt her head up and brush his lips to hers. He'd meant it to be a chaste kiss but the second Aislinn groaned he lost it, tightening his grip and thrusting his tongue into her mouth. She melted against him, long hair tickling his bare chest and her arms raising to wrap around his neck. Someone was growling and when Aislinn smiled into their kiss Tobias realised it was him; a steady, lusty growl which he couldn't have contained if he wanted to. When Aislinn pulled gently away, both of them panting, blue lights danced beneath the skin of Tobias' hands and arms and, judging by the expressions on the faces of the people around him, very likely the rest of his body.  He didn't care about those people, though, didn't care that they stood on the middle of the common lawn with helicopters behind them and houses around them and the blistering Australian sun sheening his skin in sweat. All he cared about, in that moment, was the woman in front of him, his heartmate, his *everything*. "I want to lick you everywhere."

Someone snorted a laugh; someone growled. Jerking his head up at the aggressive sound, Tobias locked eyes with Andre and frowned. Aislinn's hands found their way to his chest but he shook his head, accepting the surge of transitional rage and channelling it rather than attempting to block it out. Blood pounded heavily in his veins and the blue lights beneath his skin began to multiply exponentially but he felt in complete control. Fur spread up his arms and down his back and Tobias bared his teeth as pointed incisors lengthened into proper fangs.

Startled, Andre took a step back. When Aislinn made no move to interfere, the other Alpha barked; "Midday - and not a minute later!"

"Sure," Aislinn replied, but her father had already spun on his heel, disappearing inside Grandma Redding's house as fast as he could manage without fleeing outright. The door slammed behind him and the rest of both packs watched in fascinated silence as Tobias reversed his energy, dismissing fur and fangs in favour of skin and - well, slightly less fanged fangs.

Triumph surged and he looked down at his heart mate. "You were right. I can control my midform."

"Told you." She winked. "About time you realised I'm always right."

"Hah!"

Grandma Redding, her face stretched into a grin wider than he'd seen in years, announced; "The Greenwood pack has full sanctuary and are to be treated as your own. Any arguments can be taken up with me, and me alone." When nobody protested, the older woman nodded.

"Good. Aislinn, take the Greenwood house for your pack house; Rupert and Stephanie can stay with me the night."

"Are you sure?" Tobias asked his mother.

Stephanie nodded. "I said it was more your house than ours now and I meant it. Go home, my son. Rest. And… might I visit in the morning? To discuss the travel arrangements?"

"Of course," Aislinn answered. "Join us for breakfast."

"Breakfast!" Jaxon immediately protested. "Can't we do brunch?"

"Midday, remember?" Aislinn looked thoughtful. "How about a late breakfast? Let's say ten o'clock, down in the den."

Stephanie looked surprised to be invited to the den, but she nodded nonetheless. "Can I bring a date?"

"Sure. Bring Achilles," Aislinn returned.

"Achilles? Achilles Heliope-Flint?"

Aislinn looked amused. "Yeah. Don't know any other Achilles, do you?"

"No." Stephanie looked confused and perhaps a little disappointed but she nodded. "Ten o'clock, at the den. With Achilles."

"Excellent. Dom and Jax, you're in charge of setup. Rory and Sienna, food. Zeke, booze. Flynn, bring the interlopers." She grinned at Kaira, Brayden and Jacques.

"Isn't Flynn technically an interloper?" Marguerite queried.

Aislinn raised an eyebrow at her mother. "He's blood bonded to both myself and Tobias, Ma, which makes him closer than family." She paused. "Want to come, too?"

Marguerite looked shocked, then, quickly seizing the opportunity for peace, nodded. "I'd love to."

"You, too, old hag."

"Don't speak to your grandmother like that, you insolent whelp," Grandma Redding snapped, brandishing a fist. "You're not too old to bend over my knee."

"Uh huh." Aislinn grinned and got one in response. "Just be there."

Looking mystified, the three women nodded and went on their ways. When they'd collected Rupert and disappeared inside Grandma's house, Zeke murmured; "You're handing the den to Achilles tomorrow, aren't you?"

"Yeah. Seeing as we're not going to be needing it any more, I figured he'd put it to good use." Aislinn grinned, her smile brighter than the sun. "Him and the rest of those barefoot vagabonds who follow their future Alpha around like a bad smell."

Zeke chuckled and said something but Tobias didn't hear. He couldn't take it any more; not the shine of Aislinn's hair nor the sweep of her collarbone nor the smooth texture of her skin. He bent and swept her up in his arms, turning away without waiting for the discussion to end naturally. Ash started laughing and didn't stop until they were inside his house, up the stairs and in his room, where he kicked the door shut with a decisive slam.

The bed was still rumpled from when they'd last slept in it with Flynn draped across their legs and Tobias was sure if he looked closely he'd find tiger fur in the sheets. His bedside clock blinked the same as it always had, the few possessions and framed pictures of himself and Aislinn resting where they always did. And yet it felt different; *he* felt different.

As though sensing the turn of his thoughts, Aislinn tightened her fingers around his wrist. "Did you ever think, as kids curled up in wolf form on your bed in the middle of the night, that one day we'd end up here like this?"

"Yeah."

She blinked, twisted to look up into his face. "Really?"

"At least twice a day." Smiling in the face of her astonishment, he shrugged. "I told you I've loved you as long as I can remember. I wasn't kidding." Tobias bent and placed her in the middle of his bed, straightening up just so he could stare down at the sprawl of her limbs, the flush of her cheeks and the way her thick, brown-red hair spread across the pillows. "And now I have you."

********

Aislinn stared into the intensity of Tobias' love and for a blinding second it was almost too much. Swallowing heavily, she managed; "I hope I can live up to your expectations."

"I don't have expectations." He shook his head in emphasis, hair flopping forward into his face. After a long moment he crawled onto the bed, six foot four inches of solid, muscular male in bad need of a hairbrush and a shower, sweat and mud and blood spattering his chest

407

and impeding Aislinn's view of the spectacular light show taking place beneath the surface of his skin. He was, in a word, perfect.

"No expectations at all?" She asked breathlessly, feathering her hands across his shoulders as Tobias made his slow, determined way up her body. "Not a single one?"

Tobias paused above her, palms either side of her head, deliciously heavy hips wiggling their way between her legs. "The only thing I've ever expected from you is that you'll do whatever it is that I or anyone else least expects."

Laughter bubbled up in Aislinn's throat and she wrapped her arms around his neck, burrowing her fingers into his tangled hair. "I guess that makes a certain amount of sense," she allowed, tugging him closer. "Maybe that's why I love you so much. You never ask me to be anything other than who I am."

"I *love* who you are," he whispered, nipping at her nose, her cheeks, her lips. "I love who you were." Kisses now, along the line of her jaw, down one side of her throat and back up the other. "I love that it all belongs to me." Tobias pressed her more firmly into the bed, dropping onto his forearms to speak against her lips. "And more than anything, I love that I belong to you."

"I'm about to take you away from your home," she reminded, gasping as Tobias began rubbing the hard length of his erection against her core. "For a long time. Maybe forever."

"You're my home," he replied, and kissed her.

Aislinn groaned into his mouth, their kiss very quickly escalating from tender to desperate. Tobias rolled off long enough to strip out of his shorts and yank off hers, whilst Aislinn struggled with her sports bra. When they were at last naked, he tackled her back onto the bed and buried his face in her neck, inhaling deeply as his hands shaped the curves of her body.

Wondering if Tobias was planning to take things slowly and not in the mood for it, Aislinn reached between them to grab his erection, smoothing her hands up and down the shaft and tracing her fingers over the head until he began to growl and squirm on top of her.

"Ash," he groaned, "You're killing me."

"Do something about it, then," she panted - and a second later Tobias yanked her hand aside and buried himself to the hilt. Nothing had ever felt so good as that moment, their bodies joined, hearts thundering and gazes locked. Then he began to move and it took all Aislinn had not to scream as pleasure arced through her veins, turning her breathing ragged.

Tobias kept his strokes strong and steady, his eyes never leaving her face. One hand fisted in her hair, the other playing expertly across her skin, over the side of her breast, all while his hips kept up their exquisite torture. Aislinn could do no more than hang on, clinging with her arms and her legs and her heart as sweet pressure built between them. The blue sparks dancing under Tobias' skin began to multiply and she knew the moment he was hit with the energy surge, because he twined the fingers of his free hand with her own, bent to take her lips and picked up the pace.

Aislinn moaned into Tobias' mouth as he took her higher, faster, harder. Pleasure barrelled up her spine and her eyes flew open to see electricity dancing across both their bodies; a build-up of kinetic energy second only to the time Tobias had been struck by lightning. Then there was no more time for thinking as sensation overcame her, tearing that scream from her throat at long last as Aislinn's world fractured into millions of brilliant, glittering pieces.

Tobias growled against her lips, the tendons in his throat standing out in stark relief as his spine locked and his body jerked, his release shoving Aislinn over the edge a second time. She clawed mindlessly at his back and shoulders, her body shaking and her thoughts in tatters. Her heartmate collapsed on top of her, instinctively understanding that Aislinn was not only strong enough to bear his weight but also wouldn't let him move away.

They lay like that for some minutes, until Tobias raised his head, swallowed heavily and said; "Do you hear that?"

"Hear what?" Blinking to clear the pleasant haze of their lovemaking, Aislinn turned her head to the side to hear better. "It sounds like swearing."

"Jaxon swearing," Tobias agreed. He pushed up on his elbows, brows furrowing as he fought to make out the words. "Maybe we should - "

"I'm telling you," Jaxon's voice drifted through the window, "I don't know! The power just *died*."

"The power?" Aislinn glanced at the bedside clock and discovered that, true to Jaxon's word, it was blank. She looked back at Tobias, frown still in place while he strained to hear the rest of the conversation, and noticed that the electricity which had been dancing under his skin was gone. "Oh."

"What?" Tobias turned back to her at once. "Are you okay? Did I hurt you?"

"No, no," she tightened her arms when he made to move and added; "It was you."

"What was me?"

"The power. Look." Daring to unwrap one arm, she spread her palm over his chest.

Tobias reared up enough to stare down the length of his own body and, a moment later, collapsed to the bed with a groan. "Solaeden save me, Ash. Are you saying when I - when I -"

"Came?"

"That I blew out power to the whole house?"

Aislinn bit her lip to keep from laughing. "From the sound of it, I'm thinking it might be the entire pack."

"Shit." Tobias buried his face in her hair.

"Are you blushing?"

"I took out the power!"

"With your magic cock," Aislinn agreed, tilting her hips in emphasis. "Your still-hard magic cock."

"You're not helping." He tried to stop her body's movement by shunting his hips hard against the bed, but that only drew a gasp from them both. "Dammit, Ash, how is that even possible?"

"Well, when mummy and daddy are loving each other very much -"

"The blackout, not the boner!"

This time she did laugh, because his expression was so adorably tortured there was simply no other option. "Transition."

"So you're telling me that I can't control the EMP on purpose but I can shag it out?" Tobias shook his head. "How much worse is this going to get?"

"Well, considering you've already taken out power to the whole pack, I'd say -"

"The transition," Tobias growled - but he was smiling at last, the golden starbursts in his steely blue eyes glittering. "How much worse is the transition going to get?"

Aislinn chewed on her lip, watched his eyes track the movement. "A bit."

"A *bit*?"

"Probably a lot. Getting control of your midform is a huge deal, but your other powers are just getting started. I could have damped you," she admitted, looking up from under her lashes, "But it felt so good."

He paused at that, male satisfaction warring with Tobias' ingrained need to do the right thing. Finally, his body relaxing ever so slightly, he rocked his hips against her with erotic purpose. "Really."

"Yes," she gasped, pressing a kiss to his jaw. "Really."

"Well then," Tobias said in that slow, deliberate way Aislinn adored, "I suppose if it felt good, and I've already taken out the power, then it can't get any worse, can it?"

"Oh, Mother Moon, no," Aislinn agreed as he began tracing a path down her throat with his lips. "Definitely not."

"And it would be a shame to waste all that energy. While you're in heat, no less."

"Such a shame," she managed, back arching as he closed his mouth over her nipple and sucked. "*Tobias!*"

"What?"

"For the love of all you hold dear, don't stop!"

He chuckled, the sound vibrating through Aislinn and hitting her right in the heart. With Tobias' eyes once more locked to hers and his lips brushing her breast, he whispered; "Never."

Taking that promise on all the levels with which it was intended, Aislinn twisted her hands into Tobias' tangled hair, closed her eyes and surrendered completely.

# ~ The End ~

Thanks for reading!

Can't wait for the next instalment?

Keep up to date with all the latest shenanigans at:
www.sliceofsammy.com

# About the Author

Hi, I'm Sam!

I've been writing my whole life, scribbling stories on anything close to hand – from the shopping list to napkins to post-it notes (don't mention post-its to hubby haha).

I grew up reading fantasy of the likes of Anne McCaffrey, Terry Pratchett, and their peers. I'm also a lifelong vampire fan, along with all things spooky. In my late teens I was introduced to paranormal romance and discovered a whole new layer of storytelling with a bit of a spicy edge! Taking what I learnt from all of the above, I devoted myself to creating full-bodied characters, meaty plots, epic adventure, and a little bit of naughty sauce on the side.

I completed a Diploma of Professional Writing and Editing after high school and spent the next several years in my writing cave, working on a novel that is now in a drawer somewhere, followed by a couple of others who shared the same fate. (What can I say? I'm a recovering perfectionist.)

I came close to debuting my novel career in 2009, then ended up pregnant and took some time off to have kids. I debuted for real in 2019 with *Sorcery and Stardust* and won ARRA's Favourite Debut Romance Author for 2019, which was extremely cool!

I write speculative fiction that is a fusion of multiple sub-genres and therefore doesn't fit particularly well into any of them, but after many years and a lot of angst, I'm okay with that. I love all my characters and their stories for different reasons, but have a soft spot for an excellent villain and a tortured protagonist.

I currently live in south east Melbourne, Victoria, with my hubby, two kids, a Golden Retriever and a turtle. I volunteer with the Romance Writers of Australia, and I'm passionate about great writing, interesting characters, chai tea and happily ever afters.

www.ingramcontent.com/pod-product-compliance
Lightning Source LLC
Chambersburg PA
CBHW020010120726
47903CB00004B/1219